ALASKA NATIVE WRITERS, STORYTELLERS & ORATORS

The Expanded Edition

D1452908

ALASKA NATIVE WRITERS, STORYTELLERS & ORATORS
The Expanded Edition

Executive Editor
Ronald Spatz

Contributing Editors
Jeane Breinig
Patricia H. Partnow

Original Edition
Nora Marks Dauenhauer
Richard Dauenhauer
Gary Holthaus

UNIVERSITY OF ALASKA
ANCHORAGE

Alaska Quarterly Review is a journal devoted to the full range of the literary arts. It is published twice a year by the University of Alaska Anchorage, an Affirmative Action / Equal Opportunity Employer and Educational Institution. Send correspondence to *Alaska Quarterly Review,* University of Alaska Anchorage, 3211 Providence Drive, Anchorage, AK 99508.

   E-mail address: *ayaqr@uaa.alaska.edu*

   Web Site: *http://www.uaa.alaska.edu/aqr/*

Distributors: B. DeBoer, 113 East Center Street, Nutley, NJ 07110

   Ingram Periodicals, 1240 Heil Quaker Blvd., Lavergne, TN 37086

   University Microfilms International, 300 North Zeeb Road, Ann Arbor, MI 48106

Alaska Native Writers, Storytellers & Orators: The Expanded Edition was made possible, in part, by a Heritage and Preservation Grant from the National Endowment for the Arts. Grateful acknowledgment is made to The Rasmuson Foundation and Alaska Airlines for supporting the second printing of this edition.

ISSN 0737-268X

About the cover: "Shaman Flying" is a late prehistoric Iñupiaq Eskimo artifact from Point Hope, Alaska. It is made of whale vertebra and the eyes are of walrus ivory. Although many shamans flew, only the greatest flew to the moon where they communed with the spirits. Cover photo © 1986 Sam Kimura
(Courtesy of the Anchorage Museum of History and Art)

ALASKA NATIVE WRITERS, STORYTELLERS & ORATORS
The Expanded Edition

INTRODUCTION:
LITERARY GAMBLING STICKS

"Turn around the way the sun goes and come in," says the giant to a rich man, some time ago, in "The Gambling Story" by Peter Kalifornsky. The rich man has lost everything, his wife, children, and even his gun to a young shaman. The giant courts the rich man to outwit the shaman with the right spin of the gambling sticks. The Alaska Native stories in this outstanding anthology are the literary gambling sticks that win back a native spirit, consciousness, and sense of presence. There are giant storiers here who create a wise, bright, visionary sense of native survivance.

Native stories arise in those imagic moments of meditative associations with nature, animals, shamans; and mythic stories are sustained in the many great language games of tricksters and visionaries. Native stories are the very spirit of creation on this continent, an interior vivancy. Native memories endure in the imagination of storiers; endure in the diverse tease of creation, tradition, and survivance in sound, gesture, and shadows in literature. Stories, in this sense, are the literary gambling sticks of native cultures.

"The Gambling Story" by Peter Kalifornsky was recorded in the Dena'ina language, transcribed, and then translated by the author and others. Katherine McNamara interviewed Kalifornsky and points out that there are four associations of mighty characters in his stories: shamans, of course, characters of true, mythic words, dreamers, and the last are skywatchers. The associations of these characters are common in most native stories, and the traces of myths have outlived the silence of translation. The imagic memories of these associations, shamanic memories, and mythic words are created in contemporary narratives. That "shaman was in the wrong, using his power to do wrong against this person through gambling," says Kalifornsky. "And for the shaman doing wrong, it was reversed back to him: the same punishment he gave out." The shaman loses the last throw of the gambling sticks. McNamara asks him how it was right to gamble. "We take chances," says Kalifornsky. "Human life is a gamble. You have to go out and gamble, take chances, do things." Native stories are a gamble on life, the chance and credence of survivance.

Kalifornsky, in "The Old Dena'ina Beliefs," says that those who pursue the power of dreamers "read the stars." There are traditional skyreaders, or skywatchers, shamans, dreamers, and wise speakers "whose words come true," and there are native artists who pursue the same sources of power in their stories. The strategic points of native presence are not the same, sound to silence, oral to written, trickster to semantics, but there are traces of shamanic visions, dreamers of the future, and artists of true written words.

Kalifornsky says the Dena'ina "lived life through imagination, the power of the mind." That native sense of presence is common in this anthology; that "power of the mind," ancestral memories, traces of shamanic visions, are new acts of imagination and native survivance. Shamans and creative artist encounter good and evil, but visions are risky and never easy. "To try to become good is dangerous. Struggling against evil is dangerous."

Native storiers learn that words have power in sound and scripture, and resistance is not the same as survivance. Kalifornsky recounts, in "The Boy Who Talked to the Dog," a spoiled boy who would not listen, an instance of the power of words. The boy talks to his dog "all the time. When he ate, it would eat with him and he would command it, 'Talk to me!' He would take hold of the dog's tongue and say, 'This is your tongue. Your tongue is for talking.' His parents said not to do that to the dog, but he would not listen." Then, one day, the dog "faced the boy and said, 'I will do whatever you tell me to do. But I am an animal. I am not made to talk.' This is what it said to him." The boy listened, "keeled over and died. And the dog went out. The boy had caused this to happen by his words." Later, the dog is found dead near the boy's grave.

The storiers and poets presented in this anthology create a mighty sense of native presence; a sense of presence that teases the cause of nature, the circles of ancestors, and many conversions in translation. The stories trace the native names, hearers, readers, and totemic survivance with an inimitable literary vivancy. These stories are traces of native reason and memories as the birch trees are traces of the catkin, and salmon are memories of the rivers.

Anna Nelson Harry, for instance, recorded "Lament for Eyak," one of the last songs of a great coastal people. "However sorrowful her earthly existence and tragic the fate of her people, Anna's Eyak spirit rises in triumph for herself, for her people, and for us all," observes Michael Krauss in *In Honor of Eyak: The Art of Anna Nelson*

Harry. Anna laments an entire native nation in the name of her poor ancestors.

The song is included in this anthology; here are a few lines:

> My poor aunt
> I couldn't believe you were going to die. . . .
> All alone here I'll go around.
> Like Ravens I'll live alone. . . .
> I sit down on a rock.
> Only the Eyaks,
> the Eyaks,
> they are all dying off. . . .
> Yes,
> why is it I alone,
> just I alone have survived?
> I survive.

"The final chapter in the history of the Eyak nation began in 1889 with the establishment of the first American cannery in Eyak territory. Until then, Eyaks had had relatively little contact with Europeans," writes Michael Krauss. "The cannery crews brought with them uncontrolled vice: alcohol, opium, disease, violence, and tragic disruption and degradation of the Eyak community, outnumbered each summer by the all-male crews of these canneries, where everything but sustenance and employment awaited the Eyaks."

"Lake-Dwarves" is an ironic story. The dwarves, stone babies, or little people are characters in the stories of many native cultures. Anna told stories about the dwarves and the "Giant Rat" at about the same time, more than thirty years ago. "The two tales fit together perfectly," notes Michael Krauss. The dwarves are out hunting in canoes and take a mouse, in the scale of their perceptions, to be a bear. Actually, the dwarves shoot two mice with their tiny bows and arrows. They butcher the mice as bears and then, as the dwarves are loading the bear meat in their canoes, a "man reached down and plucked up one of the wee people. He took him and tucked him under his belt." The dwarf pleads to be released, and promises that with his secret weapon, a "lucky hunting leaf," the man could be a great hunter. "The man set him free."

The monster in the "Giant Rat" story overturns a canoe of native berry pickers. "The woman was lost. The man grabbed the child and jumped onto the back of the rat." They live for a long time with the monster in its hole. The rat hunts at night to feed the man and child. The two escape at last and return to their people. Later, on the night of a full moon, and with many ravens, the people sharpen their knives and kill the monster. "The monster rat was more massive than a very big whale, and had enormously long upper teeth." The people butcher the monster and find many people "who had been killed and eaten by the big rat." Only chiefs sit on the skin of the monster, but others are envious and that causes wars over the rat skin. "When the battle ended" the people put the chief's corpse inside the tail of the rat, wrap that in the skin and burn the bundle. The remains are thrown in the water, and that starts more wars. "These people were just like each other, though living in a different land," the story ends. "But these people waged war over that rat skin, people just like each other. What good is a rat skin? They did that, though, and nothing more could happen to them, no more wars with anyone. They were wiped out completely."

Haida means "the people" in translation, and the people are eminent, creative storiers. A child becomes a salmon, and later returns to his mother, a shamanic reincarnation in "Moldy Collar Tip" by Victor Haldane. His story is about the natives who teach their children to respect the salmon. The narrator shows a reciprocal tradition between humans and the salmon. "A long time ago a child kept on scorning fish," a moldy fish, and the salmon lure the child to "really nice land." They eat and dance for four winters. The child returns home with the salmon, and when he sees his mother on the beach "he jumped out of the water at a spot where she would notice him." She catches him and tries to cut his head off, but he is "wearing a small whetstone around his neck." A shaman tells the mother that her child has returned. "Lay him on the roof of the house. And then it will rain on him. And your child will return again." Three days he later loses his fish skin and becomes a human. "That's the way the tradition is."

Haida stories create a sense of natural honor, and that "implies proper attitude and behavior, not only towards other humans but to all creatures," writes Jeane Breinig in "Commentary on Haida Texts." The salmon, as in the "Moldy Collar Tip," are "especially revered and continue to be a valued source of food and spiritual sustenance for Haida and other Southeast Alaska Native peoples; hence, any disparaging remarks about them are strictly forbidden."

The trickster is a comic character, a healer by contradiction, by the tease of conversion, the ruse of envy, and by humor in native stories. The mode of trickster stories is comic not tragic, and the encounter is in the mind, a language game, not a representation of victimry. Ivan Durak is a trickster character of many conversions in native stories. Richard Dauenhauer points out that the source of the name is in Russian folklore: "Ivan Durak means John the Fool or John the Idiot. The name is sometimes translated as Ivan the Simpleton."

"There was this fellow named Ivan Durak. He was a liar about everything," is how the story, "Ivan Durak Steals a Ring," is told in Alutiiq by Dick Kamluck, Sr. "Was he a good liar, or was he a good liar." The comic choice, of course, teases the listener, and that is a tricky start to a trickster story. Ivan tells a Man of High Position, "If I want to get a wife, I can get your wife." The listener is always in on the comedy. Ivan Durak digs up a dead man from the cemetery, and that night he presses the body "against the window." The Man of High Position, warned, waits at the window with his gun. "As soon as the body came up, he shot it," and the "body buckled over." His wife thinks he has killed Ivan Durak. "Take him far away," she says. "People will forget all about Ivan Durak." The Man of High Position carries the body away. Meanwhile, the real Ivan Durak enters the house and pretends to be the husband. He caresses her hands, and takes her ring, fakes a search in the blankets, and then leaves the house. The next morning he returns, wearing the wife's ring. Naturally, they wonder how he came back to life. The Man of High Position learns about the ring and says he will kill Ivan Durak. "You already did," says Ivan Durak.

"Ivan Durak is a trickster," observes Patricia Partnow. "Like Raven in other stories in this volume, he is clever, selfish, and generally successful. However, two elements distinguish the two tricksters: Raven is also a creator figure, while Ivan is rooted firmly in the human world with no special spiritual or creative powers; and Raven's actions often provide lasting benefit to the world despite the selfish motives that inspire them, while Ivan's are strictly self-serving." In other stories, she points out, the "boundary between humans and nature, natural and supernatural, life and death is perceived to be permeable even today in the Alutiiq world view."

Robert H. Davis, in his poem "Saginaw Bay: I Keep Going Back," creates a sense of native presence, the first light over the sea and land, in the cocksure character of the trickster Raven. Near the end of the poem, in the seventh and eighth stanzas, he writes: Because Raven tracks are locked in fossil, clam beds still snarled in roots because it has been told to us this way, we know for a fact Raven moves in the world.

> The old ones tell a better story in Tlingit.
> When I was small everyone used Tlingit
> and English at once.
> Tlingit fit better. . . .

You wonder why sometimes you can't reach me?
I keep going back.
I keep trying to picture my life
against all this history,
Raven in the beginning

hopping about like he just couldn't do enough.

Sister Goodwin creates humorous scenes in "Piksinñaq," a delightful play of images, old and new, in Inuit culture. Popcorn arrives, the new century awakens, and, for hours, Aana, the grandmother of this poem, waits for the popcorn "to make her bounce around." Here are the first and last stanzas of the poem:

when popcorn
first came up north
north to kotzebue sound
little iñuit
took it home from school
long long ago when
the new century first woke up. . . .

for hours
Aana sat hunched over
with her eyes squinched shut
she grasped onto neat rows
of willow branches
waiting for the popcorn
to make her bounce around

Glen Simpson, a Tahltan and Kaska Athabaskan, creates a natural, comparative scene at a hotel bar after a moody day in a museum, the absence of natives. The narrator in "Traveling in the Land of the Native Art Historians" asks how "many would puke their cafeteria lunches if they learned that hunting people hunted?" He mentions "the smack of a bullet striking flesh," and "that special quick laughter" in times of fear. Here are the last six lines of the poem:

Indians, under the lights,
gave more answers than were theirs to give.
But who am I to talk like this;
a man alone with a designer beer,
just an excuse for not going back to that costly room
with its windows permanently sealed against the night air.

Old World diseases decimated natives, and smallpox "became the single most lethal disease Europeans carried to the New World," writes Henry Dobyns in *Native American Historical Demography*. Russell Thornton, the native sociologist, notes in *American Indian Holocaust and Survival* that smallpox was the most "destructive during the nineteenth century."

The Russians colonized Alaska, and in the nineteenth century, "Yankee whalers from New England hunted extensively in arctic waters," write Susan Andrews and John Creed in *Authentic Alaska: Voices of Its Native Writers*. "These Yankee whalers brutalized many of the Native peoples they encountered, while driving the arctic's whale population, on which the coastal Iñupiat depended, to near extinction. In addition to new diseases, the New England whalers also introduced alcohol to Natives who had no previous experience with this addictive drug." Many natives thought that "they had been overcome by evil."

Mary Jane Nielsen writes with courage about a frightening and devastating disease, Acquired Immune Deficiency Syndrome, in her personal, emotive story, "What Hope Can Do." Arnold, the author's brother-in-law, "looked like a starved holocaust victim, his cheeks sunken into his bones. His once-thick dark hair had thinned and turned an odd reddish color. Weak eyes stared back at us out of his pale gaunt face." Arnold, a Vietnam veteran, is hospitalized and uses a wheelchair. He "had been trying for seven months to kick a drinking and drug problem," and later, "struggled to gain back his strength at the Alaska Native Medical Center." As soon as he is able to walk again, the family arranges for his return to South Naknek.

"Arnold expressed fear that people in the community might shun him, be afraid of him, or talk about him," writes Mary Jane Nielsen. "Fortunately, we have learned that people have become generally far more informed about AIDS than when this dreaded disease first began spreading around the United States in the early 1980s. Friends and family visited Arnold at home in South Naknek. Some people shook his hand. Some even hugged him, much to our relief and joy."

He recovers in the care of his family and spirit of his community. Arnold gains weight over the months. The doctor says he is a "miracle patient," and Arnold attributed his recovery to "family support, a good doctor, and prayer." Soon, he is strong enough to travel and talk to groups about his disease, and his recovery. "I used to wonder what I was here for," he tells the author. "Maybe, this is why I'm here."

Native stories create a sense of presence and survivance, and the storiers are artistic or scriptural shamans. The visions of many storiers are similar to shamanic ecstasies in the sense of separation, the conversions of time, totemic mediation, and creation, return, or source of spiritual power. Shamans and native storiers, at the same time, encounter evil, dominance, and victimry.

Peter Kalifornsky, in an interview with Katherine McNamara, says that the "shaman is trying to receive a power from good things." McNamara asks, uneasily, "if the bad spirit is part of humans," and he "laughed wryly." Kalifornsky says, "We live alongside bad things." Kalifornsky's "work is a network of literacy," and the "power of this literacy, of course, stems from a certain relation to life, from being able to use writing with regard to what is already one's own," observes Dell Hymes in *A Dena'ina Legacy: The Collected Writings of Peter Kalifornsky*. His "life and work teach that where there is intelligence and sharing of knowledge, the potentialities rooted in a human language can flower in our lives, even at the last hour."

Shamans "believed in what they could see," and that "belief involved the spirit of every living animal and every living plant," says Kalifornsky in "About Shamans and the Men with Gashaq." The shamans "would contact the living being with their mind and they would start gathering the spirit of that thing through a transfer of power from one to the other."

Likewise, many creative storiers are the aesthetic shamans of scripture; they see the spirit of characters, and envision the scenes of a narrative by nature, by action, by myths, by ancestral names in the power of words. This anthology of native storiers creates shamanic listeners and readers.

– Gerald Vizenor

Gerald Vizenor is professor of Native American literature at the University of California, Berkeley. He is the author of more than twenty books on native history and literature, including *Manifest Manners: Narratives on Postindian Survivance*. His novel, *Griever: An American Monkey King in China*, won the American Book Award. His most recent book is *Fugitive Poses: Native American Indian Scenes of Absence and Presence*.

EDITOR'S NOTE

Alaska is rich in Native culture and heritage as illustrated by the fact that there are about twenty distinct Native languages spoken here. Sadly, however, many of the languages are in danger of dying out. Eyak, for example, has only one Native speaker left; Haida has about ten. This compelling reality reinforces our strong belief that it is important for our readers to have an appreciation for the diversity of the original Alaska Native languages. To that end, we have selected ten works to appear in their original Native language versions and in English. The impulse to tell stories is, of course, universal to the human condition, and language is the lens through which we convey who we are. These primary texts emphasize the distinctiveness of Alaska Native people and their respective literary traditions and heritages. And while we recognize that most readers will not be able to read the original language versions, we believe it is essential nonetheless to include them; culture and heritage are nurtured and shared by their publication.

By including the original Native language texts we further hope to suggest the deeper levels of *all* of the translated texts and perhaps even inspire interested readers to learn an Alaska Native language.

Finally, we wish to express our admiration and our deepest gratitude to the living Native language speakers and tradition bearers who keep their cultures alive through their stories and through their words.

– Ronald Spatz

Íñupiaq

Gwichin

Han

Koyukon

Tanacross

Tanana

Upper Tanana

St. Lawrence Island
Yupik

Holikachuk

Upper
Kuskokwim

Ingalik

Denaiina

Ahtna

Central Yupik

Eyak

Tlingit

Tsimshian

Haida

Aleut (Unangan/Unangas)

Alutiiq/Sugcestun

Alaska
Native
Languages

ORAL TRADITIONS &
WRITTEN TEXTS

Anna Nelson Harry

I·YA·QDALAHGAYU·, DAŁI'Q' LAG̣ADA'A·ŁIṄU·

1 Ayanh si'aht*.
2 Dik' waẋ qu'xłale·q qi'yisinh.
3 *K'e·t iẋ k'uqu'di·xłch'a·q'?
4 Al waẋ i'xle·,
  u·t ich' q'e' iqe'xła'e·.
5 Daqi·kih sałe'ł.
6 *Anh siyahsh waẋ sitl' tsin'dale·.
7 *Anh ts'itwaẋ ki·nẋ siẋa' sałe'ł da·ẋ aw q'aw.

8 Da'a·nt dlag̣axu· yaẋ qu'xda·.
9 Ch'i·lehyu·g̣a' dlag̣axu· qu'gali·xta·.
10 Si'ahtgayu·* siẋa' lag̣ada'a·ł da·ẋ dlag̣axu· q'al qu'gali·xta·.
11 A·nt ala· de·lehtshdal waxyu· g̣axle·ł?
12 Sig̣a·kgayu·dik* siẋa' łi'q' i·nsdi'ahł da·ẋ dik' uk'ah
   laxstahłg̣inu·.
13 Ahnu· sig̣a·kgayu· siẋa' lisdi'ahłch'aht q'uhnu·,
   si'ahtgayu· siẋa' q'e' lag̣ada'a·ł.
14 Daxu· dlag̣axu·.

2

Anna Nelson Harry

LAMENT FOR EYAK

1 My poor aunt.[1]
2 I couldn't believe you were going to die.
3 How would I hear you?[3]
4 I wish this,
   to go back to you there.
5 You are no more.
6 My child speaks to me that way.[6]
7 I just break out in tears and lament.[7]

8 All alone here I'll go around.
9 Like Ravens I'll live alone.
10 My aunts are dying off on me and alone I'll be living.[10]
11 Why, I wonder, are these things happening to me?
12 My uncles also have all died out on me and I can't forget
   them.[12]
13 After my uncles all died off,
   my aunts are dying off next.
14 I'm all alone.

Anna Nelson Harry, Eyak from Cordova and Yakutat, Alaska.

15 Saqe·gayu· six̣a' atgax̱łala·ł, al anhq'ach'a'.*
16 Ch'itwax̱ ki·nx̱ six̣a' a'łe·k'.
17 Aw ulah yax̱ adi·lihx̱ła'ya·x̱ da·t ahnu· si'ahtgayu·.
18 Si'aht q'a'anh da·x̱ anh gał'ihtya· si'aht six̣a' k'a·dih sałe'ł.
19 Da·chi·dal q'e' qu'xda·?
20 Da·chi·dal q'e' qu'xda·?
21 Datli· dałi'q' ahnu· i·nsdi'ahł.
22 Ahnu· i·nsdi'ahł.
23 Daxu·sh k'e·'shuw da·al Qa·ta·' k'e·'shuw wax̱ six̣ä' ileh,
dlagaxu· galagaxtahx̱.
24 Ts'itwax̱ awa· atq' da·xdadza·nts' da·x̱ k'udzu· sidagale· siya·
q'e' dałe·k'.
25 A·ndax̱,
awleht q'aw al anh,
qi' atk'udadadza·nts',
yax̱ axda·k.'
26 A'xq'e·'k' awch' ixiyah.
27 Dlagaxu· q'aw,
dlagaxu·kih a·ndax̱ lu·di·'daxyu· yax̱ axda·k'.
28 Ts'itwax̱ ki·nx̱ six̣a' łe·k'.
29 Tsa·dli·na'q' ya·n' axda·k'.
30 Ts'itwax̱yu· I·ya·qdalahgayu·, I·ya·qdalahgayu·, dałi'q'
lagada'a·łinu·.
31 Ts'itwax̱ dax̱k'nu·shduw u·t I·ya·qda·t.
32 I·ya·qch'aht adiłilahł, ahnu·dik daqi·kih gałe'ł.
33 K'a·dih ulah u·ch' q'e' i·łi'e·.
34 Sitinhgayu·dik* six̣a' i·nsdi'ahł.
35 Sitinhg̱ayu· six̣a' lisłi'ahłch'aht q'al ahnu· si'ahtg̱ayu· q'uh ya·n'
q'e' disłiqahqł, al i·sinh.

36 A·n,
de·lehtdal dlagaxu·,
ts'it dlagaxu· atxsłilahł?
37 Atg̱ax̱łala·ł.

15 With some children I survive,
   on this earth.[15]
16 Only I keep bursting into tears.
17 I think about where my aunts are.
18 She is my aunt and my last aunt is gone.
19 Where will I go next?
20 Wherever will I go next?
21 They are already all extinct.
22 They have been wiped out.
23 Maybe me, I wonder, maybe Our Father wants it this way for
   me, that I should live alone.
24 I only pray for it and my spirits recover.
25 Around here,
   that's why this land,
   a place to pray,
   I walk around.
26 I try to go there.
27 Alone,
   alone around here I walk around on the beach at low tide.
28 I just break into tears.
29 I sit down on a rock.
30 Only the Eyaks,
   the Eyaks,
   they are all dying off.
31 Just a very few at Eyak there.
32 They survived from Eyak,
   but they too are becoming extinct.
33 Useless to go back there.
34 My uncles too have all died out on me.[34]
35 After my uncles all died out my aunts next
   fell,
   to die.

36 Yes,
   why is it I alone,
   just I alone have survived?
37 I survive.

– *Collected, transcribed in Eyak, and
translated by Michael E. Krauss
Originally published in* In Honor of
Eyak: The Art of Anna Nelson
Harry, *edited by Michael E. Krauss,*

Alaska Native Language Center,
University of Alaska, Fairbanks,
1982.

NOTES

Recorded on tape, Yakutat, June 15, 1972. It was difficult in spots for me to transcribe this, both because I did not have the help of a native speaker of Eyak and because the sounds are sometimes difficult to recognize in the singing style, which interferes especially with vowel length, glottalization, etc., and also because Anna's language here is often very poetic. I am nevertheless fairly confident that I have correctly interpreted it in most cases. Sentences 1–7 are a kind of spoken introduction; the chanted lament itself is sentences 8–34.

1. -'aht (Tlingit aat) is father's sister. Perhaps specifically Wa·njangaq, wife of Old Man Dude, Cordova, who died in 1930. See Birket-Smith and de Laguna 1938, pp. 220–221, for account of her death, Genealogical Table, and Plate 6.2 for a photograph of her grave.

3. More literally 'How will I hear anything of you?'

6. Perhaps to be interpreted Anh "Siyahsh" waẋ sitl' tsin'dale· ' "My child," that way she speaks to me', that is, 'my aunt calls me "my child"'. This is usual for a mother's sister, but not for a father's sister.

7. Perhaps to be interpreted 'She just became tearful with me' in accordance with footnote 6; da·ẋ aw 'and it is', 'and so', as direct introduction to the chanted lament.

10. -'aht-gayu· (Tlingit aat hás) 'father's sisters' or 'father's sister's side of the family'.

12. -ga·k-gayu· (Tlingit káak hás) 'mother's brothers', or 'mother's brother's side of the family'. Perhaps specifically Blind Sampson O'Shaw (1866–1948) (Tlingit name Yaanduɫsín, Eyak Wa·ndaɫsan, also name of Anna's son Johnny) or Billy Jackson (died about 1949, Tlingit name Eitisée), both of Yakutat. The aunts and uncles whom Anna mentions are mother's brother and father's sister, the relations which are called by the same terms in Tlingit as in Eyak (káak = -ga·k, aat = -'aht), except in 34–35 below.

15. al anhq'ach'a' also perhaps '(by moving) to this area'.

34. tinh-gayu· 'father's brothers' or 'father's brother's side of the family'.

LAKE-DWARVES
(told in Eyak)

A man was out hunting on foot. He came upon some lake-dwarves. He stood there and watched. Before him, boating around, were two little canoes filled with these lake-dwarves.

Just then a mouse came out. To their eyes it was a brown bear, that mouse. The dwarves got into a scurry over the mouse. Many dwarves shot at it with their bows and arrows, until at last they killed it. Then, lo, they saw a second mouse, and they were going to kill this one too.

The man was watching that. "Wha – ? What is that?" he pondered.

After the dwarves had killed the second mouse, they landed their canoes and proceeded to tow the two mice to shore. These wee people began butchering the mice the way brown bears are butchered. They took off the skin. Then they cut up the carcass. It was quite a struggle to load that mousemeat into their boats. It took two dwarves to carry the hindquarter, the mouse-thigh. They worked very hard until all the meat from the two mice was loaded into their boats – the ribs, the spine. They took the mouse-spine too. That lesser little mouse, for them, was a black bear.

While they were bustling about over their work, preoccupied with the mice, the man reached down and plucked up one of the wee people. He took him and tucked him under his belt.

The dwarf pleaded with the man. "Please, these things I hunt with, I'll give them to you if you release me. They are yours if you let me go. You will become a great hunter if you free me." The little fellow was begging the man quite pitifully. "I will show you my weapon." He handed it to the man. It was the size of the man's thumb, like a strawberry leaf. Then the dwarf said, "Put this inside your rifle whenever you are going to shoot anything." The man set him free.

The other lake-dwarves were at their boats and ready to leave, waiting for their comrade who was missing, who had disappeared from their midst. The hunter had freed him and he was running back to his people. When he arrived they asked him, "Where are your weapons?"

"I gave them away. That's how I managed to get back here. A huge man, big as a tree he was, grabbed me. I got him to release me by giving him all my things."

"Maybe it was a tree-man," they said to him.

"No, no. He was a person. He was the size of a tree, though. A huge person. He was enormous. He had clothes on and he stuck me under his belt. I offered him everything to pay him off. I finally gave him my lucky hunting leaf and for that he let me go."

"Quick! Hurry up! He'll come upon us again!"

The dwarves put out their boats, paddled across the lake, and got home.

My, how their women came running down to meet them! Their little husbands had killed a brown bear and a black bear and had come boating home to them. The little people brought the meat ashore. Although it was already evening, the women hung the meat in the curing-house, right away, just as it was. The next day they would cut it into strips. Some went to bed, but it was expected that at any time the man would come.

They had boated clear across the lake. There was no way for the man to walk across, because it was such a deep lake.

He too went home. After all, he was out hunting for black bear when he came across these lake-dwarves.

– Collected, transcribed in Eyak, and translated by Michael E. Krauss Originally published in In Honor of Eyak: The Art of Anna Nelson Harry, *edited by Michael E. Krauss, Alaska Native Language Center, University of Alaska, Fairbanks, 1982.*

GIANT RAT

A man and woman and their child were boating along, looking for berries, when they came upon the cliff where the monster reputedly had its hole.

'I wish we might see it,' said the woman.

The man said, 'Shhh! Don't ask for trouble!' And just as he spoke the rat emerged behind them, capsizing their canoe. The woman was lost. The man grabbed the child and jumped onto the back of the big rat.

It took them into its hole, where they jumped off. The man held the child. She was afraid of the monster. Nevertheless, they lived a long time with this giant monster rat.

When it got dark the rat would go out hunting. It would bring home seals and ducks for the man and his child. Then it would lie down on top of them to cook them. When the food was cooked, the rat gave it to the man and his child and they ate it. They were living this way for some time. The man would try climbing the spruce-roots which hung from above, while the rat was gone. He got out. But he knew the rat would look for them as soon as it came back, so he hurried back in. When the rat returned, they were sitting there. It lay in under itself what it had killed and gave it to the man and his child to eat.

His child was a little girl.

When it was pitch-dark the rat would leave, returning as it began to get light out. One day just before it got light the man put the girl on his back and climbed out of the rat-hole. He was going along, and had not yet gotten very far, when the rat returned. It immediately missed them and started banging its tail around, knocking everything down.

The man and his daughter returned to their people safely. He told them, 'Go get some young ravens. Snare them. Snare lots of them.' They did as he asked.

When the moon was full, they went there. (The rat would stay in and never go out when the moon was full.)

They sharpened their knives and axes, packed the young ravens on their backs, and headed for the rat-hole. 'Now dump the ravens down into the rat-hole to see if they'll be quiet.' (If the birds remained quiet, that would mean the hole was empty.) Immediately they clamored. The rat jerked his tail partway down but the people chopped it off, thus killing the monster.

The rat moved forward as it died, but only about halfway out. They were going to tow it down to shore but it was too big. They had to leave it there, until a big tide came and carried it down to the shore.

The monster rat was more massive than a very big whale, and had enormously long upper teeth. Its hair was longer than a black bear's fur.

The corpse of the giant rat floated out and as it washed around, they towed it ashore. They butchered it to get the skin. When they cut it open, they found all sorts of things in its stomach. People who had been disappearing mysteriously, they now found, had been killed and eaten by this big rat. They found people's skulls in its stomach. The people butchered it for its skin. The hair was already going in some places, but where it was good they dried it.

After this, they called a potlatch and exhibited before the people's eyes what had been killing their relatives. Now, not just anyone could use that rat-skin, only a chief could sit on the monster rat-skin. At the potlatch the people kept saying, 'No cheapskate will sit on it. Only chiefs. Too many people have fallen victim to this rat. Those poor wretches, all killed. That's why only chiefs will sit on it.'

Word spread of the giant rat-skin and a tribe from some distant land wanted it for themselves. These people from another land came and made war over it. Many people died, but the rat-skin was not wrested from them. The chief who used to sit on it was the first to be killed in the war for that rat-skin. Therefore it could not be abandoned. It was of no concern to them how many would perish on its account, or how many would die in the pursuit of that skin. They fought to a finish.

When the battle ended, they took the chief's corpse from among the other dead people and put it inside the rat's tail. Then they wrapped it in the rat-skin and burned it.

(In the old days people didn't bury one another. Whoever died was cremated and his charred remains were gathered in a box.)

Thus they did to their chief's bones. But then the other tribe found out about the box and stole it and packed it up the mountain and threw it in the water.

Then there was another battle, between that other tribe and those whose chief's bones had been thrown into the water. They were all wiped out, except for old men and women and children. They killed all the young men. That's what happened to those whose chief's bones were thrown in the water.

Their children grew up and wanted revenge, but never got revenge. They got wiped out, those whose chief's bones were thrown in the water.

These people were just like each other, though living in a different land. There are people from Sitka living here at Yakutat just like we do. Though they are foreigners, they live harmoniously with us. But these people waged war over that rat-skin, people just like each other. What good is a rat-skin? They did that, though, and nothing more could happen to them, no more wars with anyone. They were wiped out completely.

That's all.

– Collected, transcribed in Eyak, and translated by Michael E. Krauss Originally published in In Honor of Eyak: The Art of Anna Nelson Harry, *edited by Michael E. Krauss, Alaska Native Language Center, University of Alaska, Fairbanks, 1982.*

Victor Haldane

KUL K'ALUUDAAY

Húutl'an Gasa.áan eihl naháangaan-dluu,
Gaadáa-'aa-tl'ts'aagáas-dluu,
chíin gáakw-uu tl'íijaangaan.
'Wáadluu gaa xadalgáayk tl' súutgaangaan,
5 'wáadluu chíinaayk tl' sk'ínggaangs-dluu,
tl'áak tl' gyaehlántgaangaan.
Tl'áak tl' ḵ'íigaang[gaangaan].
'Wáadluu wéit chíin ḵíigaang is tl'áak tl' súutgaangaan.
Awáahl gagwíi nang gaa xajúu chíink sk'ínggaang sgwáanang-
gaangaan.
10 Gudúu ḵ'áludaas-dluu, hal súugaangaan,
"Íi! Gám ga díi gudáng'anggang!"
'Wáadluu láa tl' súutgaangaan,
"Jáa gám [huk'ún hl] súu'ang.
Dáng súugang ḵáwt-uu chíin xaat'áay dáng isdáasaang."
15 'Wáadluu chaaw salíi-'aa hal náanggan-daan, [Gaadáahl],
sahgúust [án tl' dáng stlúudaalt'a.eilaan].
'Wáadluu láa-'an tl' gidatl'áas-dluu tl'eihl hal kyáenaangaan,
"Gitl'áank-uu dláng íijang?

12

Victor Haldane

MOLDY COLLAR TIP
(told in Haida)

When they lived in Kasaan,
when they moved to Karta Bay,
they went to get salmon.
And then they told the children
5 when they refuse and turn up their noses at the fish,
they told them stories,
they told them legends.
Then they told them traditions concerning fish.
A long time ago a child kept on scorning fish.
10 When it was a little moldy, he would say,
"Ee! Yuck! I don't want it!"
And then they would say to him,
"Hey! Don't say that!
If you keep talking like that, the fish people will do something
    to you."
15 And then while he was playing on the beach at Karta Bay
[a southeast wind was blowing].
And then when they came to him he asked,
"Where are you folks going?

Victor Haldane, Haida from Hydaburg, Alaska.

Jáa! Gitl'áank-uu dláng íijang?"
20 "Jáa, tlak 'láa-'aa tl'áng ts'at'a.íidang-gwaa.
Hawíit íitl'-'eihl is."
'Wáadluu tl'eihl hal [káaydaan].
Chíin xaat'áay-uu 'láa isdáayaan.
'Wáadluu tl' isdáal káwt-uu tlak 'láa gusdl.yáaykw-uu tl'
[istl'aagáan].
25 Kálk xitkw-uu na íw'aandaa tíiwaanggaangaan.
Ts'at'áan náay isgyáan sk'ak náay isgyáan sgwáagaan náay.
Asgáaykw-uu tlak tl' guláagaangaan.
Gáa tl' [xyáahlsgaangs]
Tl' gatáa 'láa áwyaa.
30 'Wáadluu sánggaat stánsang-dluu gu tl' íijaangaan.
'Wáadluu gu tl' gáayaas-gyaen isíisan tl' íw'aandaagaay[s tl'áa]
háwsan sahlgáang ts'at'a.íidan.
'Wáadluu ts'at'iit-s-dlúu tl'eihl sahlgáang hal ijáan.
Nang gaa
xajúu tl' gál [káaydaan].
35 'Wáadluu húutl'an Gaadá.ahl háws hal gidatl'a.áas-dluu
hal aw chaaw salíi-'aa [k'atga] k'idáas-dluu 'láa hal kínggaan-
gaan.
'Wáadluu 'láa k'yuuk hal gadiyáanggwaanggaangaan.
Hal íijang káwt-uu hal aw 'láa hal [k'ahlkíyaas]-dluu, hal gat-
l'a'áas dlúu,
"[Áyáw!]" hín hal súugaangaan.
40 "Áyáw! hal [gat'uwáahlwaan] 'láa hal súut.
Gíidang káwt-uu 'láa hal duungéihls-dluu 'láa hal gitsgíihl-
daayaan.
[Asgáay-dluu] hal kats 'wáast 'láa hal k'ik'íitl' sánsdlaas-dluu
húuk'us gyaa tl'ak'gyáa hal kán xagángs-uu
ahljíi 'láa gat'uwáas-gyaen-uu.
45 Asgáayst-uu [nang sgáagaas-'aa 'láa hal dliidáan].
'Wáadluu nang sgáagaas 'láa súudaayaan,
"Jáa, dáng git awáahl gagwíi dáng gúutgan-uu
sahlgáang dáng-'an gidatl'a.áang-gwaa.
Náay úngkw-hl ['láa] dlahlandaa.
'Wáadluu 'láa gwíi gwa.áaws-gyään.
50 Háws sahlgáang dáng git sdíihlsaang!"
'Wáadluu huk'ún 'láa hal isdás-gyaen.
[. . . .]
'Wáadluu náay úngkw 'láa hal dlahlándaayaan.
Sáng hlgúnahl gu hal dluudáa[yaan],

Hey! Where are you folks going?"
20 "Hey! We're moving off to a fine land, you see.
Come on; come with us."
And then he went along with them.
[Actually] the salmon people were taking him.
After traveling for a while, they came to a really nice land.
25 Under the ice there stood huge houses.
Pink Salmon House and Dog Salmon House and Sockeye
Salmon House.
They liked the land very much.
They were dancing there.
They ate very well.
30 And then they stayed there four winters.
And they grew fat there and again, [the ones that were fully
grown] moved back again.
And then when they started to migrate, he went back with
them.
They led the child away.
And then when they arrived at Karta Bay,
35 he kept seeing his mother, who was cutting fish down on the
beach.
And then he jumped out of the water at a spot where she
would notice him.
After a while, when his mother noticed him, when he jumped
out of the water,
she said, "Ayaww!"
"Ayaww!" she said [when he jumped].
40 After a while when he came close to her, she caught him.
And when she was trying to cut his head off,
he was wearing a small whetstone around his neck.
This is what her [knife] struck.
They brought a shaman there.
45 And then the shaman said to them,
"Hey! The child you lost a long time ago has come back to you,
see!
Lay him on the roof of the house.
And then it will rain on him.
And your child will return again."
50 And then they did what he said.
And then they laid him on the house.
He lay there for three days.
Then after a while his fish skin came off.
He again became a human.

55 asgáayst-uu
   gíidang ḵáwt-uu chíin ḵ'ál 'wáast 'láangaa is-gyáan,
   sahlgáang háws hal x̱aat'a.éilaan.
   'Wáadluu ahl'áanaas-uu Gasa.áan eihl nang sgáagaa
         tláats'gaa gusdliyéi-uu hal
   ijáan 'láa tl' súud[aawaan].
60 'Wáadluu tluk gin wáadluwaan [isáasii] tl'áak hal súutgaangaan.
   Hín gat'u wáa áwyaa'angḵasa.aas-dluu tl'áak hal súudaas-
      gyaen-uu
   húujii tluwáay áangaa tl'ḵagántgalgaangaan.
   'Wáadluu hal [k'ut'ahldáal]s-dluu tl'áa[k] hal súudaayaan,
   [. . . .]
65 húutl'an Gaadáa [ḵ'yúuk ḵwaa] íw'aan x̱íilaas aa,
   asgáaykw-uu 'láa-tl' dluudiyéik hal gudáangaan,
   hal k'udahls-dlúu aa.
   'Wáadluu gíi 'láa tl' [isdáas guu] hawáan tl'áak gin súutgangang.
   [. . . .]
   Ahljíi uu gáwjuwaay hawáan 'láa tl' gudánggang.
   [. . . .]
   Ahljíi uu tluk tl' ḵ'íigangaay gíidang.

55 And they said he became a very powerful shaman in Kasaan.
And then he told them how everything [was going to be].
He told them when it was going to storm hard, and
they would bring their canoes up to safety.
When he went away to die, he told them
60 on the outside of Kasaan there is a cave.
He wanted them to lay him in there.
And when he died,
he still spoke to them after he was put in there.
They still hear his drum.
That's the way the tradition is.

– Told and recorded by Victor Haldane
in Hydaburg, Alaska, on February
3, 1973
Transcribed and translated by
Charles Natkong, Sr.
Edited by Jeff Leer and Richard
Dauenhauer

NOTES

This story was first told in Haida. See "Fish Story: Karta Bay," following, for the same story told by the same storyteller, but in English.

The tape recording from which the Haida is transcribed is severely damaged in many places, so that some words and lines are unclear or lost entirely. Parts in question are marked by angle brackets [ ]. Because of the missing lines, the line count is slightly different in Haida and English. Some words in the Haida text are transcribed in a provisional orthography reflecting Hydaburg pronunciation; these spellings may change in future publications. The present text and translation were drafted as a project of the Sealaska Heritage Foundation with grant support from the Administration for Native Americans.

– R.D.

FISH STORY: KARTA BAY
(told in English)

I will translate the story of the fish as it originated in Karta Bay years ago. It almost coincides with the findings of Fish and Wildlife about the migration of the salmon as it leaves the stream, but it must be borne in mind that when these legends were made, the Natives themselves, the Haidas, Tlingits, or whoever made these legends, believed that these fish that went up the creek and died had spirits, and that their spirits actually went into the next fish that were spawned; or in other words, life was passed on just like a human being passes its own self into another human being; therefore reproducing in that manner so that these stories were actual visions that were supposed to have been seen by Indian doctors or people of vision and even prophecy. They had some who were prophets and told stories.

So the story goes, in Karta Bay there was a family who went there during the summer to put up fish, and they had a little boy who was always skeptical about the fish and he would say, "Eee! I don't like this fish because it has mold on it."

So in order to make him eat the fish, his parents tried to scare him and told him that if he said that too many times, that fish people would come and get him, or take him away.

So one day when he was playing on the beach there at Karta Bay where the river comes down, he saw a great number of people coming down from the river towards him, and they were filing by and he asked them, "Where are you folks going?"

And they told him, "We are going to a far country. We're traveling a long ways." And of course these were the fish people – spirits of the fish people, as it refers to them in the legend.

And the boy said, "I would like to go with you." So they said, "Come and follow us."

So he went with them and they traveled a long ways until they came to a great big city with a lot of buildings scattered around, and these buildings were composed of different clans. Some were the Herring Clan, Humpy Clan, Dog Salmon Clan. And they, the people, belonged to the Sockeye Clan. Those were to his way of

18

thinking actual people, so that when they arrived at this place he looked up into the sky, and saw nothing but ice over his head.

So it was visualized then, that the fish traveled way up into the Bering Sea to get fat and stay for a certain time to grow up. He stayed there (the boy) and attended these potlatches and got fat and became big for a period of four years, and the clan he was with decided to travel back to the place where they originated from. That is their home town and so they started back.

And they came to Cape Chacon and a group went up towards Hydaburg or Cordova Bay which is on the map now, and a group traveled on towards Kasaan or Karta Bay.

So when they arrived at Karta Bay he spotted his mother sitting on the beach there carving up fish for drying and putting up for the winter, and he was so happy to see his mother that he began jumping around in the water there, and finally his mother spotted him.

Every time he jumped, she would say "Ay-oh!" so now that expression has been passed on from generations and most all Natives in our area say "Ay-oh!" when a fish jumps, which is a sign of pleasure in seeing a fish arrive or jumping in the bay.

This fish, a Sockeye, kept jumping around and came closer and closer, and finally this woman grabbed the fish and started to cut its head off. And her knife hit a piece of brass that was the collar that the son had worn around his neck, when he disappeared from Karta Bay.

So they went to the Indian doctor and asked him what to do. And they explained what happened, and the Indian doctor told them, "That is your son, who disappeared four years ago. He has come back in the spirit of a Sockeye. So in order to bring him back to his own way of living or state, place him on top of the house and leave him there for three days."

So they took this Sockeye and put it on top of the house. And it rained on there for three days. And after three days they heard a tapping on the roof, and they went up and got him down, and here it was their son who had disappeared four years ago.

And the story goes on, when he grew up he became one of the most powerful Indian doctors that was ever around Kasaan amongst the Haida people. He was famous for predicting storms. And what he did was, he noticed the waves beginning to get large and the wind blowing from the Southeast, and he was sure according to the size of the waves, whether it was going to be a storm or just a breeze. And incidentally he would notify his people and they would pull their canoes up off the tide line, and save their canoes that way from being bashed against the shore.

So when he grew old he performed many other things that were of note. And when he was ready to die, he made the request, there's a cave at Karta Bay in which half of it is in the water, and half of it is showing on top of the water, and that is where he wanted to be buried.

He said, "You will know, every time the storm is building up. My warning will be the beating of the drums inside the cave."

So now to this very day this same thing happens. When the waves begin to get big from the Southeast, they pile into the cave there and you hear the sound of the drums – boom, boom, boom – in that manner.

So to this day they claim that he is there to warn them about saving their canoes out of the storms that are to come.

– Collected by Vesta Johnson
Transcribed by Erma Lawrence

SHAG AND THE RAVEN
(told in Haida)

A long time ago the Shag and Raven went fishing. Raven caught more halibut than the Shag. So the Shag asked the Raven, "What are you using for bait?" Although the Raven was using octopus for bait, he fooled him and said, "I'm using my privates for bait!" So the Shag proceeded to cut off his privates! So he also got a lot of halibut, even more than the Raven!

When their canoe was full they started back, and Raven started to scheme again about what he would tell the people, so before they arrived Raven thought of a trick and said to the Shag, "Let me see your tongue." So the Shag stuck out his tongue and immediately Raven cut out his tongue so the Shag could not talk. So when they landed the people asked them, "Where did you get so many halibut?" Raven said, "I caught it all by myself" and turned to Shag and said, "Isn't that right?" And all the Shag could say was "Aang, aang," which in Haida means "Yes, yes."

And so in time the Shag became angry and grabbed Raven but Raven got away. He chased Raven for some time until they came to a river. Raven took some kelp and stretched across the river and walked over on it. So the Shag followed, and when he got about halfway over Raven flipped the kelp over and the Shag fell into the river and drifted way out to sea, and so the story goes because the Shag is ashamed of himself he swam deep under water. So when they tell the story now they say the moral of the story is "You shouldn't believe all you hear, as all may not be the truth."

– Collected by Vesta Johnson
Transcribed in Haida and translated
into English by Erma Lawrence

NOTE

A shag is a seabird, a cormorant.

STORY OF THE DOUBLE FIN KILLER WHALE
(told in Haida)

A long time ago two young men went fishing. They were brothers. They went away out to sea. They were out there for quite some time when it became very foggy, so they just drifted around out there. While out there they noticed some small birds. It is said that the Haidas never killed these birds. It is when they killed these birds, that things began to turn bad for them. They drifted around for some time longer when suddenly someone, a person, came out of the ocean and began speaking to them, "Say! What you have done is very wrong. You have killed a very sacred bird, that's why it has become foggy for you. Nevertheless, we will help you. Come follow us."

So they followed this person or persons into the sea. They were taken to a place where people lived in large houses and it actually had roads leading here and there. These are the places where the porpoises lived. They were taken to the Chief of the Porpoise People and he said to the brothers, "We will help you now, and put this mark upon you." This marking is referring to the Killer Whale, with two fins. So the Chief of the Porpoise People said to the brothers, "We give you now this (garment) marking. Go back to your canoe." So they returned to their canoe and to the place where they lived, as two fin killer whale and one fin killer whale.

– Collected by Vesta Johnson
Transcribed in Haida and translated
into English by Erma Lawrence

Jessie Neal Natkong

BEAVER AND GROUND HOG WERE PALS
(told in Haida)

Beaver and Ground Hog were getting to be friends.
They were getting to be pals.
And eventually Beaver went everywhere together with
   Ground Hog.
After a while, Beaver swam Ground Hog out to his island.
Ground Hog was not able to swim.
He lived only underground.
After he stayed with him for a while,
Beaver swam away from him.
The [beaver] lodge formed an island.
He left him on the island.
Beaver was gone for a while.
After he left, he started to worry and
his food ran out.
Beaver went around in the woods eating tree bark.
He would go about felling trees and eat the bark.
When he didn't come back,
he started to worry, and

Jessie Neal Natkong, Haida from Hydaburg, Alaska

when the hunger hit him
he went outside and
when there was no sign of Beaver returning,
he started to sing.

    "Aa gwíikw gudéi, gudéi
    sax̂aaníidei, gudéi, gudéi
    sax̂aaníidei, hák'anaĝuhl tíixiityuutii k'ula tuu kusii
    gudéi, gudéi, sax̂aaníidei.

After this, he went inside again.
Again, after he stayed in the house
for a long time
he kept singing for freezing weather.
He kept feeling this water.
After singing this for a while, pieces of ice began to float.
He kept singing,
and after singing for freezing weather for a long time,
while he was singing, the water froze.
He ran out across the ice.
He was saved in this way.
And they stopped seeing each other.
There! It's finished.

      – Told by Jessie Neal Natkong in
        Hydaburg, Alaska, on March 8,
        1973
      Recorded, transcribed and translated
        by Charles Natkong, Sr.
      Edited by Richard Dauenhauer

NOTES

    We have supplied nouns in English translation. The Haida text uses only pronouns. The song is puzzling. It is not in Haida. Many words could be Tlingit, but it doesn't make complete sense in Tlingit either. It seems to be some kind of spirit song or incantation.

                                                            – R.D.

George Hamilton

HAIDA HUNTERS AND LEGEND OF THE TWO FIN KILLER WHALE
(told in Haida)

Right below Howcan, there's a little village they call "K'wíi Gánd-laas." Our uncles used to live there. The schooners would come there and they would go up North to go hunting. Haidas were good hunters so they would take them clear up to the Bering Sea. They would be gone for nine months. After that they would come back. They would bring back blankets, and food. That's all they got paid. When our uncles went back up there, I don't remember their names, one of them said, "If we don't come back, we will come back as Killer Whales, but we will have two fins, it will be us," they said.

Sure enough, late in the fall they were lost at sea and never found. During the winter, some children while playing outdoors became very excited. They saw Killer Whales with two fins. Everyone ran outside to see it, as the two fin Killer Whales circled around in the bay. That's how we claim the Killer Whale with two fins.

– Collected by Vesta Johnson
Transcribed in Haida and translated
into English by Erma Lawrence

George Hamilton, Haida from Craig, Alaska.

Willie Marks

YÉIL KA LÁX'
KÉET YAANAAYÍ
X'ÉIDAX SH KALNÉEK
KEIXWNÉICH KAWSHIXÍT

Wé láx' áwé
áa ajikawulneegí.
Du wakkáax' áwé awsinóot'.
Wé x'wáat' gíwé.
5 Wé láx'ch.
Áwé I dunno what kind of aliman.
Áa ajikawliník.
Yú láx' xánt woogoodí áwé
atx awudagootch a xánde,
10 "Yóo áyú idaayaká,
yú yú hobo yóot áa."
Héix' áwé tlél ash éex x'eitaan.
Ch'a aan áwé yéi ax'akanéek.
Awsikóo ku.aa áwé de du yíx yéi kanaléin
15 wé xáat.
"Du een kuxlagaawú

Willie Marks

RAVEN, SEAGULL AND CRANE
(told in Tlingit)

It was Crane
to whom Raven egged the Seagull on.
Before his eyes Crane swallowed it.
Maybe it was a trout
5 that he swallowed.
I don't know what kind of animal it was.
He egged them on.
After he went up to Crane
he'd turn around and go from one to the other, and say,
10 "That guy over there is talking about you,
that – that – bum, the one sitting over there."
Here he hadn't really been speaking to him at all.
But still he keeps on saying that's what he said.
Because he knows that fish
15 is already dissolving inside him.
"When I fight

Willie Marks, Tlingit from Hoonah, Alaska.

ax̱ x̱ooni ḵáa
du wóow shuyee áwé s'é ux̱latseix̱ch kíndei."
Yéi áwé ash shukoojeis'
20 du x̱'éináx̱ kei x̱lagáas'eet ásgé wé
wé x̱áat.
Wáa nanée sáwé du x̱'ayáx̱ wootee de.
Has ḵuwlihaa
wé láx̱' tín.
25 Ch'a aadéi ash koo.aaḵw
yáx̱ áwé aawatséx̱ a x̱'óol' kíndei.
Du x̱'éináx̱ yóot wuligás'
wé awsinóot'i x̱áat.
Wás at gadaḵín Yéil ku.aa.
30 "Déi áwé! Déi áwé! Déi áwé!
Yax̱ wooch yayeeydlijáaḵ."
Héix̱' áwé awsinóot' hóoch tsú de.
Yéi áwé x̱wsikóo.

28

with a guy like me,
first I usually kick him upward under the edge of the ribcage."
That's how he coaches him,
20 so that the fish
will pop out of his mouth, right?
Eventually he did as he said.
He began fighting
with Crane.
25 He kicked his belly upward,
just as Raven instructed him.
The fish he had swallowed
popped out of his mouth.
But then Raven flies in on the scene, as if by coincidence.
30 "Enough! Enough! Enough!
You're gonna kill each other."
But here he'd already swallowed it up again.
That's the way I know it.

– Transcribed and translated by
Nora Marks Dauenhauer

David Kadashan

SPEECH FOR THE REMOVAL OF GRIEF
(spoken in Tlingit)

My father's brothers, all my brothers-in-law,
   [Keet Yaanaayí: Áawé.]
we are feeling
your pain,
5 feeling it.
I will imitate my mother's brother
son of Ḵáak'w Éesh
your child
Tsalxaan Guwakaan
10   [Héiy!]
Yakwdeiyí Guwakaan.
   [Héiy!]
I will imitate your brother-in-law
   [Áawé.]
15 my brother-in-law Keet Yaanaayí
   [Áawé.]
Ḵaatooshtóow.
   [Áawé.]

David Kadashan, Tlingit from Hoonah, Alaska.

I will imitate your brother-in-law
20 Gusatáan.
[Héiy!]
I will imitate your child.
   [Thank you.]
Surely this is
25 a hard thing to do.
It is difficult to handle
things of this nature
and sensitive.
We are in need
30 of my mother's brothers.
The river would swell,
the river.
In the river
the rain would fall on the water in
35 this lake.
When it had swollen it would flow
under the trees
this river.
The earth would crumble away.
40 That's when it would think
of breaking.
When it had broken, down the river
it would drift,
down the river.
45 It would think of going to the world.
On this great ocean it would drift.
From there the wind would blow over it.
   [Naawéiyaa: Your brothers-in-law are listening to you.]
50 The wind would blow over it. It would begin
to roll with the waves to fine sand.
When it rolled on the waves to the sand
it would drift ashore. It would be pounded there by the waves
55 it would be pounded there.
Here the tide would leave it dry
would leave it dry.
It would lie there.
In the morning the sun would begin to shine on it
60 in the morning.
After the sun had been shining on it
it would begin to dry out.
From this

my hope is that you become like it
65 my brothers-in-law,
whoever is one.
    [Naawéiyaa: Thank you.]
You created me, Chookaneidí.
You created me.
70 This is why I feel for you.
Yes!
This is the way Xwaayeenák is.
    [Keet Yaanaayí: Áawé.]
In this world
75 we're still holding each other's hands.
We too don't overlook
  our dead.
Yes!
This moment
80 when the sun shines on it, my hope
is that it dries out
[Keet Yaanaayí: It shall be.]
the flowing from your faces.
Let it turn to joy,
85 is my wish for you.
[Naawéiyaa: Thank you. Thank you.]
You all know your brothers-in-law
your fathers' sisters.
    [Keet Yaanaayí: Thank you.]
90   [Naawéiyaa: Thank you.]
This is the way it is.
Yes!
You will stand.

    [After asking some of his clan members to rise,
    the orator rested for a few moments.]

95 What your fathers' brothers
used to do
when such things happened,
yes,
these are the things that might warm your feelings.
100 The people I'm living in place of now
  yes,
used to show you.
This is the way it is.

32

[Keet Yaanaayí: Thank you.]
105   [Naawéiyaa: Thank you.]

[The orator rests again.]

My brothers-in-law
those who are my father's brothers
    [Keet Yaanaayí: Áawé.]
110 those who are my father's sisters
    [Aan Káx Shawoostaan: Áawé.]
there is no way we can do anything for you.
We will only imitate them.
You can now see them standing in these,
115 yes.
We will try.
This is the way it is.
    [At this point, two songs are sung:
    Frog Hat Song, and Mountain Tribe's
120   Dog Hat Song.]
This is all.
This is all.
    [Kaakwsak'aa: Thank you. Thank you, my fathers.]
    [Keet Yaanaayí: Thank you.]
125   [Aan Káx Shawoostaan: Thank you.]

– Collected by Rosita Worl
Transcribed and translated by
Nora Marks Dauenhauer

NOTE

See Contexts section for extensive line notes for this "Speech for the Removal of Grief" as well as those by Jessie Dalton and Austin Hammond.

Jessie Dalton

SPEECH FOR THE REMOVAL OF GRIEF
(spoken in Tlingit)

    Does it take pity on us
      too
    my brothers' children
      [Keet Yaanaayí: Áawé.]
 5 my fathers?
    All my fathers.
    It doesn't take pity on us either,
    this thing that happens.
      [Unidentified: Yéi áawé.]
10 That is why you hear their voices like this
    your fathers,
    that your tears not fall without honor
      [Naawéiyaa: Thank you.]
      [Keet Yaanaayí: Thank you.]
15 which flowed from your faces.
    For them
    they have all come out this moment.
    Your fathers

Jessie Dalton, Tlingit from Hoonah, Alaska.

have all come out.
20 [Naawéiyaa: Hó, hó.]
They are still present.
That is how I feel about my grandparents.
    [Keet Yaanaayí: Thank you.]
Someone here stands wearing one,
25 this Mountain Tribe's Dog.
It is as if
it's barking for your pain is how I'm thinking about it.
    [Keet Yaanaayí: Thank you.]
My fathers, my brothers' children
30 my father's sisters,
yes.
Here
is someone standing next to it:
it's Raven Who Walked Down Along The Bull Kelp.
35 Someone is standing closer, next to it.
L yeedayéik's robe.
That is the closer one.
    [Naawéiyaa: Thank you.]
Someone is standing next to it.
40 Yes.
    [S'eilshéix: Thank you.]
It's The Beaver Robe
from Chilkat.
A Chilkat Robe.
45 Lutákl your father
it was once his Robe,
once his
Chilkat Robe.
    [Unidentified: Hó, Hó.]
50 [Naawéiyaa: Thank you.]
He came out
because of you.
    [Sei.akdoolxéitl': Hó, hó.]
Yes
60 at this moment
all of them seem to me as if they're revealing their faces.
Your fathers' sisters
my mother
Saayina.aat
65 her Robe
the Tern Robe.

Yes.
  [Unidentified: That's it.]
  [Keet Yaanaayí: Thank you.]
70 Someone who is feeling like you
would be brought by canoe,
yes,
to your fathers' point
Gaanaxáa.
75 That is when
the name would be called out, it is said
of someone who is feeling grief.
Yes.
Father! Sei.akduxleitl'
80   [Sei.akduxeitl': Áawé.]
Yes.
My grandfather's son Koowunagáas'
  [Koowunagáas': Áawé.]
My brother's son's child Keet Yaanaayí
85   [Keet Yaanaayí: Áawé.]
yes,
my father's sister's son Xooxkeina.át.
   [Xooxkeina.át: Áawé.]
How much
90 for your grief
your father's sisters are revealing their faces.
My brother's son
Kaatooshtóow,
  [Kaatooshtóow: Áawé.]
95 Kaakwsak'aa,
  [Kaakwsak'aa: Áawé.]
Yes,
my brother's wife, Aan Káx Shawustaan.
  [Aan Káx Shawustaan: Áawé.]
100 Yes
how much it is
as if they're revealing their faces is how I'm thinking about
   them,
your sisters-in-law.
Yes,
105 they are revealing their faces.
Weihá, his shirt.
It was only recently
we completed

the rites for him.
110 That is the one there,
The Raven Shirt.
    [Keet Yaanaayí: Thank you.]
You also heard him here,
Weihá
115 this brother of mine
this Peace Maker of yours.
It will remain in his hands, in his care.
    [Unidentified: Thank you.]
Weihá's shirt:
120 this moment, it is as if he will be coming out for you to see.
    [Keet Yaanaayí: Yes.]
Yes.
How proud
he used to feel wearing it
125 he too, this brother-in-law of yours.
    [Unidentified: How very much.]
Here one stands wearing
The Raven Nest Robe, your father's sister.
But on the far side
130 is Yaakaayindul.át your father's sister,
yes.
We had long since given up hope for their return,
    [Unidentified: Hó, hó.]
these fathers' sisters of yours, your fathers.
135   [Unidentified: Thank you.]
Raven Who Walked Down Along The Bull Kelp Shirt,
your father,
    [Unidentified: Áawé.]
Kaadéik,
140 it's your father's Shirt,
that is the one.
    [Unidentified: Your brothers' children are listening to you.]
That's the one there, but I don't feel that it burned.
Yes.
145 It is the same one in which your father's brother is standing
    there in front of you.
    [Keet Yaanaayí: Thank you.]
    [Tsalxaan Guwakaan: Thank you.]
That is why,
yes,
150 Gusatáan

[Unidentified: Áawé.]
it will be just as if I will have named all of you
those who are my sisters-in-law,
yes.
155 Can I reach the end
my brothers' children?
Yes.
Can I reach the end?
These terns I haven't completely explained
160 yes,
these terns.
Your fathers' sisters would fly over the person who is grieving.
[Keet Yaanaayí: Áawé.]
Then
165 they would let their down fall
like snow
over the person who is grieving.
[Tsalxaan Guwakaan: Your brothers' children
are listening to you.]
That's when their down
isn't felt.
170 That's when
I feel it's as if your fathers' sisters
are flying back
to their nests
with your grief.
175 [Naawéiyaa: Thank you indeed.]
Yes.
The one standing here
here
my mother's mother's brother, his hat.
180 Yes,
to the mouth of Taku he went by boat
for that hat,
to his grandparents
to his grandparents.
185 Yes,
from there it's said he acquired The Frog Hat.
Along side of it came
[Tsalxaan Guwakaan: Thus it is.]
the shirt from Weihá.
190 Yes,
it also came from Taku.

That is why
I keep saying thank you
   [Keet Yaanaayí: Thank you.]
195 that they're standing in front of you at this moment.
Yes
during the warm season
this father of yours
would come out.
200 That's when it's as if your father, his hat,
came out for your grief.
Yes,
   [Naawéiyaa: Thank you indeed.]
your father's grandfather's hat.
205 With it
he will burrow down,
with it
with your grief
   [Tsalxaan Guwakaan: Your brothers' sons
210   are listening to you.]
he will burrow down.
Not that it can heal you
my brothers' children, my fathers
   [Unidentified: Thank you.]
215 my fathers' sisters
my sisters-in-law.
And now
yes,
it is like a proverb
220 "we are only imitating them
lest it grope aimlessly"
   [Tsalxaan Guwakaan: Thank you indeed.]
what your grandparents used to say.
That's why it's as if your fathers are guiding them.
225 Here is one.
Here is one.
Here one stands wearing one:
this grandfather of mine
Yookis'kookéik, his hat.
230   [Unidentified: Hó, hó.]
He too has stood up
to face you.
Yes.
   [Unidentified: Hó, hó.]

235 Your father, his hat
Koowunagáas'.
  [Unidentified: Thank you indeed.]
  [Keet Yaanaayí: Thank you.]
He has stood up to face you,
240 yes,
The Loon Shaman Spirit,
yes.
Here,
yes,
245 the one this brother of mine explained a while ago:
how that tree rolled on the waves.
When it drifted to shore
the sun would put its rays on it.
Yes.
250 It would dry its grief
to the core.
This moment this sun comes out over you,
  my grandparents'
  [Unidentified: Thus it is.]
  mask.
255 This moment
  [Unidentified: Hó, hó.]
my hope is your grief be like it's drying to your core.
  [Tsalxaan Guwakaan: It shall be.]
  [Keet Yaanaayí: Thank you. It shall be.]
260 Géelák'w Headdress
yes.
Your fathers' sisters would reveal their faces from it
from Géelák'w
yes.
265 That is the one there now.
Someone stands there with it, that headdress
my grandfather, his headdress.
  [Keet Yaanaayí: Thank you.]

– Collected by Rosita Worl
Transcribed and translated by
Nora Marks Dauenhauer

Austin Hammond

SPEECH FOR THE REMOVAL OF GRIEF
(spoken in Tlingit)

I too
would like to speak, my father's brothers
my father's sisters,
yes!
5 How
very much
I too feel grief,
yes,
that I am here
10 yes,
but I can't even find anything to show you.
At this moment
he came out
here with it.
15 [Unidentified: Your father's brothers
   are listening to you.]
In many ways when this would happen to you
K'eedzáa

Austin Hammond, Tlingit from Haines, Alaska.

used to talk.
20 Here is his robe, here he stands with it.
    [Keet Yaanaayí: Áawé.]
    How he used to speak of it
    when things were like this and when he expressed affection
    for his father's sisters.
25 At this moment we need them.
    And the one standing on this end
    Kaatyé
    he too.
    My mother's brother Tsagwált, his robe,
30 yes!
    I own it in place of him.
    [Keet Yaanaayí: Áawé.]
    And there is one more
    [Tsalxaan Guwakaan: Thank you.]
35 There is one more.
    Yes,
    I will just explain it.
    It wasn't here.
    My father Keet Yaanaayí!
40   [Keet Yaanaayí: Áawé.]
    This brother-in-law of yours spoke proudly of you.
        [Keet Yaanaayí: Thank you.]
    This Naatúxjayi whom we have
    he too
45 has also come here for your grief,
    yes,
    to remove it
    from you.
    And now, that blanket:
50 it will be as if it has just become
    a kerchief in my hand.
    This is how I feel too
    my father's sisters.
        [Thank you.]
55   [Thank you.]
        [Thank you.]

– Collected by Rosita Worl
Transcribed and translated by
Nora Marks Dauenhauer

HUMAN FIGURINE (St. Lawrence Island Yupik)
This human figurine was carved of mineralized walrus
ivory during the Okvik Period (300 B.C. to 0 A.D.).
Photo: Chris Arend.
(Courtesy of the Anchorage Museum of History and Art)

William Beynon

NDA CKSHUN TCKAIMSOM DIS LAGGABULA

Ada wil yaas Tckaimsom, yaka da gishee Kloosums
Hlat 'waa na dsugga ax ada wilt yaka hahl dsugga ax
wa giet wil 'waa na agga Ksheeyen.
5 N-nee wilt tckal 'waa wak'id as Laggabula. Na 'wai
giadit Laggabula a spaggiet moagg. Hlat tckal 'waat did
Tckaimsom wak'id ada nees gga aam willa waalt. Awil aam na
uaaka Ksheeyen. Ada wil hows Tckaimsom
a wk'id "Wai Waggi, shim aam dim ckshanum.
10 Dim 'bil ckshanum na uaaka na kkala axan, dihl na uuaka
na kkala axoo, Kloosums." Anoaggash Laggabula. Ada wil
hows tckaimson, "Go wilsh ckshan dim dsabam?" Ada wil
hows Laggabula,
"Dim hoyam ha oyam ggan."
Gwa-a willa waalshga oyam ggan.
15 Hawaal hoys dip gwa-a
Baaldidumt ggalksa oy hawaal da wil dsoosgan ggalksa ggagg.
Dawil gwildum ggodees Tckaimsom dis Laggabula.Oys Laggabula

William Beynon

WHEN TCKAIMSON AND LAGGABULA GAMBLED
(told in Tsimshian)

Tckaimson was walking, following down the Nass River.
He came to the coast and kept on going along the coast
until he came to the mouth of the Skeena River. This was
5 where he had first met his brother Laggabula. Laggabula had
been found by some people on the kelp. When Tckaimson met
his brother he saw that he was well to do, because the oolichans of the Skeena were very good. So Tckaimson said to
his brother, "Well, brother, it will be good if we gambled.
10 Our stakes will be the oolichans of your river and of my
river, which is the Nass." Laggabula agreed. Tckaimson
said, "What kind of gambling shall we do?" Laggabula said,
"We will use our throwing sticks."
Well this was how this game Laggabula spoke of was
15 played: A shaft, which was like a spear, was used. They
would try to shoot this through a hole by throwing it.
Tckaimson and Laggabula were prepared. Laggabula shot and
at the same time Tckaimson wished to himself, saying, "Make
your throw short." And Laggabula did just that. His shot

William Beynon, Tsimshian from Victoria, British Columbia, Canada.

hawaal, dawil hows tckaimsom, "dse dalpahl ma wil oyt.
Ada n-nee willla waal ayeas Laggabulablga
20 'nakhl wil daawhla ayeat. Ada wil hietgas Tckaimsom dim dee
ayeat
Shil ggalksadaawhla hawaal da a-neesh. Ada wil hows Laggabula
"Ckstant wagi Howna go willa
waal na amckshanum." Ada wil hows Tckaimsom
"Dim 'wee laiksa kkowtsee da uuam kloosums ada dim 'wee
hailt.
25 Ada ahlga dim waal uuam Ksheyen. Dsoo dim dagla uua da
Ksheeyen
ada kkap ahlga dim 'wee laixhl dim kkowtseet. N-'nee gwa-a
ggan ahlga dsuuhl uua a Ksheeyen.

20 did not go far enough. Then Tckaimson stood up to shoot.
He shot right in the knot hole. Then Laggabula said to
him, "Well, my brother, you have won. You will now say
what shall be done about our stakes." Then Tckaimson said,
"Well, only the Nass oolichans will give oil and be plenti-
25 ful. Not so with the Skeena. Even if the Skeena should
have oolichans they will not have any oil." This is the
reason the Skeena River does not have many oolichans.

*– Transcribed by William Beynon in
his orthography of the 1930s.
The storytellers may have actually
been Alice and Jessie Woods who
are listed as "informants."
This Manuscript is part of the
Columbia University Library of
Rare Books and is reprinted here
with the permission of Columbia
University.*

NOTE

Tckaimson translates loosely as "Giant," which is also a name for "Raven."
– R.D.

Reginald Dangeli

TSETSAUT HISTORY: THE FORGOTTEN TRIBE OF SOUTHERN SOUTHEAST ALASKA

Adawak: Chief Mountain Story

This story does not include where the Eagle Clan originated or where they started from. It's only assumed from the far north. Some stories say the Yakutat area or close to the Copper River area. The Chief Mountain story opens when they arrive at Prince of Wales Island in Southeast Alaska.

The known name of this Clan is "Runaways" (or Hagwenhudit in Tsimshian), as told on the totem and Chief Mountain. They were not "Hagwenhudits" running away from enemies, as many believe, but were looking for the river Lisims, Nass River, also known as the "Great Food Basket."

Six canoes full of our ancestors landed at Thlawak'on (Klawock), on Prince of Wales Island in Southeast Alaska. They meant to settle there, but this place did not agree with their needs.

Reginald Dangeli, Tsimshian/Tsetsaut from Tombstone Bay, Portland Canal, Alaska.

They did not know where they were at that time. They kept on moving down the coast, still looking for the Nass. This migration lasted several generations. Many died, others were born. After paddling a long time, they arrived at Kahsanee (Kasaan?). Other people had left, who used to live there.

While they rested at Kahsanee, one of the young men went down at low tide on the shoreline to look for shellfish. A large rock stood exposed above low tide. This large rock had a hole under it. He poked a stick under the rock, thinking that an octopus (devil fish) might be lurking under the large rock. This devil fish was a great delicacy for the Native people.

This large devil fish got ahold of the stick. Aitl tried to pull the stick out, but the creature was too strong. He then tried to pull out his hand, but the devil fish caught his arm and would not let go. Aitl tried to hold on to another rock and pull his arm out. To his dismay, a large shellfish near the large rock closed on his other hand with its huge two valves. This giant shellfish "K'ahl'un" is known never to give up its enemy until the enemy drowns.

Aitl's brothers saw his predicament, came down to try to free him, but to no avail. Nothing could be done. They inflated a seal stomach, and tied it to him as a float. In hopelessness, Aitl spoke to them in Tlingit, as it was the language of our ancestors, "Cry for me." He kept repeating this, until the tide came over him and his brothers repeated this cry with him. So this "Cry for me" became a dirge for us in Tlingit, "Higanaway" – cry for me.

After Aitl's body floated free, they cremated it. After this tragedy, they paddled on, more determined to find the destination.

After leaving Kahsanee, they paddled day and night until they crossed a large body of water (Clarence Straits), south of Stikine River. They came upon "Alk-Nebahk" and arrived at a river in Tongass Narrows; "Mahk'La'an'shehawn" – where you catch fish for food.

Salmon was plentiful at the narrows, mostly sockeye. They caught some and roasted some on the beach, as it was warm and sunny. Their stop was content, so they relaxed.

Gunas, a young man, went into the water to swim. A giant halibut rose from the bottom and swallowed him. They looked for him, but could not find him. An Eagle swooped down to the edge of the water looking for salmon. When the fishermen saw the halibut coming to the surface, they caught it and opened it. They found Gunas' body in the halibut. He was already decomposed, but a copper shield hung around his neck like a collar. Gunas' uncle stood at the head of the halibut and lamented his nephew's death. The words of his dirge, which have become traditional in the Eagle Clan, are "This is where we encountered the Supernatural Halibut."

After Gunas' body was cremated and buried, they continued on their journey down the coast.

Near the open ocean water, north of Akstaqhl near Cape Fox, the people beheld Man Underneath – Git-dem Tsu Ooghu. He had long hair. This monster of the sea looked like a statue holding in each hand two king salmon. Sitting in the ocean, the monster was eating the salmon. While they looked at him in awe, the people decided to take him as an emblem, Man of The Sea or Man Underneath.

A frightened canoeman sitting in the stern urged, "Let us flee from here. Man of The Sea might devour us all!!!" While the canoes were turning, he asked his brothers facing him, "Is he still eating the salmon?" They replied, "Yes, he is eating it." These words were never forgotten to this day. They are repeated in another dirge, used at the death of Chiefs in our family.

The clan resumed their journey a little farther down, in good weather. They came upon Akstaqhl (Cape Fox), near the mouth of Portland Canal. There they saw the Bullhead, "Masklha Yait," a huge fish, and they made haste for the beach on a small island. From this vantage point, they looked for a long time at the monster, whose body was covered by human faces. They were so impressed, that they took him as an emblem, like the others. It has been represented since on some totem poles.

Seeing the monster, an old man said, "What is it I behold? What is the being there whose body is covered with human faces?" And these words were kept as another dirge.

They returned a few miles back from where they came from, Lahksail, Foggy Bay area, the opposite Clan. There our ancestors started the village of Lahksail – Cape Fox. The present Lahksail is in southeast Alaska. Kasaiks of Saxman, south of Ketchikan, is their head Chief and our close relative.

While at Lahksail, a young man and his sister went out in a canoe. Soon after, he placed on his head an eagle cap with a stuffed eagle's head. Their canoe capsized because of the strong wind that suddenly came from the sea. The man was drowned and his sister saved. Their Chief, dressed in his regalia, walked down to the beach chanting the loss of his nephew. Then the spirit Halibut came to the top of the water, looking like an eagle. The Chief, in mourning, felt his long leather earrings with haliotis pearls sewn on them. They were large haliotis pearls. He said, "The Prince whose canoe capsized shall wear my earrings," saying it to the supernatural Eagle Halibut in the water, who was the nephew, now transformed after drowning.

The Chief's chant became the fourth dirge, which we still use, "Dear Boy Wear These Earrings After Death."

Before his chant ended, a strange canoe landed on the shore, with the body of his nephew. Standing near it, he cried out "Dear son, the Eagle cap still sits on your head," and their words are part of the fifth dirge. The body was cremated and buried at the village at Lahksail. They decided to move south, down the coast, to continue their quest for Lisims – the Nass.

They went around Akstaqhl and stopped at Tongass, which they called "Lahk-Tawq." Here, they saw many canoes filled with people. Here, they met with the Grandfather of La'ee, the Chief of another Eagle Clan, now located on the Nass, also the Grandfather of Chiah-Mass, Chief of a leading Wolf Clan, now also of the Nass. Other Eagle and Wolf Clans had gone ahead in their migration down the coast.

They did not linger long at Lahk-Tawq. They continued their journey, with Chiah-Mass and La'ee and their people, in the quest for the Nass. They traveled up Portland Canal, turned right at Reef Island, then up at Ramsden Point (present day names) without knowing they were at the mouth of the Nass River. They made two camps at a place called Tsemadin – Nass Harbor area.

At a mouth of a river, they built a fish fence across the river, a trap for catching salmon, which were plentiful, the king salmon – "Ya'a," the humpback – "Sta-mawn," dog salmon – "Qa it," but no sockeye.

Chief Pahl (Charles Barton)
Adawak: Story of Portland Canal

A year later, our people decided to move after they had prepared their salmon supply and dried it. They filled their canoes with salmon so completely that they had to sit on the bundle, also to sleep on them while on their way. Once more, they wanted to look for Lisims – The Nass, and they started paddling again.

This time they discovered it. La'ee who had gone before them there, and also Chiah Mass, welcomed them, and received bundles of salmon – "luks" – as gifts. They went back to Portland Canal to get the rest of the Tribe.

The whole Tribe or Clan returned and built a new village at Lis-ims, and called it "Lahk Luks" – "on bundles" – because of the bundles of smoked salmon which the earlier occupants had presented to them upon their arrival.

Our people had taken in the Tsetsaut people as part of our own Clan and before separating they had agreed that they would all be "Brothers Together" – Eagles and Tsetsauts. Some Eagle Clansmen adopted three Tsetsauts, others four, and took care of them, supplying their needs. The Tsetsauts returned the kindness with fur and meat, for they were great hunters and woodsmen. Our people were seafolk and fishermen.

Among the Tsetsaut Chiefs, they adopted "Tsedzeen," "Quiyah," and "Aladazaw." These Chiefs' names are still preserved in our Clan. These names are in Tsetsaut language. To this day, we remain brothers with the Tsetsauts.

The Tsetsauts were numerous in those days, and working together with them we became strong and prosperous. Unfortunately, the Tsetsaut have died out. This was due to warfare with the Tahl-tans, and the Lahk Wi Yip, the Prairie People up the Stikine and Nass Rivers. The Lahk Wi Yip used to be at the head of the Nass. Later, warfare in Behm Canal with the Tlingits, and also the diseases of the whiteman such as smallpox really decreased them. The Prairie People also have dwindled in numbers. Not many survived. A few of the Nass People have intermarried with the Tsetsauts.

Our story which we all know well, ends at Lahk Luks, "on bundles," near the mouth of the Nass. We used to be Tlingits, but adopted the ways of the Nass River People. But we kept our dirges which are still in Tlingit today. The need for food is always strong, and we return to the country of the Tsetsauts – up Portland Canal – according to season, and with them we harvest our food.

[The manuscript continues, covering East Behm Canal place names, personal names, land use, and battles for the land, with the Tsetsaut being set upon by Haidas, Tlingits, Interior Atha-baskans, and Whites. As we move from the prehistoric era to the historic period, more family history comes into account. Levi Dangeli's father is killed in war and his mother taken captive. She escapes with the Child Levi around the 1850's by making a canoe and paddling home. The Tsetsaut population is now less than 30, and the group eventually settles near the Anglican Mis-sion at Kincolith, BC. At the mission the people are drawn into the new culture and language, at the cost of their own. At this point in the narrative we meet Levi Dangeli, an ancestor of the author and famous in anthropological literature as the Tsetsaut informant for Franz Boas.   – the editors.]

The Last Days of A Tsetsaut Chief

"Chief Quiyah," Levi Dangeli, was the last chief of the Tsetsauts. He experienced many adventures during his lifetime in the Misty Fjord National Monument area of Southeast Alaska – warfare, unknown sicknesses, occasionally famine, and most of all, the happy moments of successful Nomadic Hunting Expeditions.

After having led the remnants of his tribe to the Kincolith mission, and joining the church at the mission, and having made their new homes there, Chief Quiyah would lead his men back to hunt the Portland Canal area. The families made a good living, also their subsistence gathering.

It was about fifteen years later, in 1894, while Levi was in the Canal, hunting, that a whiteman, an anthropologist by the name of Franz Boas, was drawn to the Kincolith mission, when he heard of an Indian tribe living there, originally from Portland Canal. No one had heard of these people, except the coast tribes of the area. Boas waited several days for the Chief Levi, who he learned of, who could tell him many stories of the history of the Tsetsaut Tribe.

My Grandfather Timothy Dangeli remembers this meeting, and I remember Timothy telling me. Timothy was in his teens then. He thinks Levi was over sixty years old at that time.

According to Boas, in his journals and letters home, the meeting was very difficult, due to four different language translations: Tsetsaut translated to Nishga, then to Chinook jargon, then to English, as Boas' Nass interpreter was not good in Chinook jargon. This Nass interpreter was a Christian and half the Chinook jargon was swear words. So they went back to just Tsetsaut and Nishga. Boas' Nass interpreter was also limited in English, but somehow they managed to complete some sentences in Tsetsaut. Levi knew the Nass dialect, but translating to English was the hard part.

Franz Boas did an excellent job under these conditions. All the ethnological and historical data was given by Levi. According to Timothy, these meetings lasted just a few hours each day, when all were able to meet together. It was not more than a week. After completing the words, Boas had Levi make miniature houses they would use while hunting, and also their traps, which Boas drew for his journals.

There are interesting accounts in his letters. He asked Levi, "How do you say in Tsetsaut 'If you don't come, the bear will run away?'" Levi's answer: "The Nishga could be asked a thing like this; we Tsetsaut are always there when a bear is to be killed. The Tsetsaut have no words for that." Boas asked him another one: "What is the name of the Cave of the Porcupine?" His answer was only: "A whiteman could not find it anyway, and therefore I don't have to tell you."

Franz Boas had difficulty with the Tsetsaut language. It is an extremely difficult language, especially the verbs. And Levi wanted to go back to Portland Canal to check on his traps. So with all the handicaps Boas encountered, he managed to get around fifty pages of some words and sentences, and some stories. During this time, he wrote 170 pages on the Nass Indians. But during this brief encounter with the Tsetsauts, Boas documented a very significant period of the Tsetsaut history in Alaska.

Several years later, Chief Quiyah (Levi) having enjoyed this new peaceful life at the mission, not having to worry about enemies with arrows, etc., was on a hunting trip in Portland Canal with his tribe, to trap bears and hunt mountain goat in a familiar favorite hunting valley, when he was seized by violent cramps, so they returned to their base camp on the beach. It was during the night, when they laid down to rest, the tribesmen heard Levi praying. In the morning, they found Levi dead.

Levi's remains were brought back to the mission by the other Tsetsaut hunters, under a flag at half mast. Later, Levi was given a Chief's service. Many of his Nishga friends and brother Chiefs accompanied him to his grave, where he was given the Chief's burial, and Christian services. So ended a Tsetsaut era of history. But Levi's oral stories and history will be told to the newer generations, both the Tsetsaut and the Nishgas of Portland Canal.

NOTE

The samples of Dangeli's work excerpted here are from his unpublished manuscript "Tsetsaut History: The Forgotten Tribe of Southern Southeast Alaska," Alaska Historical Commission Studies in History No. 147, 1985, researched and written with support from the Alaska Historical Commission.

—R.D.

"CIING'QUTAIYUK," A WRETCHED, WOULD-BE SHAMAN (Yup'ik)
Jack Abraham made this mask from cedar, horsehair, deer antler,
acrylic pigment, and walrus ivory. Photo: Chris Arend.
(Courtesy of the Anchorage Museum of History and Art)

Isidor Solovyov

SAĜIM TAYAĜUU ULUUQIDAX̂

1 Saĝim tayaĝuu Uluuqidax̂ asagaan Siimluudax̂ asix alaĝuĝiiĝan ayugikux̂ awa. 2 Malix iqaĝilix, Kisxan akayugan chuqaan aĝaagiim, txin aaĝatikux̂ awa. 3 Asagaan asix laaqudan lalix, usilalix aqadaagiim, tanaanuuĝan txin iqaĝitikux̂ awa. 4 Tanaanulix̂takuĝaan, kachix aqalix, angaliĝiqadalix, imachx̂iliin asagaan ngaan agiitaasaqalikux̂ awa. 5 Alaĝum taagaa aqaqaliguun, taagam ilaan iqiliiĝdagalikux, txidix ukux̂taqadadaqalikux awa. 6 Txidix ukux̂taĝulux aygaxchx̂iqadaamdix, txidix uux̂tukux, amaan kinguuĝix̂ asagam, Siimluudam iqaa tunux̂taqalikux̂ awa. 7 "Amamatalix amamada. 8 Ayagamin angaan ax̂tagalikux̂txin-aan, qachx̂imin uuĝnaasaa nung utadaĝultxin malix, txin akuuĝaasaaqalanaĝulting."

9 Siimluudam iqaa tunux̂takux̂ tutaaqaltakum, iqaan kayux igiim tunux̂takux̂ tutaqalikux̂ awa, awan Uluuqidax̂. 10 "Aang, amamatalix amamada. 11 Ayagamin angaan ax̂txumin, ayagamin-aan qachx̂iin utanaan nung ulixsadanax̂txin malix, txin akuuĝaasaaqalnaqing," iilanaan tutikux̂ awa.

Isidor Solovyov

THE MAN OF SAĜIX̂ DRIED MEAT
(told in Unangan/Aleut)

1 The man of [the village] Saĝix̂ [named] Dried Meat together with his cousin Little Guillemot went out to hunt at sea. 2 After he had paddled to Unimak Pass he stopped. 3 Together with his cousin he killed a lot of fur seals and loaded them in and then headed home. 4 On his way home a storm arose and it got dark, and he kept contact with his cousin only by voice. 5 When a billow came, they would escape from it but began to lose sight of each other. 6 When they had gone along for a while without seeing each other and then came close to each other again, the baidarka of the younger cousin, Little Guillemot, began to talk, 7 "Take the consequences.[a] 8 Since upon rising from your wife's side you would not touch me with your warm skin, I will not carry you to shore."

9 After he heard Little Guillemot's baidarka talk, he began to hear his own baidarka speaking too, Dried Meat [did], 10 "Yes, take the consequences. 11 Upon rising from your wife's side you used to rub against me your skin which touched your wife, so I will carry you to shore," he heard it say to him.

Isidor Solovyov, Unangan/Aleut from Akutan, Alaska.

12 Alaĝum taagaa aqaqaliix̂tukuĝ-aan, asagaan asix taagam ilaan iqilix, daĝikiimdix takaax̂tukux awa. 13 Asagaan imachx̂itagalikuun, tununaa tulakan, tanax̂ akuuĝaasakux̂ awa. 14 Malix iqaĝilix tanaam Saĝim chuqan tigikux̂ awa.

15 Ingan qilax̂ slatuĝulux ulaalaangan, ayugikux̂ awa. 16 Iqaĝilix amamalix̂takum, qangum sinigingin yaagam anikaa ukux̂talix̂taagiim, adan uyalix, ilaan aĝakux̂ awa. 17 Aman asagaam iqaa uda utmakiigiim sixsax̂talix udamtax̂takux̂ ukuugiim, ngaan txin ayugnilix, aĝitikux̂ awa. 18 Asagaan wa iqaam ilan changalix asx̂alaaĝanax̂ ax̂takux̂ ukux̂taqaliigiim, qichx̂ux̂txin daĝan achisix, aman ilaan ukunaam adangan aguxsix, tigusakux̂ awa. 19 Iqaam ilaan igalix, iqaan akuuĝatxadaagiim, asagaam adan sakaanulix, iqaa sayulix, asagaan unĝigan sitxikiin sulix, iqagan ilaan idgitxadaagiim, awangun aqadaagiim, iqagan adan sakaanukan, ilaan aĝakuu[n], uluĝiim aslaan sixsalix udamanax̂ ax̂takux̂ ukux̂takan, amakux sixsax̂takix dax̂kin qisatxadaagiim, kumsikan, iqagan ilan angachx̂ikan, sukiixsxan, iqagan snangakin nayux umsxan ax̂sxan aqadaagiim, alaĝux̂ ngaan tadasxan, iqaan awaagan kumsilix alaĝum ilan ax̂six, ilan angalix, asagaam angaan aĝaqadaagiim, qichx̂ux̂txin daĝan achisix, igiim iqaĝidusakux̂ awa. 20 Iqaĝiisakan tanaam Saĝim chuqan tigusakuu awa.

21 Waaĝakuĝ-aan, Siimluudam ayagaa chaam ilan laan sux̂talix adangkiigiim sakaaĝaangan, aman laa adan uyakan, ingaagan sitxaan kumsikan, alaĝum adan sakaanusakan, alaĝum ilan taangalĝitakan, ngaan tunux̂taqalikuu awa. 22 "Txin ayagalĝigumin, ayagamin angaan ax̂txadagumin, ayagamin-aan qachx̂iin utanaan iqamin-aan utadaqalinaaĝnaĝulux ax̂takux̂txin?" iistakan, alaĝum ilan ingumixtakan, qidachx̂ikan aqadaagiim, anagan-aan akuunusakan, chuqan ax̂sxan, ngaan tunukuu awa. 23 "Txin ayagalĝiguun, ayagaa ngaan agachiidax̂tachx̂iimin aqaliqaan ax̂talix waya i? 24 Uknan ugiin ukuda!" 25 Malakakin-iin ulaaqaltakutxin malix, iingun txin ungutxadaagiim, qidaqalikux̂ awa.

26 Asagaam-aan sakaaĝalix, unĝigan sitxakiin kumsilix, angaasalix, ulaakax̂ ngaan agulix, asagaan ulaakam ilan tanasix, ingaagan ulaam adan uyalix, ulaan uqadaagiim, asagaam agalaan txin chuuknuuĝdax̂sinaan ix̂talix iĝanayii.

12 When a billow came again, the cousins escaped from it [but] became separated again. 13 Although he called his cousin, he didn't hear his voice, and he reached land. 14 Paddling along, he landed below his village of Saĝix̂.

15 The next morning, when it was calm weather, he started out. 16 He paddled along until he saw a log floating in the kelp and went over to it. 17 Seeing that it was his cousin's baidarka lying there broken in the middle, he moved to it and turned it over. 18 When he saw that his cousin, being in his baidarka, had died, he attached his lines to it and towed it to the shore in from where he found it. 19 Having gotten out of his baidarka and pulled it up on the beach, he went down to his cousin, pulled up his baidarka, and, taking his cousin under the armpits, pulled him out of his baidarka, and, having put him down there, he went down to his baidarka, and, seeing that it was broken in two by the hatch, he tied the broken pieces together, lifted him back into his baidarka, tied the baidarka skirt on, and, having inflated two floats and put them on both sides of the baidarka, launched it in the sea, and then he lifted his own baidarka and put it into the sea, climbed into it and, having got alongside his cousin, attached his lines to his baidarka and began to tow him. 20 Towing him, he landed with him below his village of Saĝix̂.

21 When he arrived and Little Guillemot's wife, holding her son by the hand, came down to the beach to meet him, he went up to the boy and, lifting him up on his arm, carried him down to the sea and, holding him in the water, said to him, 22 "When you marry, after having risen from your wife's side, won't you touch your baidarka with the skin that touched your wife?" he said, and, having pushed him several times into the sea and made him cry, he took him back up to his mother, put him down next to her and said to her, 23 "When he gets married, you won't let him keep his wife for himself only, will you? 24 Look at your husband down there!" 25 Doing as she had not done during the night,[b] she sat down there and began to weep.

26 [Dried Meat] went down to his cousin, lifted him up by the armpits and carried him up, made a burial hut for him and buried

---

a. Lit. Being in that way (as in the past) be so.

b. Jochelson's free translation [by implication]: "said that she will do what she failed to do before."

his cousin in the hut, and having gone over from there to his own house, he died of apathy [sorrowing] after his cousin—he said, it is said.

– Dictated by Isidor Solovyov,
Unalaska, 1910
First transcribed and translated by
Leontiy Sivtsov.
Originally published in Unangam
Ungiikangin kayux
Tunusangin: Unangam
Uniikangis ama Tunuzangis:
Aleut Tales and Narratives,
edited by Knut Bergsland and
Moses L. Dirks. Alaska Native
Language Center, University of
Alaska, Fairbanks, 1990.

Cedor L. Snigaroff

ATKAN HISTORICAL TRADITIONS
(told in Unangas/Aleut)

After some time, however, they [Eastern Aleut] took the Atkans by surprise at Seguam, spearing them all right outside the cave they were living in there. Then two [Atka] men, cousins, went in to the bottom of the cave, with two spears they had broken in the middle. But the chief called "Wren", the chief of the Eastern men, gave his orders. Having seen for himself that those two men were left and had gone in to the bottom of the cave, he told a man to go in after them and pull them out. But the man who together with his cousin had just gone in to the bottom of the cave heard everything that was being said about him and hid himself and his cousin there in the bottom of the cave, for he knew what the bottom of the cave was like: on the cliff side it is as if it had a shelf made on it, where one can stay, so he got up there and had his cousin hide himself in a corner. Then, when a man came in from the daylight, without seeing him, he, looking out, saw him, and when he was on his way in towards him, passing right below him, he thrust his spear into him along his neck, and turning around he rushed out but did not get

Cedor L. Snigaroff, Unangas/Aleut from Atka, Alaska.

farther than to the entrance of the cave, to the daylight, where he dropped dead.

That chief, however, was still giving orders, and again a man came in to them. As he was coming in exactly the same way as the other one and was passing below him, he again thrust his spear into him, down along his neck. Repeating what the other one had done he turned around and started on his way out, but in turn fell there where the body of the other one had fallen. Seeing that, looking out, and having nothing more in his hands to fight back with, as he had made up for his death by revenging his cousin and himself, he decided to surrender.

The chief, seeing all that was happening, just continued giving orders, and again a man started to come in after them. Considering surrendering to him, because he had nothing more to fight back with, he jumped down, jumped down on the ground from that shelf of his. However, a small pointed rock sticks up there, at the passage into the bottom of the cave, and having got down to it, he held it with both arms and clung to it, just when the man came inside, passing in the direction where they were supposed to be. When, on his way inside, he was passing right above him, he stood up with him and pushed him against the ceiling of the cave, stretching both his legs, crushing him against the ceiling and, that side of the cave being low, jammed him up there under it. From the back of his neck he made resistance, but having him jammed up against the ceiling of the cave, he made movements with him and heard cracking sounds within him. Having done that three times, he threw him down towards the mouth of the cave, where he dropped, but whereas each of the men he had speared had got out, this one stopped right there where he threw him, he said, it is said.

After that, the fourth time, a couple of men were ordered in to them, and because there were now two of them coming in, they surrendered. Having surrendered, they were taken out and then, outside the cave, they were laid on the ground on their back and held by several men, to get cuts in their skin across the forehead. Then they were loaded into boats and transported across the strait towards Amukta, with their forehead cut across (when a warrior was captured, his skin was never left intact, it is said). With their forehead cut, they were almost bleeding to death in the course of the day they were being taken across the strait, they said.

When they arrived at Amukta, they were not killed but were put to use as workers there.

Being kept alive as such, they lived on one and the same island, but their life was such that they did never see each other.

In fall, when the time came for having the birds called shear-water collected by bird catchers, when people went walking around on the island, then they began to see each other secretly. The two cousins did. And they started to plan what they might do. They started to look for a boat to sneak from there over here with.

One of them lived towards the east side of Amukta. At an appointed time they set the change of the weather into eastern gales.

When the bad storms they had set as a time started, when as usual the fall weather began to look real bad with easterly winds, the partner began to sleep little. However, he had a guard. Their plan was not known but they were watched all the time, it is said.

He was watched like that, but when the time for his partner's appearance had passed by and he wondered where he could be, when he was on the point of falling asleep, he used to pinch his own skin to become sensitive by the pain. Then, being in doubt about his coming, he got the feeling that he would be coming, and he actually heard him coming, making his call to him, and he got up from his bed and ran down to the beach, where he had a boat ready for him too. As it was, having in vain looked at his guard, thinking that he would have needed to find something to kill him with, he could do nothing to him and so hurried down into his boat, and they took off, they said.

But the watchman, who was on his guard and saw what was going on, called his people, and they saw that a host of warriors started out after them as they took off in the direction of the strait, heading west, with the wind behind them.

At first, as he was passing the shore towards the strait, trying his best to catch up with his partner, who was going on the high waves like a feather blown by the wind, he was deathly afraid of being overtaken from behind, but when he got to the rough sea in the strait, his partner no longer was ahead and he himself was in front. While he had not caught up to his partner along the shore, the situation was reversed when he got into the strait, and he worried about his partner that he might be overtaken, for when his own bidarka started to go, it just hopped along the waves, he said.

So he went on, and when he got into the strait, they did not see anymore the warriors who had come after him, they said. Indeed, they were no sea animals, those warriors who came after him, and the cousins did not think that they made it back safely – at least not all of them, they used to say. The agitated sea was as if covered with smoke all over.

From Amukta they crossed the strait over to Seguam, passed along the south side of Seguam, and in the morning, at daybreak, they came ashore on Amlia. There they landed in the bay called Agulganunax̂, where they hid their bidarkas and their few belongings, and went to bed, started to sleep. They must have slept a day and a night, they said.

From there they went westwards, parted company at some of the islands around here, and began to live normally.

So they went on until warriors from the East were no more seen and one could live normally. Also, they did not fight with each other so much any more.

– Told in 1952 by Cedor L. Snigaroff
Excerpted from Niiĝuĝis
   Makax̂tazaqangis (Atkan
   Historical Traditions), *by Cedor*
   L. Snigaroff and Knut Bergsland,
   Alaska Native Language Center,
   University of Alaska, Fairbanks,
   1986.

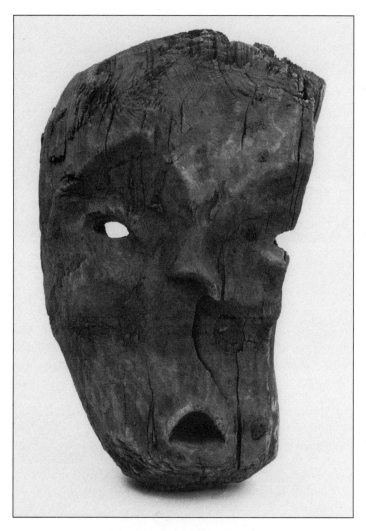

MASK (Aleut or Yup'ik)
This unusual wooden prehistoric mask, collected in the Bethel area of Alaska, bears some resemblance to Aleut masks, but has no provenance. Photo: Walter Van Horn.
(Courtesy of the Anchorage Museum of History and Art)

Ignatius Kosbruk

PUGLA'ALLRIA

Una ggŭani unigkuaq qangiq makunek nitniqetaalleqa taugna angun, *his name was Wasco Sanook. He used to tell me stories.* Unigkŭa'itaaqiinga maani kapkaanirwigmi, etaanemteni kapkaanirtaanemteni.

Awa'i kangircigkunaku caqaimek unigkŭa'itanga. Cunang una ggŭani kallagalek pimakii. Awa iqugcingamku, unigkŭa'itesggŭagta unigkŭa'aq taugna, *telling stories.*

Ggŭaken-i Katmaayamen – agluni angii ggŭaken-i Naknimek esggŭarluni angutegnun. Awaqutengqerllutek-gguq allrilumek.

Nutaan taug'um angiin awaqutaa taugna kallagalelliaqlluku. Nutaan castun niu'utegkunakek angayuqaak. Ankutarngami anulluku taugna kallagalelliani etqacugmen eklluku. *It was about in the fall, in September, I guess, or October, whatever.*

Nutaan tawaken uksurpak tawani uksigkŭarluku qanitami. *We call it a garbage hole.* Uksurpak tawani ell'uni.

Nutaan ugnerkaryarngan, taugna angii Naknimek ggŭaken-i es-

Ignatius Kosbruk

PUGLA'ALLRIA
(told in Alutiiq/Sugcestun with italicized portions originally told in English)

I used to hear this story in the past from that old man, *his name was Wasco Sanook. He used to tell me stories.* He used to tell me stories there in the trapping grounds, when we used to be there, trapping.

Then, I didn't understand what he told me. He was really talking about a shaman. Then, when I thoroughly understood it, he made me tell that story back to him.

From Naknek to Katmai, a maternal uncle went down there to two old people. They had only one son – one.

Then that uncle made that son into a shaman – but the uncle didn't tell the nephew's two parents anything. When he was about to go home, he took that boy out, the one he had made into a shaman, and he put him into a garbage pit. *It was about in the fall, in September, I guess, or October, whatever.*

So he made him stay there the whole winter, through the entire winter, in the back of the pit. *We call it a garbage hole.* He was there the whole winter.

Then when spring came, that uncle went down from Naknek to

Ignatius Kosbruk, Alutiiq from Perryville, Alaska.

ggŭarluni Katmaayamen. Nutaan angayuqaak apllukek, "Naamami-llu-gguq awaqutartek?" Nutaan aanii usgui'art̲epiarluni nalluniluku ima'i uksuaninek; tamarniluku taugna, (her) boy.

Nutaan taug'um angiin piluku iwaraasq̲elluku k̲eggani etqacugmi. In the pit – garbage pit.

Nutaan aaniin pisqucaatun taug'um esggŭarluni tawa'ut etqacugmen. Nutaan tang̲erlluku tawani etqacugmi kumkiiqataa'arlukigguq ggutni sisuq yuularluku ggutminek. E̲sggŭaucaagluku atiinun.

Nutaan taug'um tan'uraam caqiq tamarpiarpiarpia'an llaami nallugkunaku. Caqait suu'ut tamaita umyugaat nallugkunaku. Suu'ut castun suu'uciqat nallugkunaku. Nallutainani suu'uluni nutaan.

Nutaan tawaken a'ularnirluni taug'um angiin canallra kallagal̲elliaqlluku. Nutaan tawaken kallagalluluni sull'utni pigkunaku, sull'utni anirtuqainarluku. Kallagalluluni. Suu'ut nalluluku taugkut nunat castun suk taugna et'a. Taug'um Pugla'allriim, he knows everything what was going on. Tawang angagni taugna pitaqlluku elliin. Angayuqaagmi qiagkŭaucillrak pit̲ekllukek. The only person he killed, that was the only person.

Ankutarngan angitekutarngan angagni taugna, nuyaminek qil̲lerlluku uyaquikun. Nalluluni, taugna angii, he didn't know he tied a hair around his neck. He didn't know. So he went back, back to Naknek, and that same year, one year after that, he went back. He went back to Naknek, and looked at him. He was almost cut by the hair what he put around his neck. Tawarpiarpiaq taugna awa'i angagni tawang sugtaqlluku. Kallagalgurlluni nutaan.

Agem qaingani tawani suu'ut anirtualuki. Cali nutaan cangami arn̲asurtaan'atni qayatgun imarmi unani ellratni qayat paitaalget – amlerlluteng arn̲asurluteng. Aqllaq t̲ekilluni, aqllangluni maallurpiaq piwigkainani. Nutaan taug'um Pugla'allriim enqaqlluki taugkut arn̲arsullret, the ones that went out for sea otters. And all of a sudden tamarpiarmeng-gguq taima qayat ellmegt̲enun katurtut. Nobody touched them. They were out in the storm. They didn't know. And they all gathered in one place and made a path for them to go back to Katmai.

Sugmek pistainateng – nobody touch them and they didn't know what happened. They all go through that one path – right up to Qa'irwik, right where they live. And when they landed, Father, Apawak.

Nutaan tawaken elliin taugna kallagalek suu'uluni suu'ut ilagarluki. Ugauluni. Sull'ut̲esteng tamakut anirtuaqainarluki. Taugna kallagaucini aturluku.

Nutaan, nutaan cangameng taima-gguq ukuk ggŭani tamallkuk usiillraraak qaturluni iqalluum nen'a kapuc'arluni igmautiinun

Katmai. Then he asked the two parents, "Where on earth is your son?" Then his mother got all excited, not having known where he was since the fall; she had lost him, her *boy*.

Then that uncle told her to look for him out there in the garbage hole. *In the pit – the garbage pit.*

His mother did as she was told, she went down to that pit. Then she saw him there in the pit, in the process of leisurely cleaning his teeth, taking fish eggs out from his teeth. She took him down to his father, to his dad.

Now that boy knew every last thing in the world. He knew what was on everyone's minds. He knew how people would live in the future. He was a person who knew things.

Now that uncle was just beginning to make him a shaman. From then on, being a shaman, he didn't hurt his fellow humans; he just helped his fellow humans. He became a shaman. People in those villages didn't know what kind of person he was. That Pugla'allria, *he knows everything what was going on.* He only killed his uncle. He killed him because of the fact that he had made his parents cry. *The only person he killed, that was the only person.*

When he was just leaving, when that uncle got ready to go home again, Pugla'allria tied a hair around his neck. That uncle didn't know it, *he didn't know he tied a hair around his neck. He didn't know. So he went back, back to Naknek, and that same year, one year after that, he went back. He went back to Naknek, and looked at him. He was almost cut by the hair what he put around his neck.* As a shaman, the only person he killed was his uncle. On the way, he helped people out.

Then again one time when people were hunting for sea otters in the sea, when they were way out in qayaqs, in three-man baidarkas, there were lots of them hunting sea otters. The wind came up, it blew really hard, and they had absolutely nowhere to go. Then that Pugla'allria, he called those who were hunting sea otters, *the ones that went out for sea otters. And all a sudden* suddenly all the qayaqs went towards each other, they gathered without anyone doing anything. *Nobody touched them. They were out in the storm. They didn't know. And they all gathered in one place and made a path for them to go up to – back to Katmai.*

There was no human agent – *nobody touch them and they didn't know what happened. They all go through that one path – right up to Qa'irwik* [Katmai], *right where they live. And when they landed, Father,* Apawak [the Russian priest told him not to do that any more].

Then he, that shaman, lived among the people. He was kind and nice to the people. He only helped those people. He used that magic.

Now, once, unexpectedly, this couple's child got a fish bone stuck ggut-i. Angayuqaagken taugkuk tasqaurluki tamakut kallagallget anirturtestengnaqlluku. Taug'um Pugla'allria tangerniqlluki imanigguq kallagallget amlellriit, tawani *in their home. They couldn't do nothing to him. And Pugla'allria was watching them from his home – and wondering what kind of kallagalek are they. At last, finally they think of him. They call Pugla'allria down. And he went out. And when he entered the house he told them,* "Gğua'i caqairkauluci kallagalluluci? Sull'utegci metqeqainarluku sull'utegci tuqutengnaqeqainarluku anirtuagkunaku. Gğua-qaa una usiillraaq ggğuani nangteqellria? Ellpeci anirtuumagkunaku."

So he just take the child and put him on his lap. I don't know what he did. And he take the bone out and show it to them kallagaleks, every one of them. "Gğua-qaa una ggğuani kayagnalleq?" *He take the bone out and show it to them – every one of 'em.*

Awa'i tawaken niu'ulluki tangrru, "Kallagallunaurtuq suk ellminek takukellria. Sull'utegteng anirtualuku. Caqaimek asiillngurmek pigkunaku."

And they tawaken anluteng – *they said some of 'em were real criminal, in that group. He seen them, their mind. And then after that,* awa, kallagalek suu'ulluni tawani suu'ut anirtualuki.

Una-ggğuani tuyullrat maani – *the one I told you about, the chief, he never hire nobody, only Pugla'allria for partner. He say he never carry no gun. And fall of the year when they watch for bears at night, he let the bear come right close to them, up to them right there. He had no gun. [laughs] That's something amazing. He never let the bear see him.*

Nutaan tawaken elliin anirtuateklluku taugna kallagallucini aturluku. Suu'ut anirtualuki kallagalluciminek. Nutaan tawaken suu'uluni suu'ut anirtuaqainarluki.

Nutaan cangami awa umya'alinguarluni, "Ggui-qaa ggua picitun arrignaartua?"

Nutaan tawaken – nutaan tawaken umya'alinguarngami tawaken umya'alinguarluni a'ullai'ucugluku taugna picini, kallagallucini. Nutaan tawaken qenaluni a'ularnirluni. Qenaluni tawaten-pi. Awa cangami-gguq cangami taima-gguq cangameng kallagalli taugkut tai'ut. Makut-ggğuani ipii, *[his] arms and legs were broken up without nobody touching 'em. And he hollered,* "Whoa! I wouldn't come with you guys!" *And his arms and legs started to break up without nobody touching them. And he hollered,* "I wouldn't come with you guys, because I think that we are doing something that is wrong."

Aakakaarluni picuumaniniluku tamana piciq. *"It's not right. It's all devil's work." And it got worse and worse and worse. His legs start to break without nobody touching them.*

in his throat – in the village – a bone got stuck in his throat. His parents asked shamans to come help. That Pugla'allria watched all those shamans from somewhere or other, *in their home. They couldn't do nothing to him. And Pugla'allria was watching them from his home – and wondering what kind of* kallagalek [shaman] *are they. At last, finally they think of him. They call Pugla'allria down. And he went out. And when he entered the house he told them,* "What are you shamans good for anyway? You just torture people in their minds, you're just killing people instead of helping. Is this child suffering here? You can't seem to help him."

So he just take the child and put him on his lap. I don't know what he did. And he take the bone out and show it to them kallagaleks every one of them. "Was this hard?" *He take the bone out and show it to them – every one of 'em.*

Then he told them to look, that "a person who pays attention to himself can be a shaman. He helps people, doesn't do anything bad to them." *And they said some of 'em were real criminal, in that group. He seen them, their mind. And then after that* then the shaman lived there helping people.

This chief there, *the one I told you about, the chief, he never hire nobody, only Pugla'allria for partner. He say he never carry no gun. And fall of the year when they watch for bears at night, he let the bear come right close to them, up to them right there. He had no gun. That's something amazing. He never let the bear see him.*

Then he used his shamanism as a means of helping people out. He helped people out with his shamanism. Then he lived and just helped people.

Then once he started to ponder, "Am I doing the right thing?"

Then, then when he started to think about it, he started to think he wanted to quit it, what he was doing, being a shaman. Then he started to become sick. He was sick then. Then one time, once, all of a sudden his shaman helpers came back to him. They broke his joints. *Arms and legs were broken up without nobody touching 'em. And he hollered,* "Whoa! I wouldn't come with you guys!" *And his arms and legs started to break up without nobody touching them. And he hollered,* "I wouldn't come with you guys, because I think that we are doing something that is wrong."

He screamed that it wasn't right. *"It's not right. It's all devil's work." And it got worse and worse and worse. His legs start to break without nobody touching them.*

Then it got worse and worse. *His arms and legs start to break without nobody touching them.*

Nutaan tawaken anagnengluni tawaten. *His arms and legs start to break without nobody touching them.*

Nutaan aakakaarluni maligningainiluki illai picitun arrignaa'uman'iniluni. Una Agayuteggut kesiin picuusqaq maligciqniluku. Nutaan tawaken tuqusaagluni. Qayumek miryaqainarluni Asisqamen. Taugna niitaa'aqa Good Friday-mi, tuqusaagluni, qayumek miryaqainarluni.

Tawaken qumtukisaaq nang'uq.

Then he screamed, saying he will not go with his spirit helpers, they're not doing right. He said he would follow only the true God. Then the poor thing died. He just vomited blood until Good Friday. I heard this, that the poor creature died on Good Friday, vomiting blood.

That's the end, it's all done.

– Recorded on March 24, 1992, in
Perryville, Alaska, by
Patricia H. Partnow
Transcribed and translated by Jeff
Leer and Patricia H. Partnow

Dick Kamluck, Sr.

IVAN DURAK STEALS A RING
(told in Alutiiq)

There was this fellow named Ivan Durak. He was a liar about everything. Was he a good liar, or was he a good liar?

Once, he asked himself, "Can I get the wife of the Man of High Position? If I'm clever, I can get her." He found a way.

The Man of High Position liked him. His wife liked him too.

As soon as it was night, just as it was becoming night, he went to the cemetery. He dug up a grave, a grave they'd just put in, before the body was three days old, long before it was spoiled. He dug as fast as he could. As soon as he had dug it up, he took the casket out and broke it open.

Then he went back to the Man of High Position, and went in. The Man said to him, "Ivan Durak, why did you come here? Why are you hanging around here? Why don't you go someplace else?"

No response. Then he said to him, "If I want to get a wife, I can get your wife."

The Man of High Position replied, "How are you able to get my wife? I am a Man of High Position."

Dick Kamluck, Sr., Sugpiaq/Alutiiq from Port Graham, Alaska.

Ivan Durak left. The dead man, the one he had dug up, he pulled closer to the side of the house.

As night fell, as it was getting dark, the Man and his wife went to bed. Ivan Durak took the body to the window. He pressed it against the window.

The Man said, "Ivan Durak, get away from there!"

He pressed even harder.

The Man said, "I'm going to shoot him!"

"Don't! Don't! Don't! Don't shoot him! Don't shoot him! You like him. Don't touch him. Just talk to him."

Looking through the window, knocking on the window, he had the dead man dressed up like himself.

They couldn't get to sleep. The man finally got up, took his gun, and went to the window and waited. As soon as the body came up, he shot it. He made the body buckle over.

His wife said to him, "For God's sake, why did you kill Ivan Durak? Don't let the light of day find him out there!"

Now the Man of High Position got fully dressed. His wife was lying in bed. But when he was ready to go, Ivan Durak went behind the door.

Watching her husband, the wife said, "Take him far away. People will forget all about Ivan Durak."

She watched him as he went. The Man of High Position carried the dead body off.

Not long after he left, Ivan Durak went in the house. It was dark. He made noise on purpose. He took off his shoes. He pretended to take off his clothes. He lay down beside her.

She asked him, "Now, did you take Ivan Durak and throw him far away?"

Somehow he tried, tried to pretend he was the Man of High Position. He pretended to be the Man of High Position.

"Yes," he said to her. He didn't talk to her. When she turned her back he took her hands, caressed her hand, her fingers, her ring. He found her ring.

She didn't touch him in return. He caressed her ring, like so. Like so he touched it.

Now he was getting anxious. When he got anxious, he pulled it right off, like so.

Ivan Durak pretended to get excited and started mumbling, "Your ring – I dropped it – . It fell from the blankets," he said to her. "I'll get up. I'll look for it."

But he had the ring in his hand while he was saying he'd look for it. Now she too was getting anxious.

Ivan Durak said, "First, I'll go outside." He put his clothes on. He put his shoes on, and went out.

Before too long the Man returned. His wife said, "Now, did you take Ivan Durak far away?"

"Yes, I put the body far away."

Yet he was listening out there. Daylight came. When daylight came, Ivan Durak put the wife's ring on. He went in.

They asked, "Now, Ivan Durak, how did you come to life?"

"I just now woke up. I'm just now getting up." Again he answered, "I just now woke up. I'm just now getting up."

He sat beside him at the table. Before long, the Man of High Position noticed his hands. He asked Ivan Durak, "How did you get my wife's ring?"

No reply.

He asked his wife too. "How did Ivan Durak get your ring?"

"I don't know," she replied.

"If you don't know, look at his hands."

She too, the wife, asked him about it. "How did you get my ring?"

Ivan Durak replied nonchalantly, "Because I felt like it, I took it yesterday when your husband killed me. I just walked in and pulled it off," Ivan Durak answered her.

"Don't you ever do this again!" the Man of High Position said. "I'll kill you!"

"You already did," Ivan Durak said to him. "Remember? You carried me off. You threw me away."

The man thought the dead man he had carried away was Ivan Durak.

And with that, Ivan Durak took off.

– Collected and transcribed in Alutiiq
by Derenty Tabios
Word for word interlinear English
by Derenty Tabios
Revised translation by
Richard Dauenhauer

Walter Meganack, Sr.

A BEAR STORY
(told in Alutiiq)

A young man once was out hunting, it is said, going after bear. When he came upon a cave, he looked in. When he looked in, he saw a female bear, it was a woman, inside the cave. She invited him in and, it is said, he entered.

The male bear was gone and was out hunting, the wife told him. These two bears were a married couple.

The man looked into the cave. The bear's wife was a woman. When he looked in, she let him in, it is known. When he went in, she fed him.

Before long, her husband returned. He reached the entrance. He entered the cave. Then his wife, it is known, hid the young man, this hunter-man, behind her.

Her husband exclaimed as he entered, "Ha! the smell of man!" smelling man.

Then his wife threw out his glove, the young man's glove. "You smell this," she said.

There they wintered. They prepared to eat stored food, vegeta-

---

Walter Meganack, Sr., Sugpiaq/Alutiiq from Port Graham, Alaska.

tion, and fish. When they prepared the food they had a fire, a small fire, in the center, in the center of the cave.

She would place her hands above the fire. Above the fire she would melt her body fat, when she was about to prepare food.

All winter the two of them stayed there, all three lived there, the male bear not knowing he was there behind his woman.

Then when spring came, when it was time for bears to go out, her husband went out, saying he would see how it is outside. When bears come out of their caves then, it is known that they circle them, like the sun circling.

He went circling . . . singing . . . and playing out there. The third time around he made a mistake, it is known. Ha! He made a mistake.

"I will not see you again," he said to his wife, toward the cave. "Someone will capture me this summer or this fall."

Then his wife did not come out. It was too cold for her. Two children they had, little bears in the cave. Also in the cave was the young man she had kept, the young hunter.

Then after a time, after a few days, following her husband's parting, it was known, they came out, then the young man. When she was ready to go out, the woman bear put on her clothes, her skins. She then clothed her children with their skins when they were ready to leave.

Then when they all were ready to leave, she advised the young man, "These two children are yours. When you arrive home and you hear dogs bark, be sure to run to the sound. Dogs may tear my children up, at the edge of your village, when we come."

Now when the young man, the hunter, arrived home, he told them that he had lost track of where he'd been all winter. (He'd been at the bear's cave.)

It was known he ran whenever dogs barked, seeing those little bears. But once, after a number of times with the dogs, when they began to bark when he was occupied, he did not go and check. When he was with her, and near her, with a woman he liked, because he liked what he was doing, he did not go and check.

After a while, it is known, then he went to check out of curiosity. Already, it is known, the dogs had torn the bear cubs to pieces.

Their mother then came out, it is known. Then from her face she removed her skin and exposed a human face. Speaking to the man, she said, "Remember, I advised you about the dogs, that each time they barked, you were to run to your children to check on them? You've made a foolish mistake with me."

Then she put her skin back on and tore the young man completely to pieces.

– Collected and transcribed in Alutiiq
by Derenty Tabios
Translated into English by Derenty
Tabios and James LaBelle

Leo Moses

QULIREQ

Tawa-llu-ggur-am-ukuk,
anuuruluqnassiilriig-am-ga,
ukuk maurluquralriik,
cuulliniaqelriik,
tawa nunayararramegni-wan',
·imarpiim yaqsinrilkiini.

Tauna-gguq-taw',
tutgararulua,
taw' calistailami-llu.
Ellmineng-llu nallunrirluk' pikngailamiki,
elliriqlutek taukuk,
anuuruluqelriik cuugaqelriik tawa,
imarpiim yaqsinrilkiini.

Tawa-gguq-taw',
pitarkar-llu-taw',
caperqerrluamiu caperqengamiu-ga,

Leo Moses

TALE
(told in Yup'ik/Cup'ik)

The two people in this story,
as in so many stories like this,
are a grandmother and her orphan grandson,
who stayed
in a little place
not far from the ocean.

Now
the grandson
had no one to make tools or equipment for him,
and without those things, he could not learn to hunt.
Oh, those two were poor,
that grandmother and her grandson
living by the sea.

Well,
game animals
were beyond his reach

Leo Moses, Yup'ik/Cup'ik from Chevak, Alaska.

cassuutaunani.
Umyugami piyuumillra-tawa,
antaqkii,
umyugarramikun.

* * *

Piqerluni-tawa,
waten-taw' kiagutaqatek,
imarpiim ciñiikun,
cinirtellininaurtur-taw' mallussuareluni.

Mallungaqami-taw',
quinakevkenak' pilagluku caviggerrangqerrami,
pilagluku-taw' ut'rulluku-taw' neqkartaqaqluku.

Cuna-ggur-taw',
taw'-cinirpiirluni cauyuumillni-taw' qaillun qacikluk',
umyugami pitaciani.

Imarpigkun cinirtelliniluni,
makuneng tengmianeng-ll' ayuqniarluni.

Ayuqniarpakarluni-taw' caneng makuneng unguvalriarneng-llu,
waten,
cullritneng.
Qaillun qaciggluki makut pitaqellerkait ellaicitun,
piyuumiryaaqluni.

Cucukek'ngaini-gguq-taw',
tunucillget makut,
taw'-cucunanqurraullruu'-taw' cakneq,
ellaicitun ayuqsuuminaqluni,
waten tengautuluteng pagaani,
cillakun.

Tamte-llu-ggur-imarpigmun mic'ameng,
tamte-llu-ggur-angllurluteng camavet,
mer'em acianun pissurluteng neqkameggneng pissurluteng
    pilluteng,
pugulluk' teng'aqluteng ataam.

Ayuqniaqengamini-ggur-taw' tamakuni,

since he had no equipment.
So his mind
ridded itself
of all wishes for success in hunting.

One day
during the summer,
he was walking along the seashore,
looking for dead sea mammals.

Now whenever he found one,
the smell did not bother him, and he just cut it up with his little
   knife,
he cut it up and brought it home as food.

And so
as he was beachcombing one day, he thought it would somehow
   be easier for him to be what he wished he were
through the power of his mind's yearning.

He walked along the seashore,
and wished he could be like the birds.

He yearned to be like all the animals,
and get a living
as well as they did.
He admired the way they caught game so effortlessly,
and he wished and wished that some day he could hunt as they
   could.

But more than anything else,
he wanted to be
like the arctic loons,
for they were an inspiration,
the way they flew up above,
through the sky.

They landed on the water
and dove down to the bottom,
hunting and catching their prey underwater,
and then emerging with it, and flying right off again.

More than anything else,

tamakut ayuqnianrulqai,
tunucillget,
tengautulit,
kuimatulit angllutuluteng epsurtuavkenateng.

* * *

Piqerluni-gguq-taw' taw' cinirpiirluni-taw',
ivarutmeng aturtuurluni-taw' umyugami-taw' piyuumiryaaqellran
   pitaciani,
ivarutmeng aturtuurluni,
cinirtelliniluni.

Ivarutii-gguq-gga-taw' waten ayuqelr':
(Ivarutii-ll'-am-cal' tamana taw',
arulacilingqerrluni-cal' ayuquq
waten-taw' yurautnguuq maa-i,
mat'um nalliini.)

*The repeating figure represented with ♫ has a strongly accented first element, and
a somewhat lengthened second element that is slightly lower in pitch than what is
written for it.

* * *

Anglluraqameng-ggur-taw' tawaten,
makut tunucillget,
Uuiiq!
waten pitullernaari'-taw'
ayuqeliliku-taw' anglluryuumirlun' cali ellii,

he wished he were
like the arctic loons,
which flew,
swam, and dove without needing to come up for air.

* * *

And so one day as he was beachcombing,
he was singing a song which came to him through the power of
   his mind's helpless longing,
he was singing this song
as he walked along the shore.

And his song went like this:
(His song
is accompanied with arm motions,
since nowadays
it is used in traditional dancing.)

DRUM

I am traveling, on and on,   I am flying, on and on,   I am traveling, on and on, I am flying, on and on,

Aa-yaye-eya-aa   yaa-yaye-eya-a   aa-yeya   aa-waya aa.

I am traveling, on and on,   I am flying, on and on,   I am traveling, on and on,   I am flying, on and on,

Aa-yaye-eya-aa   yaa-yaye-eya-a   aa-yeya   aa-waya   aa.

*The repeating figure represented with ♫ has a strongly accented first element, and
a somewhat lengthened second element that is slightly lower in pitch than what is
written for it.

* * *

When the arctic loons
dove underwater, they cried
Uuiiq!
And just like that
he imitated them, wishing he could dive as they did,

imarpigkun-taw' cinirtellinilun',
ivarutmeng aturtuurluni tamatumeng.
Ellii-cal' piqeryuumiryaaqlun' tawaten.

Mallung'ngami-am-taw',
tawa-i malluni taun' ut'rutliniluku.

* * *

Umyugam-gguq-taw' kayutacia capriutaqur-tawaten.

Ayuqniaryaaqvakarluni-gguq-taw' cuucim ayuqucianeng
    mat'umeng,
umyugaq capriutaqan.

Caprit'taciani umyugam,
makut-llu piyuumilriit
ayuqeqeryuumirluki
cuuvakarluni cuum,
nukalpiat-ll' makut,
tangerkengani ayuqeqeryuumirluki
cullran-gguq tawaam cuk,
elluarrluku-taw' pivkarciqaa,
ayuqelingnatugluki elluarrluteng pilriit cuukuneng.

Tawa-i-taw' mat'um quliram apalluqaa,
ayuqniaruciq.

Cuk,
umyugaan tawaam
piurtarkauluku-gguq,
ayuqniallran tawaam,
piyukek'ngaanun tekiutarkauluku,
tukuutem tekiuyngaitaa piyuumatacianun-gguq,
tawaam-gguq ayuqniallran.

Kina elliriqevkenani cuukuni,
ayuqniarciquq tawaam ilamineng,
piyuumalrianeng.

Maligtaqungnaqluki-ggur-tawken ayuqniallni maliggluku niilluku
    pikuni-taw' cuuguluni.

Tawaam.

all while he walked along the shore,
singing that song.
Oh, how he wished that he could do what the loons could!

Well, he found a carcass,
and he brought it home with him.

* * *

By the power of his mind, he was able to succeed.

He tried long and hard to approach the life he admired,
whenever his mind overcame the barriers to success.

Through the power of the mind,
those who want to
can wish to be like those who are successful,
and throughout his life,
a person can wish to be
like the great hunters he sees around him;
but a person
will only succeed in life
if he lives correctly, trying to imitate those who are successful.

The theme of this story
is a person's will to follow those who are successful.

Only the mind
will make a person
continue on,
only his will to follow those who are successful
will bring him finally to his goal.
Great wealth will not bring him all that way,
only his will to follow those who are successful.

Whoever has very little
must aspire to do
as others around him who are more successful do.

He must try to imitate, follow, and listen to those he wants to be
  like, and only in this way can he succeed in life.

The end.

– Told by Leo Moses on November 8,
   1978
Translated by Leo Moses and
   Anthony C. Woodbury
Originally published in Cev'armiut
   Qanemciit Qulirait-llu: Eskimo
   Narratives and Tales from
   Chevak, Alaska, *compiled and*
   edited by Anthony C. Woodbury,
   Alaska Native Language Center
   and University of Alaska Press,
   1984.

NOTES

Anthony C. Woodbury explains in his introduction to *Eskimo Narratives and Tales from Chevak, Alaska* that the translation was guided by the principle that "a translation that sounds natural and is faithful to the meaning of the original is in the end more useful." To achieve a "natural-sounding" translation, the translators "departed from Yup'ik structure per se" by "not mechanically translating particles like *tawa* (or taw'), which variously means 'well', or 'then' (among other things), and =gguq 'it is said'." Woodbury concludes that the translation "reflects at every turn" Leo Moses's deep understanding "of the relationship between textual meaning in Yup'ik and in English."

Mary Worm

THE CROW AND THE MINK
(told in Yup'ik)

Once Crow was walking along the shore.
As he walked,
he came upon
a fish skin mitten
which was mending itself.

"Oh, you poor thing!
Whoever tore you up so?"

"It was that old grass bag
who tore me up.
And so I have to mend myself."

After staying a while and watching
the Crow left.

As he was walking
he came upon an old grass bag
weaving itself.

Mary Worm, Yup'ik from Kongiganak, Alaska.

"Aling aren,
oh, you poor old bag.
Why do you have to mend yourself?"

"It was that old fish skin mitten
who fought
and tore up parts of me, so now I am mending myself."
And after watching a while,
he walked on again.

As Crow walked on
right along the shore,
he saw several beluga whales
breaching and diving as they swam down the river.

One enormous beluga
slowly surfaced
and just as slowly submerged.

Well,
so then,
that cunning old Crow
lighted at the edge of the water,
sat down,
and proceeded to address that huge beluga as it surfaced.

"Hey!
you great whale down there!
You should surface close to the shore
with your mouth open.
You would surely show more of your greatness
if you would come up
with your mouth wide open!"

So then,
in a little while,
that great beluga emerged very close to Crow,
its huge mouth open wide.

And then,
Crow suddenly stood up,
and went right into the whale!

Well,
he found himself in a porch
and further inside was an entryway
(even though he was inside a whale!).

He went further in through the entryway,
and found himself in a house
in which there lived a young girl,
who was busy sewing
a gutskin rain parka,
a parka made out of the dried intestines of a beluga.

And in there,
in the middle of the far wall,
was an oil lamp.
How bright that light was!

When the girl suddenly saw Crow
she said,
"Oh! Crow!
However did you get in here?"

(Nonchalantly) "Oh,
I just decided to come in,
since your place is right on my way . . ."

"Oh, well then, let me go
and get some food for you.
Wait for me
but be sure not to touch that light back there.
Don't even reach for it."

And so she went out.

After being gone a short while,
she came in
with a bowl of tomcod.

Well,
of course Crow had been very hungry
and so he ate and ate
and finished off the tomcod.

And after finishing off the tomcod,
Crow said,
"I sure would like some more to eat!"

Then, the girl said,
"Well, I will get you some more.
Now, remember not to touch that light."

Then,
she left carrying the bowl with her.
And, although the girl had warned him strictly,
Crow started toward the light
and reached for it.
And, the moment he touched it,
he was engulfed in darkness!

Oh no!
There he was
in the dark
and the girl didn't come back.

And so,
he had to stay there in the dark.

So then,
after he had been there for a while,
he heard voices overhead.

"Oh!
I wonder how this giant beluga died?
It doesn't seem to have been wounded.
How could it have died?"

And Crow thought to himself,
"I wish those men out there
would cut this whale open right above me!"

Pretty soon,
he saw a knifeblade
coming through above him.

And, as they opened up
the area above him,

he spread out his wings,
and gathering all his strength,
he sprang straight up.
Up, up he went.

When he got high enough,
he glided down
and landed some distance from the group.
And after staying there a while,
he started walking toward them,
then stopped to watch them
from a distance.

He could see them down there near the shore,
cutting up that huge beluga whale.
They had a lot of the skin and blubber cut into pieces.

And then, after they had it all cut up,
and after the meat was cut up too,
Crow approached them.

Well,
when he got there
they said to him,
"Oh, Crow, it's too bad
that you got here
after all the pieces were claimed,
and now there is nothing left
for you, you poor thing!"

"Oh, that's quite all right.
I don't mind if there's none left for me,
because when I was watching you
back there,
a while ago,
when you cut into it
I saw something
(what a liar that Crow is!)
fly out
and it shot up into the sky
and disappeared!
Just don't give me any
because I'm kind of squeamish about it.

Anyway, I've got to be going,
so just don't bother."

So then,
he went off
but he landed not far away,
and hid himself where they couldn't see him.
Then he heard them talking among themselves,
"That Crow . . .
I've never known him to be squeamish about *anything* before.
So what's he afraid of now?"

And then one of them said,
"Just when we started
to cut the whale open,
I saw something, too.
Something came out in a flash
and went somewhere."

"Yes, maybe we
should leave this whale alone, too.
We have other food.
It's not the only thing we have to eat.
Because if Crow,
who'll eat anything,
is squeamish,
after seeing what he saw,
then . . ."
And so, they didn't take the meat after all.

And Crow was delighted
that they had left all that meat.
And, as soon as their kayaks
were out of sight,
he went down to the shore
and started packing the pieces
up from the shore.

As he carried the meat up,
a nice little mink came by.

"Hey! little Mink!
Help me carry all this food

for the two of us,
and we will have enough for the whole winter,
and the summer, too.
Let's carry it back up there!"

Well,
Mink was very pleased!
And so, they went back and forth
carrying all the pieces of skin and meat.
They made pits in the cold ground
to store some parts of the whale.
They hung the meat up on racks, for a fine store of dried beluga.
Before they knew it, it was evening
and they were still busy hanging up the meat.
For Crow had put up many drying racks.

And so, after hanging up all that meat,
and since there was driftwood all around them,
they built themselves a home.

And since it happened
that the mink was a female,
Crow took her as his wife.

And so, they made themselves a home
and finished it.
They also built a food cache,
and stored the whale skin there.

And now
they had all that to eat
besides the other food they had stored.

And then,
winter came
after the long stretch of summer.

Then, Crow would make trips
to gather wood for the two of them.

Back then,
people did not have stoves,
and so Crow and Mink built their fire

in the center of the house on the floor
and with the skylight open to vent the smoke
they would warm themselves while cooking.

And since they lived this way,
Crow would go out wood gathering.
He would bring back a large supply
of good dry wood.

And so,
it was before one of those wood gathering trips one day
that he said to Mink,
"Gee, you should make some akutaq."

So,
since he asked her to make akutaq
she did so.
She mixed seal oil with some berries,
since they had stored away quite a lot of this
and other food, too.

Really they had everything they needed!

And so it happened that
night fell while Crow was gone.

(Ominously) Well then,
shortly after nightfall,
and since they had an underground passageway that you had to
    crawl through,
Mink heard someone out there in the passageway singing,
"Qamyumaa-aa-aa, Qamyumaa-aa-aa,
(My one in there . . .
My one in the . . . re!)
If you don't give me any akutaq,
I am going to eat you-u-u-u-u."

Oh my!
Mink grabbed half of the akutaq
and flung it out into the entryway!
And as she did so,
she heard a slurping sound out there.

And then came another song.
"Qamyumaa-aa-aa, Qamyumaa-aa-aa,
(My one in there
My one in there!)
If you don't give me a little akutaq,
I'm going to eat you-u-u-u-u!"

(Excitedly) Mink then tossed out
the rest of the akutaq!

And again she heard that slurping sound.

And then
the singing stopped.

Shortly after that,
Crow came home.

And since Mink prepared him food to eat,
he ate.

"Oh Crow,
since you had asked me to make akutaq
I did,
and here was my pan.
I had it full of akutaq
but something came to the door
and sang,
and said that if I didn't give it any
it would eat me.
When I threw some out
something would slurp it up and sing for more.
And finally it stopped,
after it finished up all the akutaq!"

(Crow) "That's terrible!
I wonder what it was!"

And so, again, on another day
while he was getting ready to get wood,
Crow said,
"Make me some more akutaq.

Maybe someone will sing
'qamyumaa' for it again."

So, Mink made some akutaq again
as Crow had asked her to,
and she waited.

And so,
it happened again that night fell before Crow got home.

As it started getting dark,
Mink thought to herself,
"H-m-m-m, I wonder if it is Crow
who is doing this to me,
who is trying to scare me?
Why is it that when he asks me to make akutaq
that ghost just happens to come to me?"

And so,
soon after she made the akutaq,
there came that singing again.

"Qamyumaa-aa-aa, Qamyumaa-aa-aa.
If you don't give me a little akutaq,
I'm going to eat you-u-u-u-u!"

Again she tossed half of the akutaq out.
And after the slurping sound,
she heard more singing.

"Qamyumaa-aa-aa, Qamyumaa-aa-aa.
If you don't give me a little akutaq,
I'm going to eat you-u-u-u-u!"

The Mink threw
the rest of the akutaq at it.

"Qamyumaa-aa-aa. (He would sing again and again)
Qamyumaa-aa-aa . . . (My one in the . . . re!)
If you don't give me a little akutaq . . ."
And then
this time, since Mink didn't have any more to give him,
she took a charred stick

from the firepit
and held it ready. '

"If you don't give me a little akutaq
I'm going to eat you-u-u-u-u!"

(With force) Mink then hurled that stick out toward the door
and said,
"The akutaq is all gone!"

And as she hurled the wood out
she heard,
"Q'ruk" from out there.

And then the thing was gone.

And so, again,
after some time,
Crow came home.
He came home complaining of a sore eye.

And then
he said his poor eye was hurting him so.
He must have hit it with something.
It was terribly sore, he said.

(Mink) "Here,
come over,
and let me open it and see.

That akutaq I made
is all gone again.
I gave it all to that one
who kept asking for it."

And so,
after Crow lay down in front of her
she pried his eye open.
And there in his eye
was a huge chunk of charred wood!

Well,
She took it out,
And, sure enough, it was a piece of charred wood!

Then, being really ticked off at him,
she shook her finger at his nose
and said to him,
"So! It was you, you louse,
who was scaring me like that.
And it was I who got charcoal in your eye
when I hurled that piece at you!"

At this,
the crow started chuckling.

And after a time,
his poor eye was no longer sore.

So then
after that
Crow continued to be Mink's husband
and never tried to play tricks on her again.

As he lived with her
he continued to gather wood.

In time winter passed and summer came.

And they stayed there all summer.
And during this time
Crow would go looking for beached seals.

And as berries ripened
Mink made woven grass containers,
filled them up with berries,
and placed them in lakes to keep them fresh,
anchoring them in place with pieces of wood.

And
it is told that Mink stayed on as Crow's wife
and though he was her husband
they never had any children together.

*– Transcribed and translated by
Elsie Mather, with assistance
from Phyllis Morrow.*

Kirt Bell

THE FIRST WHALES
(told in Yup'ik)

There were these two –
a man and his wife
who lived by the sea.

They were all alone.
They lived there by themselves,
with no one else,
these two,
a man and a wife.

There were mountains near
where they lived.

And the mouth of their river
was not far away.
The ocean was also close by
and the river flowed out to that sea.

Kirt Bell, Yup'ik from Hooper Bay, Alaska.

The woman's husband
was a nukalpiaq,
a good hunter and provider.

But though he frequently went out hunting,
he never had anything to say about his trips.

He would be gone all day
hunting somewhere,
out in the wilderness.

Often,
after going
on his trips inland,
after being gone for some time,
he would come home
back to their place,
and not have a word to say about his adventures.

But he would sometimes remark,
"It's strange,
there isn't anyone else around here
or even in the land beyond here!

"And even when I am paddling
out there in the ocean,
I've never seen
anyone –
not even a sign of a kayak."

That was how it was.

At times,
when he took a break from his work,
he would say to his wife,
"How is it that we
have never had a child
together?

"And yet,
when I'm traveling on land,
or paddling out in the ocean,
I see the birds out there,

for instance,
accompanied by their young
when the time is right. .

"Then why is it that
a child has never come to us?
Why is it that we have never
had a child?"

He would go on.

"It's a pity
that we don't have a child."

And so. . . .
Sometimes the wife
would go outside, too.
She did not always stay in the house
doing her work,
but she would go outside
and scan the inland area.
She would look towards those mountains back there
hoping to see something.

But no matter how hard she looked
she never saw anything unusual
or any sign of a human form.

That one,
her husband,
would return and say,
"Ali, one could be out in the wilderness
from sun-up to sundown
and never see another person anywhere,
except for those cranes
who pose here and there
looking like human forms."

So then. . . .
one of those times
the wife was feeling lonely
while her husband was gone.
Setting aside her work

she lay down on her back on the bed
and ran the palms of her hands
over her belly.

While feeling around on her belly,
she felt something,
something inside her belly.
There was something firm in there
which, when she pressed on it,
would give her some discomfort,
a kind of a dull ache.

"Oh!
I wonder what that is inside?"

And
as she pressed and felt around
inside,
she would feel something and say
worriedly,
"I wonder what this could be?
Is it some kind of a growth
inside me?"

So then,
when her husband came home
as usual in the evening
she said to him,
"Hey, listen!
While you were gone,
when I was feeling my belly,
I felt something in there.
When I pressed on it
it felt firm
and it felt like something was throbbing
in my belly."

"Oh, my!
I wonder what it could be?"
I hope it is a baby beginning to grow
and not something else!"

"Yes, I hope so, too!"

Before long,
the growth inside her became bigger.
It started growing quite rapidly.
And soon
her belly
was quite swollen.

"Oh, what is that
growing inside of you?
What could it be
that is causing your belly to swell so much?

They did not know what to make of all of this.

And then,
not long after,
that one,
his wife
said,
"I wonder why
my belly hurts today?
It stops now and then,
but it is getting worse."

Soon she could not walk around any longer
because the pain was increasing.

"Perhaps,
by some chance . . .
maybe it is a baby!

"Why don't you stop walking around.
Sit on the bed
and stay still.
There is nothing we can do."

Soon after
while she was sitting there
she started to feel the urge to push
and bear down.

"I'm feeling the urge to push
and it is hard to stay still."

"Well then –
why don't you settle down somewhere
and try pushing
if that is how you feel."

As she started bearing down
she felt something coming out down there.

Her husband was beside her
as she bore down
and then he suddenly started exclaiming
that it was a baby.

Well,
he was so-o-o-o thankful!
He was so very, very thankful!

"Well now,
be very careful.
Be very careful not to hurt it
as you care for it."

My! How happy they were!

"Well,
we finally have a child.
Take good care of him."

And so,
the woman,
the mother,
recovered.

After her recovery
the man, her husband
said to her,
"After you are able
to sit up and sew,
please make me a gutskin rain parka.
Make it with plenty of room inside.
The rain parka I have –
the sleeves keep working up
and I am tired of that.

And when I tie the bottom edge
to the opening in my kayak
it keeps working its way off."

But
she always had made his rain parka
as wide as the opening on the kayak.

And soon,
the newborn had passed the stage
where the navel was healed.   ˙

In the meantime,
the husband continued to hunt as usual.

And so,
his wife sewed,
working on the rain parka.

And then,
as she had been sewing steadily,
she was soon done with the parka.

And what a great parka it was!

"Please,
put it away somewhere.
I'll take it with me
when I go hunting
one of these times."

So she folded the parka neatly
and put it safely away.

So then
after some time
the man awoke early one day.

"My,
what a fine day it is outside.
It is such a beautiful day
with no wind at all!

"You must be tired of being in the house all the time.
Why don't you come with me in the kayak
and we will go out for a ride.

"You have been in the house so much.
Come out today
and breathe the fragrant air outdoors.

"You two can ride behind me in the kayak
while I paddle.
You are both in need of fresh air."

So his wife
agreed
and quickly got herself ready.

And then
he said to her,
"That rain parka you made,
that you finished –
have it ready.
We won't leave it behind.
We'll take it along with us."

This he told his wife.

So he pushed his kayak down
to the river.

"Come on over now
and get in.

"The weather is so fine,
and there's not a breath of wind!"

And so it happened that they went down to the river,
the husband paddling and taking the other two with him.

And then,
when he reached the mouth of that river,
when he made his way out of that river,
he went straight out into the ocean,
straight ahead.

The land started to recede behind them into the distance.
And as soon as the land was out of sight,
they saw land ahead of them,
emerging into their sight.

As it came into view,
as the land appeared ahead of them,
it looked like an island.

As they got closer,
the island came into view.
And when they were nearly there . . .
There was no wind at all.
How calm the sea was,
its surface smooth and unruffled.

They reached it
and it was a sandbar.
There was no land around it
nor could they see any beyond it.
The land they left was out of sight behind them.

"Well then,
you two must be uncomfortable and you probably need to empty
    your bladders.
Get on out and go back there,
and take the rain parka along.
You can nurse the baby back there too.

"Sit down
and let him nurse in comfort.
Take along that rain parka,
the one you sewed,
and go sit down."

So the mother and baby got out.

She spread out the parka,
the parka she had worked on,
on the sand there.
And she put the baby down,
that baby of hers,
there on the parka.

Then she got up to relieve herself.

After she relieved herself,
and since she had had her back to her husband,
and had been facing her baby,
she got up and turned around –
and saw her husband,
who was already paddling away
towards the land they had left.

She started to call after him,
"Hey, you!
Where are you going?
Why are you leaving us?"

And he answered,
"Stay there.
You can just stay there."

And then she called after him,
"So this was what you were planning to do with us.
And this was why you had me make the rain parka.
I see now that you wanted me to make this parka
for the baby and myself."

And she quickly put the parka on.
Because the water,
the tide,
was already starting to come up.

The water was rising quickly.

Quickly donning the rain parka,
she put the baby on her back,
that little baby of hers.

And it wasn't long before
the water reached her feet.
They say that the water rose very fast
as the tide came in.

And then
she let out her voice.

"Ngaayangaa
Ngaayangaa
Ngaayangaa-a-yaraa qukaa-rrangaa-a-yaraa
Qukaa-rrangaa-yaraa.
Now it's coming, co – ming up to my feet
It is reaching my feet.
Qukaa-rrangaa-yaraiy."

"Well now,
we are in a real fix.
That one, your father,
is so cruel.
It is so senseless
that it is for this reason
he pretended to care about
our need to get out in the fresh air,
so that he could take us out here
to this place.
He just wanted to take us here,
and abandon us!"

And then she wailed,
"Ngaayaraa
Ngaayangaa, Ngaayangaa-a-yaraa
Qukaa-rrangaa-yaraa
Qukaa-rrangaa-yaraa
Now it's coming, coming
up to my shins
It is reaching my shins
Qukaa-rrangaa-yaraa
Qukaa-rrangaa-yaraiy.

Ngaayaraa, ngaayaraa
Ngaayangaa-yaraa
Qukaa-rrangaa-yaraa
Qukaa-rrangaa-yaraa
Now it's coming, coming
up to my knees
It is reaching my knees
Qukaa-rrangaa-yaraa
Qukaa-rrangaa-yaraiy.

Ngaayangaa
Ngaayangaa Ngaayangaa-yangaa
Qukaa-rrangaa-yaraa
Qukaa-rrangaa-yaraa
Now it's coming, coming
up to my hips
It is reaching my hips
Qukaa-rrangaa-yaraa
Qukaa-rrangaa-yaraiy."

She kept on singing
while she patted her baby
on her back.

That baby on her back,
the little one she carried
was starting to cry.

"Ngaayangaa
Ngaayangaa Ngaayangaa-yangaa
Qukaa-rrangaa-yaraa
Qukaa-rrangaa-yaraa
Now it's coming, coming
up to my navel
Qukaa-rrangaa-yaraa
Qukaa-rrangaa-yaraiy.

Ngaayangaa
Ngaayangaa Ngaayangaa-yangaa
Qukaa-rrangaa-yaraa
Qukaa-rrangaa-yaraa
Now it's coming, coming
up to my chest
It is up to my chest
Qukaa-rrangaa-yaraa
Qukaa-rrangaa-yaraiy.

Ngaayangaa
Ngaayangaa Ngaayangaa-yangaa
Qukaa-rrangaa-yaraa
Qukaa-rrangaa-yaraa
Now it's coming, coming
up to my neck

It is reaching my neck
Qukaa-rrangaa-yaraa
Qukaa-rrangaa-yaraiy.

Ngaayangaa
Ngaayangaa Ngaayangaa-yangaa
Qukaa-rrangaa-yaraa
Qukaa-rrangaa-yaraa."

And now it was up to her head.

And then they were gone.

The cries of the little one on her back
broke off in mid-air.

In a little while,
after being under water,
she surfaced,

and there she was – a killer whale!

And the baby,
her child,
had become her dorsal fin
there on her back.

And then she sped away
after the father.

"That foolish father of yours!
So this was why he had me make this rain parka,
so he could do this to us.
Oh, we are going to give him what he deserves,
and plenty of it,
when we catch up with him."
She went after him furiously.

And
it wasn't long before
he was in her sight.

She sped on after him.

When she caught up
she stayed out of his sight,

then shot up in front of him!

There he was, paddling along
when this whale suddenly breached
in front of him.

She dug into her upper jaw
and peeled it up
to reveal her human face.

"You fool!
So you had a plan in mind
when you took us down to that island.
You planned to leave us there on purpose.
And you asked me to make this parka for you
when it was really for us.
You had it all planned!

"And your little child here –
you didn't even think of him
when you took me along with you
and left us behind!"

"Well,
never mind!
Don't be so upset!
Let me help you into the kayak!"

"It's too late now.
We are going to stay the way we are.
I'm going to be a whale.
I'm going to make it worse for you
than you made it for us!"

With that she turned furiously.
As she twisted around
she drenched him with spray.
And whenever she came up next to him
she would thrash her tail to toss the water on him.
The kayak rocked about

from her twisting and thrashing.
And she tortured her husband
with the waves she made,
almost capsizing the kayak!
She would also come up behind him
and with her tail
splash water on him!

He was terrified!
"Stop!
and come here.
I'll let you in!"

She paid no attention to his pleas.

After she'd tortured him
as much as she wanted
she dove under his kayak
and with the flip of her tail
she tossed him, kayak and all,
high up into the air.

And he was gone.

In a little while,
after being underwater a short while,
he surfaced.

All three of them
had become whales.

That woman,
his wife,
had her little child on her back.
Now they were all whales.

So now,
you have that story.

They say that that thing on her back,
that fin that protrudes out of her back,
her dorsal fin,
was really her baby.

They say that
these whales
are really people.

That was when
the first whales appeared.

That is all.
That is the end.

*– Transcribed and translated by Elsie
Mather, with assistance from
Phyllis Morrow*

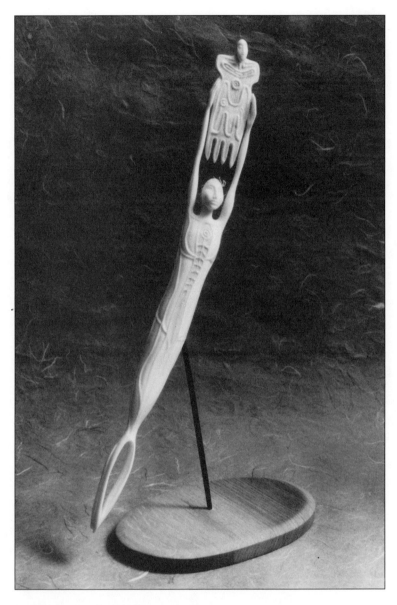

SHAMAN WITH COMB (St. Lawrence Island Yupik)
Susie Silook, whose prose and poetry also appear in the Contemporary
Works section of this volume, made this carving from walrus ivory,
red ochre, baleen, sinew and wood. Photo: Jimmie Froehlich.
(Courtesy of Susie Silook)

Pelaasim Apellgha

IVAGHULLUK ILAGAATA

Ighivganghani, eghqwaaghem elagaatangi taakut atughaqiit. Ila-
gaghaqut angyalget taakut. Ivaghullugmeng atelget.

Elngaatall, repall tusaqnapangunatengllu. Nangllegsim angtalanganeng, wata eghqwaalleghmi tawani nangllegnaghsaapigllu-
teng ilaganeghmeggni iglateng qughaghteghllaglukii piiqegkangit.
Nangllegsim angtalanganeng Kiyaghneghmun.

> Uuknaa-aa-aanguu-uuq.
> Saamnaa-aa-aanguu-uuq,
> Taglalghii-ii-ii saa-aamnaa.
> Ketangaa-aan aghveghaa-aa saa-aamnaa-aa
> Aghvelegglaguu-uu-lii.
> Ellngalluu-uu-uu.
> Qagimaa iluganii-ii-ii.
>
> Uknaa-aa-aanguu-uuq.
> Saamnaa-aa-aanguuq,

Lincoln Blassi

PRAYER SONG ASKING FOR A WHALE
(told in St. Lawrence Island Yupik)

Before the whaling season, the boat captain would sing ceremonial songs in the evening. The ceremony of singing was called *ivaghulluk*.

The boat captain would sing these songs in such a low reverent voice that you could hardly make out the words. Especially before the whaling season began, the songs of petition were sung to God in a prayerful pleading voice.

> The time is almost here.
> The season of the deep blue sea . . .
> Bringing good things from the deep blue sea.
> Whale of distant ocean . . .
> May there be a whale.
> May it indeed come . . .
> Within the waves.
>
> The time is almost here.
> The season of the deep blue sea . . .

Lincoln Blassi, St. Lawrence Island Yupik from Gambell, Alaska.

Taglalghii-ii-ii saa-aamnaa.
Ketangaa-aa-aan ayveghaa-aa saa-aamna.
Aghvelegllaaguluu-uu-lii
Elngaa-aa-aalluu-uungu-uuq
Qagimaa iluganii-ii-ii.

Uuknaa-aa-aanguu-uuq.
Saamnaa-aa-aanguu-uuq
Taglalghii-ii-ii saa-aamnaa.
Ketangaa-aan maklagaa-aa-aanguuq.
Aghvelegllaguulii-ii-iingii.
Ellngalluu-uu-uu.
Qagimaa iluganii-ii-ii-ngiy.

Bringing good things from the deep blue sea.
Walrus of distant ocean . . .
May there be a whale.
May it indeed come . . .
Within the waves.

The time is almost here.
The season of the deep blue sea . . .
Bringing good things from the deep blue sea.
Bearded seal of distant ocean.
May there be a whale.
May it indeed come . . .
Within the waves.

– Originally published in Sivuqam
Nangaghnegha Siivanllemta
Ungipaqellghat Lore of St.
Lawrence Island: Echoes of Our
Eskimo Elders, *edited by Anders
Apassingok, Willis Walunga, and
Edward Tennant. Bering Strait
School District, Unalakleet,
Alaska, 1985.*

Ignitchiaq

KIVALLIÑIGMI PILGURUAQ AGNAQ

Taikanigguuq tavra Piŋumilu, uvanilu, Igluġruaġnik taikka piraġi-gaich, taipkua sivulliavut iñuuniaġviat. Naugaluaġniqsuagguuq iñ-ugiaksivluni taikani nuŋutitqataġutiŋ tamatkunuŋa aŋuyyiaqtua-nun, atqunaqtuqtillutiŋ. Tainnaasiii iñua una nuŋuanmun ilivluni.

Tavra tamaunaqpaatigun umiaqtuġiaqqaaġutiŋ tagraagaqsilgiñ-ñiqsut taavavrumuuna Kivalliñikun. Kivvaasiiñ tatkivuŋa Masut-tuum kiŋuġauraŋanun nullaaqtuġutiŋ. Panapkaaqtuamigguuq tamaani qiñiġnaitchuq, qiñiŋitchut. Tamarra umiatiŋ akivillugich iigutaaġiiksillugich inillagataqtut. Tuttusiuqsaġumavlutiŋ aŋutigik-kaŋiich.

Qammasugrukkii qamma. Masutuuq upinġaami siñiġraqtuni, kuuŋan avatik ivigaaqaqtuk masum nakautaŋanik tatqamma tatqa-vuŋa. Nausuŋŋilanik qiliġruattanik tainna takiŋilaanik uqpiiruq taatkimñaqpak. Takiruanik uqpiitchuq.

Uvvaliasiiñ una aġnaq. Aġnamliuma aġnat aullautiniġai masuli-aġutivlugich. Tavra tatkivuŋa tatqamma masuuruamun iliyaqtua-ġutigalugu sivulliaqtuaġuni. Masunniagaqsirut. Taikuŋaqtaaqsaġ-nialgilluni tavra aŋuyaich ilitchuġilġataġniġai. Imma aŋutiŋich

122

Clinton Swan

THE KIVALINA WAR HEROINE
(told in Iñupiaq)

Our ancestors used to live over at Pinu and Igluġruaq.[1] There used to be a large population there, but bands of raiders would come from different places to wage war on them. The raiders killed off most of the population.

One time when the whaling season was over, a group of people went up the Kivalina River to hunt and fish. They camped near Masutuuq Creek. They did not see any tents or other signs of campers so they propped their skin boats next to each other to use as shelters and set up camp there. The men had plans to hunt caribou.

This place was quite far up the Kivalina River. Both sides of that creek were covered with grassy areas where *masu* or "Eskimo potatoes" grew in abundance, near the short willow thickets.

When the men had left to hunt caribou, one woman took a group of ladies to gather *masu* up there. When the women came to an area where the *masu* stalks grew in thick patches, the woman who was leading the group happened to notice that there were people con-

Clinton Swan, Iñupiaq from Kivalina, Alaska.

aullaŋarut. Tavraukua sapkuniŋa inillaktuanunkii kiŋuġaaġutisu-gutigguuq.

Taavruma iḷitchuġiniġai punŋaugaqtuat. Naluruatun tamaani sugagrailiqivluni, qanutun iñugiaktilaaŋat iḷitchuġisuglugu iḷit-chuġilġataġaa.

Tavra iñugiaŋniġmata utiġuni iḷitchuġipkaġniġai, inna tupak-saŋiññiġai, "Kanuŋaqtaallaguta niġiñiuraallakkisiruaguut."

Tavraasiiñ taliññami uqautivlugich, "Aŋŋua iqsiñiaqasi. Uvva pisuqtilaaqsiktun aisaġisirusi. Iñuich pamma qiñiġitka punŋaruat. Pisuqtilaaġusi aisaġumausi aasii iglillavsi amaġuq tasamma maguk-pan sivunnavsiññiñ, iqsiginiaŋitkiksi tuŋaanun igliġisirusi."

Tavra tiliqqaaġlugich utiġuni tavrani nakutchaġataaqsigai, sap-kua aisaqukkani ayuuqugaluaġlugich. Tavra iḷimasuliġuŋnaġma-taguuq tikilġiñaġai. Tainna akkupasugruk ayuuġuŋnaqsiŋmiullu, makkiqigaat pananik aġnaq. Avatiqamitruŋ quugaqsiḷiġaat pa-nanik.

Tavra pisargaġaluaqtinnani qiviuġuġuni tiŋiliqtuq. Anauniaqtu-ġaalguuq qiviulġiñaq. Taatpavuunaasiitai qiviuġuġluni.

Sivuniŋannun aġnat tunnami, amaqqutun maguulalġataqtiġaq-tuq. Tikisaaġlutiŋ. Tavra annaktitkaigguuq aŋuyaŋniñ.

cealed among the willows. In the meantime, the men went to hunt caribou. Apparently, a band was planning to raid the women during the hunters' absence.

The woman remained calm and pretended not to notice them because she wanted to determine how many of them there were.

When she realized that it was a large party, the woman went back to her group and said in a calm voice, "Why don't we move a little further down there to eat?"

When they were out of sight she said, "Do not panic. But do try your best to make it back home. If you should hear a wolf howling up ahead of you," she instructed, "don't be startled. Just keep moving towards the sound."

Then, to give the women a head start, she went back to distract the raiders. Knowing that the raiders suspected something, the woman revealed herself. The raiders rose up, pointed their spears at her, and closed in.

Before they could harm her, the woman turned into a down feather and floated in the air. The raiders tried desperately to stab at the little feather. But the woman floated up away and landed ahead of the ladies who were escaping.

She then howled like a wolf. The ladies followed her instructions and moved toward the howl. She kept this up until they got home. That is how the woman from Kivalina helped the others escape.

– Originally published in Uqaaq-tuangich Iñupiat: Lore of the Iñupiat, The Elders Speak, Vol. 1, *edited by Hannah Mendenhall, Ruth Sampson, Edward Tennant. Kotzebue, AK: Northwest Arctic Borough School District, 1989.*

NOTE

1. Igluġruaq is about 15 miles north of Kivalina. Pinu is about five miles further north.

Frank Ellanna

SHAMANIC FLIGHT
(told in Iñupiaq)

Frank Ellanna:
> Because I used to play outside so much, I do not have many
> stories to tell.
> In the wintertime, I used to play outside a great deal.

Aloysius Pikonganna:
> Myself, I would sleep.
> Whenever I got sleepy while they were telling stories, I would
>   stay
> in the qagri and fall asleep,
> leaving the storytellers behind.

Frank Ellanna:
> There were those shamans who made magical flights,
> the very first people to fly through the air,
> before white men began to fly.
> *"Ilima.tuat"* they called those who could fly.

Frank Ellanna, Iñupiat from King Island, Alaska.

A person who was going to fly – in the qagri
they would tie him up,
tying him with skin rope so that he was thoroughly bound.
Below them, at their feet, they tied his arms up behind him.
They laid him on the floor,
tying him up so they were sure he could not move.

Then they hung up his sealskin breeches.
There were two posts supporting the roof and a cross beam
called "the paddle carving place."
They hung the breeches over there out of a person's reach;
they hung them there.
These were to be his wings,
the one who was going to fly, the "*ilima.tuaq.*"

Then they put the lights out in the qagri, making it entirely dark,
and they began to sing his songs for him from all around the
    floor,
the qagri members.
Then, after many songs were sung,
you could hear the sealskin breeches fall,
the sealskin breeches which would be his wings,
his pants.

It would not take long after that.
You know the sound of many birds flapping their wings at
    once –
they can be heard very loudly when they are close by.
Then he could be heard very clearly making a flapping sound,
using his sealskin breeches for wings.

He used a piece of walrus hide rope like the tail on a kite
as his dragline.
They called them their draglines.

When he had flown around there awhile –
the air vents in the houses weren't very big,
you know those air vents –
he went out through the air vent.

Then he would fly away in whatever direction he wanted.

Finally, when he returned, when it was time to return,
he would come in through the air vent
and could be heard as he did that.
They would light the lamps.
And there he would be on the floor, all tied up.

Aloysius Pikonganna:
He would tell about where he had come from.

Frank Ellanna:
He would tell about where he had come from and what he had seen.

– Told in Iñupiaq Eskimo by
  Frank Ellanna
Transcribed and translated by
  Margaret Seeganna
Originally published in
  Ugiuvangmiut Quliapyuit King
  Island Tales: Eskimo History
  and Legends from Bering
  Strait, *compiled and edited by*
  Lawrence D. Kaplan, Alaska
  Native Language Center and
  University of Alaska Press, 1988.

Laura Norton

THE BOY WHO FOUND THE LOST
(told in English)

This is a story
about a boy
that went and found the lost.
This happened a long time ago
in a small village along the coast.
In this village
there was a rich man with a son
and the people in the village
would hunt out on the sea.
They would hunt seal and ugruks
and what have you –
all the water fowl
they could get.
And all summer
they prepared these and other things.
They were real
smart people

Laura Norton, Iñupiaq from Kobuk, Alaska.

that is, they lived off the land
and off the sea.
One day
there was a group of men that went out hunting to the sea
and they did not come home. They were lost.
And among these men
was the rich man's son.
The father was really grieved.
He wanted his son back.
The men –
the men that were in the village –
went OUT to look for the missing group
and they also did not come home.
So the father
of this boy
offered
a reward. If any person
found the group and brought them home
he would give h a l f
of everything he had
(and he was the richest man in the village
never in want).
When the people heard this
there was a poor boy –
ORPHAN boy –
who lived with his grandmother
in the village.
There were some men –
they kept going out looking for them
but they could never find them.
And the grandmother told this boy
"Now if I get things ready for you
and prepare you for your journey
you will find them.
But if you do
you must FOLLow the rules
that I lay out for you.
When you find them
I want you to tell them
please shout and say
'Who will go home first?'
and then close your eyes
and paddle your

paddle, your qayaq paddle
as much as you can
and do not open your eyes
until you are home."
That's what his grandmother told the boy.
So
he started out
all alone
toward the sea.
Just when he got in the middle of nowhere
where he could hardly see the land in any direction
he saw a seal.
It would come up from the water
and down again.
And all the little boy had was his knife and a spear.
So he chased the seal
all over.
Chased it and chased it
until he caught it
with his spear
and put it on his qayaq.
But he looked –
he could not see the land
in any direction.
He was in the middle of nowhere
way out
in the water.
He did not give up.
He did not turn back.
(I don't think he knew which way to go anyway.)
But
as he went on
he saw a duck
a small duck
swimming.
So he started chasing that too.
He c h a s e d it and c h a s e d it
and finally caught it
with his spear.
When he finally caught it with his spear
he looked to see
whereabouts he was.
And then

he saw
he was close
to the land.
And when he saw
he was close to the land
he went that way
and there he saw
an iglu.
[He paddled to the shore
and got out of his qayaq.
He went into the iglu.][1]
He saw that
there was absolutely nothing wrong.
All he saw was a window
that faced on the ceiling.
Well, when he got inside
he put the seal and the duck and the spear
on the floor
of that little iglu
and while
he was just staying there
he heard a sound
like somebody was coming.
A walking sound.
And pretty soon
he heard somebody climbing up the iglu from the side –
from the outside.
He watched
and there
pretty soon
a m o n s t e r
looked in
through the window
from the outside and he called the boy by name
and he said
"If you don't give me what you caught
I'm going to swallow you."
The monster had a mouth from ear to ear.
The boy
picked up
the seal.
He picked up the seal.
He t o s s e d it up toward the window

and the monster caught it in his mouth.
Then the boy heard it
going down
the side of the house
and he heard it going behind the house
[and beyond.
And after a while
he heard it coming back
climbing up the iglu from the side.
The monster had a]² mouth from ear to ear.
And he called the boy by name
saying, "If you don't give me what you caught
I'm going to swallow you."
The boy picked up the duck
and t o s s e d it
toward the monster.
The monster caught it in his mouth.
Then
the boy heard him going down
the side
and up beyond the building –
beyond the iglu.
And there was no more sound.
And after a while
it came back.
The same thing over again.
When it got to the window
it called the boy by name
and he said
"If you don't give me what you caught
I'm gonna swallow you."
Well, the boy had nothing left
except the spear.
So he picked up his spear
threw it at the m o n s t e r
as h a r d as he could.
And he caught the monster
right through the neck.
He heard it tumbling down
tumbling down the side
of the iglu
and up and beyond.
Well, the boy was curious to see

where the monster
had gone.
So he went out of the house.
He went behind the house
to see what he could see.
There was a little trail
that led away
from the house
and over the ridge.
So the boy followed it.
And when he got over the ridge
he saw a small village
beyond there.
He waited until it got dark.
And then he saw all those people
rushing around
like something was going on
down there
in the small village.
He waited until it got dark
and then he went down
to the small village.
He went inside the first
little iglu that he got to.
And in this little iglu sat an old woman
all by herself with a parka on
and she was twisting sinew
to make thread for sewing.
The boy lost no time.
He caught the little old woman by the neck
and choked her.
He took the parka off of her
and hid the body
inside her little sleeping bag.
And HE put the parka on
picked up the sinew
and pretended to be an old lady.
When he heard two people coming
he turned the light off
and sat in the dark.
And when these two men came
they informed him
saying

"Our hunter
our hunter is very sick.
We came to get you."
So the boy pretended he was aged
it was hard to get around
had a hard time getting up.
These two men
helped him.
So he went by the door.
They helped him walk.
And when they got to the place
where the people gathered
sort of like a community
place
he went inside.
And there was the same monster
in the middle of the floor
tossing in pain.
And he asked these people
to turn the light off
saying "I can work better
in the dark."
And
then they turned the light off.
(Of course all they had
were the seal oil lanterns –
nothing bright –
it was really dim anyway.)
When he walked up to this monster
and he asked the monster, and said
"Where are you hurt?"
the monster was really in pain.
He pointed to the place where the spear
had caught him in the neck.
And
the boy
walked up
and he felt around this monster's neck and he found the spear
where it got stuck.
So he got his knife out
and CUT his spear out
took the parka off real fast, ran to the door
and got it.

He ran out
started running through the little trail
toward the place
where he left his qayaq.
While he was running he heard
a lot of people
running after him.
And then he remembered what his grandmother told him.
His grandmother had told him "If you find them
shout and see
who would go home first.
And then when you get to your qayaq
close your eyes
and p a d d l e
as hard as you can
your eyes closed."
And that's what the boy did.
He shouted
"Let's see who goes home first!"
When he got to his qayaq he got in
and p a d d l e d his qayaq
as h a r d as he could
without looking.
He p a d d l e d and p a d d l e d and p a d d l e d
for a long trip – (it seemed a long time to him).
Finally
when he stopped
he got out of the qayaq and
he was on land.
He looked back –
a view of these men
that had been lost for days.
And among them
was the
rich man's
son.
The rich man was so h a p p y
then
this boy brought his lost one home.
He kept his promise.
He gave half of everything he had
to the boy.

And the boy and his grandmother
were never in want
any more.
The end.

– Collected by Hannah Loon
Transcribed by Richard Dauenhauer

NOTES

1. There is a very brief gap in the recording at this point as a result of the tape recorder having become unplugged for a few seconds.

2. There is a short gap in the recording here where the tape ran out and the cassette was being ejected and flipped over.

Peter Kalifornsky

K'EŁA SUKDU

1 Suk gheli łuq'u Dena'ina qghelach'. Tak'hnelt'eh ch'u tan'i qełchin ch'u łuq'a uquqel'an tach'enił'i eł. Yeh łuq'a naqaqelash tach'enił'i eł. Heyi niłtu k'qezdelgha.

2 Ts'ełt'an quht'ana yeh qheyuł ch'u ch'qidetnik'. Heyi niłtu k'usht'a q'u niynik'eset'. Yethdi k'ełaggwa gheni q'ileshteh gheyuł ch'u q'inggwa iditnal'un. Yigheni yighetneq ch'u dan'i jenyegh-ełghel.

3 Yegheni shughu hey qwa qizdlan ch'u chik'enaq qbetudinzet. Na'uni qizdlan ch'u yadi ninya qbek'uhdi'u ch'u. Heyi niłtu niqey-dalkidi qwa k'qusil. Qdichin. Chik'enaq qwa dinzet.

4 Yin kił ghunen k'ełaggwa dani jenyeghełghelen ghun qil'i niłtu tiniyu. Dghilikenh tazu. Yehghu gheyuł, gheyuł, gheyuł, ch'u nich-iłka aniyu. Ch'u dasgedi qughe'u. Yeh dukaq'di qul hq'u yuqech'-hdi, "Aa, hunch'dal'an. K'tu'ushch' naqanlgheł ch'u qinldush," yełni. K'tu'ushch' naqalghel ch'u yethdi naqandalghel. Yethdi da-kaq' ch'ak'tnintun. Qighel'ets. Qichika yuyuh ezdu. Tuyanq' detsen dazdlu. "Shqen nutujuł. Gu zidu. Hunch'dal'an," yełni. Yeghuk'enił-kit. "Ch'aduch' hghuda t'ent'an qit'anideshni. Qit'anch'itni," yełni. "Shqen nutujułda yetdahdi neł nuqtulnek," yełni.

Peter Kalifornsky

THE MOUSE STORY
(told in Dena'ina Athabaskan)

1 Long ago this is the way the Dena'ina lived. They drove poles for a fish weir where they fished with a dipnet. They brought in fish with a dipnet, and they made ready for winter.

2 One man only walked around, and he was lazy. He wasn't preparing for winter at all. Then a little mouse was going in the brush with a fish egg in its mouth, but it couldn't get over a windfall. The man lifted the little mouse over the windfall.

3 Then winter came to them and sickness struck. Bad weather came, and they couldn't find any animals to hunt, and what they had stored for winter was gone. They were hungry. Sickness struck them.

4 The young man who had helped the little mouse over the windfall went out walking without hope. He went to the foothills. There he walked, and walked, and walked, and came to a big brush shelter. Smoke was coming out. There was no door, but from inside he heard a voice, "Yes, we were expecting you. Turn around the way the sun goes [clockwise] and come in," someone said. He turned around the way the sun goes, and, as he turned, a door opened. He

---

Peter Kalifornsky, Dena'ina Athabaskan from Unhghenesditnu ("farthest creek over"), Kasilof River, Alaska.

5 K'usht'a k'dit'al k'enli t'et'an. Ełnen ghenu. "Aa shqen dungh-ejuł," yełni. Uch'en qech' k'kegh'i qt'ingheju.

6 "Yaghali," yełni. "Qit'anideshni ch'aduch' qghuda t'ent'an. Nełch'indaqna łuq'u qdichin. Chik'enaq qutudinzet. Ndesnaqa beł itighełyeshi uqu nughenyuł. "Yaghali, nuntgheshtuh," yełni. "Nen k'u shnunintun."

7 Łuq'u qughesht'a q'inggwa dahdi k'tsenggwa dahdi ghenalggeni łuq'a denłts'ek' ggwah k'eyesggwa yiyełdeł. Ts'anesdets'ek' ggwah diyełdeł ch'u. Łuq'u ya k'ighałchet. Hał k'u k'ushu k'usht'a iłagh. Ditushi yeł didghełdatl'.

8 "Ginhdi nqayeh quht'ana nach'u haztunh gin eł nininjuda q'u niditighecheł ch'u ditushi gini beyditighełtesh. K'tu'ushch' naqantghelghełda, ba dinlchetda ndahkugh ni'ilyuh tut'ał. Yethdi nutghejuł ch'u neł ch'indaqna un detghenił ch'u. Yinahdi nen eł snuqiditulyash. Neł ch'indaqna beł itighełyesh yina ghutghełket yigheni nagh htusegh qech q'u łuq'u nunqiditultesh. Łuq'u tik'u nuqtudedeł ch'u chik'htuł'ish. Itighedyesh," yedgheni.

9 Yeqech'a besukt'a qdilanch'a, "K'eła yethdi łuq'u k'qezdelgha łuq'u gin ninya en'ishla k'usht'a shqidinil," yełni. "Nenhdi ch'qidghendnik'. Nughenyuł. Sha ninyu ch'u shighendneq ch'u dan'i q'in eł dan'i deshghełgheł. Yethdi yeqech' shnunintun. Yeqech' hguda yech' nen eł niqdalnen," yełni. "Shi sh'izhi K'eła Dnayi shi ghelihdi sh'izhi qdilanch'a Gujun. Gujun dnayi shina'i łuq'u yadi ninya qilan."

K'eła Sukdu Egh

Gun kił hdi k'egh t'eynizen, hq'u ch'qidudnik'. Q'ilish teh nuhuk'ulkeł, ch'u k'ełaqwa ghen dan'i jeneyghełghel. Yi ghen yaghalich' talghel, ch'u hey k'undet qayeh qadinzet, ch'u yin kił ghen, tik'u niyu yeh ghu nugheyuł, ch'u ninya dnayi gheniyu Gujun qyełnihen, ninya dnayi, kił ghun yeghudgheni. Ch'u yu qadi nuqiłchin, beł dnayi yeł ułyeshi. Yaghalich' talgheli ghen benuynastun. K'ełench'qghe'uyi, k'egh t'ich'eynizeni, ch'qich'dednik'i qil nabut' egh.

went in. A big old lady was sitting inside. A fire was burning in the center of the room. "My husband is coming back. Sit here. We were expecting you," she said to him. She fed him. "I know why you are here. We know you," she said. "When my husband returns, he'll explain it to you," she said.

5 Not long after, it hailed. The earth shook. "Yes, my husband is coming back," she said. From outside, a giant came in.

6 "Hello," he said. "I know why you are here. Your relatives are all hungry. Sickness has struck them. You are going about to try to save your relatives. Good, I'll help you," he said, "because you have helped me."

7 The giant put all kinds of small little fish eggs and little meats and dry fish into a little skin a pinch at a time. Pinch after pinch he put in and then he wrapped it up. It didn't come to much of a pack. He put down feathers in the pack.

8 The giant said, "Take this to your village. Before you arrive, put down the pack and spread out the food. Then sprinkle the down feathers over it. Turn around the way the sun goes, and, when you touch it, it will turn into a large pile of food. Then go to your village and tell your relatives to come with you. They will help you bring the food the rest of the way to your village. With this food you will save your relatives. You will feed them and before it is all gone, they will regain their strength. They will go to the woods and they will kill game. You will be saved," the giant said.

9 "The mouse you saved was getting ready for winter like everything else. But no one took pity on it when it needed help," the giant said. "You were lazy. You were walking about when you should have been helping. But you lifted me over that windfall when I had that fish egg. You helped me. That is why it has turned out this way," he said. "My name is Mouse Person, but really my name is *Gujun*.[1] *Gujun* is related to all of the animals."

About the Mouse Story

This man is a lazy person, and you would expect something bad to happen to him. But he is also gentle and kind. When he lifts that little mouse over the log, he is doing something good. When adver-

---

1. In this story, *Gujun* is a benevolent giant, but in other stories, he is a malevolent avenger.

sity strikes his people, it is his proper behavior toward the mouse that brings him to the right place for help. His attitude, that laziness is bad, saves his people.

– Originally published in A Dena'ina Legacy: K'tl'egh'i Sukdu: The Collected Writings of Peter Kalifornsky, *edited by James Kari and Alan Boraas, Alaska Native Language Center, University of Alaska, Fairbanks, 1991.*

THE GAMBLING STORY
(originally written in Dena'ina Athabaskan)

The Dena'ina once used to tell stories. In this story, two rich men met and said, "Let's play the gambling game." One young man was a shaman. The other fellow followed the traditional beliefs [He was a True Believer, *'K' ech' Eltanen'*]. That shaman was winning everything from the rich man. He took all of the rich man's possessions from him. Then, all the rich man had left were his wife and children.

"What will you bet me?" the shaman said. He had his wife and children, one a small boy. He longed to keep them. The shaman had taken all of the rich man's belongings from him. He longed to keep the young boy and his wife. He bet his three girls, and lost. He only had his wife and young son left.

"Bet me your wife and boy against all your things and the three girls," the shaman said. Which one did he love the most, his wife or his young son? He bet his wife, and lost.

All his belongings and his daughters and his wife he bet for that boy. The shaman took the boy from him too. He had nothing. The shaman had won all that he had, even his last gun.

That young man went outside and walked a long way. When he came to a trap he had set in the foothills, a squirrel was caught in it. The squirrel was chewed up and only a small skin was lying there. He picked it up and put it in his pocket.

He walked a long way and then came to a big house. From inside someone said, "I heard you. Turn around the way the sun goes [clockwise] and come in." It was big inside. A big old lady was sitting there. "My husband is away, but he'll return to us," she said. Not long after, a giant came in. "Hello. What happened to you that you come to see me?" the giant said.

The man explained what the shaman had done to him. "The shaman took from me my daughters, then my wife, and even my young boy. And somehow I came here."

"Good," the giant said. "Rest yourself well and I'll fix you up." The man rested well, and then that little skin he had put into his pocket started to move, and it jumped from his pocket. It became an animal again. "Yes, you have come to us with our child," the giant said. "And I had searched all over for my child that I had lost. You said the one who gambled with you is a shaman. Good. I too have powers. I'll prepare you to go back to him," the giant said.

There were animal skins piled in the house. The giant cut little pieces from all of them and put them into his gut bag. He put down-feathers in with them. "You'll return with this and sprinkle these down-feathers on the gut bag when no one is looking at you. It will turn back into a large supply of animal skins. You will bet with these." And he lay down three sets of gambling sticks. He wrapped these up.

"The first time you play with the shaman, sometimes he'll win from you and sometimes you'll win from him. As you continue and he thinks, 'I'll take everything from him again,' you will throw down this set of gambling sticks. They will spin the way the sun goes [clockwise] and you will take back all your belongings and wife and children," the giant said.

"Then you tell the shaman, 'Do to me as I did to you. I went out and went to the one they call *K' eluyesh. K' eluyesh* resupplied me and gave me the gambling sticks. With them I won everything back from you.' Go to *K' eluyesh* and tell him, 'Give me gambling sticks,'" the giant said.

The True Believer went back. This is why the True Believer won everything back from the shaman when he gambled again. When he went to *K' eluyesh, K' eluyesh* blocked the shaman's powers by means of the pieces he had cut from all those skins. As the shaman tried magic, as he tried to transform himself, he couldn't take the form of an animal again. He failed at magic and left, and there was not any more word of him.

About the Gambling Story

In this story, the shaman's belief is in something tangible, that is something he could see. The other man's belief is *'k' ech' ghelta'*, that is belief in something intangible which one cannot see. The story shows how one can have reversals in life because of bad luck. But the man is also a "True Believer" and that little skin represents how, through belief and proper attitude, one can rebound from adversity. In the end, it is the shaman who goes broke.

– Originally published in A Dena'ina Legacy: K'tl'egh'i Sukdu: The Collected Writings of Peter Kalifornsky, *edited by James Kari and Alan Boraas, Alaska Native Language Center, University of Alaska, Fairbanks, 1991.*

RAVEN AND THE HALF-HUMAN
(Originally written in Dena'ina Athabaskan)

Raven was flying through a canyon in a mountain pass. And he saw something but couldn't quite make it out. He sneaked over to it and looked at it, and it was human on one side and animal on the other side. So he made himself into an old grandma and went to him.

"Wherever did you come from?" the half-human said to Raven. "I've traveled all over, but I've never found a living thing."

"I've come to you," Raven said to him.

"Good, for I too am alone," the half-human said to him.

That Raven said, "I want you to be my baby. And you will make a cradle, and I'll rock you and put you to sleep."

"All right," the half-human said. He made a cradle. Over there on the bank was a good place with a little breeze blowing.

"Pack that cradle up there," Raven told him. The half-human packed it up onto the bank of the canyon and lay down in it. And Raven rocked the cradle with him and sang to him.

"Aah, my baby, aah."

Then the half-human pretended to cry: "Wa wa wa." That Raven said, "This spoiled thing, this cry-cry-cry baby!" And he kicked the cradle. Down the canyon it sailed in the wind along with the half-human. "It's not my baby anymore," Raven said.

He (Raven) went down to the half-human's house. "Now I'll eat well," he was thinking.

Inside, the house was very big, with all kinds of half-dried meat. There was a big knife there. He took it and cut the meat. "Mm, mm," he said, "this will taste good – no, this one!" He hadn't eaten yet when he heard a noise outside.

At that, the half-human came home. And Raven cried, "My dear baby!" And he rushed to meet him.

Then Raven made himself stumble, and stabbed the half-human in the belly. But when he pulled the knife out, there was no wound on him.

And then the half-human said, "I am one of the things which the humans you call Campfire People call evil," he said. "But you came to me and treated me well," he said. "And now, turn back into whatever you really are," he told Raven. And he turned back into a raven.

Then Raven flew back to Camprobber and told him the story: what kind of baby he had, and how badly he treated him, and how the half-human said he liked the mistreatment. And Raven said, "Then he sent me back. He was human on one side and animal on the other, but he didn't look like any ordinary animal."

That's a Raven story.

About the Raven and the Half-Human

In this story Raven treats the half-human badly. He lies, he is abusive, he invades the half-human's territory, and he steals. The half-human is the embodiment of evil. He knew what Raven was thinking all the time. But to the evil half-human, bad treatment was good. He reversed bad to good and did not punish Raven; instead he set him free. To spread the news, Raven describes the experience to Camprobber.

– Originally published in A Dena'ina Legacy: K'tl'egh'i Sukdu: The Collected Writings of Peter Kalifornsky, *edited by James Kari and Alan Boraas, Alaska Native Language Center, University of Alaska, Fairbanks, 1991.*

THE BOY WHO TALKED TO THE DOG
(originally written in Dena'ina Athabaskan)

This boy was spoiled. He would not listen. He would not listen whenever he was told not to do something.

He got a dog. He would talk to it all the time. When he ate, it would eat with him and he would command it, "Talk to me!" He would take hold of the dog's tongue and say, "This is your tongue. Your tongue is for talking." His parents said not to do that to the dog, but he would not listen.

They were staying in a smokehouse. He bit that dog's ear and he said, "Listen to me." He pulled the tongue in the dog's mouth. He said to it, "This is your tongue, it is for talking."

And then the dog got up. It sat down and faced the boy, and it said to him, "I will do whatever you tell me to do. But I am an animal. I am not made to talk." That is what it said to him.

And the boy keeled over and died. And the dog went out. The boy had caused this to happen by his words. [Literally 'his own words went back against him.']

Later they found that dog at the boy's grave. The dog was dead, and it lay on the boy's grave.[1]

– Originally published in A Dena'ina Legacy: K'tl'egh'i Sukdu: The Collected Writings of Peter Kalifornsky, *edited by James Kari and Alan Boraas, Alaska Native Language Center, University of Alaska, Fairbanks, 1991.*

---

1. The Dena'ina had many taboos concerning the treatment of dogs.

ABOUT SHAMANS AND THE MEN WITH GASHAQ
(originally written in Dena'ina Athabaskan)

The shamans had their specific way of belief. They believed in what they could see. Their belief involved the spirit of every living animal and every living plant. Through prayer, they would contact the living being with their mind and they would start gathering the spirit of that thing through a transfer of power from one to the other.

The *Gashaq*, the Dreamer, the Doctor, and the Sky Reader, who get visions—they all had the same belief as the Shaman [*El'egen*], but they also had something more. Their belief involved something that was not visible. They would take a cup of water and bend down on one knee and hold the water still. Then they would make a wish and take three sips of water so the spirit could interact with them. If two spirits sipped together, this would help their minds to receive a revelation.

They were always learning about the animals and how plants could be used for medicine. The Dreamer did this too.

– Originally published in A Dena'ina Legacy: K'tl'egh'i Sukdu: The Collected Writings of Peter Kalifornsky, *edited by James Kari and Alan Boraas, Alaska Native Language Center, University of Alaska, Fairbanks, 1991.*

THE OLD DENA'INA BELIEFS
(originally written in Dena'ina Athabaskan)

Whatever they wanted to be as they were growing to adulthood, they fasted and tried to become that. They tried to have shamanistic dreams, to speak words that would come true, and to read the stars.[1] And they always fasted.

Their chief would spread the news about the one seeking spiritual powers and they would respect that person. They didn't pass in front of him. If you met him on the trail, you didn't look at him, you moved to one side of him. Then he would pass you thinking gratefully toward you.

Whatever is on this earth is a person [has a spirit], they used to say. And they said they prayed to everything. That is the way they lived.

Then it would become clear to them, what they were trying to become, and they would keep their minds set on it. To try to become good is dangerous. Struggling against evil is dangerous. They got into that state of mind and it stayed with them. They began to have nightmares, and they would suffer for a long time. Then finally they would become what they were trying to be.

They always prayed to plants and to all living things.

And the novice shaman had a doll,[2] and when his spirit was out of his body, the doll temporarily housed his spirit [so he would not die]. And the shaman could transfer his spirit into some animal. When he returned to his body, he became his normal self again. He also had a "help me" song and people would help him sing it. Then he would accomplish his magic.

After that, he would suffer for a long time and then become powerful. Evil things would keep tormenting him. They didn't become shamans to do evil. Another shaman from another village

---

1. This passage refers to one seeking the powers of the Dreamer, the Doctor, the Prophet, or the Sky Reader. This story outlines the roles of a class of specialists in shamanistic powers.

2. An effigy of himself.

might do evil toward them, or take their territory. A shaman would protect his people from an evil shaman.

And the Sky Reader would tell the shaman various things. He would say what the month would be like, by the moon. And he would look up into the sky at midnight and say, "Night and day is divided" [i.e. predict when the solstice occurred], and by that means they counted the days [kept a calendar]. And he would say, "Ration the food, the animals will turn away from you," and that would happen.

And the Dreamer [literally 'the one with prescient dreams'] he too foretold what would happen in the future, how it would be. And he would dream about sickness, too.

The Prophet [literally 'the one whose words come true'] is really dangerous. Because of his power, he might unintentionally say something harmful. He always stayed away, isolated from the village.

The shaman would advise people who were seeking *k' ech' eltani* ['beliefs,' 'convictions'] that one might see too many sinister things. "If you're a coward, or if your heart is small, don't seek those powers. It's too dangerous [because it takes a strong person to confront evil]."

Then as they were working in the daytime, they would see strange things. Things would change on them: a stump would turn into something else, that is how it would happen with them. Then when they had become what they were trying for, the dangerous things would leave them.

Once there was a young man whose heart was weak. "Let me try for *k' ech' eltani* ['spiritual convictions']," he said. And he tried for them. And he started seeing all kinds of things.

And they were bringing fish out with a dip net. A sculpin swam into his net and turned into something terrifying to him. At that, he had a heart attack. A person with medical knowledge worked on his heart in the steambath. But his nightmares became severe and he didn't wake up again. The shaman said: "It is not possible to turn back from *k' ech' eltani.* Turning back is even more dangerous."

There was another shaman, or *el' egen,* and there was a *K' ech' Eltanen* [a 'true believer' one who had acquired spiritual powers]. The *el' egen* said, "I want to compete with him." So he sent word to him. "If it gets rough, someone will throw a stick on the fire for you." And "I too," he said.

Then the *K' ech' Eltanen* said, "Whatever will attack me, the same thing will attack him back." And, "Water!" he said.

They put water by him and he put his hands in it. Then they

covered him up with something. And his body felt as if it were being beaten with a stick. He was aching all over and tired.

There is nothing as dangerous as a brown bear digging up ground squirrels in the springtime: they call him "riptide," or "the whirlwind," or "the tidal bore." He spoke these names as he moved his hands in the water. And he exhaled and inhaled, and with his power he moved the water. After that he didn't feel any pain anymore.

Now there was no wind where the *El' egen* was, but a wind blew him out of the smokehouse and blew him into a puddle outside.

Both of them were exhausted and could barely move around. The doctors massaged them with hot compresses in the steambath. Then the *El' egen* said, "The *K' ech' Eltanen* whose words come true, the one they call *Gashaq*, is not the kind of person to challenge. He is the only one who can use the wind and water powers." These men didn't use their powers for evil. He, *Gashaq*, was a whale hunter.

– Originally published in A Dena'ina Legacy: K'tl'egh'i Sukdu: The Collected Writings of Peter Kalifornsky, *edited by James Kari and Alan Boraas, Alaska Native Language Center, University of Alaska, Fairbanks, 1991.*

Shem Pete

THE SUSITNA STORY
(told in Dena'ina Athabaskan)

I'll tell you a little more. I am Shem Pete. My father had an older brother. He was a powerful shaman. He used to say this: "Susitna will disappear. It will disappear. Only grass will grow there. That grass will cover the whole village. The Tanainas of Susitna will disappear." Thus he spoke.

Brother, six hundred Tanainas lived there. Yusdislaq' was too small for all the people that were there. They gathered rocks upriver for the steambath. There were houses one after another all the way to Tsadukeght. There were lots of houses. They speak of a place called Tan'i'i. It was my father's older brother's village. He would make magic, they say. "Susitna will disappear. All the people living there will disappear," he would say. This would make the people mad.

There were six hundred of us. Every year twenty or thirty more would be born. "Why would we disappear?" they would say. "I tell you that's how I see it," he would tell them. "It will disappear. There will be only Americans. Do you understand?"

"No! We won't disappear! There are lots of people. How could we disappear?" they would say. "No!"

"Only grass will grow after you."

Shem Pete, Dena'ina Athabaskan from Susitna Station, Alaska.

"Is that so?"

There were also people at Kroto Creek. There were also people at Alexander Creek. Yusdislaq' was too small for so many people. "And how could we disappear?" they said.

"Only grass do I see after you. I tell you as I see it will happen." Thus he told them. "After me plants will grow so high. And then what will happen to this land? The people do not know what will happen. Turn to the land! On the shortest day of the year turn to it," he said to them. He would make magic. On the floor he would turn around the way the sun goes. "The people do not know what will happen. After me, plants will grow this high, that's what will happen." The people didn't know. I didn't know either.

"After I'm gone, don't go where the Americans have come from. There will be many Americans. Do not turn to them. There are no airplanes yet. This is what will happen when the airplanes land. They will put two hundred people in the airplanes and fly back outside with them like the geese. Only you will be left here cowering.

"Then store away matches somewhere, and shells and axes there with them. Whatever you need to save yourselves, hide it all away. All the Americans will fly away and only you will remain here. And when the Americans return outside, only the clouds will cover their tracks. Even the mountains won't rise above them. The mountains will rise halfway above this land here. Land will appear above the clouds here. Hurry, go there! Before you fall, after I'm gone, go there and you will save yourselves. There you will be safe."

Thus he would say. That's how he would warn the people. Now you see what has happened to Susitna. Only grass is there. Not one Tanaina person lives there. Everything he used to say has happened. He knew just how the flu would come. All their tracks will disappear from this earth. One after another they are dying off and all Susitna is gone. Do you understand how it will come to be? I have told you as he used to tell it. I tell, but who would listen to me? Now my friend has come to me here. My words will be on the recorder and you will understand. I too will die, but you will hear my words. Then you can save yourselves. That is why I say this now. I have said enough.

– *Originally published in* Susitnu Htsukdu'a, *told by Shem Pete, edited by James Kari, Alaska Native Language Center, University of Alaska, Fairbanks, 1975.*

John Fredson

RAVEN AND THE MALLARD GIRL
(told in Gwich'in Athabaskan)

Long ago, it is said, there was a very beautiful mallard girl. Many men wanted to marry her, but all in vain. Raven, behaving in his usual manner, went to work. He made clothing of grass and plastered it well with mud. As he was nicely dressed, he appeared to be a big chief, and in his important chief's disguise he went to the mallard girl's father, so they say. "I come from far away; I am a great chief, and having heard a great deal about your daughter, I have done this because I wish to marry her." The father didn't like it, but since the chief seemed so fine, he gave his daughter in marriage.

She started back with him, so they say. He had not paddled far when it began to rain. The mud became wet and dissolved. "It's nothing," he said, but through the grass his black feathers became visible here and there. She was sitting behind him and he didn't know what she was doing. She sewed his coattails to the canoe.

"Let me get out for a little bit," she said. "No," he said, but she insisted. After he had tied a fairly long rope to her, she got out of the boat and left him. She climbed up the bank out of sight. There

---

John Fredson, Gwich'in Athabaskan from Sheenjek River, Alaska. ˙

was a spruce tree there, and she quickly tied the rope to it and set off running back home.

"Enough!" he said, but there was not a sound in answer to him, so he tugged on the rope, but without result. "What's going on?" he suddenly thought. "Hurry up, I'm telling you!" he said, and shouted, but once more there was no answer. He became furious and jumped up in anger, but his coattails were sewn down and he fell abruptly back into the canoe on his rump. Since the canoe was quite frail, he broke a hole right through it with his rump.

With difficulty he caulked the canoe with pitch and paddled back downriver. When he landed, someone said to him, "What have you done to your canoe?" Without a sign of laughter, he said, "I was getting a little fish for my starving children when I did that, that's what happened."

– Transcribed by Edward Sapir in 1923
Retranscribed by Katherine Peter
Edited and translated by
Jane McGary
Originally published in John
Fredson Edward Sapir Hàa
Googwandak (Stories Told by
John Fredson to Edward Sapir),
Alaska Native Language Center,
University of Alaska, Fairbanks,
1982.

NOTES

This typical trickster story is one of the best known and liked of all Gwich'in tales. In many versions, Raven's marriage is followed by an episode in which his identity is almost discovered when he sneaks out and eats a dead dog's eyes, leaving three-toed tracks. In the other versions we know, Raven makes his fancy clothes not with mud but with his own white excrement; this makes the grass look like dentalium (ornamental shell), something only wealthy people wore.

– J.McG.

WOLVERINE AND THE WOLVES
(told in Gwich'in Athabaskan)

Long ago Wolverine traveled around one winter with the wolves, so they say. A certain wolf woman was married to him. As there was no game all winter, they hunted in vain. Wolverine always camped back on their trail. While they went around hunting ahead of him, he always stayed behind hunting beaver. As it was getting dark in the evening, he would come along the trail, pulling a big load of beaver. Every evening, while he ate well, his companions were almost starving beside him. "Give us some food," they said to him, and what did he say but, "My poor children are about to fall over; what are you saying?" he said.

When they were eating in the evening, the wolf woman who was married to the wolverine tied meat to a rope that ran underneath the snow. She pulled on the rope and they drew it back and forth beneath the snow. "What a lot of meat you're taking for nothing!" the wolverine said to his wife.

"What a lot of children you have eating it – what do you mean!" she replied. He got angry and flopped over on his back with his stubby legs in the air.

All winter he killed many beaver, but he never once thought, "My brothers-in-law next door are starving." After midwinter, as usual, the wolverine was going along hunting behind them, when the wolves unexpectedly came upon caribou sleeping by a creek; they fell upon them and killed many. They packed home heavy loads of meat and fat. As it was getting dark, he came along pulling a young beaver which he had killed, as usual, back on their trail. He saw his tent set up in the middle of the camp and stood above it, looking at it. "What's the matter with you?" his wife said to him. "Your brothers-in-law have packed food home. We're just preparing it. Come, eat with us, what is the matter with you?"

"Ah, thank you, they are truly my brothers-in-law, it is done properly. Back on the trail, I killed some young beaver with great effort, thinking as I did so, I shall relieve my brothers-in-law from starvation. The young beaver are tender, and my mothers-in-law and my grandmothers[1] have poor teeth and will swallow them; but

157

never mind, here!" So saying, as he had never done before, he distributed them among his mothers-in-law and his grandmothers. The beaver which he gave to them, they threw right back. "Why didn't you do that before, when we were starving?" said one woman to him, as she hurled the beaver at his chest.

"Hey, my grandmother and I are joking together again. Of course, we are relatives; it is right for us to do that."

They were crowded together in the tent, and they made a place for him in the middle. Saying, "Here he comes, our brother-in-law," they gave a shout. Saying "Evidently my brothers-in-law have hunted again as before," he sat down in their midst with a black expression. Meat and fat were roasting on sticks before the fire. That evening, after having starved all winter, they all ate well, of roasted heads, marrow, and stomach fat, and after he had eaten a great deal, the wolverine flopped down comfortably on his back. After he had quickly fallen asleep, they took a stone which they had ready, red-hot, and while they held him down, they threw it onto his belly, on which they had put some fat. "My relatives, I only live with you. Why are you doing this?" The hot stone and the fat quickly burned right into his belly.[2] While he was still saying, "My poor dear brothers-in-law, my children, what will become of them, and what are you doing?" he quickly died.

NOTES

Most storytellers incorporate an episode in which wolverine's wife lies to him about her brothers' success in hunting. The killing of wolverine is usually related in rich comic detail. In stories, wolverine is always a villain, perhaps because he was a hated animal for his habit of robbing and spoiling people's caches of meat.

1. Wolverine means all his female relatives of his mother-in-law's and grandmother's generations; this is the regular respectful form in Gwich'in.

2. Some storytellers say that this is why the wolverine today has a spot on his belly.

– J.McG.

Sally Pilot

GGAADOOKK
(told in Koyukon Athabaskan)

In the time very long ago there lived a boy named Ggaadookk. All he did was sleep. He slept and slept.

One day his mother said to him, "Ggaadookk, get up! Why don't you go out and hang some rabbit snares in the trees for your brothers and sisters to eat," she told him.

He got up and dressed and went out. He walked and walked and hung a snare wherever he came across a rabbit trail. Then he came home and went back to bed. He slept and slept.

Then one day his mother said to him, "Ggaadookk, get up! Remember those snares you set? How about checking them."

He replied, "Snares I set. Snares I set. What snares I set? You told me to hang them on the trees and that is what I did," he said.

"Oh no! I told you to set them. I didn't tell you to hang them in the trees," she told him.

Once again he got dressed and went out. He picked up all the snares he hung in the trees and set them properly. He came home and went back to bed. Then he slept and slept and slept.

Sally Pilot, Koyukon Athabaskan from Koyukuk, Alaska.

Then once again she said to him, "Ggaadookk, get up! Remember those snares you set? How about checking them," she told him.

He got up and dressed and checked his snares. He brought home a pack full of rabbits. Then he went back to bed. He slept and slept.

Then one day his mother said to him, "Ggaadookk, get up! Go out and stick a fish trap into the open water in the ice," she told him.

He got up and got fish trap wood. Then he made a fish trap. He then went out and found an open water in the ice and stuck the fish trap into the water with part of it sticking out. The part where the fish were supposed to go into the trap was out of the water. He came home and went back to bed. He slept and slept.

Then one day his mother said to him, "Ggaadookk, get up! Remember that fish trap you set? How about going out and checking it," she told him.

He said, "The fish trap I set. The fish trap I set. What fish trap I set? You told me to stick it into the water and that is what I did," he told her.

"Hey!! I told you to set it," she told him.

Once again he got dressed and went out. He then set the fish trap properly. He came home and went back to bed. He slept and slept.

Then one day she said to him, "Ggaadookk, get up! Remember that fish trap you set? How about going out and checking it," she told him.

Then he got up and dressed and checked the fish trap. He brought home a pack full of blackfish. He went back to bed and slept and slept.

Then one day she said to him, "Ggaadookk, get up! Go out and look for some crooked things for your brothers and sisters to eat," she told him.

He got up and dressed and went out. He walked around in the woods in search of crooked sticks. He then came home bent down under the weight of a big pack of crooked sticks.

His mother opened the pack and said, "Hey!! I told you to hunt for porcupine," she told him.

"Porcupines, porcupines. You didn't say porcupines."

Once again he went out and then brought home a pack full of porcupines. Then he went back to bed and slept and slept.

Then one day his mother said to him, "Ggaadookk, get up! Go out and chop some wood into the fireplace," she told him.

Then he got up and chopped and piled wood in the fireplace. Soon he was roasting his brothers and sisters.

"Hey!! Now he is roasting his brothers and sisters," she complained. "I suppose if you go out and chop a tree, it will say, 'Ouch,' and bleed," she told him.

He went out and chopped a tree. It said, "Ouch," and bled. Then he chopped another tree. It said, "Ouch," and bled. He kept doing that. Then a woodpecker landed right where he was about to chop. He chopped at it and missed. It landed on the next tree. He chopped at it again and missed. He kept doing that, going further and further into the woods. He kept trying to chop it and he kept missing it. He didn't know it, but it was leading him to the sky world. Soon he came to an area that looked like a pretty grass lake. He looked in all directions. It was a beautiful sight. He was now in the sky world. There was a path around there. He followed it upstream. He was following the path and soon came to where an old lady lived. He began living there. He lived there for some time. He always stayed home while grandma went hunting.

Then one day before grandma went out hunting she said to him, "Grandchild, don't move that rock, if you move the rock, you will regret it and think, 'I wish I didn't move that rock,'" she told him. Then grandma went hunting.

He wondered why grandma told him not to move the rock. Then he moved the rock.

Then he heard lots of excitement down below, it sounded like people were dipnetting for fish, going up and down the river. Then he heard another sound, that of someone crying. Heard someone crying saying, "My child, my child." He recognized it as his mother crying for her son, he who chopped his way into the sky world.

When he heard his mother he got very sad, and cried for a long time.

When grandma came home she noticed that he had been crying.

Then she asked him, "Grandchild, what happened? It looked like you had been crying. Did you move that rock that I told you not to move?"

He answered, "Yes, I moved it and I heard my mother crying.".

Then grandma started to ply sinew for rope. She plied and plied sinew. Soon she had a pile of plied rope. Next she made a big bag for him. Then she put him in the bag and tied it closed and made sure it was tied securely. She also put some food in there for him to eat.

Then before she lowered him she instructed him, "When I lower you to earth, very carefully undo the rope the bag is tied with. Don't cut it, if you do it will say, 'Ouch,' and bleed. Then in the future when another of the people are made, they will use the rope for suicide."

Then she lowered him to earth. He came out of the bag and cut the rope, ignoring the careful instruction he had been given, and what would happen if he cut the rope.

Then he gave the rope a couple of jerks. Then grandma started pulling the rope back up. It was going up and up until he couldn't see it.

Then he heard grandma say, "Hey!! I told him not to cut the rope."

Then he left for home. When he came home his mother was gone. There were signs of her leaving with a sled load on a nomadic hunt. He started following her. He walked and walked. Then he saw his mother up ahead pulling the loaded sled, while crying. She was crying and saying, "My child, my child."

He snuck up behind her and stuck a stick through the back of the sled, and into the snow.

Then his mother kept jerking on the sled and then said, "I hope the one I am suffering for anchored this thing that is stuck." Saying that she turned around. There stood her great big son.

*– Transcribed in Koyukon and
translated into English by
Eliza Jones.
Originally published in* Ggaadookk,
*Alaska Native Language Center,
University of Alaska, Fairbanks,
1982.*

CONTEMPORARY WORKS

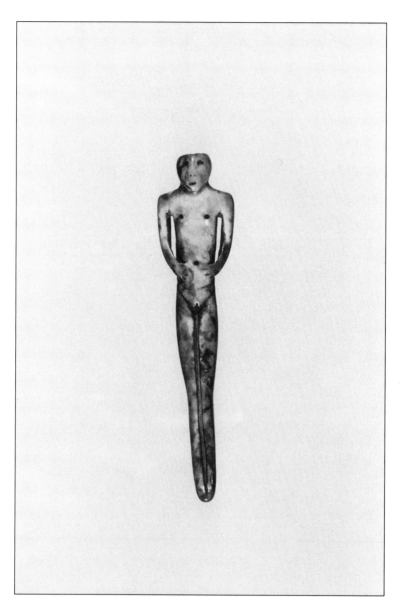

NEEDLE CASE (Yup'ik)
Made of mineralized walrus ivory, this rare and elaborate needle case is in
the form of a human figure. It was collected in the St. Michael area of
Alaska where Yup'ik women sewed clothing using walrus ivory needles
that were as finely made as today's steel needles. Needles were stored by
inserting them into a leather strap that was pulled into a bone or ivory
case. (Courtesy of the Anchorage Museum of History and Art)

Robert H. Davis

SAGINAW BAY: I KEEP GOING BACK

I

He dazzles you right out of water,
right out of the moon, the sun and fire.
Cocksure smooth talker, good looker,
Raven makes a name for himself
up and down the coast from the Nass River,
stirs things up.

Hurling the first light, it lodges
in the ceiling of the sky,
everything takes form –
creatures flee to forest animals,
hide in fur. Some choose the sea,
turn to salmon escaping.
Those remaining in the light
stand as men, dumb and full of fear.

Raven turns his head
and laughs in amazement,
then dives off the landscape,
dividing the air
into moment before
and instant after.

He moves north, Kuiu Island, Saginaw Bay –
wind country, rain country,
its voices try to rise through fog.
The long tongue of the sea
slides beneath the bay.
Raven is taken in by it all:

Robert H. Davis, Tlingit from Southeast Alaska.

sticky mudflats horseclams squirting,
rockpool waterbugs skitting,
bulge-eyed bullheads staring through shadow,
incessant drizzle hissing.
Oilslick Raven
fixed against the glossy surface of infinity.

II

The Tsaaqueidi clan settled there first,
it was right. Beaches sloped
beneath canoes greased with seal fat.
They delivered the Seal clan
to these same creeks
shaking with humpies and dog salmon.
Everywhere eyes
peered from the woods and mist.
The berries were thick and bursting,
and there were always the roots.

They knew how to live,
by the season.

Sometimes it felt like the center of the world,
mountains circling within reach.

At its mouth on a knoll a fortress
guarded against intruders.
They came anyway,
from the south.
A swift slave raid
destroyed the village.
The people fled every direction.

A captured shaman
tortured and ridiculed
scalped before his very people.
Through blood running in eyes
he swore revenge
and got it.

After the massacre the battered clan
collected themselves and moved
north to Kupreanof Island.
That became the village of Kake.
They became the Kake-kwaan,

and every once in awhile
one sees in his mind
Raven tracks hardened in rock at Saginaw
where Raven dug his feet in
and tugged the mudflats clear into the woods
remaking a small Nass
because he grew homesick there,
and in those moments
they feel like going back too.

III

Kake is the Place of No Rest. It is.

I've heard men in black robes
instructing heathen natives:
outlaw demon shamanism,
do away with potlatch,
pagan ceremony,
totem idolatry,
get rid of old ways.
The people listened,

dynamited the few Kake poles –
mortuary poles fell with bones,
clan identifiers got lost in powder,
storytellers blown to pieces
settled on the new boardwalk
running along the beachfront
houses built off the ground.
In the middle of Silver Street
my aunt drove the silver spike
that sealed the past forever.

People began to talk different,
mixed and tense.
Acted ashamed of gunny sacks of k'ink',
mayonnaise jars of stink eggs.
No one mashed blueberries
with salmon eggs anymore.

They walked different,
falling all over.
A storekeeper took artifacts for credit
before his store went up in a blaze.

Grandpa went out in his slow skiff
and cached in the cliffs
his leather wrapped possessions
preserved like a shaman body
that can't be destroyed, that won't burn.

IV

Grandpa's picture hangs in the church
next to Jesus.
He was a great minister. He traveled
with the Salvation Army band,
the famous Kake band
called to San Francisco
to play for President Harding.

My father as a young man
was sent away,
Sheldon Jackson Industrial School, Sitka.

They changed him.

Separated from his family
years at a time,
one of the conditions.
He was punished
for speaking his own language.

He graduated.
He was sent off to college,

a handsome man.
A ladies' man, I've heard,
shy and sad, but likeable.
But goddamn, you had to catch him sober
to know what I even mean.

Now they say I remind them of him.
But you have to catch me sober.

V

I turn ten or fifteen or something.
Pentilla Logging Co. barges into Saginaw.
Floathouses, landing craft and cranes.
Cables to the beach, cables in the woods.
Dozers leave treadmarks in mud.

Redneck rejects, tobacco spitters
drink whiskey in rowdy bunkhouses
at the end of the drawn out day,
brag how many loads, how many turns,
who got maimed, flown out
and did they take it like a man.
Climb all over each other
gawking at the spare camp women
and their minds turn to tits and ass.

Some men can't help it,
they take up too much space,
always need more.
They gnaw at the edge of the woods
till the sky once swimming with branches
becomes simply sky, till there is only
a scarred stubble of clearcut
like a head without its scalp of hair.

They hire a few Indians from Kake,
what for I don't know.
Maybe it looks good,
maybe it's the stories they come with,
maybe it's just they do things so quietly,

even sit speechless
in the stalled speedboat
while high power rifles
chip at the cliff painting –
the circle with three dashes
warning the invaders
from the south centuries ago
who destroyed with such precision.

VI

When my uncles were younger
they crawled on their bellies
through kelp draped rocks
at Halleck Harbor, Saginaw Bay
at a tide so low
and almost remembered;

uncovered in the rubble
of boulders from the cave-in
a hundred skeletons
in armor and weaponry –
slave hunters
piling over each other,
still hunting.

VII

Because Raven tracks are locked in fossil,
clam beds still snarled in roots
because it has been told to us this way,
we know for a fact
Raven moves in the world.

VIII

The old ones tell a better story in Tlingit.
When I was small everyone used Tlingit
and English at once.
Tlingit fit better.

But I forget so much
and a notepad would be obtrusive
and suspect. I might write a book.

In it I would describe
how we all are pulled
so many directions,
how our lives are fragments
with so many gaps.

I know there's a Tlingit name for that bay,
it means "Everything Shifted Around."

I'm trying to remember
how that shaman was called.
I can't.
Except of course he was the most powerful
and I feel somehow tied to him (and was he
the one wrapped in cedar mat
sunk in the channel
only to reappear at his grieving ceremony
ascending the beach at Pt. White?)
I don't know, I get mixed up.
But I know my own name,
it's connected with some battle.

Listen, I'm trying to say something –
always the stories lived through paintings,
always the stories stayed alive in retelling.

You wonder why sometimes you can't reach me?
I keep going back.
I keep trying to picture my life
against all this history,
Raven in the beginning
hopping about like he just couldn't do enough.

– *Originally published in* Soul
Catcher, *Robert H. Davis,*
Raven's Bones Press, Sitka, 1986.

Nora Marks Dauenhauer

EGG BOAT

In the fall of every year Keixwnéi and her family went trolling for coho salmon. The season for trolling usually opened mid-summer and the run became intense toward the end of the cannery season when the whole family went to the cannery to earn their money. Her father seined for the canning company while her Aunty Anny and sometimes her mother worked processing the catch from the salmon seiners. Because the family worked for the cannery, they lived the summer season in the company houses.

Some years the catch of salmon seiners began to decrease before the seining season came to an end, but around this time coho trolling began to pick up. In order to get in on the favorable runs when the salmon began to migrate to the rivers for spawning, trollers had to be ready.

This was one of the times they were going to go fishing early. Her father had observed on their last trip that there were signs of

Nora Marks Dauenhauer, Tlingit (Raven, Lukaax.ádi Clan, Sockeye Crest) from Alsek and Chilkat, Alaska. A contributing editor to the original edition of *Alaska Native Writers, Storytellers and Orators,* she is a native speaker of Tlingit, a published poet, and a co-editor of three major volumes on Tlingit oral literature.

coho, but he wasn't catching too much salmon in his seine. So he stripped his seine off the boat and began to replace it with trolling gear.

While Pop prepared the gas boat for trolling, the rest of the family packed their belongings from the company houses and transferred them to the boat. Everyone helped get everything aboard.

Mom packed things from their house while Grandma and Aunty packed things from theirs. Keixwnéi and her younger brothers and sisters carried things they could carry easily, and the little ones carried things like pots and pans.

The older boys were big enough to help their father get the boat gassed up and get fresh water for the trips. So they had plenty to do, too, besides helping Grandma and Aunty pack their belongings down to the boat.

When the *New Anny* was finally ready, they left port in the early afternoon and headed toward Point Adolfus. The tide was going out, and they got on the right current which would carry them fast to their destination.

* * *

It was on a similar tide the previous year while they were coming to Hoonah from Cape Spencer that Keixwnéi's father spotted a little square-ended rowboat floating on the Icy Straits water. He picked it up and he and the boys put it on the deck of the boat. They had it on deck when they stopped in Hoonah. Everyone saw it and commented on what a nice boat it was. Everyone noticed it wasn't one of the family's rowboats. When they arrived in Juneau, people noticed it too, but no one claimed it. There wasn't a fisherman who didn't know another fisherman or about another's boat and no one knew who the boat belonged to.

So, Pop brought the boat up on the beach at their home at Marks Trail in Juneau and started to work on it. He checked the boards to see if they were strong enough to hold the new materials he was going to apply to it and he found that indeed it was strong enough and would hold them.

He began to renew it by stripping the old paint off. Then he caulked up the seams and finally put on some green paint left over from some other boat that he painted before. He put a pair of oars in that didn't quite match. He tied an old piece of manila rope on the bow that could be used to tie it up.

It was a good-looking boat. It looked just like the flower chalice of a skunk cabbage. And when he tried it, it had balance. It glided across the water very nicely. It was almost as wide as it was long. It was almost round and because it looked like an egg shell, they called it "Egg Boat."

Ḵeixwnéi liked it very much and wanted to try it. She thought the boat was so cute. But when her father told her it was hers, she thought it was the most beautiful boat she had ever seen.

Her own boat! Why, she thought that it was going to be for one of her brothers. She could hardly believe the boat was hers. She was so happy she went around day-dreaming about it for the longest time.

Now that she had her own boat it meant she could go fishing on her own boat alongside her brothers, Aunty, and Grandma all by herself. It also meant she might catch a record-breaking salmon that she would fight for so long that she would get exhausted from just the thought of it.

Or perhaps she and her Aunty and Grandma would hit a school of fish like she heard some fishing people talk about. She would fill up her little boat, empty it, then go back out and fill it again.

Or perhaps she would catch her first king salmon, and she wouldn't care what size it was just as long as it was a king.

Her rowboat took her through many adventures during her day-dreaming. How exciting the next coho season was going to be! She was so happy.

* * *

And now they were actually going to the fishing ground. The boat moved along at a good speed. They all worked on their gear, giving it a last minute check for weak spots and sections that needed replacements.

Mom steered the boat while Pop checked the tackle he would use on the big boat. She ran the boat a lot, taking over completely, especially when Pop had to do work on deck or when he started catching a lot of salmon. Sometimes she even engineered. There was no pilot house control, so Pop would ring a bell to signal "slow," "fast," "neutral," "backwater," and so forth.

The boys were playing some kind of game on deck. They said their gear was ready. Ḵeixwnéi's Aunty wound her line onto her wooden fishing wheel. Grandma was taking a nap. She had been ready for quite some time. She was always ready for things.

As for Ḵeixwnéi, she had her tackle that her Aunty had helped her get together from discarded gear left by various members of the family. She and her Aunty had made a line for her while she was still fishing in her Aunty's rowboat. Her spinner was the one her father had made for her the previous year from a discarded spoon. It was brass.

Her herring hook, however, was brand new. It was the one her Aunty had given her for her own. She was ready to fish, completely outfitted with rubber boots her brother loaned her that were slightly too large.

She was so excited she could hardly eat. The family teased her that she was probably fasting for the record-breaking salmon.

When they finally got near enough to see the fishing ground, there were a lot of power boats trolling and others were anchored. A lot of the hand trolling fleet was there too. Some of the hand trollers lived in tents out at Point Adolfus for the duration of the summer. When there was no salmon, the fishing people smoked halibut they jigged from the bay over past Point Adolfus. Some of the people were relatives of the family.

When they finally reached the fishing ground, everyone was anxious to get out and fish. They all took turns jumping into their boats while Pop and the two boys held the rowboats for them while the big boat was still moving along.

Grandma went first, then Aunty Anny, then at last K̲eixwnéi's turn came. The boys followed in the power skiff that was converted from a tender boat from seining.

They immediately began to troll. Grandma and Aunty Anny went close to the kelp beds along the shore line. The boys stayed just on the outside of the kelp while K̲eixwnéi was all over the place and sometimes dragging the bottom.

She didn't even know where her father, mother, sister, and brothers were. She didn't notice a thing – just that she was going to catch her own salmon. Every time she dragged the bottom she was sure she had a strike.

Evening came and people began to go to their own ports. Grandma and Aunty waited for K̲eixwnéi for such a long time they thought she wasn't coming in for that night. When they finally got her to come along with them to go back to *New Anny,* all of a sudden she realized it was near dark and uneasiness came to her. She had completely forgotten all about the *kooshdaa k̲áa* stories she had heard, where the Land Otter Man came and took people who were near drowning and kept them captive as one of them. She quickly pulled up her line and came along with her Grandma and Aunty Anny.

Everyone had caught salmon except K̲eixwnéi. It was so disappointing, especially when her brothers teased her about being skunked by saying, "Where's your big salmon, K̲eixwnéi?" The rest of the family said she would probably catch one the next day and she shouldn't worry. She slept very little that night. Maybe she never ever was going to catch a salmon at all.

The next day the fish buyer who anchored his scow said that there were fish showing up at Home Shore and that he was going over there to buy fish on his tender.

Pop pulled up the anchor to start off for Home Shore. But half way between Point Adolfus and Home Shore, the boat started to rock back and forth from a storm that had just started to blow. Chatham Strait was stuffed with dark clouds and rain. So they had to make a run for shelter instead of trolling that day – another disappointment for K̲eixwnéi, especially after standing on deck most of the way straining her eyes to see if anyone was catching any salmon.

They holed up all night. She heard her father getting up from time to time during that night. He never slept much on nights of a storm.

Daybreak was beautiful. It was foggy, but through the fog they could see that the sun was going to be very bright. Where the fog started to drop, the water surface was like a mirror except where the "spine of the tide" – the rip tide – made ripples of tiny jumping waves on one side and the other side had tiny tide navels. Sounds carried far. They could hear gulls, and a porpoise breathing somewhere, and splashing from fish jumps. It was going to be gorgeous.

They ate quickly and went off to the fishing ground. Once again they took their turns getting into their boats while the big boat moved along.

This day K̲eixwnéi stuck really close to her Grandma and Aunty. They stayed on the tide spine, circling it as it moved along. She did everything they did. They measured fathoms by the span between their arms from fingertip to fingertip. K̲eixwnéi also measured her fathoms the same way. She checked her lines for kinks whenever one of them did theirs. She especially stayed close by when Aunty got her first strike of the day. She had hooked onto a lively one. K̲eixwnéi circled her and got as close as she dared without the salmon tangling their lines.

Then Grandma got her first salmon of the day.

K̲eixwnéi had just about given up hope of getting a salmon for that day when she got her first strike. It was so strong that the strap on the main line almost slipped from her hand. She grabbed for it just in time.

Splash! Out of the water jumped the salmon! At the same time – swish! – the salmon took off with her line! The line made a scraping hum on the end of the boat where it was running out.

In the meantime the salmon jumped out into the air and made a gigantic splash. She could hear her Grandmother saying, "My little grandchild! It might pull her overboard!" while her Aunty said, "Stay calm, stay calm, my little Niece. Don't hold on too tight. Let it go when it runs."

Splash! Splash! Splash! Splash! The salmon jumped with her line. It was going wild. It was a while before she could get it near enough to see that it was a coho and a good size one too. She would get it close to the boat and then it would take off on the run again. Just when she had it close enough to hit with her gaff hook club, it would take off again. Several times she hit the water with the club instead of the fish because it kept wiggling out of range. Each time the salmon changed its direction the little boat did too, and the salmon pulled the little boat in every direction you could think of. The boat was like a little round dish and the fish would make it spin.

At long last the salmon tired itself out, and when she pulled it to the boat it just sort of floated on top of the water. She clubbed it one good one. It had no fight left.

She dragged it aboard and everyone around her yelled for joy with her. Grandma and Aunty looked as if they had pulled in the fish. They both said, "Xwei! She's finally got it!" Keixwnéi was sopping wet. Her face was all beaded with water.

It was the only salmon she caught that day but, by gosh, she brought it in herself! She sold the salmon and with some of the money she got for it she bought a pie for the family. What a feast that was! Everyone made pleasing comments about her so she could overhear them.

They mainly wished she wouldn't spend all her money on pie and that she was going to start saving her fishing money for important things that a girl should have as she grew older.

It was great to be a troller. That fall was a very memorable one for Keixwnéi. Rain or shine she tried to rise with her Grandma and Aunty each dawn.

One day they all timed it just right for the salmon to feed. Everyone made good that day. There wasn't a fisherman who wasn't happy about his or her catch that day. Keixwnéi also made good. When her Aunty and Grandma lined up their salmon on the beach for cleaning, she also had her eight salmon lined up. What a day that was!

When they got to Juneau after the season was over, everyone bought some of the things they'd said they would buy once the season was over. Pop bought some hot dogs for dinner and a watermelon that Grandma called "water berry."

Keixwnéi bought herself a pair of new hip boots. What dandies they were! They had red and white stripes all the way around the sole seams. And they also had patches that read "B. F. Goodrich" on each knee. And they fit perfectly if she wore two pairs of sox.

Her mother told her they were a very fine pair and that they would wear for a long time. Now she wouldn't have to borrow her brothers' boots anymore. In fact, they could borrow hers from time to time. And she could use the boots to play fishing with boats she and her brothers made from driftwood bark at Marks Trail. And very best of all – she would wear her boots when she went with the family to get fish for dryfish camp on their next trip.

– Originally published in Neek: News of the Native Community, *Sitka, Alaska, edited by Andrew Hope III, vol. 1, no. 2, January 1980.*

GRANDMOTHER ELIZA

My grandmother Eliza
was the family surgeon.
Her scalpel made from a pocket knife
she kept in a couple of pinches of snoose.
She saved my life by puncturing
my festering neck twice with her knife.
She saved my brother's life twice
when his arm turned bad.
The second time she saved him
was when his shoulder turned bad.
She always made sure
she didn't cut an artery.
She would feel around for days
finding the right spot to cut.
When a doctor found out
she saved my brother's life
he warned her,
"You know you could go to jail for this?"
Her intern, my Auntie Anny, saved my life
when I cut a vessel on my toe.
While my blood was squirting out
she went out into the night
and cut and chewed the bark
of plants she knew.
She put the granules of chewed up bark
on my toe before the eyes of the folks
who came to console my mother
because I was bleeding to death.
Grandma's other intern, Auntie Jennie
saved our uncle's life when his son
shot him through the leg by accident.
A doctor warned her, too,
when he saw how she cured.
Her relative cured herself of diabetes.
Now, the doctors keep on asking,
"How did you cure yourself?"

– Originally published in Rolling
Stock, *Boulder, Colorado,*
No. 19/20, 1991.

MUSEUM

Alaska Native youth
flickering
in strobelight:
disco diorama.

AFTER ICE FOG

1. *Overexposure*

Barely distinctive
where the fog begins,
where the frosted
trees begin.

2. *Negative*

Driving home at night,
distinctive where fog
settled on trees, white
against the black sky.

3. *Positive*

Working in the morning:
black skeletal trees
against gray clouds
stripped of frost.

John Active

WHY SUBSISTENCE IS A MATTER OF CULTURAL SURVIVAL: A YUP'IK POINT OF VIEW

BLACKFISH

Once there was a little blackfish swimming up a stream. Every so often he would swim up to the surface and look around.

The first time he had surfaced he saw a camp where people were living. The people there were very careless. Their camp was unkempt and their belongings were strewn around.

He noticed that when the people ate, they ate very carelessly. Bits of whatever they were eating would drop from their hands or out of their mouths as they talked, onto the ground.

The little blackfish heard much wailing and crying at this camp. Those cries were the weeping and wailing of the bits of food that had fallen to the ground.

The dogs were given the leftover scraps of food and these dogs

---

John Active, Yup'ik from Bethel, Alaska.

would also leave uneaten bone and bits of food around the ground. These bits of food and bones were also crying.

The little blackfish said to himself, "I'll not swim into this man's fish trap. He's too careless with his food. I don't want my bones stepped on underfoot." The blackfish swam on.

By and by little blackfish came to another camp and there he also saw people eating. These people also were very unkempt and, just as at the first camp, were dropping bits of food onto the ground and throwing their bones to the dogs who were leaving them strewn on the ground. There was much wailing and weeping coming from these bits of food, too.

Little blackfish also noticed that the children were playing with their food, throwing bones at one another as in a game. He thought to himself, "I'll not swim into this man's fish trap. They are also too careless with their food. His children are playing with their food. I am not a game to be played with."

Blackfish swam on and soon he came to another camp. This next camp seemed to be deserted. There were no dogs about or people. But again little blackfish heard much wailing and weeping.

These cries were coming from the stores of many fish rotting in the fish cache. There were no cries coming from strewn-about bones and bits of food on the ground, but the cries were just as horrendous coming from the caches.

Little blackfish said, "I'll not swim into this man's trap. He must be greedy. For all those poor fish are crying and not being eaten. I don't want to be wasted. I'd rather be shared with others in need."

Soon blackfish came to another camp. He listened and there were no cries to be heard. A man, his wife, and two children lived there. Their father also had many dogs which were tied around the camp.

Blackfish noticed there were no bones or bits of food lying about, and, when the family ate, they ate very quietly, being careful not to drop bits of food on the ground. He also saw that they set the edible bones aside for the dogs, and those bones which they knew the dogs would not eat went to a separate pile.

When the family was done eating, their father took the leftovers for the dogs to them and placed them in the dogs' bowls. The other unedibles were taken aside, where people never walked, and buried there. There was no carelessness at their camp and indeed it was very quiet.

Little blackfish said to himself, "At last, a family which appreciates their food. They don't waste or leave bits of food or bones on the ground. They bury their unedibles so there is no crying and wailing at this camp."

Blackfish was overjoyed. He swam about immediately looking for the man's fish trap and, upon finding it, swam into it because he knew he would be eaten very carefully and his bones would not be strewn about on the ground.

LESSONS IN STORYTELLING

The preceding was a story my late grandmother, Maggie Lind, of Bethel, used to tell me when I was a child: her Yup'ik way of teaching me to be careful with my subsistence foods. I think you get the point. If you are wasteful you will become unlucky during your hunting and gathering because the animals will stay away from you. Might be a fable or might not.

Young Yup'ik people are taught by example and through story telling. Here's another regarding waste of subsistence foods and stealing. The late Jimmy Chimegalrea of Napakiak told this story at our kitchen table one day when visiting my grandmother. Chimegalrea was relating a story he had heard from another man, who had the following dream.

The man relates that he dreamt he was drift-netting on the Kuskokwim River. The man drifted and drifted and he didn't seem to have caught anything so he decided to take his net in.

As he pulled the net in there were no fish caught in the first half of the net, but then, near the end, he felt a tug and eagerly waited for the fish to appear.

When it did appear the man was horrified to find what appeared to be a salmon which was nothing but skin and bones but was quite alive.

The man was about to pull the fish into his boat when the fish spoke to him. It said, "Please, wait a moment. I have something to tell you."

The fisherman sat down quite surprised and listened. "Look at me," said the fish. "I am skin and bones. This is because your people have been so wasteful. There is coming a time when we fish shall be scarce to you. The people have begun to use us to become rich (probably referring to the commercial fishing industry).

"We fish were not put on this earth to be used this way. We were placed here for you to eat. Look where it has led you. You fish us only to make money and some of you fish us only for our roe and throw the rest of us away.

"Listen, I hear crying and wailing coming from your fish caches. Many of us from last year hang rotting in them. Why should we make ourselves available to you when you waste us and only use us in this way?

"Go and tell your people there is coming a time when there shall be very few fish returning to this river, the Kuskokwim. Those of you who fish honestly for food must go and lock the doors to your caches. The days of want and stealing are coming. Many hearts will be broken when they find that their subsistence-caught fish have been stolen. Even their set nets will be taken without the asking. Be watchful. There, I have said it. Now you can take me if you want."

The man, needless to say, released the fish and told his story to Mr. Chimegalrea, who related it to us so we could pass it on to others who would listen.

Indeed, along the Kuskokwim river of late there has been some reported waste and stealing of fish from fish camps.

People have resorted to locking the doors to their fish caches as fish have been stolen from them, sometimes a family's whole winter's supply.

Only several years ago there was a chum salmon crash on the Kuskokwim and commercial fishermen were broke for a whole year. Even now, there is always the question of whether or not to have a commercial opening because of these low returns.

Elders say fish return to the rivers for a purpose: for us to eat. Not to make money off of, but for subsistence purposes.

They have always said, "While there are fish in the river, fish for them as much as possible. They will sustain you."

BEING A "GENUINE YUP'IK"

Now, in this cash economy some people fish commercially and others even go so far as to fish to sell them illegally. Unfortunately, those who know about people who do this turn the other way and pretend not to notice. This is not the Yup'ik way of doing things.

A cash economy and stealing are not a part of our culture. Subsistence is everything to us. Our traditions teach us this.

I am so very fortunate to have been raised by my grandmother. I am so happy to have had the opportunity to live with her and learn from her.

Maggie Lind was a "genuine Yup'ik," as she used to call herself, and I hope by remembering her teaching I too am a genuine Yup'ik. There are so many things that she taught me by her example that they are too numerous to mention. Perhaps a book might be in order.

Let me give you some examples of what I learned from her about being a genuine Yup'ik.

First and foremost: subsistence is our life. I used to go weeks on end out into the far reaches of the tundra with her to pick berries and watch my uncles hunt and fish.

For instance, when we went picking berries about fifty miles west of Bethel up into the Johnson River, a tributary of the Kuskokwim, we would travel by boat all day, and then somewhere in the Johnson River we'd veer off into one of the many small sloughs.

I would watch my grandmother as she sat at the front of the boat directing my uncle, who was running the outboard motor, to go this way and that, until she would point at the bank and tell him to stop.

I remember thinking to myself: berries don't grow here; there's no tundra. It's a swamp. We'd stop nonetheless and immediately my grandmother would take me and bring me ashore.

Then she would take me into the tall grass until we came to what appeared to be a small mound on the ground and say, "This is where my mother is buried. She was your great grandmother."

We'd linger there a moment and then return to the boat, where she would take out a lunch for us. Before saying grace, she would take a pinch of everything that we were going to eat. A pinch of bread. A pinch of butter or jam. A pinch of dried fish. A pinch of tea or coffee. A pinch of everything that we were going to have for lunch and then take these and go back up onto the land and bury them there.

She told me that she was feeding our ancestors, her family, who were buried there. She also said this was done for a good journey and for the abundance of the subsistence foods we were going after. Today, I still do this. It is my – our – tradition. It is a part of what makes me a "genuine Yup'ik."

I thank my grandmother who taught me these things, who taught me to appreciate our subsistence lifestyle. To take care; not to waste, but to share. To take care not to steal, but to provide for myself so I don't need to steal. To remember my elders, those living and dead, to share with them also. To be watchful at all times that I do not offend the spirits of the fish and animals that I take for food.

To give the beaver or seal that I catch a drink of water so its spirit will not be thirsty. To take from the land only what I can use and to give to the needy if I have enough to share.

Today Yup'ik elders shake their heads and say we Yupiit are losing our culture. Our subsistence lifestyle IS our culture. Without subsistence we will not survive as a people. We Yupiit are different from the many other Native groups in Alaska.

If our culture, our subsistence lifestyle, should disappear, we are no more and there shall not be another kind as we in the entire world.

– Originally published in Cultural Survival Quarterly, *Fall 1998, Vol. 22, Issue 3 ("Crisis in the Last Frontier: The Alaskan Subsistence Debate").*

Sister Goodwin

ASRAAQ, THE GIRL WHO BECAME A SHE-BEAR

Up north when springtime comes around, the real people come alive with the birds singing in the air, the plants sprouting, and the fish and sea life jumping out of the water. They come alive with the bears waking up, and the little squirrels darting everywhere.

Asraaq was born during this time when the tiny blueberry blossoms grow on the tundra. She was born at the blueberry camp, up by Agvagaaq, near the mouth of the Kobuk River. Her name means blueberry. Her family loved her deeply. She made everyone smile and entertained everyone with her gift of humor. Even when Asraaq was young, she could tell funny stories that made real people laugh until happy tears rolled down their eyes. Sometimes she would get into trouble when she made everybody laugh out loud when they were out in the country. The elders scolded her for being too noisy.

After salmon fishing along the Bering Sea coast, Asraaq and her family always moved up to the mouth of the Kobuk to pick berries. Asraaq loved her birth place, this place called Agvagaaq. She loved

---

Sister Goodwin, Iñupiaq from Kotzebue, Alaska.

to laugh and dance on the tundra, and that usually got her into trouble. At Agvagaaq, her ancestors had first cleared a space for their camp among the spruce and hemlock trees, on the bank of the river. It was their place, their camp.

As soon as the boat landed on the bank, Asraaq would jump out of the boat and run as fast as she could to her favorite tree to see if the great grey owl was still there. That year it was gone, so the family named that time When the Owl Disappeared. Asraaq thought about the great grey owl throughout the day, the owl she nicknamed Qavlaq, big brown eyes. It was one of those rare times when she felt sad. And feeling sad made her think of fall-time, coming up close, when the darkness would return. Asraaq did not like the time of darkness, too many real people get shut up in their sod houses.

At Agvagaaq, the time When the Owl Disappeared, Asraaq came out of her sadness and danced a Raven dance. She liked to imitate the ravens in flight. Asraaq and her sister Aanaluq laughed and played string games. Asraaq made a jackrabbit hop in her string story. Her grandmother scolded her, reminding her that the jackrabbit story cannot be told during the coming of fall. Her grandmother told her that whenever anyone played the jackrabbit string story something bad happens, and sometimes it means someone is going to die.

That evening before Asraaq went to sleep, she went outside to relieve herself. She never came back into the tent. The next morning her family found big brown bear tracks.

Her family missed her but they also knew that she would not return. When the Owl Disappeared, Asraaq also disappeared, probably because she made a jackrabbit hop in her string story. After a year, the next spring time, Asraaq came back in human form to tell her family what had happened.

Asraaq began her story by remembering the time When the Owl Disappeared. She remembered going out behind a tree and just as she headed back to the tent, a big brown bear grabbed her. The Aqlaq pulled her skin from the nape of her neck over her face so she couldn't see where he was taking her. She must have blacked out from the pain because when she was able to think straight, she was in some sort of a pit. The pit was lined with grass and there were dead animals all around her. She felt these furry things and found a jackrabbit. With the soft fur of the jackrabbit, she cleaned away the dirt and grass that had stuck to her head. Next she pulled the skin back into place over her face. When she did that, she felt a long bear nose and a furry face instead of her own. She frantically felt over her body and found out she had become a she-bear. Then she realized that the bear meant to marry her. The Aqlaq thought she would be happy with a full cache of meat in the pit.

When Asraaq finished her story, her family cried but understood that she was happy in her life as a bear. Asraaq told them to look for her and her cubs across the river each time they returned to pick berries. Every year her descendants go back to Agvagaaq to pick berries and marvel at the handsome bear cubs dancing on the tundra. And they say, just look at my relatives, Asraaq's grandchildren. Before they leave Agvagaaq, they leave something nice for the bears. The family leaves Asraaq's favorite foods, sometimes it was sourdock greens preserved in seal oil, or sometimes it was a barrel of blueberries.

WHEN THE OWL DISAPPEARED

for my sons Andy & Ishmael

You have come of age to hear my story
my story about my grandmother's grandmother
my story about Asraaq
Blueberry girl who became a she-bear
I will tell it to you many times
until you can form the sounds
as clearly and correctly
as my grandmother did for me
for now your voice
cannot repeat this story
in your heart you are still
confused about the feelings of my story
in your mind you are still
confused about times and names
and where you fit in this story
for now remember how
you are related to the
brown bears of the Arctic

SACRIFICE: A DREAM / A VISION

i looked over toward the steep snow bluff
and on the edge

stood a serene young man
he was wearing a fancy squirrel parky
and high wolf maklaks covered his feet

he gently held his grandfather
by the throat

grandfather Owl
in his human form was also dressed
in fancy squirrel and wolf

they did not exchange words

as the old man died

the love and north wisdom
flowed into his grandson
he remembered the lessons
of making stone tools

and the ceremonies performed
in order to live in harmony
with polar bear wolf and wolverine
kings of the arctic beasts

and he remembered
grandfather had chosen him
to carry on his name
Ukpik
Owl

in this way
he will keep the memory alive
with the tales and adventures
told by his owl grandfather

                    grandfather the wise one
                  had chosen his time
                        Tingmirat Tatqiat
              Beginning Spring Moon

when the song of birds and ducks returned
and when the soft snow
            melts into the earth
so did his life

– *Originally published in* A Lagoon Is
in My Backyard, *Sister Goodwin,*
I. Reed Books, Berkeley and New
York, 1984.

NOMADIC IÑUPIAT FOR KAPPAISRUK

Illivaaq
　　how many times
mom & dad took us
out of school
　　one month ahead
ahead of the coming water
　　　we rode on an
oaken sled over spring ice
　　the dogs excited as
children
　　　　　race without directions
east to Illivaaq
opening up the summer home
　　is a special thirst
saved for the nomadic change
　　　we drank the freshness
　　of the new-fallen snow
　　　the last of the year
we ran
as the snow crunched under us
we felt
we touched
happy to be home again
we ran across both creeks
on the rocky shore
we ran up to the top
of the hills named
for each of us
we ran over to the
old drifted up scow
we couldn't wait for Nelsons
to move to their camp
from Napaatauchaaq
　　how many games of
norwegian ball kept us happy
we held onto driftwood boats
on a pole making waves on a
calm arctic shoreline

Agvagaaq
   summer home for grandparents
the spruce is tall
   roots for baskets & carved dish
     you bounced on a
   wild duck carved of driftwood
       while the owls
   just sat around
watching
      big robins
   fly by tree to tree
golden eagles & hawks glide
on a quiet wind current

Kitikliquagaaq
   fall season
   where we pick barrels of berries
& dine on kutugaq a wild duck

Qugluktaq
   last berry camp
   last duck hunting camp
evening becomes a reality
    as the first hours of
   darkness
hold a blanket over the sun
   the northern lights fill up
the sky with a bright speeding
   polar force
legends are remembered from
parents of parents & retold
     how special for
a whole family to sit
together
reminiscing laughing planning
for the winter
always the squirming children
    sit wide-eyed for hours
   listening to old-time powers
hushed by folks telling them
     the bears outside will hear
them laugh and come to take
    them away

fall
a glint
a last chance to take home the earth
a beginning of subdued sleep

– Originally published in A Lagoon Is
in My Backyard, *Sister Goodwin,
I. Reed Books, Berkeley and New
York, 1984.*

PIKSINÑAQ

when popcorn
first came up north
north to kotzebue sound
little iñuit
took it home from school
long long ago when
the new century first woke up

Aana sat on neat
rows of willow branches
braiding sinew into thread

Uva Aana niggin
una piksinñaq
for you grandmother
eat this
it is something that bounces

after Aana ate it
the little iñuit girls
giggled hysterically
for sure now, they said
old Aana is going to bounce too

for hours
Aana sat hunched over
with her eyes squinched shut
she grasped onto neat rows
of willow branches
waiting for the popcorn
to make her bounce around

– *Originally published in* A Lagoon Is
in My Backyard, *Sister Goodwin,*
I. Reed Books, Berkeley and New
York, 1984.

Andrew Hope III

Shagoon 1

Thunderbirds flying
Like giant planes
Moving silently
Across the gray sky
Thunderbirds flying

Shagoon 2

Brown bears dancing
Leaving footprints
In the mud and snow
Brown bears dancing
Into the woods
Brown bears dancing

Shagoon 3

Killer whales flying
To the mountains
Becoming rock
Turning to stone
Permanent landscape
Eternal Killer Whales flying

Andrew Hope III, Tlingit from Sitka, Alaska.

Shagoon 4

Killer Whales multiplying
Like grains of sand along the shore
Killer Whales multiplying
Killer Whales multiplying

– Originally published in Rolling
Stock, *Boulder, Colorado*
No. 19/20, 1991.

DIYEIKEE

Intangible
Mountain spirits inside
Brothers and sisters
Family
Unscientific
That tattoo
That design
That spirit inside
Unmeasurable
Crests speaking
Through the ages
In dreams
I don't think it ever changes
If your grandchildren
Could hear your voices
Your history
Your spirit coming down
They would surely remember

Eleanor Hadden

NATIVE IDENTITY: WHAT KIND OF NATIVE ARE YOU?

In Western culture, stories usually have three sections: a beginning, middle and end, or an introduction, body and conclusion. Since this is a story of my life, the introduction will become apparent, the body of the story is here in front of you, and there is no conclusion, as my life has yet to end. I have talked with my elders, and they have given me permission to discuss my life story. However, in the Kwakiutl custom, I can talk about myself only if I wear a special mask. *Since I do not have this special mask, this Raven's Tail weaving is a symbolic curtain that will hang between you and me so I can talk about myself to you.*

Traditionally, the Tlingit/Haida/Tsimshian way to tell a story is long and complex. The elders would say, "This is a long story, so I'll try to make it short for you." This is what I will try to do today. My story is long, but I'll try to make it short and not so complex.

The word "Native" can convey a variety of meanings to the person interpreting the word. In Alaska, the name for the indigenous people is "Alaska Native." This is because Alaska's indigenous

---

Eleanor Hadden, Tlingit, Haida, Tsimshian from Ketchikan, Alaska.

people comprise several different groups: Aleut, Athabaskan, Eyak, Yup'ik, Iñupiat, Tlingit, Haida, and Tsimshian. However, the use of the generic term Alaska Native might seem to suggest that there are no distinct, separate groups of indigenous people. It could mean to someone who knows only about Yup'iks or Athabaskans that all Native people are Yup'iks or Athabaskans. Or the term Native might mean "Eskimo" to those people who think that is the only Native group in Alaska. And if I tell someone that I'm from Southeast Alaska, they might automatically think I'm Tlingit, not knowing there are other Native groups or tribes in Southeast Alaska. I am an indigenous person of Alaska. In order to understand what kind of Native I am, it is important to know my background. Here is my Tlingit introduction with a translation and brief description of the meaning.

1. *Ax aat hás, ax sani hás*
1. my father's sisters, my father's brothers

2. *Ch'áak' Naa ka Yéil Naa áyá xát*
2. I am Eagle and Raven (this in itself is another story)

3. *Gunalcheesh haat yeey.aadée*
3. Thank you for coming

4. *Eleanor yóo xat duwasaakw dleit káa x'éináx*
4. My white man's (English) name is Eleanor

5. *Aan-kee-naa yóo xat duwasaakw lingít x'éináx*
5. My Tlingit name is Aan kee naa which means an Eagle flying high above a village, the name given to me by my maternal grandmother.

6. *Ax aal Elizabeth Kininnook Baines yóo duwasaakw dleit káa x'éináx*
6. My maternal grandmother's name was Elizabeth Kininnook Baines

6a. *Ax tláa Mary Jones yóo duwasaakw dleit káa x'eináx*
6a. My mother's English name is Mary Jones

6b. *Ax éesh Willard Jones yóo duwasaakw dleit káa x'éináx*
6b. My father's English name is Willard Jones

7. *Neix̱.ádi naá ayá x̱át*
7. My clan is Neix̱adi, Eagle and Raven; my land crest is Beaver
and my sea crest is Halibut

8. *Taas-laa-naas (Deikeenaa) yadí áyá x̱át*
8. I am the daughter of a Haida, Brown Bear, Taas-laa-naas clan
(My father is a Kasaan Haida)

9. *Ts'ootsxán dachx̱án áyá x̱át*
9. I am the granddaughter of the Tsimshian Wolf
(My mother's father, Joel Baines, was a Metlakatla Tsimshian)

10. *Taanta-k̲wáan Teik̲weidee dachx̱án yádi áyá x̱át*
10. I am the great-granddaughter of the Tongass Teik̲weidee
(My maternal grandmother's father, William Kininnook, was a
Brown Bear of the Tongass)

11. *Yaadaas (Deikeenaa) dachx̱án áyá x̱át*
11. I am the granddaughter of the Yaadaas (Haida clan)
(My paternal grandfather, Louis Jones, was of the Kasaan Yaadaas)

12. *Scottish dachx̱án yádi áyá x̱át*
12. I am the great-granddaughter of a Scottish man
(My paternal great-grandfather was Scottish: William King Lear of
Wrangell)

13. *Sanya k̲wáan ax̱ shagóon aanée*
13. My ancestors are from the Sanya k̲waan (Cape Fox)

14. *Gunalcheesh haat yeey.aadée*
14. Thank you for coming

15. *Ax̱ eesh hás, ax̱ sani hás*
15. my father and my father's brothers

16. *Ka ax̱ aal hás*
16. and my grandparents

This is my traditional Tlingit introduction which places me
through my family and by place of origin. This is part of my heritage
and lineage which is important in understanding issues regarding Native identity. In my family's research and our knowledge of
our lineage, we discovered an extension to our family which has

brought interesting results. In addition to my family in Southeast Alaska, I have blood ties to Tsimshian families in British Columbia, Haida families on the Queen Charlotte Islands, Kwakiutl families on Vancouver Island, and Upper Chinook families in the Columbia River area.

The Tlingit introduction is my immediate maternal and paternal connections. The extended family tree includes many more. My maternal great-grandfather was Chief Ebbets (Kinanuk) of the Tongass Brown Bear. Kinanuk's sister was Mary Ebbets; she married Robert Hunt, a Hudson's Bay Company employee. The couple moved to Fort Rupert, British Columbia, where they raised 11 children. One of their sons, my great-grandfather's first cousin, George Hunt, taught Franz Boas much about Northwest coast cultures. Until a few years ago, our family knew only that we had family "down south." The Hunt family knew only that they had Tlingit relatives. Approximately five years ago, through extensive research of Alfred Hunt, the Hunt family found my mother and the Teikweidee or Tongass clan. We attended a three-day Kwakiutl potlatch at Fort Rupert. A traditional Kwakiutl potlatch could include a memorial service, a naming ceremony, the raising of a totem pole, dedication of a long house and a wedding, and, in this particular potlatch, a celebration for the Hunt family in finding their Tlingit relatives: my mother and her descendants.

My mother's father's people came from Old Metlakatla, British Columbia. William Duncan, an Anglican lay minister, moved over 800 people from British Columbia to Alaska. My grandfather, Joel Baines, was four years old when he, along with his family, moved from Old Metlakatla, B.C., to New Metlakatla, Alaska. We believe this family is from the Coastal Tsimshian group. My mother continues to research this part of our family through the Anglican church records in Prince Rupert and in the U.S. federal archives.

My paternal grandfather, Louis Lear Jones, was from Kasaan, though he was born in Wrangell with familial ties to Masset, B.C. The name Jones comes from his aunt who raised him after the death of his mother. The family of his wife, Anna Frank, is also from Kasaan. My paternal great-grandfather was William King Lear, an Army Quartermaster in Wrangell, Alaska. We thought we were his only surviving family.

My grandfather was born in 1877 to a Kasaan Haida woman and to a Scottish man, William Lear. He was stationed with the Army and based in Wrangell. At the end of martial law in Alaska, the Army sold the standing fort and buildings to William Lear. When the Army later returned, the sale was considered null and void, so he no longer owned Fort Wrangell. About four years ago, my father was in Wrangell to search for information about his grandfather. What we did not know was that there was another family who was also doing research on their ancestor.

The city of Wrangell hired a researcher to document its history. One name appeared more than others, William King Lear. The researcher decided to find out who this man was and what his significance to Wrangell was. While she was doing research, she received a letter from someone requesting information on their ancestor. Carol was looking for information on her great-great-great-grandfather, William King Lear. William Lear married a young Indian girl from the Columbia River in 1856. Their daughter was born in 1857, 20 years before my grandfather, Louis Jones. Carol's great-great-great-grandfather is my great-grandfather, William K. Lear. He had other children but we do not yet know who the descendants are, and we continue to do research on his family and history.

I introduce myself in the Western style in the following way. My name is Eleanor Jones Hadden. I've been married for 25 years and I have two children. I am a graduate of the University of Alaska Anchorage with a B.A. degree in anthropology. My husband retired from the Air Force as a lieutenant colonel. This means we spent 23 years living around the United States (Alaska, Arizona, Kansas, California, Texas, and Massachusetts) and in Italy and Germany. We also traveled extensively throughout Europe and England. However, as a child, I lived in Southeast Alaska and in Oakland, California, a product of the Relocation Program of the Bureau of Indian Affairs. I attended University of Alaska Fairbanks, Glendale Community College in Arizona, and Anchorage Community College. I am currently contemplating graduate study in anthropology.

My parents and I have spent several years researching archives, interviewing elders, and trying to remember stories from the past in order for me now to write this information. (The next goal is to have it all memorized and be able to pull the information from any section of the family tree, find the relationships between people which means a clan or family historian.)

Some here may understand the significance of my lineage and the information I have provided today; others may not. Lineage to Alaska Natives is more than knowing one's ancestors. It is an essential link in knowing and understanding one's ties to the culture. What does this information and knowledge mean to me? It means, "That's the kind of Native I am": one who knows who I am and where I come from – a Tlingit, Haida, Tsimshian, with some Scottish ancestry, who has lived in Alaska, the "Lower 48" and in Europe;

and I understand my ties to my ancestors and to my culture of Southeast Alaska which includes fishing for and smoking salmon, picking berries (hunting and gathering), eating traditional foods, weaving, showing respect for elders, and singing and dancing traditional songs. You can use your knowledge of your past for the future. When people know their past history and family, there is an understanding of self and relationship to today's culture.

Now that I know who I am, what does it mean? There are obligations that come with this knowledge. My great-grandfather, William Kininnook, sent my grandmother, Elizabeth Baines, to Chemawa Indian School in Oregon to learn English and to understand the white man's culture. My parents went to Sheldon Jackson Mission School to continue their knowledge of the Western culture and to "forget" their Native ways. My grandmother worked to make the world a better place for her grandchildren, as have my parents. Now, it is my turn to continue this work, study the Western culture and make the Western culture better understood for my children and future grandchildren as set in place by my grandmother and to pass this Native cultural knowledge on to the next generation. As with all societies, the outward description of an individual's identity defines the person.

And in the traditional way of ending a story, the elders would say, "This is the short version of a long story; one day I'll tell you the longer version. *Dei awei*. That's all."

Gunalcheesh. Háwaa. Thank you.

Glen Simpson

NIGHT WITHOUT DAWN

In the endless night
we are in the moths who knock twice
in the hissing sun of the gas lantern
and are gone.

Glen Simpson, Tahltan Athabaskan from Atlin, British Columbia, Canada.

TAHLTAN COUNTRY

It was necessary to draw the line in blood once again;
Timid trespassers become arrogant all too quickly.
They purified themselves near the river,
sharpened the long knives, and called on their spirit helpers.
Others might fall like wounded bears,
but not the man whose spirits fought with him.
They left silently, bound in the aura of each man's power.
Their screams would pierce the mists of sleep at first
light as they raced through the cold wet grass.

TRAVELING IN THE LAND OF THE NATIVE ART HISTORIANS

After a day of viewing the world of Native Art,
sometimes dried and preserved,
I sat in the contrived coziness of a hotel bar.
How many would puke their cafeteria lunches
if they learned that hunting peoples hunted?
"Raise your hands everyone who knows
the smack of a bullet striking flesh
and has seen the last breath plume
like a small white cloud.
Hold them high please.
Our researcher, in the back of the bar, is counting."
Indians scared some of them;
obvious in that special quick laughter
that surfaces at times like that.
Indians, under the lights,
gave more answers than were theirs to give.
But who am I to talk like this;
a man alone with a designer beer,
just an excuse for not going back to that costly room
with its windows permanently sealed against the night air.

FRONT STREET

Nome,
where cultures meet in the mud:
Hunters,
whose eyes swept the horizon,
search in a thickening fog,
lost on the drifting ice of an unknown sea
while foraging for one more beer.
Sons of farmers,
seeking what they couldn't find at home,
seek even harder
as they step too heavily
on this last thin edge of America.

Who can tell them
that they are formed in the image of angels?

Julie Coburn

SEED POTATOES AND FOXGLOVES

$\mathbf{W}$e have today potatoes that were originally brought into old Kasaan over a hundred years ago. One of our great-aunts on Dad's side of the family brought the seed potatoes from Puget Sound or Victoria, B.C. She and her sisters would travel by canoe to the Seattle area and work in the fields picking crops and probably thought the potatoes especially tasty. Some people call them "finger" potatoes. The missionaries or traders also introduced a type of potato to the Haidas (probably the "Irish" variety). The kind my great-aunts brought to old Kasaan are long, skinny, and bumpy, especially tasty with "setow" (ooligan oil). They have a mealy texture and are more yellow than ordinary bakers. Haidas couldn't pronounce "sweet seed" so they coined the word "sgoo seet." The Tsimshians pronounce the words exactly like we do. Today, I've given the same seed potatoes to friends and relatives. Some just plain put them in a pot to cook and eat, others have replanted them. A friend in Eureka, California, showed them to a professor at an agricultural college and he said that this potato that my great-aunts introduced is the

Julie Coburn, Haida from Kasaan, Alaska.

original potato from Peru. My understanding is that the potatoes that are normally found in the grocery store are a type of hybrid, supposedly "improved" by someone named Luther Burbank.

Back in the '30s an old prospector called Paul Jordon lived in Karta Bay and he grew many flowers in his garden. Grandma Emma and Mom thought the foxgloves were especially beautiful, so they got the catalog from Mr. Jordon and placed an order for five cents a package. Grandma thought that five cents wouldn't buy too many seeds so she ordered $2.00 worth. They were amazed when the order arrived. They gave a package to all the ladies of the village which at that time was about 18 or 20 women. The flowers did well for a number of years and I can recall there were foxgloves blooming in everyone's garden. Then during the '50s when the population of Kasaan dropped to about seven, the weeds took over and there was no one here to tend a garden. Lo and behold, in the early '70s, when the sewer and water and light systems were started and a lot of soil was turned over and dug, the foxgloves erupted and Kasaan was in bloom again. Some of the plants stand over six feet tall today.

RAVEN SPEAKS TO HAIDAS

The Haidas say that the raven can say words that the Haida can understand. I only learned a few of the words: *gulk gulk,* the wind is coming; *gawk gawk,* a boat is coming; *aawkshh aawkshh* (it sounds like blood squirting), the salmon will be plentiful.

Perry, Annie and I took a boat ride to Kasaan Island. We stopped for lunch on a shady beach. I heard a raven say "gawk gawk" as it flew over us, and I told Perry that the Raven told me that a boat was coming. We thought nothing of it. Later we stopped at Happy Harbor, and Brots, our friend's dog, barked, and she said he always barked when a boat was nearby. The boat did not come into Happy Harbor so we forgot it. About one hour later we buzzed on back to Kasaan and the first thing we heard was that our friend John McVickers had come to Kasaan, looked for us around the bay, and around Kasaan Island. So the raven was right. He had seen the boat as it came in the bay and told me by the words "gawk gawk."

Barbara Švarný Carlson

THERE IS NO SUCH THING AS AN ALEUT

We call ourselves *Unangan* or *Unangas* (Atkan dialect). This is our autonym, our name for ourselves, the word of national identity for the indigenous peoples of the Aleutian Archipelago (including nine distinct subgroups) prior to our contact with Europeans.

When Russian explorers came to our land, charting and mapping the area for their czar, the first island group that they came upon were the people who called themselves *Sasignan*. For unclear reasons the Russians called them "Aleut." They lived in what the Russians named the Near Islands, because of their proximity to Russia at the western end of the Aleutian Islands. As they moved eastward on their journeys, the Russians continued to call the people Aleut, even as they crossed a major dividing line of language and culture, encountering the *Sugpiaq* (many of whom now call themselves *Alutiiq*), *Sugcestun*-speaking people of the Alaska Peninsula.

The Russian language became the common acculturation denominator among these diverse groups. What is my point? We

Barbara Švarný Carlson, Unangan/Aleut from Unalaska, Alaska.

"Aleuts" are actually three different maritime peoples who had our own identities and subdivisions prior to our contact with the Russians: the *Alutiiq* speakers, the Central *Yup'ik* speakers of Bristol Bay, and the *Unangam Tunuu* (language of the *Unangax̂)* speakers. Why should we hang onto that foreign name, "Aleut"? If we are to show the pride we have in our cultural heritage and reclaim and maintain our identities as a distinct people, we should revive the original words we used to describe ourselves.

Our *Unangan* identities have become so tenuous that we, as a people, are excavating, sifting, and meticulously labeling the artifacts of various segments of our society with increasing fervor. If we do not, they may disappear forever, or be claimed by another group as their own, muddying our uniqueness and diffusing our very identity. So there is inherent in this work that element of reclamation that is necessarily a part of any revitalization of an indigenous culture.

It is not just material objects that make up our heritage. The endangered *Unangam Tunuu*, the *Unangax̂* language, with its extant dialects is a virtually untapped resource containing clues to found objects, an understanding of the profound relationship with land and sea, rules to live by, history, and perhaps most importantly, a unique view of the world to be shared and appreciated. *Unangam* folklore is a vital aspect of this contribution to the world bank of knowledge. It is like a gigantic puzzle in which museum artifacts fill another missing gap.

Common among Alaska Natives who were either raised away from our home villages or had to leave at some point during our lives and had to remain away for some length of time, displaced *Unangan/Unangas* have a deepened sense of the sacred value of our origins. We feel a loss for what we have been missing, be it Native foods, songs, dance, stories, or seeing beauty reflected in artfully made objects. We miss seeing people who physically resemble ourselves and physically feeling the common elements with which our own relate – elements such as wind, fog, salty air, and horizontal rain. We need to know these things about our cultural heritage and be able to share that common knowledge with family and community. We need to delight in hearing someone shout, *"Aang, Unangax̂* (Hello, 'Aleut')!"* These are what many of those people returning from other places are searching for when they return to the village, or to Alaska. Many of us reside in the densely populated areas such as Anchorage and Fairbanks. Large numbers of *Unangan/Unangas* with close ties similarly reside on the west coast, particularly in Washington and Oregon. We consider our original villages home even if we have not been able to return there for many years. We share a need to assert, "Where we are from is important to us. What we like to eat is important. Our art is important. Our dance and music are important."

The *Unangam* foods are elemental to our culture. To have our Native foods sent to us when we are away is one of the most vitalizing, identity-rich gifts one's friends or family can bestow. Some of our traditional subsistence foods include *aalax̂* (whale), *isux̂* (hair seal), *aanux̂* (red salmon), and *qax̂* (any kind of fish). From the beaches some favorites are *chiknan* (limpets), *wayĝin* (blue mussels), *aguadan* (sea urchins), *qashiikun* (chitons or gumboots), *chuxlan* (clams), and *kahngadgin* (seaweed). *Saaqudan* (commonly called puuchkiis after the Russian word), *qaniisan* (called petrushkies, again from the Russian), fiddlehead ferns, and other native vegetables seem to make one feel healthier. My favorite is *udax̂*, dried fish with *chadux̂*, seal oil. When we eat these foods we know more strongly who we are.

These valuable links to the *Unangam* culture are validation of our origins, touchstones to our self- and group-identities. It is an awesome responsibility that pairs us with various types of scholars and researchers as partners as we search for culturally appropriate ways to document traditional knowledge and skills. We are not just an exploitable resource, but an equal partner in this compilation of our world knowledge bank. The more any of us can know about who we are and where we come from, the more sensitive and confident we can be in our interactions among culturally diverse societies.

Qaĝaasakung. Thank you for listening.

– *Excerpted from* Crossroads Alaska: Native Cultures of Alaska and Siberia, *edited by Valérie Chaussonnet. Arctic Studies Center, Smithsonian Institution, Washington, D.C. 1995.*

Mary TallMountain

O DARK SISTER

Here on the shore you lie alone,
Great blue whale,
Most vast of living beings.
Gulls dart screaming
To fret your lightless eyes.
Silent your ancient clicking song,
Unanswered the calls of your mates
Phantasmic from far plateaus.

What instinct
Magnetized you to shore
Among plastic trash and rotted fruit,
Offal of careless creatures
Who so lately found the sands
Of your millennial home.
What dim kinship
Called you here?

Great Dark Sister,
Mountain of trailing brilliance,
Where now the purple painted worms,
Skittering shapes in ebon fringe,
Gels of indigo and jade
You viewed only in pearly and grey
Who frisked and frolicked in the sweep
Of your gentle passage.

In a museum stand wired
The striding bones of Allosaurus,
Jaunty at his neck a plastic ruff.
Shall we someday see Great Blue

Mary TallMountain, Koyukon Athabaskan from Nulato, Alaska.

Daubed in dayglo green
When her bones are assembled
Like his, for the mere amaze
Of some unborn generation?

Ask the bones that dangled in carnivals;
Ask the bones traded by voyageurs;
Ask the bones of Kintpuash and Black Hawk;
Hear them at Elk Creek:
Hear them at Sand Creek, Wounded Knee.
Hear the ancestors' ghostly cries,
Hear fabulous buffalo
Begging back his giant bones
Out of the carpeted plain.

These at least lie resting
Beneath kindly soil,
Cherished by earth. Their mother
And ours.

SEAHORSE MUSIC

Mail order seahorses in the belly   *con brio*
of the jet's harsh howl.
Afloat in a dark bell,
blind eyes bulging, the
male swells, surges,
thrusts forth sons.

I unpack, unwrap swaddlings,   *andante*
Breathless
pour proud wraiths
from the shipping bell
to drift safe
through amniotic water.

Desert dawn. They call, wordless.   *ritardando*
Immense my shadow
hulks over the crystal cage.
Bright stately ghosts
hook crooked tails
around pale fingers of coral.

Slim as a silver,   *allegretto*
transparent gossamer,
the solitary
surviving baby wanders
the tremulous emerald
water-garden world.

His black fearless eye   *misterioso*
encased in pulsing shell,
dainty as a mistflower.
His song haunts the listening air,
whispers over the Sierra
to eerie dragons of ocean.

Brave, uncommon voyager,   *largo*
your sojourn brief as dream.
Sea Mother rises answering

across her murmurous tides.
Lonely she sings you home.

Glossary for Seahorse Music

con brio: with spirit and vigor
andante: in a moderate tempo
ritardando: slowing gradually
allegretto: faster than andante
misterioso: shadowed, mysterious
largo: with slow solemnity

NULIAJUK, A SEQUENCE

Old Man of all Oceans
loved Nuliajuk
dragged her under the sea
wrapped himself in her storm-black hair
named her Sea Mother.

with primal yearning
to find mystic roots
my tendrils blindly searching
again I enter the waters.
I seek Nuliajuk
beneath the green glacier

she rests upon
a couch of jade.
empty carapaces one by one
fall from her hair.
into its dark and cloudy coils
drift newborn creatures

from her stitching fingers
medallions crusted with beads
litter the centuries
around her.
no breath of sound disturbs
these unimagined rooms.

above, salt water is shining
sun throws fat noon shadows
vines hang heavy red.
women sing berrypicking songs
in late summer heat.
yet here I wait

rising from her
ancient dream she sings
Come to Nuliajuk, Nuliajuk!
She swaddles me
in a blanket of sea-anemones

Tim Afcan, Sr.

SUPER COCKROACH TALE

Kozzovac Mountains were not where they are now. In the late eighteen hundreds a Native hunter was out at his fur hunting area, fall camp. Bright and early one quiet morning in the flats near Sheldon's Point, he saw in the east a dark shadow that seemed to be moving; it was getting larger as the day broke. It looked like a pile of earth to him. The next morning it was larger and closer. Sure enough, it was a mountain. Still the next day it was larger yet. It was now on the west side of his camp. Wanting to find out who, or what, made it move each day, Enuk went to see it close. When he reached the mountain, he met other men there, and one was a shaman that went on the ball to find out how the mountain was moving. Having power and knowledge of things, the Shaman said it was a cockroach that packed it from way up the Yukon River. Shaman told the people that those cockroaches were big animals. But mountain moving made that cockroach so small, the Shaman said, that since then, all cockroaches will be tiny.

And so it was hence, the Kozzovac Mountains are the only landmark for travelers down at the flats.

Tim Afcan, Sr., Yup'ik from St. Mary's, Alaska.

Randall Johnson

SALMON IN THE POND

The day was warm and the month may have been July, and the tide was very high, the kind of tide that came almost to the road, far up under the A.N.B. Hall, and almost made the old boats and barges invisible. The tide being as high as it was made my grandmother very nervous about letting me play or swim in the water. She said, "It gets too deep for little fellas like you, so stay around the house until the tide goes down."

So, my cousin, Sherman Sumdum, and I spent the time waiting for low tide constructing miniature seine boats, with masts, booms, a stack, and a seine made out of hair nets that we had found and saved for that purpose. The boats were made of 1 × 4s and for the cabin 2 × 4s that were nailed to the hull of the boats so the 1 × 4s wouldn't crack and split in two. The mast and boom were of any wood that was about a foot long, and no bigger than ⅛ of an inch in diameter, which was then attached to the boat with the smallest nails we could find. That was a day's work, and a way to keep busy until the tide went down.

Sherman and I worked very hard and helped each other. We laughed at each other's mistakes and tried to out-do the other in

Randall Johnson, Tlingit from Southeast Alaska.

designing our boats. It didn't matter much, for they came out looking like each other except, maybe, in size. Once the boats were assembled we would find a couple of eye screws to put on the bow, so a string could be attached to pull them along. If time would permit, as that day did, we would paint the boats the best we knew how, with any kind of paint we could lay our little hands on.

When our boats were finished, and the tide was low enough, we raced with all the speed our legs could summon up, to our favorite pond. As usual, Sherman won the race. The pond was below my Aunt Martha Davis' house, and she would look out the window every once in a while to see if we were all right. The beach was full of seagulls and crows eating minnows or crabs that had been left by the tide.

Once there, we pulled off our shoes and socks and rolled up our pants above the knees. We launched our boats and waded around the pond pulling our boats while making motor sounds. Sherman stuck a nail into the ground, close to the water, and attached his net and made like he was making a set; I did the same some time after. We did this for a while at different points of the pond, and then started pulling our boats around the pond playing battleships, with Sherman being the Jap or German, and me being the *USS Port Frederick*. We had some good battles.

On this particular day, while playing battleships, we saw some strange movements in the water at the far end of the pond. We ran to see what it was. When we got to where the movement was, we saw a trapped salmon. We got very excited and first tried to chase it down and catch it. When that didn't work, we threw rocks. Finally Sherman went after a long pole, and we tried to spear it. We chased that salmon all over that pond. We tried sneaking up on him, and just before we would get near him, he would swim off with such speed he looked like he would disappear for a moment. Up, down, and around the pond we went, trying to trick him, or corner him, but everything seemed to fail. Now that I think about it, we could have drained the damned thing, but then we would have had to wait for another high tide to fill the pond back up again; maybe that's why we didn't do it.

We were so involved with this fish that we forgot what time it was getting to be until we heard my oldest sister, Vickie, calling for Sherman and me to come up to the house. I hollered back, "We're trying to catch a big fish!" She hollered back, "I don't care, now get up here!" So we threw a couple more rocks and then raced towards the house.

When we got there, we found that Sherman's mother was there,

Betty Sumdum. We were breathing hard from the run, which made it hard for us to explain the salmon in the pond. We finally got the words out and were motor-mouthing so fast, each of us trying to get his story in first, that Betty finally told us to stop, then said, "One at a time, boys." So we gave them the details of our exciting adventure with the salmon and how we tried to catch him and bring him home to get cooked and eaten. Betty just laughed and said, "A tall fish story from two little people, and you're both only five." Vickie told us to wash up and get ready to eat. That night Sherman and his mother ate supper with us. We had baked salmon, boiled rice, corn on the cob, homemade bread, and for dessert we had blueberry pie. What a way to end an exciting and adventurous day.

Later that evening, after Sherman and his mother had left for home, Grandma Johnson asked where my boat was. I completely forgot the boat trying to catch the salmon and told this to her. She just smiled and said, "Some lucky soul got two strong boats built by two little fishermen that almost caught a big fish." So that night, in bed, I wondered what lucky soul had got my boat, and what that salmon was doing right about now. . . .

Buell Anakak

MAGIC MAKER

. . . And I will leave. But the children will laugh and play, the people dancing to the drums, singing: And my home town will stay, with seals playing near the shores.

Many days the skies will be cold and silent, young lovers chasing moments of excitement as they are doing today.

The people who loved me will pass away and the village will burst anew each year. But my spirit will always wander nostalgic in the same condition in the place I left behind. The people I left behind and loved will pass and only the memory of days gone by will linger in the back roads of my mind.

The Eskimo magic maker will spin me into new worlds and with the change the world itself will change. So the people I love will be left behind. My passion was left behind, my home, people, all the things I cared for. And now I wander in feelings, and sometimes I almost reach that village. But I left. And the children still laugh and sing, people still hunt for whale. I have waves of agony and an indescribable loneliness engulfing me. I know that being a passionate

---

Buell Anakak, Iñupiaq from Northwest Alaska.

man, I have many ties in the heart, so many things I cared for and left behind.

Only a warrior can balance the terror of being a man with the wonder of being a man.

For an instant the loneliness, as a gigantic wave, is frozen before me, held back by the invisible wall of metaphor.

I think back and I cry for the glory of land which now becomes only a dream.

Mary Jane Nielsen

WHAT HOPE CAN DO

My brother-in-law Arnold looked like a starved holocaust victim, his cheeks sunken into his bones. His once-thick dark hair had thinned and turned an odd reddish color. Weak eyes stared back at us out of his pale gaunt face. "This is my brother Donald and his wife Mary Jane," Arnold told the attending nurse.

Ruth Ann, his niece, kissed Arnold on the cheek and looked up at me, eyes watering despite her effort to stay cheerful. Tears stung my eyes, too. Ruth Ann and I walked down the hall of the hospital, trying to be inconspicuous as my husband leaned over his brother Arnold's wheelchair to ask, "Where have you been?" Arnold's six-foot frame had shriveled to just 120 pounds, but what we would all later learn would shock us even more. The next several days would surely test our family's faith, compassion and hope, as it would any family's.

We hadn't seen my brother-in-law since a family wedding in Anchorage during the fall of 1995, when he was out on pass from what he called "the V. A. place." Arnold had been trying for seven months to kick a drinking and drug problem in an attempt to get his life in order.

Mary Jane Nielsen, Sugpiaq/Alutiiq from South Naknek, Alaska.

Arnold's treatment ended the following April, about the same time Bristol Bay fishermen in our home region in southwest Alaska start to prepare for the upcoming salmon season every year. Every so often, someone would inquire about Arnold. "He must be doing okay, otherwise he would call," my husband would reply. We did not know what Arnold was going through during that time.

In February, 1997, a long-time friend from Naknek had called to tell us Arnold was in an Anchorage hospital; our friend's sister had seen him there. We asked our daughter Lorianne, who lives in Anchorage, to check on him, and her report shocked us.

"Uncle Arnold looks pretty bad," Lorianne told us by telephone. Donald and I immediately flew into Anchorage from South Naknek. Arnold's godchild, his niece Ruth Ann, also flew in from King Salmon.

Later, Clara, one of Arnold's older sisters living in King Salmon, also traveled to Anchorage. Once we were all there, Clara called one morning to say that Arnold's doctor needed to meet with us at the hospital.

When we arrived at the hospital, Clara, Donald, Ruth Ann and I were ushered into Arnold's room. Arnold, in a wheelchair, stared blankly at the tied belt on his robe, his fidgeting fingers twirling the tie.

"Arnold has AIDS," the doctor said.

We sat in silence for a long time. Arnold continued to stare at his restless fingers, folding and unfolding his bathrobe tie.

For several years after Arnold's return from Vietnam and his subsequent marriage and divorce, we all had just sporadic contact with him. Donald occasionally would get a telephone call from Arnold or would sometimes call Arnold if he knew where his brother was. Once, when we lived in Anchorage in the late 1980s, we had Arnold and his girlfriend over for Thanksgiving with our family. But for much of the 1990s, there was a long period of silence when no one in our immediate family knew Arnold's whereabouts.

Our youngest daughter, a health aide in South Naknek, called the Anchorage hospital when she heard the new facts about her uncle's illness. Arnold had confided to Eva that he was waiting for a call from the "main man," meaning God. Eva immediately flew into Anchorage from South Naknek.

Daily, members of our family visited Arnold, cajoling him into eating, telling him that we were all praying for him, trying to keep his spirits up. Donald asked friends and family who called to inquire about Arnold to please add to the "collective positive thoughts" and to pray.

During Arnold's hospitalization in Anchorage, he frequently suffered from mental confusion from the HIV virus coupled with the effects of alcohol abuse. For instance, in the hospital at Anchorage, Arnold would sometimes think that a grenade was about to explode behind one of his visitors. "Incoming!" he would blurt, a term American soldiers in Vietnam called artillery or mortar shelling. Arnold would shout this out when he heard loud noises, such as a cart coming down the hall.

From early February to the middle of March, 1997, Arnold struggled to gain back his strength at the Alaska Native Medical Center. When he was finally able to walk again, he was allowed to leave the hospital with Donald and me. After a trial week in Anchorage, we prepared for the trip back to South Naknek.

In addition to his illness, Arnold expressed fear that people in the community might shun him, be afraid of him, or talk about him. Fortunately, we have learned that people have become generally far more informed about AIDS than when this dreaded disease first began spreading around the United States in the early 1980s. Friends and family visited Arnold at home in South Naknek. Some people shook his hand. Some even hugged him, much to our relief and joy.

In the month following Arnold's arrival in our home, my husband refused to travel to any of his regional board meetings. He wanted to take care of his brother. Donald made sure Arnold took his medicines on time. Donald cooked for him, talked to him, and made sure he was warm enough when he would get the chills.

Back at South Naknek, Arnold's mental confusion continued. He would sometimes go through the wrong door; for example, he might go through the outside door when he actually meant to go into the bedroom, or he might go out the front door instead of through the intended bathroom door. Such mistakes would make Arnold seethe with anger, sometimes cursing at whoever helped him, and sometimes at himself. He rarely slept more than a couple of hours at a time, then he would get up and wander about the house. Donald would get up. I would get up. Such nights would recall times long past when our own children were infants, awakening frequently during the night. These episodes gradually occurred less often, and eventually they ended.

When Arnold got stronger, he would take walks, help Donald do repairs on the house, or work outside cleaning the yard, moving rocks to mark the edge of the driveway.

By the end of May, 1997, Arnold said he was ready for a change, and Donald and I needed to get back to our work. Donald needed to get his boat ready for the upcoming commercial salmon season, and his tribal council duties and board responsibilities were calling. I also needed to get back to my job, including the local village corporation's upcoming annual audit.

Arnold's sister Clara invited Arnold to stay in King Salmon, where he soon found a modest home of his own in need of repair. He painted rooms, put in a new stove, fixed the plumbing, drove a truck around town to acquire needed equipment, and visited friends and family.

My husband and I accompanied Arnold to see his doctor the last week of July, 1997. Dr. Westby was amazed at his progress. "My miracle patient," he said. Arnold had gained weight and his T-cell count, one measure of the health of the immune system, had risen to an almost normal level. Our family all along has continued to educate itself about this alarming immune system disease. We have learned that T cells are a type of white blood cell that declines to a dangerously low level with the onset of AIDS, and Arnold's recent T-cell turn-around had us all elated.

Dr. Westby asked Arnold what he attributed his recovery to. "Good family support, a good doctor, and prayer," Arnold replied.

Arnold eventually started traveling with health education staff from the Bristol Bay Area Health Corporation's Kanakanak Hospital. He talks to groups in Bristol Bay villages about AIDS.

At a recent presentation, a health educator covered basic information about HIV and how it attacks the immune system.

"You can carry the virus without knowing it," the health care professional said. "Can you tell someone has the virus by looking at them?"

Then he introduced Arnold, knowing that most people don't know him well enough to know that he has the virus. Soon Arnold was showing pictures of himself when he was first admitted to the hospital. Then he surprised his audience. "I'm more afraid of you than you are of me," Arnold said, explaining that his compromised immune system means that he can catch illnesses from others easily.

"At first, everyone thought I was going to die, but my brother Donald said I would not," Arnold told the group, his eyes crinkling with a hint of a smile.

"I used to wonder what I was here for," Arnold told me later. "Maybe, this is why I'm here."

June McGlashan

CANDLE LITE

Blueberry candle burns,
Though no light has touched,
Smoke lifts in the room.

Long winter sleep,
blueflies hit the window.

June McGlashan, Unangan/Aleut from Akutan, Alaska.

IT IS VERY QUIET

It is very quiet.

Only sound of creaking floor,
aged to soft putty.
No small feet race.
as years ago.

Who fell down the staircase,
and who didn't.
How our candy stuck under
our bed forever.

I know each shadow
a window casts.
And the scratch mark
Mom scolded for.

Where spiders crawl,
in a secret place.
Tomorrow I'll find
that one under my boot,
and cause it to rain.

Jeane Breinig

MOOD MUSIC

My father, looking towards the sea,
his German upper lip, thin and stiff.
Blue eyes, cool as water,
a fisherman, scanning the horizon,
looking for signs of feed,
his fair skin blistered by the wind.

My mother, moving across slippery
low tide cliffs,
hunting for black seaweed,
a certain length in May.
Her dark eyes rimmed with gray,
blend in with craggy boulders.
Her brown fingers twist and pull
a sun-dried winter treat.

He learned to set free the first salmon
of the season,
a show of faith,
a thank you in advance.

She learned to make Swedish pancakes,
and how to drive
the bottle green Buick
with dented fenders.

He learned to say, "Háwaa dagwáang,"
thank you dear, in Haida.
She learned to play Gin Rummy.

Jeane Breinig, Haida from Kasaan and Ketchikan, Alaska. She is a contributing editor to this edition of *Alaska Native Writers, Storytellers & Orators*.

They netted sockeye
from the mouth of the Karta River,
smoked them in a home-built tin shed
in our back yard.

They made home brew,
pushed back the rug,
and danced to worn out 45's.

Now, "String of Pearls" or
"In the Mood" still makes me
tap my foot,
bounce my hip,
and start to rock.

George Westdahl

A HOUSE I REMEMBER

The house is old, and I am twelve years of age. The house is very large, sitting on the banks of a river in a deserted ghost town.

The house was built by my grandfather, Ketchuk Westdahl, a long time ago. Across the slough is where my other great-grand-father, George Waskey, built his cabin. The cabin's roof has caved in but the rest still stands.

I remember Grandmother bringing me to Fish Village with Axel, Augusta, Nick, and Donny. My uncle, John Westdahl, followed later.

My first time here, Grandmother says this is where I began, before I was born, and where I belong now. I feel good. The house is old and still strong. The kitchen is very large with a potbellied stove and a cooking stove. Four very large windows in the living room and a very roomy bedroom in three corners of the house with two in between.

Nobody has been here for years, says Axel, but the cooking uten-sils are still here, the beds are made, and tea is in the cupboard. My grandmother moves through the house as if she were here all along. She instructs Donny and me to go fetch some water after we've chopped wood and started a fire in the large stoves.

George Westdahl, Yup'ik from Yukon River, Alaska.

My uncle arrives and tells Axel and me to take his skiff up the slough and hunt for ducks. I remember coming back. It is dark and quiet. We can see the lights in the large windows of the house from the beach. This time the house is warm, tea is in the teapot which has not been used for years untold.

Augusta and Grandmother pluck the ducks Axel and I caught and killed up the slough, while Uncle John asks us about what we saw up the slough. After eating duck soup at the large table, Uncle John tells of his childhood here, when it was a village before TB struck. He recalls swimming in the slough as a young boy and warming by the fire, also working when the barge stopped by. He says my grandfather was a big man (and my uncle is very big), a good hunter and fisherman. Uncle John tells me of my father being born after Grandfather died and of how Grandmother raised all the boys by herself in this house, four boys and two girls. I can see the house was large enough for more.

I slept on a mattress made from goose down many years ago. My father slept in the same bed as a boy, probably with the same quilt.

My grandmother in the morning wakens me to go to the slough and wash up and start the day by greeting the world. I start a fire while everybody else is asleep, then to the slough I go and wash myself, looking around the ghost town. Trees have grown where houses have been and people have lived. A large sandbar has formed in the mouth of the slough to the Yukon River right in front of the house.

My Grandmother asks me, what did I see? I told her that the sandbar did not belong there and that the water was clear and crisp, also that the house needed painting. I told her of the two ducks swimming in the slough.

Grandmother then asks me what kind of day I'm going to have? I tell her the day looks good, clear skies, a good day to set a net for fish and hunting ducks up the slough. Grandmother says she will pick berries while my uncle and I go and hunt the ducks.

Augusta boils water for tea and cooks duck eggs that Axel and Donny have found by the little creek not far from the big house. During breakfast Grandmother tells her son, Uncle John, of what I said: The house needs painting. He asks who will stay when we have to go back to where we came from? Grandmother says someday that I will live here if I wish to.

Uncle John asks me if I will return? Of course, I tell him. My father was born here and my grandfather died here. This is a place for me.

Now I wonder about the large house in the ghost town of my father's birth.

Fred Bigjim

GASLIGHT[1]

"Yes, what will you have?"
You want to answer
"Happiness and peace of mind."
But a voice says, "Oly."

As the evening turns to night,
You notice that the Gaslight
Becomes more crowded,
And reality farther away.

You look around at all the lonely people
Looking for other lonely people.
As the night turns to early morning,
The Gaslight becomes loud, smoky,
And the lonely people become lonelier.

"Last call—"
People yell, "No!"
"You can't let us go back to reality."
Music blares, "All the lonely people,
Where did you all come from."

You leave, knowing you'll be back,
Because the Gaslight beckons you,
   Fools you,
     Seduces you,

Fred Bigjim, Iñupiaq from Nome and Sinrock, Alaska.

Drugs you into thinking
That
This is reality.

– *Originally published in* Sinrock,
*Fred Bigjim, Press-22, Portland,
Oregon, 1983.*

NOTE

Gaslight is a bar in Anchorage.

BALLET IN BETHEL

Ballet in Bethel.
Skintight dancers spinning across a stage,
Displaying only fantasies of a foreign world.

Opera in Shishmaref.
Piercing and screaming, the words unknown to all,
The sound shatters the stillness of the night.

Mime in Elim.
Stark faces of fools
Saying nothing.

Repertory Theater in Barrow.
Actors waiting for Godot
In a play that never reaches our world.

Symphony in Wales.
Instruments of time
Being blown by history
Of one world overpowering another.

Impact disguised as cultural creativity.
Upheaval replacing the entertainment
Of the ceremonial dances,
The blanket tosses, folklore,
And games of strength.

No more cultural gatherings,
Only a ballet in Bethel.

– Originally published in Sinrock,
Fred Bigjim, Press-22, Portland,
Oregon, 1983.

Andrew Evan

(UNTITLED)

I was working for Alaska Railroad at Hunter, Alaska, as section labor. I got three days pass from my foreman in 1952 and after I came back from my pass, I quit and went home to Copper Center.

While I was in Seward, I bought an old-time phonograph from a lady in Seward. She had many old-time records. I went to a record shop and bought two new records which it just got – songs by Lefty Fizzell. One was "I Love You a Thousand Ways," and the other was "If You Got the Money, I Got the Time."

While I was home I stayed in a tent outside my sister and brother-in-law's home. It was June and was really warm. My niece and nephew didn't know I had come home. As I was laying to rest I heard a bunch of children back of the log cabin. They were playing church. The next to my oldest nephew was the preacher and his brother was the altar boy. They had a collection plate and used beer caps for money. Donald the preacher asked for the altar boy, and his brother Warren came forward to collect money for church, and after the collection Donald asked if everything was ready. Donald told the congregation that the first song they were going to sing was "If You Got the Money, I Got the Time."

Andrew Evan, Yup'ik from Southwest Alaska.

I couldn't help but laugh to myself. I went inside my sister's house and told what the children were doing. She was upset about it, and I told her not to scold them or spank them. Anyway, she sold the phonograph and records to Dorothy Secondchief from Mile 31 on the Glenn Highway. She just got tired of hearing those two over and over again. I was discouraged about it but I didn't say anything.

Mary Jane Peterson

CANNERY CHILDREN

memories of childhood,
                         of playing in the canneries
among fishing boats called the David Wayne,
Shirley Carol and PJ11.
                  catching stickleback fish under the
cookhouse with my cousins, climbing in the ware-
houses, getting stuck in the gray muck under the
docks.
stealing a skiff and being rescued, the canneries
were our playground.
                  while we waited for our pots of food,
to feed our families,
                         finding and selling glass Japanese
balls on the beach, to buy cracker jacks, bubble gum
and strawberry pop.
                  being scared on the beach by brown
bears, climbing the banks to escape the tide.
Japanese and Dagos who gave us candy, fruit and
laughter on the Fourth of Julys.
                  wild flowers and bird nest brought
home to mother with love.

Mary Jane Peterson, Aleut from Anchorage, Alaska.

Dixie Alexander

WILLOW WAS HER NAME

Willow was her name
I needed her roots
the touch her soul the earth

Some stayed natural
some were dyed
some were split
but the coil stayed whole

Born again one day by these hands
that coil her into beautiful baskets

Willow was her name
when winter winds blow
she'll sway bare from side to side
but the beauty is still there

Dixie Alexander, Gwich'in Athabaskan from Fort Yukon, Alaska.

Susie Silook

THE ANTI-DEPRESSION
ULIIMAAQ[1]

Ungipaghani tamaani (Among the stories around here) there's the one of the depression so severe that I *had* to invent important reasons to live. I left my children in Anchorage, in the city, and went home to Gambell.[2]

I became the nocturnal creature I am in the absence of family responsibility. My isolation was broken only by the need to dump the "honey bucket," which always amazed me with the quantity of my shit. I also had to haul water and stove oil. Looking back, I suspect I went home to die.

All this hauling brought me in contact with what I remember most about this bleak period of soul sickness: the wind. As I walked the mile or so for the water, the wind would bully the five-gallon jugs on the sled behind me. Sometimes he shoved them over and I'd right them, knowing he'd win again by sheer unrelenting persistence. If he was in a loving mood, the full jugs would be pulling me behind them, racing to catch up.

Sometimes small things keep you alive.

Susie Silook, St. Lawrence Island Yupik from Gambell, Alaska.

I worked in short, uninspired spurts in the unheated room set aside for carving walrus ivory. Outside, the wind would furiously work to find any way he could into the house, making those mighty sounds of air claiming its domain.

The house I was born in was originally F.A.A.[3] housing – white people's housing – set far apart from the extended family lay-out of the original village site. That village I'll call "Gambell I." The clusters of *Aymaaramkat, Pugughileghmiit*,[4] and other clans, revolved around the big open space in the center where the village activities of exercise, dance, ritual, and competition took place.

Wrestling matches to the death were held there. The tug-of-war between the locals and whaling ship crews were held there. It may have served as the launch pad for many a flying *Alingnalghii* (Frightening One).[5] Today, an ugly B.I.A.[6] school sits there. Every building is a memorial of sorts. It was a place teeming with life and the occasional death of some clumsy wrestler.

People are neatly arranged in the rows of symmetrical, identical, H.U.D.[7] projects of "Gambell II." Your neighbor is determined by the next name on the list, not the ancient clan system. The old village looks ghostly but remains lived in. Every available living space is taken in Gambell I and II. Every living space is overcrowded.

So, I was born in neither Gambell I nor II. Add to this another small tale: my Iñupiaq-Irish mother was an orphan sent to St. Lawrence Island along with other orphans of a diphtheria epidemic in the late '30s. The State decided they'd make excellent new blood. *New blood.* I don't know what problems there were with the old blood, but that is what happened.

There I was, U.S.D.A.[8] new blood and all, a woman, and not essential to anyone's survival. There was never a knock at my door, mainly because no one knocks on my island. The custom is to enter and receive acknowledgment in the entrance. White people who stay for any length of time post *Please Knock* signs on their doors, unable to equate the place to Rome, I suppose.

If there is a knock at your door you know it's a foreigner, or a confused, relocated, born-again Native. I'd forget who and where I was and knock, and people would admonish me. The knock has been a very effective warning since the missionary days to clean up your reformed Native act quickly before letting the *laluramka*[9] in. If you are local (and knock) you have made people hide those stinky walrus flippers for nothing.

So, anyone ten and over scolded me for knocking, insulted. The ten and under crowd sometimes mistook me for a white lady and asked questions about me in Yupik, thinking I wouldn't understand.

I understood this much: sometimes I silenced whole rooms with my entrance, the outsider-insider. I knew this place is where I would come to die. It is *home*. Yet, I had to wonder who I was every time I resisted the urge to knock. Here, only the intruder knocks politely. There I was, then, in the middle of great despair, new blood, flirting with only the wind and wondering what side of the damn door I belonged on when the whole point of this narrative occurred, finally.

Two women I was trying to unite on the tusk, although working well independently, refused unification, like the vast world between Gambell I and Gambell II, like the need to live and the need to die in me. The piece was half done, and done poorly. I left my carving in the freezing work room and it froze.

I hadn't a plan upon beginning, and none came to visit.

My sister-in-law did, however, walking in un-knocked like the wholesome, life-long, old-blood villager she is. And she wanted to see the *Uliimaaq*. So I went to get the two women who were on the same tusk but not a part of the same story. But coming out of the frigid room they broke, almost as if they decided to go their separate ways and did so right there on my mother's linoleum floor, easily escaping my refreshing new blood to knock or not to knock hands.

It was a clean and final break.

A year later I decided the women of the carving were anti-depression *Uliimaaq* because I needed to believe in the power of such things. And I did leave that depression that was distilled in alcohol behind.

A year later I placed one of the women in the coffin of my youngest brother, for that is where she belongs. The other one I keep with me. Sometimes I take her out and hold her and think of the other side of the story, lying there with the bones of my brother.

Too little too late.

I think that if only I had had the right words or that little extra time, money, magic, he would still be alive, but he's not, though my heart doesn't completely know this yet.

One day, that inevitable archeologist is going to find his coffin with his bones and the ivory woman holding a comb. He will have to say that, although no documentation is available on the carving, the man must have been prominent and well-loved and important and highly esteemed to carry such a thing into the next world, given that he had lived and died at a time when such things, such things had been outlawed by God.

It will be the one thing any archeologist absolutely ever got right.

To Daniel Silook (Aluukaneq)

NOTES

1. Carving or sculpture
2. A Siberian Yupik village on St. Lawrence Island in Northwest Alaska
3. Federal Aviation Administration
4. Two of the extended family clans of St. Lawrence Island
5. Shaman
6. Bureau of Indian Affairs
7. Housing and Urban Development
8. United States Department of Agriculture
9. White person

UNCLE GOOD INTENTIONS

He stepped off the plane shaking
and went to the nearest bar for a quick
one or two shots of medicine.

He said he was relieved
he was
to find his long lost sisters

even more relieved to find
they were not bow-legged
and pigeon toed little
Native women
as he had feared.

His half sisters.

all these years he hadn't seen them
since their mother took to the sea
that day his, their, father caught her
beating him with his hip waders.

Said he was the reason they'd fought
Dad gave him permission to go fishing
but no one told that
mean little Eskimo woman
Susie
that

so she whipped him *good*.

My mother was born at sea
heading back to Alaska with a mother
who was a runner.

She was running from an Indian boarding school
when she begged my grandfather to help her escape
and he helped her and
himself to a mother for his sons.

My family predicament
according to half uncle Doug
read like this:
Carol was a shameful unwed mother
Johnny a no good womanizer
spreading his precious seed and
Rose was nothing but a nigger lover.

Said the only children he liked
were Barry and me.

The only children he never met were
Barry and me.

Asked my mother who she felt she
belonged to
her white
or Eskimo
side.

When she said Eskimo
he said didn't blame her
cause that's who raised her.

He liked his half brother Walter, though,
cause Walter could drink like a man,
you know.

Said only that no one was ever gonna
kill *him* in a bar
when asked what happened to
their father, Mr. Faegins,
that man with the accent
or their other brother Clairmont.

Told them their father had
searched high and low
for them after
Susie ran.

That mean little Eskimo woman.

My mother was happy to see
him coming
and happier to
see him going,
long lost
Uncle Doug of the
good Catholic intentions.

ADVENTURE IN CHINATOWN 1958

My father was a steel worker in Skokie Illinois.
  He would leave before dawn and return long after the
    sun no one ever saw in Chicago went down.

My mother says the buildings were too tall and the air
    stank.
  The only place I went was church, she remembers.

My brother Barry was a month old, making me nothing
    but
  a nagging worry in my mother's mind.
  No more babies she thought
  after the third child
  after the fourth child
  after the fifth child
  and the sixth child.

My father's hunting fed his family
  and his mother's family
  and his brother's family.

People still wonder why he agreed to the
  government relocation program and
  without my mother's consent
  took his Yupik family to Chicago.

In those days they paid the expenses to move
  Native folk out of Native neighborhoods
  and into Asian ones.

It would save them from the mistake
  of the reservation
  would solve the problem
  of that persistent Native identity.

My sister used to take all her clothes off
  and run about naked –
  that's everyone's favorite Chicago story.

My other sister got lost and only spoke Yupik
    and so they took her all over Chinatown
    looking for her non-existent Asian family.

Someone must have told them
    that child is not Asian for
    she remembers eating ice cream at the
    precinct and my father remembers
    how big her eyes were when he
    came to claim his
    relocated but not indigenous to
    Chinatown girl.

Mrs. Silook, why do you want to poison your children?
    the psychiatrist asked my mother.

My father would repeat day in and day out
    Sakuuma paneghaallequusi
    You will all starve if something happens to me.

Finally my Iñupiaq-Irish mother who spoke only Yupik
    shouted
    Then we should buy poison and prepare ourselves!

My father wouldn't go to work unless
    she stayed up all night to watch everyone.

The woman was *tired* you got that?

I didn't mean it, she told the lady,
    I was tired of Saavla saying we were going to starve.

So, Custer's Last Stand II
    or infinity
    lasted one month
    in Chinatown.

Better to starve as a Yupik than as impossible immigrant
    read the fortune cookie of my father
    who says only that
    Chicago is too big to remember.

Anna Smith

WOLVES

Fresh out of rehab and he's using again. His friends tell her. Later on, she hears the wheels of his car howl against slick, snow covered streets. Time stops. Restless, he circles around her as he explains. She thinks that everything he says is a dead end road. As he talks to her, it's like he's running, slipping, sliding and spinning around on polished ice. He pauses, lights his cigarette, rubs his eyes, and looks at a video she's rented on wolves. He turns on a light and his eyes glow yellow.

She thinks, tonight, the moon is a light that dazzles all wolves out of their lairs. She sees them running down a maze of paths that twist and turn around spruce trees. Their wolf fur brushes past tangles of spruce needles as they hasten across sculpted white dunes. They run so fast that their paws hiss as they glide by.

He sips coffee and watches the wolves with her. She presses the pause button; time stops and the wolves freeze in mid-stride. He says he read somewhere that time slows down near a black hole just before that moment it gets pulled into it. He turns on the stereo tuner and searches for a good station. He tunes in to an old Stones song called "Time Waits For No One."

Anna Smith, Tlingit from Anchorage, Alaska.

On the tv screen, a flickering image of the wolves blends together and they seem to float above the snow. She feels like her heart has paused between beats. The phone rings and no one gets up to answer it. Finally, her answering machine catches the call and the ringing stops. She looks at the wolves pressing against her tv screen.

"I know I'm running out of time," he finally says.

Now, he's sitting on the couch, eating vanilla ice-cream out of its container.

He says, "I can't go on like this, but I can't stop."

She takes his spoon and eats some ice-cream. It tastes cold and sweet; her tongue feels numb from the cold.

"Why can't you stop?" she asks.

"I don't want to."

He tries to pull her close to him on the couch. She stands up, throws her spoon at him and pushes, slaps and kicks him away from her. He reaches up, grabs her arms and tries to pull her down on the couch. She feels herself tumbling down as he pins her arms behind her and holds her close to him. She feels the stubble on his face brush against her cheek. She shivers, closes her eyes, and kisses his neck and lips. He whispers in her ear and it sounds like falling snow. Her heart thrashes like a hooked salmon on a riverbank.

When he leaves, his tires spin on glare ice. She picks up the remote and lets the wolves go.

WATSÍX SHAAYÍ MOUNTAINS

Before he died,
her father told her about them.
Now, she's driving to Carcross,
on a lost road that curves
around the shadows of those mountains.
It's night, wind whispers and hisses
as she follows the bright beams
of her headlights as they plow
a slender path through darkness.

She is afraid of shadows and feels ghosts
slip past her windshield
like moths hovering towards fire.
She turns up her music to silence
the sound of their wings
as they sizzle and melt into light.

Once, her father told her that Raven
freed the stars, moon and sun.
He tossed them up with his beak
and watched them scatter
across the night sky.

Tonight, waves of northern lights
fall back to earth like tossed buckets of paint.
The wind crackles with electricity.
She rolls down her window, reaches out
and opens her palm to let the sparks fall into it.

In the distance, she sees small homes
that line the shores of Lake Bennett.
Later, as she walks around the lake,
she feels her father's presence.

At her cousin's house,
old family photos circle the wall.
In one picture, her father smiles
and he is a young man again

posing with his hunting rifle.
In all the pictures
faded faces from the past,
dispersed around a wooden cross,
gaze back at her with the names
of Tlingit clans still on their lips.

NAATASSE HÉEN

Light years later, he's an old man,
who still remembers the salmon jumping,
glimmering silver like the sky.
After all this time,
he's finally come home again.
Outside, paint is chipped, faded,
and the wood is worn on his house.

Later on, like old times,
he sips strong coffee
at the kitchen table.
Its surface is stained with circles
and scarred with dents.
He traces each scar with his fingers,
then he closes his eyes to rest.

He dreams that he's on a skiff
following the current.
He pulls in a net brimming with fish.
His hands feel numb from icy waves.

His tongue becomes a net
that fills up with Tlingit.
He feels the words form
on his lips, grow wings
and follow the wild geese
back to the T'àkhú River.

He swims across the sky
and thinks of broken spirits
with silver scales
and the place where two rivers meet
and become one again.

When he returns to the riverbank,
he sees that he is the fish,
the mountains, the shore,
that he is the water
running through the narrows.

Diane Lxeís' Benson

RIVER WOMAN (from *SPIRIT OF WOMAN*)

The setting is a present-day fish camp.

LIGHTS UP. Heeyyyeee. I haven't seen you folks in long time. You gettin away from that city for little bit and come visit us Indians in fish camp? Huh? Heh heh. It's good to see you! (SHAKES HANDS WITH COUPLE PEOPLE IN AUDIENCE) You sit down now. I got to get these potatoes done. Hey. You remember how we used to get potatoes out of that little garden back home? Right in the middle of the village? Yeah. It's not like that anymore tho. I miss that little garden. Everyone always used to get potatoes from there. Nice brown potatotes ... from the nice brown earth, ... picked by us nice brown Indians! Ayeeee?! Ha Ha! Good times. We had good times ... fore those homestead things. I guess that what they call it.

Hey, you kids get 'way from that fish wheel, you gonna get hurt! You want sometin to do you come cut some fish strips for auntie. Come on now. Aho'. That's right, you too Charla. Dat Charla she good kid. I been takin' care of her now going on eight months. Her dad didn't get some kinda paper done or something so the government could know that was der land so they took it 'way from him. I don't know how they do that, but they did, and now they got this homestead thing on 160 acres and all these people been comin' in lookin' around like they all won Bingo or somethin. Her dad went down river lookin' for work, and I guess he's workin' some mining thing up north. Just where he don't wanna go. Poor thing. He really misses Charla. (SHAKES HER HEAD) That's how it gets for our people.

Diane Lxeís' Benson, Tlingit from Sitka, Alaska.

(GETS UP AND THROWS POTATO PEELINGS) Ha ha!! That raven sure like get into mischief. Ohhh dat reminds me! The other day, when I was in Ruby gettin mail from my sister, fore I come back out here, they was bulldozin' for some building or somethin' and I was just sittin there visiting with Norma. Well, while we was sittin there this white man got outta dat bulldozer with a hand full of Hershey bars and put them in this tin box, and then put them by his seat in the bulldozer, and then went in the woods. Go do his business I guess! Ha ha! And this raven was watchin him. After dat man go, this raven went hopping across the hood of the bulldozer and then jumped onto the seat. Dang if he didn't take out a Hershey bar! I was tellin' Norma, "Look! Dat raven's got a Hershey bar! Were both just lookin'. Then that raven set that Hershey bar out on the hood. Then he jumped in and got 'nother Hershey bar, and he kept doin that. He got must been seven Hershey bars and stacked them all on that hood. By this time, we could see that white man was comin' back, and that raven he tried to get all them Hershey bars in his beak! Me and Norma, we're just laughin'! Holdin' our mouths shut so that raven don't hear. And that raven is so greedy, he can't lift all them Hershey bars, and that white man is comin'! Finally, that raven settles on must been six Hershey bars with that last Hershey bar meltin' on the hot hood! Ohhh you should have seen dat white man's face! He look in his tin box and got no Hershey bars, and then he sees dat one just meltin' on the hood! Me and Norma can't stand it. We just busted up! That man he look over at us. I know he think we took his candy. He come over to us, and we try to tell him the raven took it, but he don't believe us. They always thinkin' we're tryin' to take somethin' from them. It was raven. Dat white man don't know but his people just as greedy as that raven. It seems like they always think everything belong to them.

(SHE PULLS A PAPER OUT OF HER POCKET) Oh. I almost forgot! I got this in the mail. I never got to learn reading too good, so could you read it to me? (PASSES IT TO FIRST PERSON IN AUDIENCE) What does it say? No, tell me, what does it say to me? Well tell me what it is then. Who's it from?

(AUDIENCE MEMBER READING): The Division of
  Family and Youth Services
So what's it say? What's it about? You have to read aloud,
  my hearing is kind of bum.

It says:
Since the documents we sent several months ago, regarding the
legal guardianship of Charla Carrie Albert have not been returned, and since it has been reported that said child has been
abandoned, it is hereby ordered that Charla Carrie Albert be
turned over to State custody until which time it is deemed in the
best interest of the child to maintain residence with an appropriate family guardian.

What does that mean? What the hell does that mean? You
  mean they gonna take her from us? I been takin' good
  care of her. You look at her. She can cut fish real good.
  She digs up potatoes and makes her own bed, and she
  even the only one who helps me with the honey bucket!
  Her father had to go to work! I been takin' care of her
  good. She likes fish camp! We have to stay here til we
  got our food for the winter. Well that's it. I won't take
  her back. That's all there is to it. We have a good life.
  She gonna have a good life. I got the best life there is to
  have. LIGHTS FADE

*– Originally premiered in Anchorage,
Alaska in 1996 at the Out North
Theater.*

WHAT SHE WANTED

(LIGHTS OUT. BEGIN IN DARK. HEAR THE HORN AGAIN. LIGHTS FADE UP AS GROUP SINGS AN ENTRANCE SONG ... Hu Hu Hu ah hei hei hei ah ha.... IN THIS PIECE LIGHTING SHOULD REACH THE FOUR CORNERS OF THE STAGE. SOMBER. NEED A SPOT SHOOTING STRAIGHT DOWN CENTER STAGE. THIS WILL BE USED AT THE END. SHOULD EXPERIENCE SENSE OF ISOLATION IN THIS PIECE.)

It probably was not what she wanted
Arranged
He took her hand with such force
feeling nothing of her
It was the way
He was Eagle
It was still this way

They say he died a sudden death
a gun shot
don't know who did it
why
was it a white man?
was it his own hand.

It probably was not what she wanted
Loving her so deeply
she would lose her breath
Remember? They'd laugh,
at boarding school you
would sneak a pie out the window,
oh, I liked the apple pie!
sitting on the ledge,
you must of dropped it three stories!
Oh, James, it wasn't that far.
Oh it was so far,
that time.
But we don't talk about it.

His sister was taken by Chinese
merchants, that's what they say.
They don't say.

He hid that thought a long time ago.
At sixteen he left his village to go
to San Francisco to look for her.
After a year, he came home
to stare at the dead volcano
with only an echo in his head
of her smile.

It probably was not what she wanted
But the snake in the bottom of her will
seared from her mouth with every tip
and turn of her own weakness
The cannibal that saturated her
blouse with his malted juices.
He possessed the house
and many generations.

I turn to the pink on the wall
trying to feel her spirit
with each gentle stroke
of my index finger
seeking to know the truth
on the other side.

Her moon came in the night
and she was so afraid of
grandmother's slurred
rage
She hid the soiled sheets in the wall.

I could hear a piano
and little Russian boots
that taped little black
leather messages into
my three year old brain.

The drum would beat
from old potlatches that
hadn't been seen in decades.

She could dance to them
but the mask of the dreamer

left only a shadow in the rain
and a tumor in her memory

You leave your mother alone!
    But why did you leave??

Don't you bother her!
    Don't ask questions!
        She's been through enough!
    But why did you leave?

That was a long time ago.
    But why did you leave . . .

It probably was not what she wanted

Could you imagine?!
A Tlingit woman ran a USO
And she wouldn't talk English, oh no.
And even the Russian man
found her too tough to break.

She raised a Yup'ik girl
and taught her all the songs and dances
She taught her to be honorable
woman of the Snail House
to share the songs of the T'akdeintaan.

Grandchild
I hear you
cry at night
Grandma is drunk again
They want to take your brothers away
Your aunts and uncles
they never come for you.

The hollow chime
of the law rang clearly
in foster homes lined
with promises

Little brown feet
widened by freedom

do not fit in
patent leather shoes

It probably was not what she wanted
But she married the white man anyway.
He kissed her only when she wanted to
and that was good enough
for a time

She could peel the pink off the wall
Two stories of family silence
locked in bottles hidden in
the darkness of the sofa,
a vanity that reflected
no mercy
Just a tear stained face
scratching for hope
in lipstick

NOW THEY WANNABE US

– Little kids
playing war. We liked that.
Playing war.
Cowboys and Indians?!!
Silence.
Maybe we play
Germans and Americans
instead –

What do you wannaBE?
I don't know.
But if the white people of Ketchikan had said
We wannaBE Indians, we wannaBE
Tlingits, We wannaBE Haidas,
We WannaBE Tsimpsians!
We woulda died
laughin'.

They called the cops on him,
I was thirteen then. He was seventeen.
Saw him hangin around waitin'
He was waitin for me. They called
the police on him. Indian boy outside
a white man's house, not wanting to be seen
by my foster family. They called the police
and they took him away.

Saw him two days later.
Cops broke his ribs. We walked, and the basketball
team from Kay-High came by, threw beer bottles
at us
Indians. At us Natives. At us
people, who tried to hide so we could talk.
They called him ugly, they called him
stupid, they called him a salmon cruncher,
a siwash, an idiot, an Indian . . .

If you had told me then,
that they'd wannaBE us, I'da
spit my gum.

If you had told me then,
they would hang on the words of an
Indian, I'da thought you were crazy.

If you had told me then,
that there would be a day when
white people would brag *they* were
Indian, and would buy
Indian books, write
Indian stories, AND . . .
dance our
dances, drum our songs, tour our
villages, buy our
art, make our crests, take
our pictures, and keep our
names,
as their own, –
WANNABE us – , I'da
left you standin' there
shakin' my head. Callin' your doctor.
Not believin' a word.

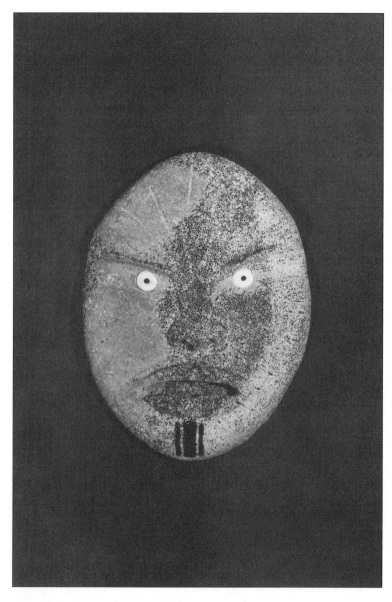

WHALEBONE MASK (Iñupiaq)
Johnny Evak, Sr., from Kotzebue, Alaska, made this mask from whale-bone, pigment, and walrus ivory.
(Courtesy of the Anchorage Museum of History and Art)

CONTEXTS

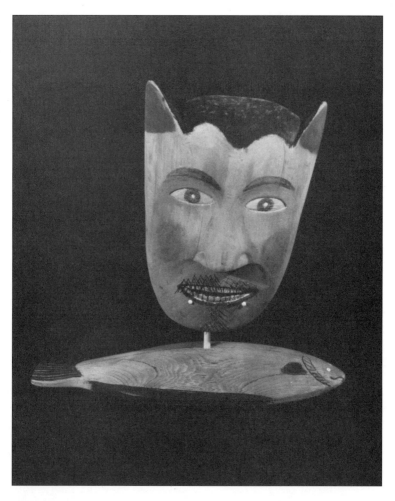

MEDICINE MAN (Yup'ik)
Jimmie Fritz from Toksook Bay, Alaska, made this sculpture from
wood, walrus ivory, and baleen of a medicine man who changes
whenever he performs his magic.
(Courtesy of the Anchorage Museum of History and Art)

Marie Meade

TRANSLATION ISSUES

In elementary school I learned to recognize written English words phonetically, but I didn't speak the language until I went to high school in Bethel. Everyone spoke Yup'ik at home and in Nunapicuaq (Nunapitchuk), the community where I grew up. We didn't have to use the individual words that we were being introduced to in the classroom. So it was only when I left the village and went to Bethel, where I interacted with classmates and new friends who were speaking in English, that I had to start practicing the little bit of English that I knew. It was difficult. I still have a hard time. By now I've been translating from Yup'ik to English and from English to Yup'ik since the early 1970s.

There are challenges in translating, partly because English and Yup'ik are from completely different language families, and because the cultures are so different. For instance, we don't have gender. There are no separate Yup'ik words for "he," "she," or "it." We just use one ending for all of them. To tell who performed the action, we look at the context, and then, when translating to English, we use either "he" or "she," "him" or "her," as appropriate.

Marie Meade is a Yup'ik linguist from Nunapitchuk, Alaska. She has worked for more than 20 years researching, transcribing, and translating Yup'ik oral histories, and also teaching and writing bilingual educational materials.

Another difference is that we have singular, dual and plural while English has only singular and plural. So if I have to translate the word *ayagtuk*, I need to remember that in Yup'ik we automatically know that there are two people who are going. In translating that word into English I have to say, "They two are going" instead of just "They are going." You have to somehow let the reader know, if it's a written translation, that there are two people who are going.

Also, there are concepts or words that are difficult to translate into a single English word, and vice versa; there are concepts in English that you can't translate by using just one word. In both cases you have to give long descriptions or explanations using many words. And I don't even bother translating some words. For instance, when the Yup'ik speaker uses *qasgiq* (often translated as "community house"), *qaspeq* (a woman's cotton over-parka), *uluaq* (a semi-lunar woman's knife), or *qayaq* (usually written as "kayak" in English), in most cases, I don't translate them. For instance, if I'm translating a sentence that means "The woman using an uluaq removed it" – *Uluarluku aug'araa* – then I use *uluaq* instead of "woman's knife."

Another example is the word for sealgut parka, *imarnin*. It's often translated as a "raincoat" or "sealgut parka." It's something that you wear as an outer garment, and does protect the hunter from the rain, but to say "raincoat" doesn't quite fit how I look at an *imarnin*. It doesn't take into account the way the shamans had always used an *imarnin* in their healing rituals. The garment had a special sacredness to it. If I just call it a raincoat, it's not adequate. It doesn't express that sacredness. *Akutaq* (often translated as "Eskimo ice cream") is like that too. It is a ceremonial food, a special dish that is important to ceremony and gathering.

There are other parts of the language that are nearly untranslatable. For example, there's an enclitic in Yup'ik, *-gguq*, that I don't translate every time. It doesn't always mean the same thing. Usually, it means something like "it is said," or "it was reported to me." This indicates that the speaker did not take part in or directly witness the events himself, but had heard about them from someone else. Because it occurs so often in the narratives told by Yup'ik storytellers, I don't always translate it in the English version.

Another challenge with translating across cultures as well as languages is the audience. You hope that your audience is everybody, Yup'ik and non-Yup'ik. And today, even if the audience is made up of Yup'iks, they might not understand a lot of the background information that I've been talking about. So as a translator I include all that, especially with the old words or those that are no longer used in everyday language. I try to give their meaning and appropriate context, usually in footnotes or a glossary. I use myself as an example to guide me in giving background information. When I hear a new word, I want to understand it, so I provide the word's definition and etymology to my readers, just as I would like to have.

Most of my translation is done from oral recordings, and it's hard to capture the rhythm and the stresses that people use when they're speaking. You try to use words to capture that. Yup'ik words are fascinating. So are English words. I just try to use the word that might get the feeling, the picture, the storyteller's style across.

My feeling about translating from Yup'ik to English and back again – whether stories, technical information, or legal explanations – is that literal translation usually isn't enough. It distorts the meaning, and the translation sounds awkward in the second language because of the different grammars. The main task is to pay attention to getting the message across, and not just the words.

William Schneider

CONSIDERATIONS ABOUT THE ORAL TRADITION AND WRITING

Most Alaska Natives grew up with a deep appreciation for things they learned from their elders, their responsibility to pass on the oral accounts, and the pleasure of listening to their elders share stories from the past. For today's elders, the oral tradition remains the primary source of knowledge, the guidepost for subsistence pursuits, and the explanation for the everyday and the extraordinary. The old stories, some serious, some funny, explain how the world was created, the correct way for people to treat each other and the other creatures that inhabit our world, and the lessons necessary to live successful lives. Such stories are told at special times, to commemorate an event, to mark the advent of the long winter season, to celebrate a Midwinter gathering, or to mark clan rights to property. The oral tradition represents a context for meaningful discourse between people who know each other very well and are privileged to participate.

William Schneider is Curator of Oral History for the Alaska Polar Regions Department, Elmer Rasmuson Library, at the University of Alaska Fairbanks.

When an elder speaks, the audience plays an important role, encouraging the teller, and giving clues to their needs for clarification and explanation. In Iñupiaq society there is often a person who serves to confirm the story by nodding and saying, "Yes, that is true." In Athabaskan groups, a young girl may be encouraged to sit near an older woman to provide the focal point for the stories. Such contexts are as important to the storytelling as the story itself.

The assumption is sometimes made that a good recording in the elder's own words can then be transcribed and translated (if need be) and reproduced on paper, thereby giving a literate audience the same benefits as actually listening to an old-timer as he/she is telling the story. In the last twenty years there have been numerous examples of this approach, from elders' conferences to life histories.

But going from the oral to the written form involves some important changes that may not be noticed by members of a literate tradition whose oral roots have been long forgotten. One such shift is in the audience. No longer is the elder speaking to the privileged few; everyone who can read becomes a potential member of the audience, regardless of how much they know or do not know about the culture. In the oral setting the audience is controlled, limited, and prescribed by the storyteller and the cultural group. When the story is written, the storyteller has no control over who will read the stories, nor does he know what clarification they will need. The level of explanation the storyteller provides is determined primarily by those present at the time of the telling, not by his/her prediction of future readers. In the written form the role of interpretation is taken out of the speaker's hands. Sometimes it is taken up by a writer who puts the book together; often it is left out, thereby creating a void. The audience which can appreciate such a book is then limited to those familiar with the culture.

Oral and written forms of communication are thus not always mutually supportive. A problem may develop when people become so concerned about preserving the stories and testimony of the elders (particularly of traditional knowledge) in a recorded or written form that they forget about the value of the spoken word. In their haste to preserve the wisdom of the elders, they forget the importance of the process of telling stories and passing on knowledge orally. It is easy then to forget that a story is a gift, and in some cultures a possession. The owner of a story chooses to share it; it becomes a gift. Often it is a gift to be listened to, but cannot be repeated except by the owner. There is an element of reciprocity here. The teller chooses to give his story to an audience he selects; the audience feels privileged to participate in the session and agrees to honor the story by upholding whatever ownership is recognized within the culture.

The interaction between the teller and the audience becomes a dramatic performance. As Dennis Tedlock has pointed out, each presentation is marked by the personalities of those present, and every telling is slightly different, shaped by the things that have happened before, the relationships between those present, and the intent of the teller. Despite the best efforts to describe what it was like to be present, the experience cannot be completely recreated in either written or recorded form. The products derived from the oral traditions, whether they be recordings, transcripts, radio shows, or written pieces, are valuable in their own right, but these forms of communication receive their sustenance from the spoken word and from the actual experiences of those present when the story is told. The writer then must convey not only the words of the story, but enough contextual material for the readers to imagine themselves present at the telling.

Storytelling is a life skill which is particularly evident during periods of rapid cultural change. It's not a matter of coincidence that Natives in the Northwestern Arctic, the Lower Yukon and the Arctic Slope have pioneered elders' conferences at this point in their history. These conferences represent a continuing search for meaningful ways to learn from their elders. I don't think this process has yet reached its most fruitful stage. We can look forward to continued searching for dialogue.

I think we'll also see a continuing interest in producing written works which emphasize first person narration as opposed to works written about Alaska Natives. This trend has been facilitated by the tape recorder, but the origins of the movement go back to a discontent by Natives with outsiders who came in, collected stories and then interpreted them incorrectly. The fallout from this has been very healthy for all of us. I suspect it will continue as we balance the need for explanation/interpretation and the vividness of reading the stories of an elder speaking in his own words.

Finally, the emphasis on original texts has created a healthy tension between oral and written traditions and new explorations into the differences between the two means of expression and the complexities of going from one to the other.

Patricia H. Partnow

ORAL AND WRITTEN NARRATIVE

The introduction of writing to the world was at first a matter of
commerce – the recording of business transactions as an aid to
memory. But once writing became more than signs for wheat
sheaves or clay pots and represented instead specific sounds and
words, once it had become a common method for communicating
ideas as well as facts, it changed the very nature of human communication. No longer did speakers – now writers – have to know and
see their audiences. They could communicate over distance, time,
and culture. However, no longer could they alter, retract or elaborate
on points the audience had not understood. Nor could readers respond immediately to writers or apply the communication skills
that helped them interpret oral communication. For instance, without knowing the author's background, readers could not "read"
between the lines" to find an unstated message or bias; without
face-to-face contact they could not "read" the face of the interlocutor

Patricia H. Partnow is a cultural anthropologist specializing in Alaska Native oral traditions.

for emotional clues. They might not understand the structure or unstated cultural values imbedded in the written communication. The communication moment's *context* – the immediate situation in which the unstated but understood norms and expectations were expressed – was lost.

The loss of immediate context results in a series of alterations in the nature of human communication. Orally communicated verbal art depends on an immediate sense of audience, the use of formulaic sayings, repetition, verses or songs imbedded in the narrative, the use of the voice to express information, a relative sparseness of description, variation from performance to performance, and a specific attitude about authorship and originality. A discussion of each characteristic follows.

Sense of audience

The most important difference between written and oral art lies in the relationship between storyteller and audience. It is immediate and changeable during oral communication but remains static and general in the written medium. In small-scale societies a great deal is mutually understood by performer and audience before speech has begun. For instance, general knowledge about the reliability of the storyteller affects the credence and attention the audience gives to a particular story performance. Also generally known are appropriate audience responses to different narrative genres – for instance, the audience may remain respectfully silent during one kind of story, periodically voice assent during another, or chant certain portions of the well-known story along with the performer during a third. Culturally specific knowledge pertinent to the story, such as the emotional impact an orphan is supposed to have, is also understood to audiences in small-scale societies. Moreover, during the performance itself the storyteller conveys information through body language, tone of voice and narrative structure which is not contained in the words themselves.

Good authors also visualize their audiences. However, the makeup of the reading audience is necessarily general. It might consist of third graders who read; or parents of preschoolers; or liberally educated adults. This is far removed from the performer's experience when he or she sees the audience and tailors the choice of story, message, and performance style and length to that audience.

Formulaic sayings

Formulaic sayings may occur at the beginning, end or middle of narratives and often signal important information about the story. For instance, when most Americans hear, "Once upon a time . . . ," we know that we are about to be told a fairy tale about make-believe characters engaged in magical situations. A happy ending is likely to result from a supernatural invention. Similarly, in Koyukon Athabaskan *kk'adontsidnee* the formulaic ending, "I thought the winter had just begun and now I have bitten off a part of it," signals that this was a story about long-ago days which should be treated with respect as a portion of truth from the past. At the same time it inspires relief at the gradual passing of winter. In contrast, we rarely see formulaic sayings in "serious" American literature. Instead, we most often encounter such sayings as parts of children's fanciful tales or jokes told for entertainment.

Repetition and terracing

Repetition is common in orally produced narratives, but when readers encounter it in a written document they may associate the practice with bad writing. To be sure, some types of repetition are encouraged. Terracing, for instance, is a common poetic device. A verbal terrace is a repetition of the last word or words of a phrase with the addition of new words. An example of terracing is contained in this selection from Laura Norton's "The Boy Who Found the Lost":

> He saw a duck
> a small duck swimming
> swimming toward his kayak.

Or,

> He finally caught it with his spear
> his long spear with the stone point
> a point as sharp as a sea urchin spine.

Verses or songs within a prose narrative

Performers have at their disposal many techniques not available to authors. For instance, they can introduce and sing the songs their characters sing, or end narratives with ritual songs inspired by the described experiences. Examples in this volume are contained in Kirt Bell's "The First Whales" and Leo Moses' "Tale." Songs, chants, and verses appear in European as well as Alaska Native lore. Many fairy tales contain verses or chants which must be said with particular tones of voice. "Not by the hair on my chinny chin chin!" must be squeaked. "I'll huff, and I'll puff, and I'll blow the house down!" must be bellowed. "Fee, fie, foe, fum, I smell the blood of an Englishman!" must be deep and ominous. Verse, songs and chants are characteristic of many oral folklore traditions but are much less common in written literature.

Tone of voice and vocal quality

Writers often try to compensate for their silence by using punctuation marks (!), CAPITAL, **bold,** or tiny letters, dr-a-a-a-w-n out words, and so on, while live performers use their voices. Some transcriptions of storytelling performances use visual clues such as those noted above to express vocal quality.

Description

Many oral narratives lack descriptions of the setting or the main characters' appearance, in contrast to short stories and novels. Oral art is generally concise, leaving much to the knowledge and imagination of the listeners. This is for one of two reasons. Either description is superfluous – everyone knows what the Yukon River looks like in July, for instance – or it is unimportant because the story's central issue revolves around something other than appearance.

As with other characteristics of oral tradition, this one is shared with many types of European folklore. In fact, some types of description are relatively recent innovations in world literature. In ancient Greece it was assumed that all humans were essentially alike, and so need not be described; what was of dramatic interest was the particular situation people found themselves in and how they dealt with it. Similarly, in Alaska Native oral traditions, visual descriptions are made only when they are central to the plot or message.

Variation

Just as a storyteller may tell a story differently each time he or she relates it, so the "same" story will be different when performed by different storytellers. The variation may be so extreme that some may question whether it is the same story at all. With the dominance of writing came an intolerance for variation. Each written work generally consists of a single authorized edition; any abridgment or editing must be so noted. When an oral narrative is written down, a similar aura begins to surround it. The written version may become canonized, considered the single "correct" version. Differences due to geographic, artistic, and individual variation are squelched or rejected as impostors. Readers may be familiar with this phenomenon among European folk traditions such as the Disney renditions of *Cinderella* and *Sleeping Beauty*. To three generations of American children these are *the original* fairy tales, even though in many details they are far removed from the versions most commonly told a century ago.

Authority and originality

Another change often occurs when the orientation of a people switches from oral to written communication: the authority of the spoken word is often undermined in favor of the written. While in most oral societies a person's word is the highest authority, the Western world tends to distrust personal testimony in favor of printed references. This is due in part to the Western convention that knowledge is objective and has reality outside the individual who expresses it. Information is considered most reliable when it comes through reason alone without the influence of emotional attachment.

In contrast to the literary demand for objectivity and originality, many oral narratives begin with the narrator's claim to legitimacy by means of a genealogy of former tradition-bearers from whom the story was learned. Within their introductions, performers often proclaim that they did not invent the story, but that it was handed down to them from knowledgeable elders.

The introduction that claims authority to tell the story – called the *narrative frame* – is often omitted from final printed transcripts of recorded stories because it is not felt to be a part of standard (*i.e.,* Euro American) story structure. From a Western literary standpoint the introduction has no bearing on the story's action and so appears to detract from the story's unity. However, the narrative frame contains vital information about the nature of the verbal art itself and indicates that the creativity in oral performance comes in the manner of performance, not in new plot elements or character invention.

A note about "titles"

Few traditional Native narratives were originally titled. It is only after storytellers and editors began to publish narratives that titles were added. Following this Western literary convention, titles have been used for all the selections included in this volume.

The above noted differences notwithstanding, the relationship between the oral tradition and the written tradition in Alaska is both dynamic and complex.

> The oral tradition still lives, and the written tradition is growing within it, not exempt from it. The one will never replace the other. The elements of the old story, of the spoken language, the myths and narratives that sustain the culture, and the speech patterns of the elders occur over and over again in the new writing. . . . The new writing now being done by Alaska Natives shares not only the characteristics of the oral tradition which is its heritage, but many characteristics of the English literate tradition it is now part of. The use of Native languages [in this text], sometimes without translation and always without apology, gives a flavor not possible any other way, and reveals a desire to protect the local languages even when working in English (from the Preface to the 1986 edition of *Alaska Native Writers, Storytellers and Orators*, Dauenhauer, Dauenhauer, and Holthaus, 10–11).

GENRES ACROSS CULTURES

Folklorists have noted thousands of motifs that recur in folklore told all over the world, including Alaska. They have concluded that these commonalities reflect issues that are so basic to human nature and society that all peoples work them out through stories. For instance, the trickster character, represented in this volume by Raven or Crow and Ivan Durak, appears in almost every ethnic folklore recorded. Similarly, the motif of the sky country, represented here in the Koyukon story of "Ggaadookk" and in European folklore by Jack and the Beanstalk, reflects in part the understanding that people are bound by the perspective of their circumstances, and only entry into a new world can help us see our situations anew.

But it would be a mistake to conclude from the many similarities between Alaska Native and European folktales that the two are in other ways identical to each other. A common assumption made by authors of children's books is that because of their strong supernatural or spiritual cast, Alaska Native stories are analogous to magical fairy tales, and are therefore children's stories. Another common misperception is that Alaska Native stories can be divided into the genres assigned to European lore. In fact, the three-part division of myth, legend, and fairy tale does not fit Alaska Native oral tradition. The primary distinction between legend and fairy tale, for instance, is that the former is believed to have been true, may have some basis in historic fact, and contains a minimum of magic, while fairy tales are make-believe and depend heavily on magic. Indigenous genre divisions are not based on this dichotomy between "truth" and "fiction." Indeed, in traditional times, all stories that were worth repeating were believed to have been true, and all stories similarly had a strong spiritual component, just as life itself did.

A common way of dividing story types in the narrative traditions of most Eskimo, Aleut, and Athabaskan groups recognized ancient stories that tell how the world became the place it is today, on the one hand, and newer stories that happened in more recent times to people who could be traced, if the storyteller wanted to take the time, to ancestors of contemporary listeners, on the other.[1]

For instance, in Alutiiq lore the oldest stories, which were once commonly called *unigkuat* [singular *unigkuaq*], took place in a time long ago when the world was different from today. It was different not just because there were no four-wheelers or airplanes, but because the very nature of the relationship between humans and animals was different. In those long-gone days, animals and people could communicate with each other directly, using the Alutiiq language. Animals could transform themselves into human-looking beings by taking off their animal skins. Humans could put on animal skins and become animals. In this distant time, humans learned how to treat animals respectfully, avoid wasting game, be careful with animal bones or skins, and follow many other rules that still apply today. Elders say that the human-animal interactions described in *unigkuat* are extremely rare nowadays but that in the past they happened to everyone. The animals have not lost their ability to understand humans, but humans can no longer understand messages from the animals.

There are more recent stories, usually called *quli'anguat* [singular *quli'anguaq*], which happened in the past, but are about people whom living Alutiiqs remember personally or remember hearing about when they were children. Some of these narratives are similar to *unigkuat*. For instance, many *quli'anguat* describe what might be considered today supernatural or paranormal occurrences. But *quli'-anguat* are different from *unigkuat* in that some of them *can* be assigned dates on a time line. When an old woman tells a *quli'anguaq* about her girlhood experiences trapping ground squirrels, she can remember how old she was when she trapped, and so remember the season and the approximate year. Similarly, if a man remembers when his father's hunting partner was fatally mauled by a brown bear, he knows how old he was when it happened and can date the event accordingly.

It is the *unigkuat* that non-Natives often mistakenly think of as fairy tales. But a comparison of the two reveals important differences:

---

1. Other recognized genres include riddles, oratory, song lyrics, clan legends, and Raven or Crow stories. Refer to the commentary for each Native group for information about culturally specific genre designations.

Setting

Fairy tales usually take place in a generalized setting, such as "in a kingdom." *Unigkuat* also often take place in unnamed settings, although this is partly because it is understood that the setting is in a time before human society or villages had been established. In *unigkuat* the vagueness of the setting is a meaningful time marker rather than an indication of fantasy. In addition, some *unigkuat* are thought to have occurred locally while others occurred at specific landmarks which took their present shape during the story. For instance, the formation of a particular bluff or rock outcrop might be recounted in an *unigkuaq*.

Time

Fairy tales happened "once upon a time" – *i.e.*, long ago, in a time that does not exist along the line of human history as we understand it. *Unigkuat* also happened long ago in an undatable time. However, this is believed to have been an actual era when the world was substantially different from today, when humans and animals freely interacted and communicated, and there were no boundaries between humans and other creatures, life and death, day and night. It was a time at the beginning of the world, much more akin to "mythical time" than "once-upon-a-time."

Characters

Fairy tale characters are usually called by "everyman" names such as Jack (in English lore) or Ivan (in Russian lore). Other names are descriptive (Cinderella, Sleeping Beauty). The individual hero is most often the focus of the story.

Unigkuat characters are also often generalized, for instance as "hunter" or "crane." A common hero type is the orphan, who, like fairy tale Jacks and Ivans, is an underdog with nothing to lose but much inner strength. The difference often comes in the story's resolution (see below).

On the other hand, some *unigkuat* are about Crow or Raven, who is a specific character with a personality that does not change from story to story.

Truth

Fairy tales are considered fiction while *unigkuat* are considered to have actually happened. There is no "fiction" genre in traditional Alutiiq narrative.

Human vs. magical agency

In fairy tales the conflict is usually resolved through magic. This is considered evidence that these are fanciful and untrue stories.

Unigkuat also are dominated by supernatural occurrences, but the implications are different. Rather than being evidence of fantasy, the magic in *unigkuat* is evidence of antiquity. Such experiences were everyday occurrences in *unigkuaq* times, while they are uncommon now. The boundary between humans and nature, natural and supernatural, life and death is perceived to be permeable even today in the Alutiiq world view.

Hero's goal

In fairy tales the hero or heroine often strives for, and attains, a rich or royal spouse, or simply money. The goal is personal aggrandizement.

In *unigkuat* the hero often plays a less central role. The point of the story may be to show how a particular part of the current world order was achieved; *e.g.,* how killer whales came about and why they act the way they do. Another point commonly made in *unigkuat* is the importance of balance and harmony between people or within the natural world. While the orphan may become rich, more emphasis is placed on the imbalance indicated by his extreme poverty at the beginning of the story, an imbalance redressed in the end.

Jeane Breinig

POLITICAL PERSPECTIVE AND LITERARY FRAMEWORK FOR THE TEXT COMMENTARIES

The Cultural and Historical Text Commentaries section of this volume provides a brief overview of each of the Native groups in Alaska, so readers may gain a greater appreciation for the diversity of indigenous experiences within Alaska. It is home and source for two major language families: Eskimo-Aleut, and Na-Dene, the language of the Athabaskan Indians. In addition to the major language families, three languages are spoken in Southeast Alaska: Haida, Tlingit, and Tsimshian.

We also have placed a list of selections under each of the headings to indicate to which cultural group individual contributors belong; however, readers should be aware of the complications such a categorization creates, especially for writers of multiple heritages. The notion of an individual storyteller, orator, or writer belonging to a particular cultural group should be understood not simply as a cultural or ethnic heritage inherited through familial bloodlines, but also within the context of the complex political relationships between individual indigenous Nations and the United States government. This requires some understanding of the historical and political similarities and differences between American Indians of the continental United States ("Lower 48") and Alaska Natives.

First, it is important to understand the distinction in terminology with how indigenous peoples identify themselves. For example, "Native American" commonly refers to the overall indigenous population of the United States. It is often used as a general label that allows for differentiation among various larger groups (*e.g.*, "African American," "Asian American," or "Euro American") and implies an inherited "ethnic" identity of sorts. While the term "Native American" may be useful in certain contexts, most indigenous peoples identify themselves first tribally and, if necessary, in more general terms, but not usually as "Native American." Rather, many Natives of the Lower 48 prefer the general term "American Indian"; in Alaska, "Alaska Native" is used. The term "First Nations" (as used in Canada) is probably a more accurate broad term to designate both "American Indian" and "Alaska Native" peoples; however, this term is not commonly used here in the United States.

This preference for "American Indian" and "Alaska Native" has developed over time for a variety of reasons. However, the distinction in terminology, for many, highlights an important difference between America's indigenous peoples and other groups in the U.S. Indigenous peoples, in addition to holding U.S. citizenship, may also be members of tribal Nations (and, in Alaska, also be shareholders of Alaska Native Corporations, formed as a result of the Alaska Native Claims Settlement Act (ANCSA) of December 18, 1971). These distinctions imply political, rather than simply "cultural" or "ethnic" differences. For American Indians of the Lower 48, the political relationship to the U.S. government is evidenced through treaties negotiated with individual Indian Nations to provide for services, such as health and education, in exchange for lands taken. In Alaska, treaties were not negotiated due, in part, to the fact that in 1871, four years after purchasing Alaska from Russia, the U.S. Congress enacted legislation that ended treaty-making. The U.S. government created somewhat different ways of dealing with indigenous ownership of Alaska via ANCSA. (For further information, see Case; Wilkinson; McBeath and Morehouse.)

With regard to early U.S. and Indian relations, Indians were first perceived as posing an actual physical threat to the newly arrived American immigrants, so the Bureau of Indian Affairs (BIA), created in 1824, was first housed in the War Department. By 1849 the BIA was moved to the Department of the Interior after the majority of the Indian population had been removed from their ancestral homelands and forced onto reservations.

Because of Alaska's vast size and its relative isolation from the continental U.S., the encroachment of American immigrants upon indigenous land came later to Alaska than it did for the Indian Nations of the Lower 48, avoiding for the most part the reservation system that still exists there.[1] The American occupation of Alaska was preceded by a period of Russian expeditions into various regions. Russian fur hunters first entered the Aleut area in 1745, massacring many and enslaving others. In their quest for sea otter skins, the Russians expanded southward along the Pacific Rim as far as California, finally concentrating at Sitka, the Russian American capital until 1867, when Alaska was sold to the U.S. (see Krauss, 1980; Dauenhauer and Dauenhauer, 1994). By the time Alaska Natives began to understand the consequences of America's sovereign claim to their land base, treaties had been ruled illegal.

Yet as early as 1912 the Natives of Southeast Alaska (Haida, Tlingit, Tsimshian) had mobilized politically and founded a pan-Native, pan-Christian organization to fight for human rights denied its aboriginal population. The Alaska Native Brotherhood (ANB), founded in 1912, and its companion organization, the Alaska Native Sisterhood (ANS), founded in 1923, won crucial political battles, including the right to vote and the right of Native children to attend public schools (see Christianson; Dauenhauer and Dauenhauer, 1994). But continuing frustration over non-Native encroachment upon the landscape and waterways of Southeast Alaska led the ANB/ANS to recommend that the Haida and Tlingit peoples unite to pursue a legal suit against the government for lands taken.

In 1939 the Central Council of Tlingit and Haida Indian Tribes of Alaska was formed. The suit was pursued and eventually won in 1959, the year in which Alaska became a state. While the settlement provided some monetary compensation for lands taken, it did not return any of the lands to Native peoples. So in the 1960s, the Tlingit Haida Central Council joined with the new larger statewide organization known as the Alaska Federation of Natives (AFN), which included people from the other Alaska Native groups – Iñupiat, Central Yup'ik, St. Lawrence Island Yupik, Athabaskan, Aleut, and Alutiiq – to pursue the question of legal ownership of Alaskan lands.

The AFN as a political organization, combined with the discovery of oil in Prudhoe Bay, helped speed the ultimate passage of ANCSA. Through ANCSA, Alaska Natives received title to about 40 million acres of land and $962.5 million dollars. However, the

---

1. The Annette Island Reserve (Tsimshian) is the only reservation now located in Alaska.

land and money did not go directly to the individuals or to tribal entities, but rather were transferred to newly created regional and village corporations. Alaska Natives born prior to the passage of the act were issued shares in corporations, and the corporations were then charged with making a profit for shareholders by development of their natural resources or creating a business enterprise.

As others have noted, ANCSA was in some respects like the treaties the United States government signed with the individual Indian Nations of the continental United States and in other respects different. In return for grants of limited land, ANCSA extinguished aboriginal title to much more extensive lands customarily used by the peoples. However, unlike treaties, ANCSA was not negotiated with leaders from each individual tribal Nation within Alaska. Additionally, ANCSA specifically excluded creating reservations and BIA trust responsibility for the land and money received (see Case; McBeath and Morehouse). Rather than tribal ownership, the land and resources were transferred to private corporations created by the act.

The financial success of the ANCSA corporations has been mixed; a few corporations have provided large dividends because they have been able to develop natural resources such as timber or oil; the majority, however, have not produced significant economic benefits for most shareholders. Many reasons exist for this situation, including the fact that for-profit corporations function very differently from tribal governments.

Unfortunately, ANCSA has also clouded the extent to which the U.S. government and the state will recognize Alaska Native tribal powers on the same footing as Indian Nations in the Lower 48 – including recognition of "Indian Country" in Alaska and the inherent powers of self-government that concept implies. Although the issue is complex, a report issued by the Alaska Native Commission in 1994 recommended tribal self-determination and self-government as the best possible solutions to the continuing economic and social problems facing Alaska Natives in one of the richest states of the U.S.[2]

---

2. The commission was formed in 1992 at the mandate of U.S. Congress with the support of the federal government and the State of Alaska. The commission was charged with conducting a "comprehensive study of the social and economic status of Alaska Natives and the effectiveness of the policies and programs of the United States and of the State of Alaska" (Volume II, Foreword). The final report includes recommendations to change the way state and federal governments deal with Native issues, thereby promoting Alaska Natives' ability to find workable solutions to their own economic and social problems.

ANCSA also left unresolved Alaska Native rights regarding hunting, fishing, and gathering on the traditional land bases used by their peoples – commonly known as "subsistence" in Alaska. Although ANCSA originally appeared to extinguish aboriginal hunting and fishing rights, Congress – recognizing that Alaska Native subsistence was inadequately protected – later included provisions for rural subsistence hunting and fishing preference in the Alaska National Interest Lands Conservation Act of 1980. The state of Alaska then enacted a rural subsistence preference in order to maintain control of hunting and fishing laws. But in 1989 the Alaska Supreme Court ruled against the rural preference after a group of urban sport hunters filed a suit based on discrimination against urban residents (see McBeath and Morehouse, 1994). The issue remains a highly charged, emotional topic, and to date no satisfactory solution has been crafted.

Given Alaska's vast size and the long distances separating small "bush" villages from urban areas, subsistence hunting, fishing, and gathering activities are important aspects of physical and economic survival for most rural Alaskans – Native and non-Native alike. Yet most Alaska Natives, regardless of where they now live, view traditional Native subsistence foods as much more than a means of physical survival; they are also a crucial aspect of cultural survival and spiritual sustenance – and a tangible means of maintaining ties to ancestral traditions and distinct tribal identities in an increasingly industrialized and ethnically diverse world.

Our goal in providing the following commentaries is to give the reader an initial framework for understanding aspects of the Alaska Native works included in this collection. We have not, therefore, provided commentaries for every selection, nor have we attempted to show all of the connections among the pieces. To do so tends to place arbitrary limits on the complexity and vision inherent in Alaska Native literary expressions and the multi-faceted life experiences they reflect. For a deeper appreciation of the wide range of Alaska Native literatures and their contexts, we have provided a selected list of helpful reading selections following this section of the book.

COMMENTARY ON EYAK TEXTS

BACKGROUND

Eyak territory at one time extended from between contemporary Cordova in the north to just beyond Yakutat in the south, north of Tlingit territory. Around 1880, there were around 200 Eyaks located primarily in two main villages: Eyak, at the outlet of Eyak Lake, and Alaganik, about 20 miles to the east. A small group also lived at Bering River village (Krauss, 1982).

Tlingit people held long-standing friendly relations with the Eyaks, and as Tlingits expanded northward they began gradually assimilating Eyaks into the Tlingit nation. By 1800 Tlingit was the predominant language spoken in Yakutat (Krauss, 1982).

In 1889, the first American canneries and a trading post arrived on the scene. This era brought the beginnings of the destruction of Eyak culture. The influx of non-Natives into the area soon over-whelmed the Eyak population. The newcomers brought with them alcohol and deadly diseases and interfered with Eyak subsistence practices. By 1892 the Eyak settlement of Alaganik had been nearly wiped out by epidemics, and by 1900 Eyak village was itself de-stroyed. About 60 Eyaks survived in Old Town (Cordova), where non-Natives had also begun to settle. By 1933 the Cordova Eyak population numbered around 30 people, of which only about fifteen could speak Eyak. It was not until 1952 that Chinese linguist Fang-Kuei Li came to study the Eyak language. By then there were only seven speakers alive. Later, linguist Michael Krauss, of the Alaska Native Language Center, at the University of Alaska Fairbanks, con-tinued to work with Eyak speakers, including Anna Nelson Harry and the other two remaining speakers, Marie Smith and her sister Sophie (Krauss, 1982). As of 1998, Marie Smith is the last living speaker of Eyak and is considered the hereditary chief.

– J.B.

WORKS

"Lament for Eyak" (p. 2)

By the year Anna Nelson Harry was born (1906), canneries had been built and the town of Cordova had been established in her home territory. Both had led to disintegration of the Eyak culture into which Anna was born.

Anna was born into this turbulent time of cultural disintegration. She witnessed the murder of her pregnant mother and as an orphan was raised by a family which neglected her. Her adult life was also marked by horror and sorrow, yet she managed to survive. She married twice, first to an Eyak man and then, after his death, to a Tlingit man. She had six sons, five of whom preceded her in death. She was trilingual, speaking Eyak, English, and Tlingit.

– P.H.P.

"Lake-Dwarves" (p. 7)

Anna's philosophical insight here is precisely that of Swift, with his biting satire in Gulliver's account of his encounters with the tiny (six-inch), laughably despicable, insignificant yet warlike Lilliputians, and then with the formidably giant (72-foot) yet wise and peace-loving Brobdingnagians. A Frenchman, Englishman, or modern American could hardly have written such a book, but only someone with the viewpoint of a smaller nation, in Swift's case Ireland, who has watched the larger nations warring with each other. It is no surprise, then, that in Alaska, Anna, an Eyak, is the one to understand so insightfully the principle of relativity in size, power, and importance of nations. She has seen her own Eyak people struggling to survive beside larger nations, Tlingit and Aleut (Chugach Eskimo), and has seen those in turn now threatened by a still more giant one. Men are foolish to forget that power and importance are relative, and that our place in this world or this universe is not a simple matter. We must not take ourselves too seriously. To laugh is to survive.

– from *In Honor of Eyak: The Art of Anna Nelson Harry,* by Michael E. Krauss

"Giant Rat" (p. 9)

Michael Krauss (1982) recorded "Lake Dwarves" and "Giant Rat" during May of 1965 when Anna Nelson Harry was 61 years old. He points out that many versions of these two stories are told in this part of the world, but that these two as told by Anna Nelson Harry are particularly noteworthy. Krauss writes that Nelson herself told earlier and different versions of the story when she was 27 years old (see Birket-Smith and de Laguna, 1938) and suggests she used the tales as a political statement at a later part of her life.

In the earlier version of "Lake Dwarves" she deals briefly with the encounter between the hunter and the dwarves and spends more time discussing the individual dwarves. The earlier version of "Giant Rat" ends after the rat is killed. The later version adds a new section onto the end of the story – the part about the rat-skin and the ensuing war.

– J.B.

COMMENTARY ON
HAIDA TEXTS

BACKGROUND

Haida people are indigenous to what is now known as the Queen Charlotte Islands in British Columbia, Canada, and the Southeast Alaska panhandle. On a clear day the mountains of Prince of Wales and Dall Islands in Alaska are plainly visible from the north end of Graham Island in the Queen Charlottes.

By the late nineteenth century the overall Haida population (estimated to be around 10,000–15,000) had been reduced by almost ninety percent due primarily to epidemics such as influenza, venereal disease, measles, and smallpox, to which Native peoples had little resistance.

Sometime prior to contact with Europeans, a group of Haida migrated northward into the southern Southeast Alaska panhandle. Although most published sources place the migration sometime in the late 17th century, some oral accounts suggest much earlier occupancy of the area; stories tell of a "great flood" that covered the islands in this area.

The word "Haida" (_Xaa das_) translates to "the people." The Alaskan Haida are sometimes called _Kaigani_, although Haida people did not use this term at the time of contact. Rather, non-Natives named them for the Haida subsistence campsite located at the southern tip of Dall Island at Cape Muzon, which was also commonly used as a trading area. The name is taken from a former Tlingit village situated there. In fact, many Tlingit place names still remain in the southern portion of the Southeast Alaska panhandle because Tlingits once controlled the area.

The Alaskan Haida established at least five villages in the southern end of Alexander Archipelago and numerous other subsistence campsites including Karta Bay. From the early 1900s forward, the steady influx of non-Natives led to rapid cultural and economic change for all Southeast Alaska Natives. With the introduction of commercial fishing, the establishment of salmon salteries and canneries, and the discovery of precious metals such as copper and gold, a wage economy soon developed. Subsistence hunting, fishing, and gathering activities began to be supplemented by a cash economy.

The two Haida villages existing today are Hydaburg and (New) Kasaan. The original village of (Old) Kasaan was abandoned in 1902 when the people moved to a new site, (New) Kasaan, because of promised year-round employment and a school. In 1911, the other villages consolidated at a new location they named Hydaburg. The move was driven, in part, by a desire to provide better educational opportunities for younger Haida, recognizing that Western education was increasingly important for their children's future well-being; yet they were not willing to send their children away to boarding school – the only other option available at the time. The U.S. government agreed to establish a local school if the villages consolidated. During this era, there was both strong pressure to assimilate and recognition of the need to acquire the skills necessary to negotiate within and adapt to a changing world. Unfortunately, as a consequence, Haida and all the other Southeast Alaska Native languages are no longer being learned as first languages; individuals under the age of 60 do not speak their Native language fluently, owing to past missionary influence and government policies.

John Swanton, anthropologist and linguist, collected Haida stories in the early 1900s and wrote an extensive ethnography. Some of the stories Swanton collected were published with full interlinear translation, others exist in English translations only. Approximately six different orthographies have been used to transcribe Haida texts.

The first Alaskan Haida to work with linguists on the language was Genevieve Soboleff, who in 1972 worked with Michael Krauss and Jack Osteen at the University of Alaska in Fairbanks. A writing system was designed, and, in June of the same year, the first Haida language workshop took place at Sheldon Jackson College in Sitka. The first Alaskan Haida books written in both English and Haida were soon produced (Lawrence, 1977).

John Enrico, in his work with Masset and Skidegate Canadian Haida dialects, has identified three types of narrative genres: q'ii-gangng (myth), q'iyaagaang (lineage history), and gya.ahlaang[1] (history, or news). Folklorists often understand the term "myth" in Na-

---

1. These terms are taken from Enrico's introduction to *Skidegate Haida Myths and Histories*. The Alaskan Haida orthography is written differently, as shown with the facing translation done by Charles Natkong, Sr., of Victor Haldane's "Moldy Collar Tip."

tive storytelling to refer to a "mythic" period in the past when the world assumed its current shape (see "Genres Across Cultures," p. 283). However, Enrico notes that the word is not temporally restricted, as the folklore definition implies. Similarly, the distinction among genres is not as clear as the English translations suggest. For example, some stories do discuss a time when the world was inhabited by supernatural characters of mythical dimension, but supernatural events and characters may also appear in genres other than "myth."

The five Haida stories discussed below highlight the important relationships among humans, animals, and spirits. Readers should be aware, however, that the distinction among these categories is not as clear-cut as the English words imply. In *The Curtain Within: Haida Social and Mythical Discourse,* Marianne Boelscher writes:

> The standard dichotomies of Western epistemology such as natural and supernatural, sacred and profane, animal and human, material and immaterial, do not apply to Haida symbolic thought. Instead, to the Haida, all beings had (and to some extent still have) multiple identities and multiple realities. The form and intent of beings and objects depend upon the perspective of the human being encountering them and his or her intent and subjective state of mind. (167)

Shifting and multiple identities, and the possibility of transformations are important aspects of Haida thought. This is reflected in all aspects of life, including literary and other artistic expressions. As renowned as the Haida have been for their artistic creations, no word exists in the Haida language for "art," because prior to contact it pervaded all aspects of life and was not conceptualized separately.

– J.B.

WORKS

Jeane Breinig: "Mood Music" (p. 234)

Julie Coburn: "Seed Potatoes and Foxgloves" (p. 211) and "Raven Speaks to Haidas" (p. 213)

Victor Haldane: "Moldy Collar Tip" (p. 12), "Fish Story: Karta Bay" (p. 18), "Shag and the Raven" (p. 21), and "Story of the Double Fin Killer Whale" (p. 22)

George Hamilton: "Haida Hunters and Legend of the Two Fin Killer Whale" (p. 25)

Jessie Neal Natkong: "Beaver and Ground Hog Were Pals" (p. 23)

"Moldy Collar Tip" (p. 12) and "Fish Story: Karta Bay" (p. 18)

These two similar stories told by Victor Haldane invite interesting comparisons. "Moldy Collar Tip" is an oral story told in Haida with facing translation shown. "Fish Story: Karta Bay" is a similar story actually told in English by the same storyteller. The one told in English provides much of the unstated context for the Haida language version. This is a good illustration of the differences between oral Native and written English stories, and the role audience understanding plays in what is or is not explained.

Portions of "Fish Story: Karta Bay" explain aspects of context in "Moldy Collar Tip" that would generally be taken for granted with an audience who understand the Haida language version. In "Fish Story: Karta Bay," Haldane explains some aspects of Haida beliefs, including reincarnation. In Haida thought, when a person dies, his/her spirit is said to return to earth in another (human) form. A pregnant woman might dream about a deceased family member, and this is taken as a sign the child will be a reincarnation of whoever was dreamed about. Haldane suggests that fish reincarnate in a fashion similar to humans.

Proper behavior and using words wisely are also important aspects of Haida thought, as it is for most indigenous groups. Implicit in the stories is a key concept of Haida thought: "respect" or *yak dang*. Respect implies proper attitude and behavior, not only towards other humans but to all creatures. Salmon are especially revered and continue to be a valued source of food and spiritual sustenance for Haida and other Southeast Alaska Native peoples; hence, any disparaging remarks about them are strictly forbidden.

Karta Bay is located on the east coast of Prince of Wales Island and is the northernmost part of Haida country at one end of Kasaan Bay. It is the traditional subsistence fishing area of the Kasaan Haidas; the area is now legally controlled by the State.

– J.B.

"Shag and the Raven" (p. 21)

This story introduces Raven, a character found in many Alaska Native and Northwest Coast stories. Farther north, "Crow" stories appear, as do "Coyote" stories in the Lower 48. Raven is a contradictory character who embodies admirable behavior, such as creating the world, sun, moon, and stars, but also displays scandalous, selfish, and often shocking but humorous behavior. Anatomical and scatological humor is common in Raven stories and is considered naughty but also funny. In general, frank reference to sexual parts and to body functions are not uncommon in Native oral literature and are not considered distasteful or out of place as they are in some contemporary Western contexts. It should also be noted that ravens as actual creatures are smart and funny, providing no doubt much fruit for story material.

– J.B.

"Story of the Double Fin Killer Whale" (p. 22)

This story illustrates the close relationship among humans, animals, and the spirit world. The spirit world, from a Native perspective, is not viewed as distinct from everyday life. While this is a Haida story, Alaska Native and American Indian cultures in general place a high value on the recognition of the spiritual as ever present. As shown here, it is important to display respect toward all creatures, or serious consequences may result. The brother's bad fortune occurred after they had broken a taboo (killed some small birds). Luckily for them, the Porpoise People were available and willing to help them out of the fog.

– J.B.

"Haida Hunters and the Legend of the Two Fin Killer Whale" (p. 25)

This is an example of a clan-owned story, belonging to the Two-Fin Killer Whale clan of the Raven moiety. The narrative recounts an actual event that occurred, giving this family the right to tell the story.

– J.B.

COMMENTARY ON TLINGIT TEXTS

BACKGROUND

Traditional Tlingit territory in Alaska includes the Southeastern panhandle coastal area between Icy Bay in the north to Dixon Entrance in the South. Tlingit people have also occupied the area to the east, inside the Canadian border. This group is sometimes called "Inland" Tlingit, with the former group known as "Coastal" Tlingit. The Tlingit population at the time of contact with the non-aboriginal population within Southeast Alaska is estimated to have been around 8,000 to 10,000 with approximately 17 permanent winter village sites. Currently, six permanent Tlingit villages remain.

The first recorded contact with non-Natives occurred between Russians and Tlingits in 1741, followed by the Spanish in 1774. In search of a Northwest passage, the British explored and charted the area, but eventually left; thereafter, Russian and American enterprises dominated. In 1796 and 1799 the Russians established forts at Yakutat and Sitka. The Tlingits destroyed both forts; however, the Russians recaptured Sitka in 1804 and it became the capital of Russian America until 1867, when Alaska was sold to the United States. After Alaska came under United States jurisdiction, martial law was administered first by the U.S. Army and later by the U.S. Navy. The American occupation of Tlingit territory ushered in many negative changes. With the steady influx of non-Natives into the area (including the military, cannery workers, gold prospectors, and other fortune seekers), many conflicts arose between Tlingits and the American immigrants. In 1868, the U.S. Army destroyed Kake, and in 1882, the U.S. Navy bombarded Angoon (Dauenhauer and Dauenhauer, 1994).

The American Presbyterian missionary influence, beginning in the 1880s and led by Sheldon Jackson, proved detrimental to Tlingit language and cultural practices. As superintendent of education for Alaskan schools, Jackson favored Native assimilation at the cost of traditional Tlingit social order and religion. He also implemented an "English only" language policy at mission and government boarding schools which contributed significantly to the decline of Southeast Native language use in general (Krauss, 1980).

Tlingit was first written by the Orthodox missionaries, who used the Cyrillic alphabet. It was subsequently written by several linguists using technical alphabets. The first popular orthography in the modern period was developed by Constant Naish & Gillian Story in the 1960s. The orthography used in the Tlingit story "Raven, Seagull and Crane," for example, is the one originally created by Naish and Story and revised in 1972. Tlingit narrative genres include *tlaagóo*, a narrative of ancient origin or time, and *shkalneek*, referring to any story or narrative in general (Dauenhauer, 1984).

– J.B.

WORKS

Diane Lxeís' Benson: "What She Wanted" (p. 262), "Now They WannaBE Us" (p. 266), and "River Woman" (p. 259)

Jessie Dalton: "Speech for the Removal of Grief" (p. 34)

Nora Dauenhauer: "About Tlingit Oratory" (p. 303), "Grandmother Eliza" (p. 179), "Egg Boat" (p. 172), "Museum" (p. 180), and "After Ice Fog" (p. 181)

Robert H. Davis: "Saginaw Bay: I Keep Going Back" (p. 165)

Eleanor Hadden: "Native Identity: What Kind of Native Are You?" (p. 201)

Austin Hammond: "Speech for the Removal of Grief" (p. 41)

Andrew Hope III: "Shagoon 1, 2, 3, 4" (p. 198) and "Diyeikee" (p. 200)

Randall Johnson: "Salmon in the Pond" (p. 223)

David Kadashan: "Speech for the Removal of Grief" (p. 30)

Willie Marks: "Raven, Seagull and Crane" (p. 26)

Anna Smith: "Watsíx Shaayí Mountains" (p. 256), "Naatasse Héen" (p. 258), and "Wolves" (p. 254)

"Raven, Seagull and Crane" (p. 26)

This is a good example of Raven at work, in this case playing a game called "Let's You and Him Fight." As is also true with the Haida story "Beaver and Ground Hog were Pals," we have supplied nouns in the English translation. Careful readers of the original language will note that although this is a Raven story, Raven is not mentioned by name until five lines from the end. Why not? Everybody knows it is a Raven story!

– R.D.

At first reading this selection has a definite Henry Jamesian flavor to it, with its foreign-sounding word order and uncertain antecedents for pronouns. This is due to two facts: first, Tlingit language structure is completely different from that of English, hence word order is different; and second, in the original Tlingit version, Seagull's name is never mentioned. The audience knows that this story is about Raven and Seagull by past association, tone of voice, and the action within the story. Thus the original has many more unexplained *he*s than does this simplified English version.

The story is similar in structure to one of Aesop's fables. Note, however, that such lesson stories were and are taken very seriously in Tlingit culture, and are not considered merely children's stories. Rather, parallels between Raven's actions and those of current politicians are seen, and adults are expected to keep the stories in mind in patterning their own behavior.

– P.H.P.

"Saginaw Bay: I Keep Going Back" (p. 165)

This poem is a condensed history of the Tlingit people, starting approximately with Raven. The arrangement is as follows:

I. The beginnings: Raven comes to Saginaw (a bay on the northern shore of Kuiu Island in Southeast Alaska)
II. First Tlingits come to Saginaw
III. First white men come to Saginaw
IV. Disintegration of traditional Tlingit culture through religious conversion
V. Desecration of Tlingit symbols as loggers came
VI. Beginning to go backward in time, back to the historical events of a slave raid
VII. Back further still, to Raven again
VIII. How the narrator fits into it all

The Nass River is just south of the southernmost part of Alaska, and is said to be the origin of Raven and the Tlingit world. In Part II, the Tsaaqueidi clan is mentioned. It is one of the Eagle moiety clans (large, extended families related through the mother's line) which has settled in Kake. According to this poem, the clan first settled in Kuiu (to the southwest of Kake) before moving to Kake. Part III speaks of the destruction of Tlingit culture by missionaries. *K'ink'* are "stink heads" (fermented salmon heads), and stink eggs are fermented salmon eggs, both traditional Tlingit foods which were ridiculed by the white immigrants who were not used to the strong smell. Ironically, fermentation in other foods was acceptable to the immigrants (*e.g.,* fermented barley or cheese).

– P.H.P.

"Native Identity: What Kind of Native Are You?" (p. 201)

This selection was revised from a presentation given at a meeting of the Alaska Anthropological Association in spring, 1997. It was presented as part of a panel on Native genealogy. Hadden's piece is a good illustration of contemporary mixed tribal identity, as she is matrilineally Tlingit, but also of Tsimshian descent on her mother's side, and Haida on her father's. In political terms, however, she is an enrolled member of the Tlingit and Haida Indian Tribes of Alaska (federally recognized by the U.S. government) and a shareholder in both Sealaska and Kavilco (ANCSA-created Native corporations).

The traditional Tlingit introduction opens by acknowledging the opposite clan ("my father's sisters, my father's brothers"), a sign of respect which can compared to the openings of the three versions of "Speech for the Removal of Grief." By identifying her clan and crests, a Tlingit audience would immediately be able to understand who she is in relation to deceased and living relatives, as well as locate her in relation to the villages and regions of Southeast Alaska to which she is tied. Contrast this with her typical Western introduction which focuses more on individual occupation, education, marital status, and where she has lived with her family.

The "Raven's Tail" Hadden refers to is a style of weaving using mountain goat wool that predates the more well-known Chilkat weaving. Nowadays, it is typically created for regalia and is also a highly valued art form.

– J.B.

ABOUT TLINGIT ORATORY

Two features characterize Tlingit culture and oral tradition – ownership and reciprocity. Songs, stories, artistic designs, personal names, land use and other elements of Tlingit are considered the real property of a particular clan. The Tlingit name for this concept is at.óow. The form, content, and immediate setting of oral tradition exist in a larger context of reciprocity or "balance." The form and content of verbal and visual art are congruent with each other and with social structure.

The two moieties, Eagle and Raven, balance each other out. They select marriage partners from each other, and direct love songs and most oratory to each other. In host-guest relationships at feasts, they share in each other's joy and work to remove each other's grief. This balancing is reflected in the oral literature itself.

Here are some examples:

1) Ravens and Eagles address each other.

2) A song or speech must be answered – not in competition, but that it be received and not "wander aimlessly."

Within speeches and stories, these components are balanced:

3) physical and spiritual,

4) living and departed,

5) humans and animals,

6) humans and land.

Oratory, the art of public speaking, is highly valued in traditional and contemporary Tlingit society. Tlingit public speaking is not easy. As these examples show, the speaker must be the master of several things:

1) genealogy – the family trees of everybody involved,

2) kinship – the Tlingit clan system,

3) visual art – the Tlingit clan crests on totems, masks, dance headdresses, Chilkat robes, button blankets, tunics, etc.,

4) tribal histories, legends, and other narratives,

5) songs,

6) protocol – rules of order.

The speaker must know these things in isolation, and also know how to connect them poetically, using the rhetorical devices of simile and metaphor. The speaker must also be sensitive to human emotion, and know how to use his or her words to give comfort, encouragement and strength to people in time of grief, and to build appropriate bridges between individuals, families, clans, and communities, and between the material and spiritual worlds.

The Speech for the Removal of Grief by David Kadashan, Jessie Dalton and Austin Hammond presented in this volume are an excellent introduction to Tlingit language and culture, because they show how all aspects of Tlingit culture are connected to each other.

The speeches are a fine example of rhetorical style and content in a sequence of Tlingit oratory composed, published, and recorded in performance at a memorial for Jim Marks in Hoonah, October 1968.

Approximately one year after a person's death, his or her clanspeople, with the support of members of other clans of the same moiety, and with indirect support from relatives of the opposite moiety, host a memorial feast. The feast for Jim Marks was held in October 1968 in Hoonah. It was hosted by his younger brother Willie Marks, with the support of relatives and friends. It took place in Gooch Hít, the Kaagwaantaan Wolf House in Hoonah. It started about five p.m. and lasted until about five a.m. the following morning. During the course of this memorial these speeches were delivered as part of an attempt by the guests to remove the grief being felt by the hosts.

About five p.m. people entered. The hosts were seated at the front, facing the guests and the back of the house. The guests who delivered the speeches in this section were seated along the back wall, facing the hosts. Jessie Dalton delivered her speech from the right back corner. Between the hosts and the guest-speakers the other guests were seated. The orphans – the children and family of the deceased – were seated at the front. The "Seagull Ladies" who sang several songs were at the right front wall. The people wearing the tribal art referred to in the speeches stood randomly among the guests in the center of the room. The only tables were at the front, on which the gifts, dry goods, and money to be distributed were assembled.

When the house was full, the hosts blackened their cheeks, signifying death. There was singing with a drum, but no dancing at this point. David Kadashan drummed on the Bear Drum of Jim Marks.

Either four or eight songs are traditionally sung, and they are the most serious and sacred of the clan songs. These are very sensitive, and people prepare themselves before the singing of such songs. Preparations include avoidance of seafood.

David McKinley was the song leader for the mourning songs.

Four mourning songs were sung, the last of which was on a tape recording by the deceased, preceded by his history of the song. The song and speech by Jim Marks were tape recorded by his stepson, Horace Marks. After the four songs, the last mourning for the dead took place. In Tlingit, there are several terms for this, including gaax, wudanaak, and gaaw wutaan.

After the mourning, the guests asked for the floor, and the activities were turned over to the guests. At this point the speeches in this section began.

The guests responded to balance out the efforts of the hosts, and to help remove the grief. After the speeches in this book, the guests "chanted the grief." The guests did a chant to remove the grief of the hosts. With this, the grief was completed, and the feast was turned over to joy.

Food was brought out (repeatedly – until the end of the activities), happy songs were sung – love songs and at.óow songs. There was dancing. In memory of all the dead – who were recalled by name – dishes for the dead were distributed; food, dry goods, other gifts, and money were distributed. After the distribution of money, shaman spirit songs were sung. This particular feast lasted all night, ending about five a.m. the following morning.

The oratory excerpted here is from a sequence of public speaking that began with the playing of a tape recorded speech and song by the deceased, followed by six speeches, of which 2, 4, and 5 are given here.

The central speech was by Naa Tláa (Jessie Dalton). Her fellow orators cooperated to set a context for her, building up to her speech and settling down again after it, creating an over-all dramatic structure similar to that of traditional European drama.

The speech by Naa Tláa opened with a rhetorical question about death, followed by a genealogical inventory in which she addressed the grieving hosts. She developed her speech through metaphor and extended metaphor (conceit), simile and extended simile (Homeric simile) based on regalia, clan emblems, and genealogy.

Other speakers, especially Kaatyé (David Kadashan) and Daanaawaak (Austin Hammond), used a similar style.

The oratory connects the living and the departed, the material and spiritual cultures, and members of the various clans present.

The meaning of the speeches is difficult to understand, even for fluent speakers of Tlingit, who describe the language as "old time Tlingit." "Old time Tlingit" involves:

1) understanding the language of oratory and poetry – especially metaphor and simile, and

2) understanding Tlingit social structure (the "clan system"), and

3) understanding the meaning and social context of visual art (the designs and regalia, other at.óow, and their owners).

The annotations provide extra background help to readers of all ages and cultures who wish to enter the world of Tlingit oratory.

In the texts included in this volume, the lines that are bracketed represent the audience's response to the speaker's words, and were spoken aloud. Where speakers could be identified, their Tlingit names are given, followed by a colon, and their response. Some responses difficult to translate are left in Tlingit. *Áawé* is something like "That's it" or "Amen." *Héiy* is something like "yo!" Most unidentified audience responses may be assumed to come from the person mentioned in the previous line.

– Nora Marks Dauenhauer

David Kadashan's "Speech for the Removal of Grief" (p. 30)

David Kadashan gave a speech because of his relationship with the deceased and because he had been educated in delivering oratory. Mr. Kadashan was of the Raven T'a̱kdeintaan clan which was also the clan of the deceased's grandfathers. He was also the grand-child of (*i.e.*, his grandfather was a member of) the Raven Lukaa̱x.-ádi clan.

This speech can be read and understood on three levels: the fact of the death of a loved one and the grief that is being expressed, the poetic metaphors within the speech, and the social structure of the potlatch. The structure of the speech is as follows:

– Proclaims solidarity with the grieving clan (lines 1–5)

– Calls on his own relatives, deceased, to help him ease the grief of the host (6–30)

– Metaphors of grief, the deceased, and tears as a river, a tree, and the water, respectively (31–57)

– Metaphor of grief leaving the bereaved (58–62)

– Explanation of the metaphor (63–67)

– Expresses his hope for the release from grief (78–85)

– A reminder of his longstanding relationship with the grieving clan (86–117)

– P.H.P.

LINE NOTES FOR DAVID KADASHAN'S "SPEECH FOR THE REMOVAL OF GRIEF"

0. The notes that follow contain detailed references to Tlingit genealogy and social structure crucial to full cultural understanding of the oratory. However, these terms and clan names need not be completely mastered for a reader to appreciate the poetry of the speeches.

Although a person has only one biological father and mother, in Tlingit culture and according to Tlingit genealogy, an individual usually has more than one person who can be considered his or her father or mother. This can be confusing in English translation due to cultural differences, and because *mothers'* (with an apostrophe following the s) at first glance seems to be a typographical error for *mother's*.

1. My father's brothers, all my brothers-in-law. Following protocol, the speaker is establishing a kinship relationship between himself and the hosts, whom he addresses as his brothers-in-law and paternal uncles. David Kadashan is a Raven of the T'a̱kdeintaan clan, and a Child of Shangukeidí. Among the hosting Eagles he is addressing, along with Willie Marks and his relatives, are Tom Jimmie and Joe White, who are members of the Shangukeidí clan assisting their fellow Eagle Chookaneidí hosts. These men are representing Shangukeidí because Tom Jimmie is a Child of Lukaa̱x.ádi (as are the host and deceased) and Joe White was adopted into the Chookaneidí clan. Emma Marks, the wife of the host, is also a Child of Shangukeidí, as is

307

the speaker. Also, David's wife is a woman of Shangukeidí. This makes the Shangukeidí men and Keet Yaanaayí his brothers-in-law. Thus the speaker is addressing the
hosts with these kinship terms as prescribed by tradition. Men can be addressed as
paternal uncles (father's brothers) or brothers-in-law regardless of their ages.

2, 3. We are feeling your pain. The guest list is partly made up of people who
are related to the host and deceased. The speaker is expressing sympathy for the
bereft family.

6. I will imitate my mother's brother. Reference here is to the maternal uncle,
who is traditionally the important figure in the education of a Tlingit male child, and
as a role model in his life. (A child is not of the same clan and moiety as his or her
father, so that clan traditions pass from uncle to nephew.) The education given to a
sister's son is usually according to the role the male child will play in his future life.
He would be trained in some or all of the following: hunting, fishing, art, and/
or leadership.

7–11. Ḵáak'w Éesh is a Kaagwaantaan name. The son of Ḵáak'w Éesh is J. C.
Johnson, a Raven of the T'aḵdeintaan clan, and Child of Kaagwaantaan and maternal
uncle of the speaker (the mother's brother referred to in the previous line). Tsalxaan
Ǥuwakaan and Yakwdeiyí Ǥuwakaan are Eagle moiety, Kaagwaantaan, and are considered the maternal uncles of Ḵaak'w Éesh. Thus they are the maternal uncles of
the father of the speaker's maternal uncle. Through the use of these names and kinship terms, the speaker is establishing his various relationships with the opposite
moiety.

9. Tsalxaan Ǥuwakaan is a Kaagwaantaan peace maker for the T'aḵdeintaan.
This position was inherited from his younger brother who is now deceased. This
Ǥuwakaan was a chosen one. With the title of peace maker goes a number of responsibilities, one of which is that a person is peace maker for life. Whenever there is a
dispute in the T'aḵdeintaan clan he can intervene and defuse or resolve it. Tsalxaan
is Mt. Fairweather in English. The T'aḵdeintaan claim Mt. Fairweather. Ǥuwakaan is
"deer" in English; from the image of the deer as a gentle and peaceful animal comes
the use of the word to signify a hostage or a peace maker. Tsalxaan Ǥuwakaan's
English name is George Dalton.

10. Heiy! This is another word used by a person to respond to the speaker. As
individuals are recognized by the speaker either by their personal names or kinship
titles, the individuals acknowledge the speaker by responding. The word has no
exact English translation, but is something like "yo" or "yes" or "here I am."

11. Yakwdeiyí Ǥuwakaan. A peace maker of the Wooshkeetaan clan, David Mc-
Kinley. He inherited the title after the death of Louie Hanson. After David McKinley's
death Eli Hanlon inherited the position. Yakwdeiyí is a place name in Lituya Bay
and means "Canoe Trail." It is a place you can go when there is a storm on the Gulf
of Alaska.

13. I will imitate your brother-in-law. He is addressing the men who are married
to Children of Kaagwaantaan.

15. My brother-in-law Keet Yaanaayí. David Kadashan is now directing his
speech to Keet Yaanaayí, Willie Marks, the host, who is the younger brother of the
deceased. Keet Yaanaayí is Chookaneidí, Lukaax.ádi yádi, and of X'aak Hít.

17. Ḵaatooshtóow. A Chookaneidí clan member but from a different house
group (Xaay Hít, Red Cedar House); Tax' Hít Taan yádi. His English name was John
F. Wilson. Ḵaatooshtóow is there as Chookaneidí dachxán, a grandchild of Chookaneidí. His father was a Child of Chookaneidí (Chookaneidí yádi). He was like a maternal uncle to Ḵuháanx' (Goox Ǥuwakaan – Jim Marks) and Keet Yaanaayí (Willie
Marks) because the mother of Goox Ǥuwakaan and Keet Yaanaayí was also Tax' Hít

Taan yádi, making her and Kaatooshtóow tribal brother and sister. (Their fathers came from the same house – Tax' Hít – Snail House.) He is also the brother-in-law of Káak'w Éesh du yéet (the son of Káak'w Éesh), J. C. Johnson, whose wife was also from Xaay Hít.

19. I will imitate your brother-in-law. Reference is to Káak'w Éesh du yéet. David Kadashan is imitating his maternal uncle. See notes to lines 6 and 7–11. The speaker is assuming the position of his mother's brother. By imitating his maternal uncle, he is presenting him to the grieving brother-in-law Keet Yaanaayí and his relatives.

20. Gusatáan. Harry Marvin. Gusatáan is named as part of the hosting family because he is a grandchild of Chookaneidí. (His father was a child of Chookaneidí.) Gusatáan is there to support Keet Yaanaayí and the departed Kuhaanx'.

22. I will imitate your child. The reaffirmation of the genealogy to the hosting group is to complete the foundation of the oratory.

24–28. Surely . . . and sensitive. In these lines the speaker expresses how difficult it is to make a speech of this kind. When he speaks, he has to remember all of his departed relatives who are related to Keet Yaanaayí. For example, the speaker's grief for his maternal uncle Káak'w Éesh du yéet is renewed every time he makes this kind of speech.

29, 30. We are in need of our mother's brothers. Had the maternal uncles of the speaker and others lived, they would be the ones making this speech. The idea is that when you tell a grieving family about your deceased relatives it is soothing, because everyone has deceased relatives, and the living can draw support from each other.

31–57. The river would swell . . . the tide would leave it dry. This is an elaborate, three-layered extended simile comparing Xwaayeenák and his song and Goox Guwa-kaan and his song to the tree uprooted by the swollen river, buffeted by the stormy seas, and deposited on a sandy beach. With the kinship relationships established by the first and second speakers, David Kadashan, the second speaker, can now begin to make further connections, and tie the various elements together. The style of the oratory now moves from the genealogical inventory or catalog into the use of simile and metaphor.

48, 49. Naawéiyaa. Harry Marvin: Kaagwaantaan; T'akdeintaan yádi; Kook Hít. Harry Marvin also had the name Gusatáan. He died in the mid-1970's while dancing with the Hoonah Mt. Fairweather Dancers during a performance in Juneau for the First Americans Emphasis Week.

58–66. It would lie there . . . whoever is one. The log would lie there on the beach. This is another simile, comparing the mourners who have been stricken and are filled with grief to the soaked log. The sun will shine on the log and dry it out. The speaker expresses his wish that his brothers-in-law will be like this. The sun is the Sun Mask to be presented in the speech by Naa Tláa (Jessie Dalton).

68. You created me, Chookaneidí. David Kadashan is a Grandchild of Chooka-neidí. His mother's father was Chookaneidí. Thus, although he is not a member of that clan, he was created or given life by that clan. As he says in the following line, this is why he feels such sympathy for the family. David's father was Kaadasháan, a Lukaax.ádi who was a close relative of Jakwteen, the father of the deceased. The name Kadashan derives from the Lukaax.ádi name Kaadasháan from the Chilkat area.

72. This is the way Xwaayeenák is. Reaffirming that Xwaayeenak is like the log. Recapitulates the simile of the log.

74ff. In this world. . . . These lines reconfirm the relationship between the two groups, the Chookaneidí and the T'akdeintaan: how the two clans both care for their dead by holding feasts for the departed, and how they support each other in these feasts by caring for each other. The speaker is emphasizing that his clan, like the hosts, are also traditional in their care for the departed, and that they also value the sense of reciprocity so important in traditional Tlingit society.

78ff. Yes! This moment. . . . These lines are a restatement of grief turning to happiness, of a beginning for new life.

87, 88. You all know your brothers-in-law, your fathers' sisters. The speaker is referring to people who are standing in their tribal regalia, waiting for Naa Tláa to speak on their clan crests, robes, hats, shirts, and Chilkat Blankets.

93. You will stand. The speaker is now addressing his fellow guests who are already standing or who now stand up.

97. When such things happened. When there was feasting for the deceased.

99. The things that might warm your feelings. The clan regalia of the guests (clanspeople of the speaker) would bring good will and comfort to the grieving hosts.

100–103. The people . . . used to show you. The speaker's ancestors used to show the clan regalia both to the living hosts and to the ancestors of the hosts. "You" refers both to the very people who are hosting, and to their ancestors as well. This is the way Tlingit tradition is.

107ff. Brothers-in-law, etc. Again, a restatement of the kinship bonds between the speaker and the hosting family and clan.

111. Aan Káx Shawoostaan. Mary Johnson. Chookaneidí; Lukaax.ádi yádi; wife of William Johnson, the next speaker. She is the maternal niece of the deceased and the host.

112. There is no way we can do anything for you. The speaker is expressing the feelings of inadequacy caused by death, and the survivors' inability to solve the problems of death and grief.

113–116. We will only imitate them. . . . We will try. The guests will imitate their ancestors who are deceased. Note the blend of the living and the deceased here and in the following speeches. The living people present are imitating their ancestors, from whom many of them inherited the regalia in which they are standing. In this way the departed are made spiritually present.

119, 120. Frog Hat Song. Mountain Tribe's Dog Hat Song. These songs were played on a tape recorder.

123. Kaakwsak'aa. David Williams: Chookaneidí; T'akdeintaan yádi. The name was inherited from his maternal uncle, the host's brother John Marks.

121, 122. This is all. This signals that the speech is over, and the guests thank the speaker.

– N.D.

Jessie Dalton's "Speech for the Removal of Grief" (p. 34)

Jessie Dalton gave a speech both because of her skill as an orator and because, like David Kadashan, she is a member of the T'akdeintaan clan. She is also child of the Wooshkeetaan clan (*i.e.,* her father was a Wooshketaan), which was one of the host clans.

The line notes to the story indicate the oral and performing nature of these selections: there is interaction with the audience and there are appropriate repetitions and pauses. Most importantly, the display of the clan regalia is important, as are the words of her speech. Anthropological literature has made much of the display

310

of the guests' regalia at potlatches honoring the dead. A common interpretation of this practice has been that it indicates intense rivalry between clans and represents a familiar image and a well-known story with its own power to comfort. There is nothing here of the arrogance noted in potlatch accounts by other authors.

– P.H.P.

LINE NOTES FOR JESSIE DALTON'S "SPEECH FOR REMOVAL OF GRIEF"

Jesse Dalton. Naa Tláa. Raven. T'akdeintaan; Wooshkeetaan yádi.

1. Does it take pity on us . . . ? Jessie opens her speech with a rhetorical question. "It" is death. This is a personification of death. She asks if death takes pity on us. She answers her question in line 7: "It doesn't take pity on us either." Her speech is to remove grief and somehow come to grips with death.

2. My brothers' children. She is addressing her paternal nephews and nieces.

5. My fathers. She is addressing the men of the Wooshkeetaan, her father's clan.

6. All my fathers. She is addressing all men who are of the Eagle moiety that is hosting. The Eagle hosts include: Wooshkeetaan, Chookaneidí, Kaagwaantaan, Shangukeidí. The main host clan is Chookaneidí.

8. This thing that happens. Again, the reference is to death.

10. This is why you hear their voices like this. Reference is to the recording played earlier, and to David Kadashan, who spoke before Jessie Dalton. The recording was of the voices of the T'akdeintaan being heard singing the Mountain Tribe Dog Song.

11. Your fathers. This line is directed to the Children of T'akdeintaan, who are Jessie's paternal nephews and nieces.

12. That your tears not fall without honor. Reference is to the traditional period of mourning, and the taboo of mourning beyond that. The relatives of the deceased mourn for approximately one year, until someone does the ritual for the purging of grief.

15. That which flowed from your faces. Reference is to the tears shed during the final weeping prior to this ritual.

17. They have all come out this moment. Two things are happening in this line: 1) the speaker is announcing the clan members who will be coming out wearing clan regalia, and 2) not only are the living T'akdeintaan coming out for the tears of the hosts, but the spirits of the deceased T'akdeintaan have come out as well.

18, 19. Your fathers have all come out. Jessie is speaking metaphorically now. The clan regalia, called at.óow in Tlingit, are physically present in the room; the at.óow have been brought out and are being worn by the T'akdeintaan Grandchildren. The fathers of the hosts are spiritually present.

21. They are still present. The deceased relatives are thought of as being present in the at.óow (regalia).

22. That is how I feel about my grandparents. Reference is to the feeling about Tlingit at.óow, and how it is regarded as the grandparent because it was once owned and worn by the grandparent. Some of the at.óow were carved by the host Willie Marks, his deceased brother Jim Marks, and their nephew David Williams as tribal commissions by the opposite moiety.

24. Someone here stands wearing one. This is a refrain running throughout Jessie Dalton's speech, and refers to the Grandchildren wearing the at.óow. She will refer to them one by one through the rest of her speech.

25. Mountain Tribe's Dog. This is a carved hat, the image of a dog, a very important piece of T'akdeintaan tribal art, and very significant at.óow. It is the image of one of the T'akdeintaan yeik or spirits of a shaman. The original hat was burned in the Hoonah fire of 1944. Jim and Willie Marks were commissioned to do the carving. (It is Tlingit tradition to commission artists of the opposite moiety to make clan regalia.) The piece became at.óow when the former owner died.

26, 27. It is as if it's barking for your pain. This is the first of many poetic comparisons Jessie will use. In this simile, the Mountain Tribe's Dog Hat embodies the spirit of a real dog acting in an appropriate way in response to the grief being experienced by the hosts.

29. My fathers, my brothers' children. As in the opening lines, a refrain showing both respect and her relationship to the hosts. She refers to her father's people, the Wooshkeetaan, and to her paternal nephews and nieces who are the children of T'akdeintaan.

30. My father's sisters. Jessie is addressing the women of the Wooshkeetaan clan. Jessie Dalton's speech shows the importance of knowing your genealogy, the genealogies of other persons involved, the meaning of tribal art, and the relationship of the tribal art to genealogy – and the art of tying it all together through the protocol and rhetorical devices of public speaking.

33. Someone standing next to it. The "it" is the at.óow she described earlier. Now she is moving on to the next. Using this refrain before each image, she lets her audience know that she is talking about the people standing with the T'akdeintaan at.óow.

34. Raven who walked down along the bull kelp. In Tlingit, Geesh Daax Woogoodi Yéil. Reference is to a shirt one of the people is wearing. The motif is taken from the Raven story in which Raven walks down the kelp to get a sea urchin to bounce on the Tide Lady's hind end, to make her get off the spot which controls the sea. As long as she stays in one place, the sea doesn't move. If she gets off, the tide will go out. Raven bounces the sea urchin on her butt.

This is an example of the connection between visual art, verbal art, the kinship system, and ceremony. Tribal art is worn or brought out by certain people at certain times; the art usually quotes, commemorates, or otherwise alludes to songs, stories, or history. All of this is happening here, and in turn providing the basis for more verbal art – the speech being composed and presented by Jessie Dalton.

36. L yeedayéik's robe. Continuing down the line of persons wearing regalia, the speaker comes to this one. L yeedayéik (English name: Eliza Lawrence) was a woman of the T'akdeintaan. When she died, someone inherited the robe. Again, Jessie is making the deceased spiritually present through the presentation of their former regalia.

38. Naawéiyaa. Harry Marvin: Kaagwaantaan; T'akdeintaan yádi. He is thanking her because he is T'akdeintaan yádi.

41. S'eilshéix. Eva Davis: Chookaneidí; Lukaax.ádi yádi, sister of Mary Johnson. She is responding to the Beaver robe because of her connection to Chilkat and Lutákl.

42–61. Beaver Robe. Reference is to the Beaver Robe from Klukwan.

45. Lutákl your father. Again, a deceased former owner or custodian of tribal regalia is made present through the regalia. Three people respond to the orator, of whom two are identifiable on the tape recording. Each has a special relationship to Lutákl, because he is of their father's clan.

Lutákl. T'akdeintaan; Shangukeidí yádi.

Naawéiyaa. Harry Marvin: Kaagwaantaan; T'akdeintaan yádi.

Sei.akdoolxéitl'. David McKinley: Wooshkeetaan; T'akdeintaan yádi; from Head House.

62. Your fathers' sisters. The orator is speaking to the Raven moiety, presenting now the Tern Robe according to the owner's genealogical relationship to the hosts.

64. Saayina.aat. Irene (Mrs. Jim) Young: T'akdeintaan; Chookaneidí yádi. Biological mother of William Johnson and tribal mother of Jessie Dalton.

65. The Tern Robe. Jessie is now introducing the Tern Robe, on which she will build one of the most beautiful and intricate metaphors of her speech. The following lines are the beginning of the metaphor; she will then move to other regalia, and return to the Tern Robe later in her speech.

74. Gaanaxáa. This is the beginning of an extended metaphor, by which the next several people are brought to the point of land, where their names are called out. Gaanaxáa is a point on the Cape Fairweather coast, near Lituya Bay. It is a tern rookery. The speaker will now continue, calling out the names of the people who are feeling grief, bringing them metaphorically to Gaanaxáa.

79. Father, Sei.akduxeitl'. David McKinley: Wooshkeetaan. Jessie Dalton is Child of Wooshkeetaan (Wooshkeetaan yádi), so according to protocol, she can address him as "Father." Metaphorically she is calling him to Gaanaxáa, where later she will call the terns to fly out over him.

82. My grandfather's son Koowunagáas'. Joe White: Shangukeidí; T'akdeintaan yádi; adopted into the Chookaneidí. Koowunagáas' was also like a maternal uncle to Keet Yaanaayí because his mother and Koowunagáas' were considered brother and sister because the fathers of both were from Tax' Hít.

84. My brother's son's child Keet Yaanaayí. Willie Marks, brother of the deceased and host of the memorial. Keet Yaanaayí's mother was a Child of T'akdeintaan, a child of one of the speaker's clan brothers. The mother of Keet Yaanaayí was a paternal niece of Jessie Dalton.

87. My father's sister's son Xooxkeina.át. Pete Johnson: Wooshkeetaan. Jessie Dalton's father was also Wooshkeetaan. Xooxkeina.át was also adopted into the Chookaneidí clan by Goox Guwakaan (Jim Marks).

91. Your fathers' sisters are revealing their faces. This line is directed to the Eagles. The fathers' sisters are T'akdeintaan, and their crest is the tern. Metaphorically, the sisters equal the terns, and are revealing their faces at the rookery to which the mourners have been called by the speaker. Gaanaxáa is the tern rookery where the terns would sit on the cliffs.

93. Kaatooshtóow. John F. Wilson: Chookaneidí; T'akdeintaan yádi. He is also one of the survivors of the people who are the original people of Kaasteen (of Glacier Bay). He is also a paternal Grandchild of Chookaneidí.

95. Kaakwsak'aa. David Williams: Chookaneidí; T'akdeintaan yádi. Maternal nephew of Goox Guwakaan. His father was T'akdeintaan of the Raven Nest House (Yéil Kudei Hít).

98. My brother's wife Aan Káx Shawustaan. Mary Johnson: Chookaneidí; Lukaax.ádi yádi. She is a maternal niece of Goox Guwakaan and married to William Johnson, a clan brother of Jessie Dalton.

102. As if they are revealing their faces. The Gaanaxáa extended metaphor ends here with a simile, in which terns (metaphorically the paternal aunts at the rookery) are imagined as revealing their faces.

103. Your sisters-in-law. This line is addressed to Aan Káx Shawustaan (Mary Johnson).

106. Weihá, his shirt. Reference is to the Raven Who Walked Down Along the Kelp Shirt. (See Note to line 34.)

Weihá. Jim Fox: Gaanax.ádi from Taku; Yanyeidí yádi.

107–109. It was only recently we completed the rites for him. The rites are also mentioned by William Johnson in his speech. (Line 24.)

113. You also heard him here. Reference is to the Frog Hat Song that was played earlier on a tape recorder by David Kadashan.

115. This brother of mine. Weihá is in the English sense Jessie Dalton's cousin, but in the Tlingit sense her paternal brother. Their fathers are of the Wooshkeetaan and Yanyeidí. Weihá is also of Jessie's paternal grandfather's clan.

116. This Peace Maker of yours. Reference is to William Johnson, who is Kaag-waantaan's peace maker.

117. It will remain in his hands, in his care. The shirt was inherited by William Johnson (Keewaax.awtseix Guwakaan; T'akdeintaan; Wooshkeetaan yádi).

120. It is as if he will be coming out for you to see. Again, a simile comparing the regalia to the deceased owner or custodian. When the shirt comes out from time to time it will be as if Weihá is coming out.

123, 124. How proud he used to feel wearing it. Weihá wore the tunic proudly.

128. The Raven Nest Robe. There was a clan house in Hoonah named Raven Nest House (Yéil Kudei Hít), which was destroyed along with all the clan houses in the Hoonah fire of 1944. The robe was made to commemorate the house.

130. Yaakaayindul.át your father's sister. Metaphorically referring to the deceased owner of the Robe. Through the blanket Yaakaayindul.át is present. This robe is one of the older ones and does not have a motif on it. It has only buttons and felt.

Yaakaayindul.át. T'akdeintaan; Jessie Dalton's maternal aunt: Bertina Peterson's great grandmother; Bertina Peterson also has this name.

132. We have long since given up hope for their return. The owners of all the T'akdeintaan at.óow are deceased, but are still referred to as being present and merged with the at.óow.

139. Kaadéik. Kaagwaantaan.

143. I don't feel that it burned. The original shirt of Kaadéik's father was destroyed in the 1944 fire. Along with much of the other at.óow, it was replaced with a newer duplicate. The shirt is made of marten skins.

145. It is the same one in which your father's brother is standing there in front of you. Kaadéik's father is merged with his shirt.

150. Gusatáan. = Naawéiyaa. Harry Marvin; Kaagwaantaan; T'akdeintaan yádi. Chookaneidí dachxan (Grandchild of Chookaneidí); one of the host group.

152. It will be just as if I will have named all of you. The speaker has been relating persons of both the guests and the host/hostess groups to each other. Here she expresses that she will be unable to name all the deceased individually, but this gesture is as if she had named them all.

155–158. Can I reach the end? She says this because there are too many of her deceased to recall them all.

159. These terns I haven't completely explained. The speaker is now leading up to her final images of the terns.

161–174. These terns. Your fathers' sisters would fly out over the person who is grieving . . . etc.

This is one of the most striking images of the speech. It is a metaphor within an extended simile. The terns are the spirits of the T'akdeintaan paternal aunts of the hosts who are feeling grief. The terns would fly out over the person who is feeling grief, and let their down shower like snow over the person who is feeling grief. The down is soothing; it is not felt. The extended simile concludes with the speaker saying that she feels as if the terns are removing the grief by absorbing it and flying back to their nests with it.

177–191. *The one standing here . . . it also came from Taku.* The speaker is giving a history of the Frog Hat, and of one way an emblem or coat of arms could be acquired.

193. *I keep saying thank you.* Jessie is thanking the hosts for having them bring out their ancestors' at.óow.

197–211. *During the warm season.* The speaker is starting another metaphor and simile. The Frog Hat is described as a real frog, and its deceased owner made present. The hat is animated, and the father of the hosts, who was the owner of the hat, comes out in response to the grief. The spirit of the departed appearing in the human world is compared to a frog coming out of hibernation in the spring. It removes the grief from the mourners, and burrows back down with it.

219. *It is like a proverb.* The following lines are a Tlingit saying, and the speaker is reiterating the theme that the group is imitating.

221. *Lest it grope aimlessly.* Lest the Xwaayeenák song resonate without response. Lest the words of the Grandfathers resonate without response. It is very important in the Tlingit system of balance and reciprocity that words and songs be answered.

223. *What your grandparents used to say.* The particular grandparent referred to here is K'aadóo, the composer of the Xwaayeenák song in Goox̱ G̱uwakaan's narrative.

224. *It's as if your fathers are guiding them.* As if Keet Yaanaayí's ancestors are leading the at.óow, the oratory, and songs.

228, 229. *This grandfather of mine, Yookis'kook̲éik, his hat.* This is the beginning of the metaphor based on the Loon Hat.

Yookis'kook̲éik. (Leonard Davis: T'ak̲deintaan; Kaagwaantaan yádi) was a custodian of Tax̲' Hít. The custom is that the same house group will refer to an older generation as a grandparent generation. Yookis'kook̲éik (Archie White) was the biological father of Koowunagáas' (Joe White: Shangukeidí; T'ak̲deintaan yádi), and the speaker is now establishing this relationship to him. Archie White was the house leader of Tax̲' Hít (Snail House) that burned in 1944.

241. *The Loon Shaman Spirit.* The Loon Spirit, a spirit helper for the shaman. In a previous line, the speaker says that the spirit "has stood up to face you." In some narratives the spirit will stand up in the path of a candidate for a shaman. The spirit stands up before him before it enters him to give him strength.

245. *The one this brother of mine explained a while ago.* Reference is to the log images in David Kadashan's speech prior to Jessie Dalton's.

246. *How that tree rolled on the waves.* This is a metaphor that works two ways. The uprooted tree is compared both to the grieving survivors and to the deceased. The deceased are looked at as someone carried by a storm. The survivors are also thought of as someone who has lost his homeland, someone who has been uprooted. Jessie Dalton recapitulates the essence of David's final comparison: the sun would put its rays on it, and would dry its grief to the core.

252. *This moment this sun comes out over you, my grandparents' mask.* Jessie has been leading up to the presentation of the Sun Mask. The sun that is drying the grief is again the at.óow. The Sun Mask belongs to K̲aachx̲ooti (no English name; Katherine Mills' great, great uncle). It then passed to Kichx̲ít'aa, her great uncle, of the Head House (K̲aa Shaayi Hít) also before the time of the English names. It then passed to K̲aakw Daa Éesh, the father of Joe White. From then it passed to S'ekyatóow (Frank Wilson). It then passed to Shaak̲wlayéix (Leonard Davis). The mask is now in the care of Katherine Mills' son, George Mills, also named K̲aakw Daa Éesh.

257. My hope is your grief be like it's drying to your core. This is the line Jessie has been leading up to. This is the line that extracts the sorrow. This is the way we cope with death. This gives us the feeling that we are not alone.

260. Géelák'w Headdress. An ermine headdress made in the image of the frontal screen of Tsalxaan Hít, better known as Tax' Hít (Snail House). See the following note for more detail.

262. Your father's sisters would reveal their faces from it, from G̲éelák'w. G̲éelák'w is another name for Tsalxaan, Mt. Fairweather. The name G̲éelák'w is an image of the part of the mountain where it separates into two peaks. G̲éel is the Tlingit word for "gunsight," the "V" where the mountain separates into two peaks. While the name G̲éelák'w refers specifically to the V made by the two peaks, the name is also synonymous with Tsalxaan in referring to Mt. Fairweather as a whole.

G̲éelák'w is the part of the mountain where Goox̲k', the little boy who became a one horned goat in David Kadashan's narrative of the One Horned Goat, went, taking all the animals with him. The One Horned Goat became a powerful spirit for the T'ak̲deintaan shaman.

This line in the speech is a metaphor of how the spirits of the mountain, who are women, would appear and come to a shaman to heal those who are ill.

There was a frontal screen on the Tsalxaan Hít (Mt. Fairweather House) in Hoonah. The base of the screen rested on the floor of the porch, and the top reached above the second floor windows. The screen was about two feet wider on each side than the door. There was a hole in the bottom center of the screen for the entrance to the house. The G̲éelák'w headdress (dance frontlet) is made in the image of the frontal screen for the house. As the headdress is displayed, the spirits are metaphorically made present.

There is another at.óow representing the spirits of the mountain. Metaphorically the woman spirits of the mountain, who are also one of the shaman spirits, are carved into Tsalx̲aantu Sháawu, a hat carved by Willie Marks. On this hat, a woman appears from the crown of the hat.

Mt. Fairweather is a spiritual ground. The One Horned Goat took place here, and the spirits of the shaman come from here. Mt. Fairweather is one of the important at.óow for the T'ak̲deintaan.

267. My grandfather, his headdress. Jessie ends the oratory with the image of the G̲éelák'w headdress, and the women coming out on Keet Yaanaayí, the hosts, and the guests. This headdress was Frank Wilson's, and was held, not worn, during the memorial.

The Mt. Fairweather Hat was James Grant's, then John K. Smith's, then passed to Leonard Davis, then Matthew Lawrence, and is now in the care of Richard Sheakley.

– N.D.

Austin Hammond's "Speech for the Removal of Grief" (p. 41)

Austin Hammond, of the opposite moiety and another clan from the deceased, was his stepson. In fact, Austin Hammond's clan, Lukaax̲.ádi, was the clan of the deceased father. This established a double relationship between Hammond and Jim Marks: Hammond was both a son and a father to the deceased.

– P.H.P.

LINE NOTES FOR AUSTIN HAMMOND'S "SPEECH FOR THE REMOVAL OF GRIEF"

1. Austin Hammond. Raven; Lukaax̱.ádi; Kaagwaantaan yádi.

2. My father's brothers. Austin is laying the foundation of his speech. He is the stepson of Goox̱ G̱uwakaan, in whose memory the feast is being held. In Tlingit tradition, there is no difference between an adopted child and a biological child and the kinship terms are the same. Here the speaker is addressing Keet Yaanaayí.

3. My father's sisters. Here he is addressing the women of Chookaneidí, and all the Eagle women.

5–7. How very much I too feel grief. Austin is expressing the sharing of grief for his father, the brother of the hosts.

9–11. That I am here, but I can't even find anything to show you. Reference here is to clan at.óow. The speaker is powerfully expressing his sense of utter helplessness in the face of grief. He will return to the theme of regalia at the close of his speech, where he will rhetorically devaluate a magnificent Chilkat Robe, implying that it is nothing in contrast to the grief and loss the host clan is feeling, but hopes that it will act in some small way to remove the grief.

12–14. At this moment he came out . . . with it. At the moment when the orator was feeling this helplessness, someone came out with a woven robe, a Grandchild of Lukaax̱.ádi.

17–19. In many ways . . . K'eedzáa used to talk. In the past, when one of Keet Yaanaayí's relatives died, K'eedzáa used to speak to them with words of comfort. But K'eedzáa is now deceased.

20. Here is his robe. . . . The robe is the Sockeye Chilkat Robe that Austin inherited at the death of K'eedzáa, his maternal uncle, and also Goox̱ G̱uwakaan's paternal uncle.

27. Kaatyé. David Kadashan, a Grandchild of Lukaax̱.ádi, who delivered the second of the guests' speeches.

29. My mother's brother Tsagwált, his robe. Tsagwált was also Austin Hammond's biological maternal uncle. Austin had inherited the robe from him.

35. There is one more. Austin is presenting another object for the grieving hosts to look at.

37. It wasn't here. The robe was not physically present at the memorial for Austin to show to the grieving family, so he will just explain about it.

39. My father Keet Yaanaayí. Keet Yaanaayí is Austin's paternal uncle, and in turn Austin is a paternal uncle of Keet Yaanaayí.

41. This brother-in-law of yours. . . . Tsagwált was very proud of his brother-in-law. Keet Yaanaayí's wife is Lukaax̱.ádi, as is Austin Hammond, and as was Austin's mother.

43. Naatúxjayi. Naatúxjayi is an image of a Shaman Spirit woven into a Chilkat tunic. The spirit was once G̱eek'ee's shaman spirit, a Lukaax̱.ádi shaman spirit.

45. He has also come here for your grief. Austin speaks of the shaman spirit Naatúxjayi as a human being.

47. To remove it. The shaman spirit Naatúxjayi will remove grief in the same way that a shaman removes illness.

41–51. That blanket . . . as . . . a kerchief. . . . This is a simile to remove Keet Yaanaayí's grief. It is as if the blanket becomes a handkerchief.

52. This is how I feel too. The speaker is expressing his sympathy and sharing of grief with his father's brother, and grief for his father, and his father's sisters.

– N.D.

COMMENTARY ON TSIMSHIAN/ TSETSAUT TEXTS

BACKGROUND

The original homeland of the Tsimshian people, like that of the Haida people, is located within what is now British Columbia, Canada, although some oral accounts suggest there was a small village located in Southeast Alaska's Portland Canal area prior to contact. In the late 1880s, under the leadership of missionary William Duncan, a group of Tsimshian moved north to Alaska, leaving their former village of "Old" Metlakatla in British Columbia, and established a new Metlakatla on Annette Island – now the only Indian reservation located in Alaska.

– J.B.

WORKS

William Beynon: "When Tckaimson and Laggabula Gambled" (p. 44)
Reginald Dangeli: "Tsetsaut History: The Forgotten Tribe of Southern Southeast Alaska" (p. 48)

"When Tckaimson and Laggabula Gambled" (p. 44)

This story was selected as an example of a Tsimshian gambling story. "Oolichans" (variously spelled "eulachons" or "ooligans") are a relatively small and oil-rich fish, similar in appearance to, but smaller than, smelt. When rendered, oolichans produce a thick oil used as a seasoning or sauce to flavor various foods including salmon, potatoes, rice, and berries. In previous times, oolichan oil, affectionately referred to as "grease" in English among Southeast Alaska Natives, was an important trade item. Tsimshian "Nass River oil" was and is especially valued.

The story has an interesting publication history.[1] William Beynon, born in Victoria, B.C. to a Tsimshian woman and non-Native father, was raised learning to speak both English and Tsimshian. When he completed school in 1915, he returned to his mother's people, as earlier agreed, to study and document Tsimshian stories and history, which he continued until his death in 1969. Franz Boas purchased the manuscripts, and later turned them over to Columbia University, where they remained undiscovered until 1979.

"When Tckaimson and Laggabula Gambled" appeared in one of the volumes that was part of the overall reprinting of Beynon's work in 1985, a task undertaken by the Metlakatla Indian Community under the direction of Russell Hayward, Tsimshian Language Coordinator, and Ira Booth, Tribal Council Historian, of Metlakatla. Beynon devised his own handwritten Tsimshian alphabet. This story shows the typed version of his alphabet, but a new one was created in 1979 by six Tsimshian elders of the Tsimshian Tribal Association.
– J.B.

"Tsetsaut History: The Forgotten Tribe of Southern Southeast Alaska" (p. 48)

The work of Reginald Dangeli represents both Tsimshian and Tsetsaut writing. Mr. Dangeli was of Tsetsaut and Tsimshian ancestry, a native speaker of Nishga-Tsimshian, and a researcher of Tsetsaut and Nishga oral literature and history.

The Tsetsaut occupied the peninsula between Portland Canal and Behm Canal in what is now Misty Fjord National Monument in southernmost Southeast Alaska. In contrast to the more coastal and marine oriented Tlingit and Tsimshian, the Tsetsaut were inland hunters. Through warfare and peaceful assimilation with neighboring groups, especially the Nishga, the Tsetsaut speaking population decreased rapidly in the second half of the 19th century.

The Tsetsaut language, a member of the Athabaskan family, is now extinct, though like Mr. Dangeli and his descendants, people of Tsetsaut ancestry are alive and well in Alaska and British Columbia. Mr. Dangeli's grandparents Timothy and Jane Dangeli were the last fluent speakers of Tsetsaut.

The term "adawak" is the Tsimshian name for the genre of oral history and literature recorded by the author.

Mr. Dangeli's account excerpted here is based on his research of oral and written traditions handed down from Chief Mountain and Chief Pahl. Chief Mountain adopted one of Mr. Dangeli's Tsetsaut

---

1. This information came from the introduction to *Tsimshian Stories*, Volume VI of the Beynon manuscripts republished in 1985.

grandfathers, and Chief Pahl (Charles Barton) was paternal grandfather of Louise Barton Dangeli, the wife of Reginald Dangeli. He was interpreter and guide for Barbeau.

– R.D.

This history indicates how cosmopolitan the pre-contact Southeasterners were. They were aware of the Nass, a far-away river abundant in food. They spoke Tlingit as well as Tsetsaut, and later Tsimshian also. Relationships with other nations of people were sometimes friendly, sometimes not. They were not the unchanging, static people which some accounts imply.

The stories recount the origins of important clan songs. Like the Tsetsaut, the Tlingits, Haidas, and Tsimshians also have clan songs which were composed by a revered elder or ancestor for some specific occurrence in the clan's history. When one learns the songs, one learns the history also. They cannot be separated. This is part of the reason Native Southeasterners may be wary of recording, writing, or singing songs out of context: the performance is otherwise incomplete.

Cremation (p. 49) was the common way of disposing of the dead.

Haliotis pearls (p. 50) are the shells of a small, white sea animal, gathered at a special place off the northern California coast.

The Lahk Wi Yips (p. 52), also called "Prairie People," are an extinct group from interior British Columbia.

Franz Boas (p. 53), known as the "father of American anthropology," trained many of the famous anthropologists of the early twentieth century, including Ruth Benedict, Margaret Mead, and Edward Sapir.

– P.H.P.

COMMENTARY ON UNANGAN/ UNANGAS/ALEUT TEXTS

BACKGROUND

Aleuts from the Aleutian, Shumagin, and Pribilof Islands and the tip of the Alaska Peninsula do not call themselves "Aleuts" when speaking their indigenous language. The Unangan (eastern dialect) or Unangas (Atkan dialect) inhabited this region long before Europeans began their journeys for furs and riches. Russian fur traders, government officials, and explorers dubbed these people "Aleuts," a name that eventually received nearly universal acceptance, even among many Unangan/Unangas.

The Unangan/Unangas were expert seamen, orienting their lives almost entirely to the ocean rather than the land. In the eastern portion of the islands they formed large permanent villages characterized by social classes and a matrilineal kinship pattern, while the more mobile western Unangan lived in smaller settlements. The Unangan/Unangas were the first Alaskans to trade with and work for the Russian fur traders, often as forced laborers akin to slaves. This relationship began four years after Vitus Bering's sighting of the islands in 1741 and continued until the United States purchased Alaska in 1867. Through the years, Unangan/Unangas islanders converted to and adapted Russian Orthodoxy, learned to speak Russian, and adopted a number of Russian customs. Today their names, religion, foods, and parts of their narrative tradition reflect this double heritage.

Like other coastal areas of Alaska, the Aleutians saw waves of other European immigrants after the territory's purchase by the United States. Most common were people from Scandinavia and Scotland for whom a sea orientation was second nature, who traveled to Alaska to fish or take part in the whaling industry. During and after World War II, the U.S. military had a strong presence as the Aleutians were seen to be the last line of defense, first against the Japanese, and later in the Cold War against the Soviet Union.

The Aleut selections in this book reflect the varied history of the islands, from Cedor L. Snigaroff's war narrative, an *ungiikax̂*, to Barbara Carlson's essay on Aleut identity in the 20th Century. A traditional *ungiikax̂* recorded in 1910 by Isidor Solovyov (and transcribed and translated by Knut Bergsland and Moses Dirks) tells a tragic tale of an unnecessary death at sea – a death caused by a man's failure to follow rules relating to the use of his boat. Three contemporary poems round out the picture, showing the continued orientation toward the sea – though now through the commercial fishing industry rather than *iqyax̂*-based hunting and fishing – and an enduring sense of belonging, whether it be to a room, a house, or a village.

– P.H.P.

WORKS

Barbara Švarný Carlson: "There Is No Such Thing as an Aleut" (p. 214)
June McGlashan: "Candle Lite" (p. 232) and "It Is Very Quiet" (p. 233)
Mary Jane Peterson: "Cannery Children" (p. 243)
Cedor L. Snigaroff: "Atkan Historical Traditions" (p. 61)
Isidor Solovyov: "Saĝim Tayaĝuu Uluuqidax̂, The Man of Saĝix̂ Dried Meat" (p. 56)

"Saĝim Tayaĝuu Uluuqidax̂, The Man of Saĝix̂ Dried Meat" (p. 56)

This *ungiikax̂* tells a tragedy of expansive dimensions, despite its brevity and succinctness.[1] It conveys lessons crucial to seamen everywhere, and serves as an allegory about life's sometimes seemingly insignificant choices. The profound sadness of Dried Meat punctuates the narrative with an infinite sigh, one that does not fall silent even in death.

Traditional Unangax̂ men's training included a strict rule that the

---

1. This *ungiikax̂*, or old Unangax̂ story, was dictated by Isidor Solovyov in Unalaska in 1910 to Waldemar Jochelson when the latter was leader of the Aleut-Kamchatka Expedition of the Russian Geographical Society. It was first transcribed and translated by the Unangan Leontiy Sivtsov. See Bergsland and Dirks, *Unangam Ungiikangin kayux Tunusangin/Unangam Uniikangis ama Tunuzangis/Aleut Tales and Narratives* (Alaska Native Language Center 1990).

In 1995, Unangan Elder Nick Galaktionoff reported that he had heard about the village in the story, and believed it to have been located on one end of Unimak Island. Unimak Pass is known to have been a favored hunting place.

morning after a man had slept with his wife he must touch or rub his skin boat (called *iqax̂* by Solovyov, in distinction with the more common *iqyax̂*) with the hand that had touched his wife's warm skin. Adherence to this seemingly quaint or mysterious custom is not at all puzzling if one considers the cultural context. First, a man depended on his skin boat for his very life and survival and the well-being of his family and village. Second, if that skin boat were to retain the ability to serve its master well, it must be taken care of well. To be well cared for required nearly constant, and certainly regular, attendance. If a man "touched" his *iqax̂* every morning, he would automatically pay attention to it and notice any needed maintenance or repairs. If the hunter did not attend his skin boat daily, such details could easily escape his notice and therefore be neglected. Third, the implied intimacy of the hunter's relationship with his boat was symbolic of its importance in the society. Without the *iqax̂*, a man could not care for a wife.

In traditional times, this story reminded men and boys that one way to stay together in blinding storm or fog was to call out to each other. This is a small but important matter to remember right away when necessary. In hearing of the words spoken by the *iqan* (plural of *iqax̂*) to their owners, and through the example of Dried Meat's examination of his cousin's skin boat as he was preparing to tow him, hunters and future hunters were reminded that it is foolish to ignore necessary boat repairs.

In the Unangax̂ culture, cousins were often very close, like brothers and sisters. They were raised together, schooled in the traditional ways together, and shared the same history. The story's end, "and having gone over from there to his own house, he died of apathy [sorrowing] after his cousin – he said, it is said," could have a variety of intended meanings. Dried Meat might have died that very day, within a week or month, or may have lived many years and experienced many other things before dying; the important point is that he cared deeply for his cousin, Little Guillemot, and mourned him until his own death.

"*Saĝim Tayaĝuu Uluuqidax̂*" is considered by some to be in the realm of *kadaangaadaan*, the Unangax̂ genre that contains narrative accounts, with elements of the supernatural interwoven. It is equally plausible that the seemingly supernatural voices Dried Meat heard might have reflected the stress he was under. If so, this text might just as easily be an example of a *tunusax̂*, or history and news story. Regardless of its genre, the story communicates the spiritual strength one can garner by living right as a human being, by walking the right path. Dried Meat spent his remaining life wishing that his dear cousin had done so.[2]

– Barbara Švarný Carlson

"Atkan Historical Traditions" (Excerpt) (p. 61)

This excerpt occurs at the end of a long history of internecine warfare between the Atkans and Unangas of Seguam Island, east of Atka. A group of Atkans had traveled to Seguam to revenge previous raids on their territory. Two Atkans, cousins, escaped the slaughter of their compatriots on enemy soil and ran into a cave. The chief of the Seguam Unangas, "Wren," sent one man after another into the cave after them. The Atkans were finally captured and taken to Amukta Island, to the east of Seguam, where they were made slaves. However, they planned escape, timed with the coming of the eastern storms, and in a hair-raising dash and hazardous ocean voyage made it westward to the territory of the Atkans, home once again.

This is one of many war narratives that make up part of Alaska Native oral tradition. The story's detail suggests that it is based on actual events; and, indeed, Russians who arrived in the islands during the mid-18th century reported that warfare had been extremely common among the islanders before the arrival of Europeans. The priest Ivan Veniaminov, later glorified as St. Innocent, noted that this period of warfare contributed to a marked decrease in the population of the islands.

Most war narratives are told by the victors, and hence recount stirring victories or, as in this case, brave and impressive escapes made possible by cleverness and skill. Still, Alaska Native war stories differ from those common in the Western world in that there is rarely an attempt to soften the harsh realities of war, nor are moral judgments made. Instead, the narratives accept warfare as a hideous struggle for resources, territory, or power between opponents who have been unable to agree by more peaceful means.

This narrative was originally told in the Unangas language, then translated into English. Readers may find it stilted or difficult to

---

2. This commentary is an excerpt from a teacher's guide Carlson is preparing to accompany the *Ungiikangin kayux Tunusangin* volume. Her guide contains linguistic analyses, expanded cultural commentaries and suggestions for teaching and studying the collection's traditional stories.

follow, a result of an attempt by Norwegian linguist Knut Bergsland, the translator, to remain as close as possible to the original. The rendition printed here illustrates many of the challenges in translation described by Marie Meade in her selection in this volume.

– P.H.P.

"Cannery Children" (p. 243)

Fish canneries abound throughout southeast Alaska and in Alutiiq and Unangan areas of the state. Cannery work is a common seasonal occupation for Alaska Natives and others in those areas. Women, more often than men, work in the canneries, while their husbands fish. Young people begin working there as early as 15.

The Japanese and "Dagos" referred to in the poem are also cannery workers, many of whom in the past were brought to Alaska especially for the cannery work, then paid low wages. The Japanese workers are technicians hired to oversee the choice and packing of salmon eggs, most of which are exported to Japan for food.

– P.H.P.

COMMENTARY ON ALUTIIQ/ SUGCESTUN TEXTS

BACKGROUND

The Alutiiq people historically inhabited the northeastern part of the Alaska Peninsula, Kodiak Island, the lower Kenai Peninsula, and the shores of Prince William Sound. Like the Unangan/Unangas, they were dubbed "Aleuts" by the Russians. In their own language, the people called themselves *Sugpiaq* (meaning "authentic, real people") and their language *Sugcestun,* but their descendants today often use the term *Alutiiq,* based on the imported word "Aleut." Linguists classify Alutiiq/Sugcestun as an Eskimo language. Indeed, it is so closely related to Central Yup'ik that some Alutiiq speakers can understand Yup'ik speakers who live as far north as Bethel.

Like the Unangan/Unangas, the Alutiiq people were oriented toward the sea, with its salmon, sea mammal, and intertidal shellfish resources. They were masters of the skin-covered *qayaq,* took part in an elaborate ritual cycle, lived together in both large and small villages (depending on locally available resources), and developed a rich material culture using ivory, wood, stone, and skins. Like the inhabitants of the Aleutian Islands, Alutiiq people have had long and sustained contact with Europeans. The first Russian settlement in Alutiiq territory was established on Kodiak Island in 1784, with smaller posts located throughout the region during the next 80 years. The heritage of the Alutiiqs is thus a dual one, melding traditional indigenous elements with Alutiicized Russian practices. The most respected elders in recent memory were bilingual or trilingual, having equal facility in Alutiiq, Russian, and English.

The Alutiiq selections in this book illustrate this dual heritage. In his *unigkuaq,* or traditional myth-like story, Ignatius Kosbruk's shaman struggles with a choice that virtually all Alutiiqs had to make during the 19th century: to cleave to the old ways or adopt the new. Dick Kamluck, Sr.'s story takes a stock Russian folk character and places him in an Alaskan context. Walter Meganack, Sr.'s bear story – like Kosbruk's *unigkuaq* – shows the endurance of precontact tradition and the continued importance of showing respect for fellow creatures and caring for one's family. Mary Jane Nielsen's personal essay carries the tradition of family care into the present as she describes her family's relationship with her ill brother-in-law.

– P.H.P.

WORKS

Dick Kamluck, Sr.: "Ivan Durak Steals a Ring" (p. 74)
Ignatius Kosbruk: "Pugla'allria" (p. 66)
Walter Meganack, Sr.: "A Bear Story" (p. 77)
Mary Jane Nielsen: "What Hope Can Do" (p. 228)

Pugla'allria (p. 66)

Pugla'allria experienced a conventional initiation into shamanhood – his maternal uncle put him into a pit used to ferment fish heads and left him there for a year. At the end of that time, Pugla'allria emerged a clairvoyant, healer, and controller of weather. The story recounts a number of his exploits, but makes a point of noting that each was for the good of the people, and that Pugla'allria, unlike other shamans of his day, did not use his powers for his own benefit or to harm people (with one exception, justified on the grounds that the murdered man had "made his parents cry"). Despite Pugla'allria's stellar career and good motives, when he was on his deathbed he realized that shamanism was essentially evil and that his spirit helpers were agents of the devil. He threw them off, dying in excruciating pain. As with Yup'ik shamans, the locus of his spiritual power was in his joints, which burst open when he expelled his helpers. He died on Good Friday, but not before he was able to accept the true God and Christ.

The story of Pugla'allria is a statement of contemporary Alutiiq values, particularly as they apply to religion and world view. This story demonstrates that shamanism was not entirely bad; when it conformed to the Christian exhortation to help others, it could be beneficial to the people. At the same time, shamanism is shown to have been powerful, regardless of the motives of its practitioners. There is no question that Pugla'allria had powerful abilities. Interestingly, the less beneficent shamans are portrayed as less successful in performing good deeds, but they had no trouble performing feats for their own benefit. The story thus shows that Christianity did not dissolve the beliefs that existed in pre-contact days. Instead, it incorporated and overpowered them. Although people claim to know little about shamanism nowadays, the bone-breaking episode at the end of the story indicates that portions of the previous belief system are remembered. It is likely that the Alaska Peninsula Alutiiqs, like the Yupiit about whom we have more information, broke the bones of a shaman when he died to ensure that he would not come back to life.

A central theme in Kosbruk's telling of the *Pugla'allria* story concerns the victory of Christianity over shamanism. In fact, the story symbolizes not just one shaman's conversion, but the conversion of all Katmai Alutiiqs. The shaman's death on Good Friday is particularly significant. It invites comparisons between Pugla'allria's life and the life of Christ, reinforcing each as a model for future generations.

– P.H.P.

"Ivan Durak Steals a Ring" (p. 74)

Like many stories from the Alutiiq and Unangan areas of Alaska, this tale shows strong Russian influence, imported during the days of Russian America (1741–1867). Ivan Durak is popular from the Pribilof Islands and the Aleutian chain to Prince William Sound. The name comes from Russian folklore and means John the Fool or John the Idiot.

Ivan Durak is a trickster. Like Raven in other stories in this volume, he is clever, selfish, and generally successful. However, two elements distinguish the two tricksters: Raven is also a creator figure, while Ivan is rooted firmly in the human world with no special spiritual or creative powers; and Raven's actions often provide lasting benefit to the world despite the selfish motives that inspire them, while Ivan's are strictly self-serving.

– P.H.P.

"A Bear Story" (p. 77)

This work dates from 1970 to 1971, and is important both for its content and its place in the history of Alutiiq scholarship. The transcription in Alutiiq was the first serious attempt since the Russian period to design a popular orthography for the language. Derenty Tabios, a native speaker of Alutiiq, and then a student at Alaska Methodist University, worked first with Richard Dauenhauer, then with linguists Irene Reed and Jeff Leer on the Alutiiq orthography.

The story is interesting for its style. The narrator frequently uses the morpheme – *ma* – always awkward in English translation, but something like "it is said," or "it is known." This is a common device in storytelling, where tradition bearers establish the reliability of their transmission. In the original as well as in English translation, the story is delicate at the end, where the hunter is too busy enjoying the pleasures of the flesh to fulfill his spiritual obligation to the bears.

– R.D.

Like other stories in this volume, this tale depicts an event that occurred in the very ancient times when humans and animals could enter the others' worlds, indicated or symbolized in the stories by the donning or doffing of appropriate clothing. People have lost the abilities to enter animals' worlds and understand their speech, but animals still have intuitive powers of knowing what humans are thinking and doing.

In this story the bear woman melts her body fat in the winter, an apt metaphor to explain why bears are so skinny when they emerge from hibernation at the end of the winter.

At one point in the story, the bear husband makes a mistake which will result, he believes, in his being caught by the humans. The mistake is not specified, but it might be that he went around his cave the wrong way, or sang the wrong words to the song, or accidentally urinated where he shouldn't have. The important point is that bears, like humans, have certain rituals which must be closely followed. This shows the analogy between humans and animals: both are subject to stringent rules of behavior.

The half-bear, half-human children can be compared with the half-human monster in Peter Kalifornsky's "Raven and the Half-Human" in this volume. Stories on the theme of human/bear marriages are common in Alaska Native oral tradition. See, for instance, Nora Marks Dauenhauer and Richard Dauenhauer, *Haa Shuká, Our Ancestors: Tlingit Oral Narratives* (University of Washington Press, 1987), Tom Peter's "The Woman Who Married the Bear," Frank Dick, Sr.'s "The Woman Who Married the Bear," and J. B. Fawcett's "Kaats'."

– P.H.P.

COMMENTARY ON CENTRAL YUP'IK/CUP'IK TEXTS

BACKGROUND

Traditional Central Yup'ik territory includes the area between Unalakleet to the north and a small portion of the Alaska Peninsula to the south. Much of this area encompasses what is known as the Yukon-Kuskokwim Delta. These two rivers flow into the tundra area known for its extreme temperatures, which may drop to −80° Fahrenheit in the winter and rise to +80° Fahrenheit in the summer. Such extreme temperatures may suggest to some a scarcity of natural food sources, but in truth the region has provided an abundance of subsistence foods from both the land and the sea.

Some estimates put the total pre-contact Central Yup'ik population near 15,000, with an average of 50 to 250 people living in individual villages. By 1995 the population had risen to over 21,000, with villages comprising 25 to 1,000 Yup'ik people (Kawagley, 1995; Fienup-Riordan, 1994).

Central Yup'ik is one of the largest and strongest Alaska Native language groups; it is still being learned as a first language in parts of the region. With the arrival of Catholic and Moravian missionaries in the late 1880s, some non-Natives began to learn Central Yup'ik, and a few Moravians even learned to write Yup'ik. Publications appeared as early as 1902, but it was not until the 1960s that a unified writing system was developed. During the 1970s, Alaska's first bilingual education programs began in the Kuskokwim region and since then many bilingual publications have appeared (Krauss, 1982).

Yup'ik narrative genres include two categories: *qulirat*, creation and origin stories, and *qanemcit*, anecdotes and historical accounts. (See Dauenhauer and Dauenhauer, 1984; Woodbury 1984.) When reading the Yup'ik traditional narratives in the volume, it is important to keep in mind the difference between the Western academic predilection for analyzing and interpreting stories, and the Yup'ik sense of the inappropriateness of doing so. Elsie Mather draws attention to this distinction in Phyllis Morrow's article "On Shaky Ground: Folklore, Collaboration and Problematic Outcomes" that appeared in *When Our Words Return,* edited by Phyllis Morrow and William Schneider:

> Why do people want to reduce the traditional stories to information, to some function? Isn't it enough that we hear and read them? They cause us to wonder about things, and sometimes they touch us briefly along the way, or we connect the information or idea into something we are doing at the moment. This is what the older people say a lot. They tell us to listen even when we don't understand, that later on we will make some meaning or that something that we had listened to before will touch us in some way. Understanding and knowing occur over one's lifetime.... Why would I want to know what [the stories] mean? (33)

– J.B.

WORKS

John Active: "Why Subsistence Is a Matter of Cultural Survival" (p. 182)
Tim Afcan, Sr.: "Super Cockroach Tale" (p. 222)
Kirt Bell: "The First Whales" (p. 101)
Marie Meade: "Translation Issues" (p. 271)
Leo Moses: "Tale" (p. 80)
George Westdahl: "A House I Remember" (p. 236)
Mary Worm: "The Crow and the Mink" (p. 89)

"Tale" (p. 80)

This is an example of *quliraq* (also spelled *qulireq*), which Leo Moses performed sitting at the his own kitchen table with his wife Mary, his son J.R., and collector/translator Anthony Woodbury present. Leo Moses was Woodbury's principal linguistic consultant for the narratives collected in Chevak, Alaska, during the late 1970s and 1980s that appear in his book. Woodbury notes that in the Chevak subdialect itself, the word "Yup'ik" comes out as "Cup'ik" (pronounced CHUPE-pick), and the people themselves prefer to call the language by that name. Woodbury also notes that

> Moses's delivery was powerful, rapid, and passionate, like his father's in using a range of expressive intonational contours, but with very marked alternation of louds and softs. The song in the *qulireq* is the refrain of a longer dance-song which Mr. Moses had performed several days earlier. According to him, traditional Eskimo dancing is an inseparable part of the full perfor-

mance of this *qulireq*, a point not lost on two-year-old J. R., who, when his father sang the song, began to giggle, waving his arms and his head like a dancer! (17)

– J.B.

"The First Whales" (p. 101)

The husband and the wife in this story, and their isolation from all other people, would indicate to a Yup'ik audience that the story had occurred in the far distant time, soon after Crow had created humans. In those early days people were few and scattered.

One problem with this old-time isolation is demonstrated by the woman's pregnancy: neither she nor her husband knew that she was going to have a baby. They did not know how to deal with the situation. Had they been living among other people, as one does now, they would have had the accumulated knowledge of older people, as well as the help of a midwife.

The husband's sudden desire to kill his wife seems inexplicable after his joy at the birth of his child. Collector Elsie Mather conjectures that this might be an instance of a man not wanting a thing as much once he has it, or an example of the frequent theme in which a man finds his wife less desirable after the birth of a child.

The fact that in the end the woman was without any hope of rescue points out another of the difficulties of a life without other people. Had she had kin, these people would have cared about her and rescued her. The audience appreciates the fact of their own family and social ties as it hears this story.

– P.H.P.

"The Crow and the Mink" (p. 89)

This story breaks naturally into three episodes: the mitten and the bag vignette, the beluga whale episode, and the mink episode. These are three of the many episodes that make up the Crow story cycle, and, as collector Elsie Mather states, they just happen to be the one chosen by the storyteller. They are *qulirat*, or long-ago stories.

The story about Crow (Raven) and the beluga whale is similar to a Tlingit story and may be evidence of widespread cultural sharing. The fact that Raven's character remains fairly constant across the cultural and linguistic boundaries in Alaska is illustrated by a comparison of this story and other Raven stories in the book.

Edward W. Nelson, in his 1899 publication, *The Eskimo About Bering Strait*, reported a very similar story from the Unalakleet area (pp.

464–466). In this story, the woman represented the spirit, or *inua* of the whale. The light seemed to be its light force. This portion of Mary Worm's story includes a common theme, that of disobeying a warning or injunction which results in the character's getting himself into trouble. This time, as usual, Crow manages to find a way out.

– P.H.P.

COMMENTARY ON
ST. LAWRENCE ISLAND
YUPIK TEXTS

BACKGROUND

St. Lawrence Island is located in the Bering Sea, approximately 120 miles southwest of Nome, on the Alaska coast, and 40 miles southeast of the Chukotka Peninsula of Far East Russia. The two major communities on St. Lawrence Island are Savoonga and Gambell. Approximately 1500 people live on the island.

The language and people have often been called "Siberian Yupik" because the language is identical to the one spoken in some communities in the Russian Far East. However, the people themselves prefer to be called St. Lawrence Island Yupik to distinguish themselves from the Iñupiat and Central Alaskan Yup'ik, whose languages and cultural practices are different. Rather than the collective term "Siberian Yupik" commonly used to refer to both groups, the St. Lawrence Island Yupik and the Russian Yupik prefer to be known as "Bering Sea Yupik." The St. Lawrence Island Yupik language is still learned as a first language and is spoken by virtually the entire population.

Edgar O. Campbell, Presbyterian minister, created the first writing system primarily to produce hymn and prayer books. Later, David C. Shinen, of the Wycliff Bible Translators, undertook work on a new orthography which was modified by linguists at the University of Alaska Fairbanks. Bilingual education began in 1972, and many books have been written by the people themselves, especially for the schools (Apassingok, Walunga, Tennant, 1985). Narrative genres include *ungipamsuk,* the term for "real events" or actual happenings, and *ungipaghaq,* the term for "fiction" or "folktale," used for entertainment storytelling.[1]

– J.B.

---

1. Thanks to Vera Oovi Kaneshiro for correcting an earlier draft and providing the St. Lawrence Island Yupik terms for the narrative genres.

WORKS

Lincoln Blassi: "Prayer Song Asking for a Whale" (p. 118)
Susie Silook: "The Anti-Depression *Uliimaaq*" (p. 245), "Uncle Good Intentions" (p. 249) and "Adventure in Chinatown 1958" (p. 252)

"Prayer Song Asking for a Whale" (p. 118)

Songs are a significant part of all indigenous oral literatures and are central to both ceremonial and non-ceremonial life. Native perspectives generally include the need to be properly prepared for a hunt, not just physically, but also mentally and spiritually, by assuming a respectful and humble attitude toward the world and all its creatures who sustain life.   – J.B.

"Adventure in Chinatown 1958" (p. 252)

"Adventure in Chinatown 1958" is a true story. Susie Silook's accessible narrative – the content of the situation – conveys what it is to be "other" in our society. The poem is set within the context of a U.S. government relocation program in the 1950s, a program whose goal was assimilation – to mainstream Native Americans and to eliminate their "special status" by "helping" them fit seamlessly into American society. The Silooks were invited to give up their subsistence lifestyle – a harsh and demanding existence in "bush" Alaska – and to take their place in a great American city. The government promised a good, new life. Here was the chance to trade in the past and its old traditional Yupik ways for the convenience and opportunity of living in the modern world. So, Mr. Silook decided to accept the relocation offer over his wife's objections, and when they arrived in Chicago, the family was placed in Chinatown, where, because of their Asian appearance, it was thought that they would blend right in. The poem resonates because the voice is authentic and the experience of being displaced from one's home, one's culture, and one's identity is compelling. The Silook family was *relocated* but other words come to mind – *hidden* and *disguised*. They were sent to a place where they looked like their new neighbors but did not share their neighbors' language, culture, or values. So close and yet so far – the situation equivalent to dying of cultural thirst. Silook affords us entry into the experience of an "impossible immigrant," and we are as wide-eyed as her lost Yupik sister in Chinatown.

                                                        – R.S.

COMMENTARY ON IÑUPIAQ TEXTS

BACKGROUND

The Iñupiat, or northern Alaskan Eskimos, traditionally inhabited the coast of Alaska from Unalakleet north and east to the Canadian border, as well as a portion of the interior reaching from the northern side of the Brooks Range to the Arctic shore. Theirs is a culture dependent on sea and land mammals and an intimate knowledge of the hazards and opportunities provided by the arctic environment. Large whale hunting villages have been in existence for 2000 years, sustained by that knowledge, which had its physical expression in an impressive collection of specialized and personalized tools. Long before the modern era made ivory carvings collectibles, the Iñupiat were fashioning beautiful implements of walrus tusks, wood, baleen, stone, and bone.

Iñupiaq ceremonial life was equally rich, based, like all Alaska Native religions, on an understanding that the world is inhabited by many different kinds of beings, each with a spirit that lives beyond the lifetime of the individual it temporarily inhabits. Survival depends therefore not simply on practical knowledge, but also on respectful practices and taboos that honor the animals taken for food. In the past, powerful spiritual practitioners specialized in knowledge of taboos and ways of repairing damaged relationships between people and animals when those taboos were broken. Both feared and needed, these healers and seers played an important role in the ceremonial and everyday life of pre-contact Iñupiat. With their widespread conversion to Christianity, most Iñupiat abandoned shamanic practices but continued to emphasize a respectful attitude toward the natural world and an intimate and personal relationship with spiritual matters.

The Iñupiaq selections in this book reflect that strong spirituality and the conflicting realities of the old and new ways. Frank Ellanna describes a shaman's flight during a shamanic ceremony. This was an ability for which spiritual practitioners were well known; a number of stories detail flights to the moon. Laura Norton's story of long ago, or *unipkaaq,* "The Boy Who Found the Lost," is a classic Iñupiaq story that combines recognition of the extreme hazards people face with the comforting news that with work and intelligence they can be overcome. As in most *unipkaat,* the boy is aided by strong spiritual powers. Clinton Swan's *unipkaaq* about a woman who saved her village combines a warning about the dangers of the human world with the reminder that one who may seem physically weak is often spiritually powerful. Fred Bigjim's hazards are of a different sort, brought about by rapid modernization and cultural change that leave people reeling. Mary TallMountain, though an Athabaskan, writes on Iñupiaq themes, basing her Nuliajuk poem on the ancient legend of the sea goddess who still has the power to reach out to people today. Sister Goodwin's poems also express the presence of the old ways in today's world, suggesting a richness available to those willing to attend to the environment and the stories. Buell Anakak expresses the unbreakable hold his home has on him, even as he lives a thousand miles away.

– P.H.P.

WORKS

Buell Anakak: "Magic Maker" (p. 226)
Fred Bigjim: "Gaslight" (p. 238) and "Ballet in Bethel" (p. 240)
Frank Ellanna: "Shamanic Flight" (p. 126)
Sister Goodwin: "Sacrifice: A Dream/A Vision" (p. 192), "Nomadic Iñupiat for Kappaisruk" (p. 194), "When the Owl Disappeared" (p. 191), "Asraaq, the Girl Who Became a She-Bear" (p. 188), and "Piksinñaq" (p. 197)
Laura Norton: "The Boy Who Found the Lost" (p. 129)
Clinton Swan: "The Kivalina War Heroine" (p. 122)

"Shamanic Flight" (p. 126)

This story was told in the King Island Island dialect of the Iñupiaq language, unique in that it is spoken only by the people from this region. Lawrence Kaplan, in the introduction to *King Island Tales: Eskimo Legends from Bering Strait* (1988, p. 30), explains why King Island is no longer inhabited year round, although former residents do return to the island in the summer to hunt animals and gather plants. Most left during the 1950s and early 1960s, when they moved to Nome to be closer to health care and other services. Eventually, the BIA closed the school because the number of schoolchildren had declined. They also said the location was unsuitable for a school because teachers would be so isolated, and the school itself was located too close to rockslides.

– J.B.

"Sacrifice: A Dream / A Vision" (p. 192)

Goodwin wrote "Sacrifice: A Dream/A Vision" after an actual dream in which the image of the owl/grandfather and the young man appeared vividly. Goodwin believed the dream itself may have derived from a story she was told as a very young child.

The author left several points ambiguous: Is the grandson really killing his grandfather? Why? Or has the grandfather committed suicide? Is the grandson to be taken as a scapegoat? A bit of cultural context may help clarify the issue. A grandfather's role in life is to impart information. Once his pupil, his grandson, has grown into a man, the elder's job is done. With no reason to live, he may (particularly, in the past, when conditions were harsher) wish not to be a burden to his family.

A similar ambiguity surrounds the owl/grandfather image. Is "owl" used as a metaphor for a wise person, as in Western folklore? Is it a name? Does the owl represent shape-shifting, as occurred in "Lake-Dwarves," "Fish Story," "Story of the Double Fin Killer Whale," "A Bear Story," "The First Whales," and "About Tlingit Oratory" (in this volume)? As these selections show, people had helper spirits from the animal world, and could sometimes change form from animal to human and back again.

– P.H.P.

"Nomadic Iñupiat for Kappaisruk" (p. 194)

The poem "Nomadic Iñupiat for Kappaisruk" lists several places:

Illivaaq, visited in the spring.

Agvagaaq, visited in the summer.

Kitikliquagaaq, in the fall.

Qugluktaq, at the end of the fall.

Kappaisruk is Sister Goodwin's oldest brother, Elmer Goodwin.

Norwegian ball is a game in which a ball and bat are used. Several dozen boys and girls, men and women may play at the same time.

The verse about Agvagaaq, the summer home, talks about bouncing on a wild duck carved of driftwood. The author explained that this was one of Kappaisruk's preferred activities.

Like other selections in this volume, this poem contains a strong note of nostalgia as it contrasts the nomadic life of the past with settled city or town life in contemporary Alaska.

– P.H.P.

"When the Owl Disappeared" (p. 191) and
"Asraaq, the Girl Who Became a She-Bear" (p. 188)

While questions about the importance of the owl are central to "Sacrifice: A Dream/A Vision," they are not problematic in the paired selections, "When the Owl Disappeared" and "Asraaq, the Girl Who Became a She-Bear." In these cases, the owl is an actual bird whose disappearance was a marker for, and perhaps spiritually tied with, the beginning of a new life for the author's great-great-grandmother, Asraaq. The same year that the formerly reliable owl, inhabitant of the fish camp's largest tree, failed to return, his human admirer, young Asraaq, was captured by a male bear. She ultimately turned into a bear herself and gave birth to cubs which were henceforth understood to be relatives of her human family.

Although it is an authored short story, the Asraaq narrative shares the motifs of shape-shifting, broken taboos, and the establishment of relationships across human-animal-spirit boundaries that appear in many of the traditional narratives contained in this volume. Its relevance to the lives of contemporary Natives is made explicit in the poem Sister Goodwin wrote for her sons. "When the Owl Disappeared" can be seen as a narrative frame for "Asraaq." It is also a reminder that each audience member bears responsibility for taking from the story what is appropriate to his or her personal circumstances and giving to it active attention and serious consideration.

– P.H.P.

"Piksinñaq" (p. 197)

"Piksinñaq" is about Aana (Grandmother) and is written by the author to honor the woman who had given her so much. The poem touches on the interaction between white and Native culture, but in a different way from many "culture clash" poems in this volume. Here we see a humorous event, told in a self-mocking but not self-deprecating tone. We also learn several surprising things about Iñupiat culture at the turn of the century: the school is the point of entry to innovative products and ideas, and consequently the children teach the elders, in a reversal of traditional practice. We also see a delight in the magical new item and a brave willingness to experiment.

– P.H.P.

"The Kivalina War Heroine" (p. 122)

Like the Unangax̂ war story told by Cedor Snigaroff, Clinton Swan's story illustrates the fact that in bygone days life was dangerous not just because of natural hazards, or even supernatural imbalances, but also because of the ever-present danger of warfare or raids by unfriendly neighbors, both Eskimo and Indian. Common as inter-group strife was, Iñupiaq societies developed a wide range of strategies far beyond warfare for dealing with strangers. The most common involved incorporating the newcomers into the existing kinship structure, either by adoption, co-marriage (the well-known but commonly misunderstood practice whereby two couples were bound by an agreement in which the wives were sexual partners not just of their own husbands, but also of their husbands' partners), and trading partnerships.

But in this story, no such bonds have been formed between the two groups; in fact, the raiders are portrayed as outside society, rather than representatives of an established group. The story combines great intelligence, planning, and bravery by one woman. This woman's heroism accords with a common contention of many contemporary Iñupiaq women that their society has "always valued women." After she has saved her friends and relatives, the woman from Kivalina seems doomed when, in a move that might be considered *deus ex machina* in a Western story – but that echoes the deeds of many a hero in Western lore – she turns into a feather and is able to lead her people successfully to safety.

– P.H.P.

"The Boy Who Found the Lost" (p. 129)

The story is from the Kobuk area (Noorvik-Selawik) and was told in Iñupiaq and English in summer of 1970 at the request of the collector, Hannah Loon. The Iñupiaq portion of the tape is much longer than the English, and has much more audience reaction, especially laughing, than the English version. This suggests, logically, that Ms. Norton's style, skill, and audience rapport are even greater in her native language than in English, although her English style is excellent.

The story is transcribed verbatim, with two exceptions. In the rare cases where the tradition bearer has corrected herself or has a "false start," the orally rejected fragment has been deleted in the transcription. Also, in a few cases, the English verb tenses have been changed for the sake of grammatical consistency. The storyteller has an excellent command of English, and out of respect for her willingness to tell a story in a foreign language, it seems in order to edit the few grammatical errors so as to make them consistent with her obvious intent and with the verb tenses used elsewhere.

The story is well paced, controlled, deliberate, slow and relaxed throughout, except where contrasted by a quickened pace at the climax. The following typographical devices are used to reflect the pace of the story, and other aspects of style or editorial decision:

(a) Line turnings reflect pauses and therefore the speed of the narration. For example, lines 21 and 22 were delivered without pauses between the words. Therefore these lines are "faster" than for delivery of an equal number of words spread over several lines, as in the lines before and after 21 and 22. Pause only at the end of the lines.

(b) CAPITALIZED words mark emphasis by loudness of voice or stress accent.

(c) S p a c e d   o u t   w o r d s are those elongated for emphasis.

(d) (Parentheses) denote almost whispered words, or a marked drop in voice, often adding editorial comment or opinion.

(e) [Brackets] identify reconstructed portions of the tape, as described in the notes below.

The Iñupiaq version of the story was transcribed as a class project by Hannah Loon over the course of two or three semesters in the early 1970's at AMU. The transcription was revised and completed during her course work at the University of Alaska, and was published by the Alaska Native Language Center in June 1974 under the title AAHAHAANGAAQ.

The English version of the story was transcribed by Richard Dauenhauer in October 1976, in conjunction with an Eskimo Folklore workshop for the Anchorage Borough teachers sponsored by the Indian Education Act Project of the Anchorage Borough School District, with the understanding that use and distribution of the English version of the tape be restricted to non-profit educational use.

– R.D.

Laura Norton's is an excellent story for demonstrating the poor orphan-grandmother theme in Eskimo (in this case, Iñupiaq) literature. The presence of this pair indicates several things to a knowledgeable audience: first, the grandmother is likely to have magical or spiritual powers, as these were the province of the old and solitary; second, the orphan boy is in need of this assistance, because he has no father to teach him the skills of survival; third, the boy is likely to be braver than an ordinary person; and fourth, the boy will be sent on a quest of some sort. These are parts of the makeup of orphan genre stories. Note the similarities to the Athabaskan Ggaadookk story.

"The Boy Who Found the Lost" is also useful in illustrating the economic leveling which was important in Eskimo culture, where sharing is stressed to a much greater extent than in Western culture. Great inequalities in wealth were seen as causes of potential social disturbance. In this story, the wealth is held by a rich man at first, and by the end we see that it is evenly divided between him and the orphan boy.

Finally, the story demonstrates the contrast between written and oral styles. Note the pace and rhythm, the repetition in the story, sometimes arranged in "terracing" (see the section in this volume on oral and written styles).

The "small" village the orphan encounters is a miniature village; hence his realization that the old woman inside the igloo (a *sod*, not *ice* house) is one of the monsters. This old woman, like the boy's grandmother, is assumed by the boy – and the audience – to have healing powers.

– P.H.P.

COMMENTARY ON ATHABASKAN TEXTS

BACKGROUND

Like "Aleut," the term "Athabaskan," which refers to a group of people and the languages they historically spoke, is a word borrowed from others. In this case, the word originated with neighboring indigenous people and was applied to a group of subarctic people, primarily interior-dwellers, in Canada and Alaska. In their own languages, people called themselves a variant of the base "dene," which means "person." Athabaskan-speakers in other parts of North America include about five groups along the Oregon and California coasts, as well as Navahos and Apaches in the southwestern United States. Linguistic and archaeological evidence suggests that eastern Alaska or northwestern Canada was the homeland of the proto-Athabaskan speakers, and that all southern groups migrated from the north within the last thousand years.

Eleven Athabaskan languages are spoken in Alaska, but these linguistic divisions did not equate with political groupings. In most cases speakers of a single language did not form a single band or tribe. The scarce food resources available in the northern interior could not sustain large human settlements, so people lived together in small mobile bands made up of extended families. During the winter, each band established a base from which pairs or groups of hunters, trappers, or gatherers set out. With the coming of summer and predictable – and often large – fish runs, several bands congregated along riverbanks. Falltime signaled another gathering time, as people cooperated to harvest caribou migrating south through mountain passes. Athabaskans needed to travel a great deal throughout the year to obtain food and engage in trade, and so developed a culture rich in verbal lore, ideas, and practical and spiritual knowledge. They placed less emphasis on material wealth, which would have been cumbersome to transport and time-consuming to produce and maintain.

The stories and poems in this volume reflect something of the richness of verbal games, humor, and mental astuteness in traditional Athabaskan culture. Sally Pilot's "Ggaadookk" is a Koyukon *kk'adonts'idnee,* or traditional story about the distant time (see the discussion of genres on p. 283). In the story, a boy learns a skill crucial to all Athabaskan adults: the ability to read the unspoken, sometimes hidden messages in the world around him. John Fredson's traditional Gwich'in stories about Raven and Wolverine illustrate a bawdy brand of humor underlain with the dead-serious message that people must help and depend on each other for survival. Shem Pete's "The Susitna Story" explores not only past reliance on the wisdom of spiritual leaders but contains a continuing prophecy. Peter Kalifornsky's six stories, each a *sukdu,* demonstrate the power of the world of ideas and beliefs, a particularly poignant message in the modern world so reliant on physical evidence and material objects.

The contemporary poems by Dixie Alexander, Glen Simpson, and Mary TallMountain show an equally deep emotional and spiritual tie to the land and its resources. Simpson and TallMountain contrast this traditional attitude with the modern materialistic world that daily surrounds them.

—P.H.P.

WORKS

Dixie Alexander: "Willow Was Her Name" (p. 244)
John Fredson: "Raven and the Mallard Girl" (p. 155) and "Wolverine and the Wolves" (p. 157)
Peter Kalifornsky: "K'eła Sukdu, The Mouse Story" (p. 138), "The Gambling Story" (p. 143), "Raven and the Half-Human" (p. 146), "The Boy Who Talked to the Dog" (p. 148), "About Shamans and the Men with Gashaq" (p. 149), and "The Old Dena'ina Beliefs" (p. 150)
Shem Pete: "The Susitna Story" (p. 153)
Sally Pilot: "Ggaadookk" (p. 159)
Glen Simpson: "Night Without Dawn" (p. 207), "Tahltan Country" (p. 208), "Traveling in the Land of the Native Art Historians" (p. 209), and "Front Street" (p. 210)
Mary TallMountain: "O Dark Sister" (p. 217), "Seahorse Music" (p. 219), and "Nuliajuk, A Sequence" (p. 221)

"Raven and the Mallard Girl" (p. 155)

John Fredson was talented and educated in the Western sense as well as according to Athabaskan custom. See Craig Mishler's "John Fredson: A Biographical Sketch" in *John Fredson Edward Sapir Hàa Googwandak (Stories Told by John Fredson to Edward Sapir),* Alaska Native Language Center, 1982, for information on this fascinating man.

The endnote contains variations and continuations of "Raven

and the Mallard Girl." In the version in this volume we see Raven up to his old tricks, motivated again entirely by his own selfish desire. We also see Raven bested for once, an experience that listeners find quite refreshing.

Note that the mallard girl's excuse for wanting to get out of the canoe is the need to relieve herself. (See also the commentary on TallMountain's "Nuliajuk, A Sequence" in this volume.)

This story adds to a formulation of Raven's personality, which, with regional variations, remains fairly constant throughout Alaska Native oral tradition.

– P.H.P.

"Wolverine and the Wolves" (p. 157)

The story "Wolverine and the Wolves" seems, at first, to present in Wolverine a character similar to Raven or Crow. Like Raven, he breaks many social rules and is motivated by greed. However, the Athabaskan attitude toward Wolverine is quite distinct. The actual animal is extremely tough, steals food from traps, and fouls any that it does not eat. It is solitary and, as this story suggests, eats beaver. It is strong both physically and spiritually. In the Koyukon area, women may not eat the animal or even speak its name. He is called "Doyonh" (meaning "chief" or "great, rich man"), and when a wolverine is caught in a trap it is brought back to camp with great respect and ceremony. Refer to Richard Nelson's *Make Prayers to the Raven* (University of Chicago Press, 1983) for a more detailed discussion of Wolverine.

The fact that Wolverine is killed at the end of the story contrasts with Raven and Crow stories, in which the trickster always manages to get away, usually after getting what he wants.

The second paragraph, in which the female wolf pulls meat under the snow, was explained by translator Katherine Peter as an indication that she had found a way to sneak the meat to her brothers and children. Unfortunately, Wolverine notices her ruse. "What a lot of meat you're taking for nothing!" he says.

—P.H.P.

"Ggaadookk" (p. 159)

Ggaadookk slept all the time because he was becoming a medicine man. This story is about the socialization of an Athabaskan, training a young man to speak indirectly and to handle metaphor. One aspect of the indirectness seen as desirable is learning to be discreet and respectful by speaking indirectly about animals, thus avoiding taboos. This story parallels the Koyukon riddle tradition, designed to train people in Athabaskan oratory. The riddles must be puzzled over, the answers memorized. They are somewhat similar to koan practice in Zen Buddhism.

– R.D.

Indirectness is important both in manners and morals for Athabaskans. An example is that a man will not declare that he is going hunting so as not to offend the spirits of the intended prey.

Speaking indirectly and in metaphor are important mental exercises beneficial in the realms of both the natural and social worlds. Traditionally, a man's task in the natural world was to feed and provide skins for his family. Because each hunting situation was different from past ones, the man needed to learn how to deal with surprises, how to improvise when faced with new situations. He had to be a problem solver, a skill honed in solving the riddles of metaphor and indirect speech.

In the social world, traditional Athabaskan culture had in common with all small, face-to-face societies a need to interact without offending, yet a way to let an offender know that he must change his actions. This is accomplished through indirect hints and actions, which a person learns to interpret. He is not told that something is wrong, but must learn to figure it out. Ggaadookk is an unbearably naïve person who has not yet learned this most basic of skills.

Richard Nelson's book, *Make Prayers to the Raven* (University of Chicago Press, 1983), and the series of five videotapes of the same title produced by KUAC Fairbanks contain additional discussion on the Athabaskan world view and beliefs.

The riddles referred to in the endnote for this story fit the following pattern: A visual image is described, and the guesser must try to guess which natural phenomenon or object that description refers to. An example is "We come upstream in a red canoe." Answer: "Red salmon." Another is "I drag my shovel on the trail." Answer: "A beaver." Other riddles are more complicated and depend for their solution on an intimate knowledge of the natural environment.

The hero's visit to the sky country is a common motif in folk literature (*cf.* "Jack and the Beanstalk") and indicates a meeting with the supernatural as well as an opportunity to view the world from a new perspective.

Another common motif involves young boys who initially show no promise because of the absence of a male role model. Because

Ggaadookk's father is not available to teach him to be a proper Koyukon hunter or shaman, he must find help in the world of spirits instead.

This story has much in common with such European classics as *Alice in Wonderland* (*e.g.*, riddles, metaphors, and aphorisms taken literally that come true) and other Alaska Native stories in this volume, including "Fish Story: Karta Bay." What follows are examples of Athabaskan (Koyukon) Riddle-Poems from Richard Dauenhauer's *Riddle and Poetry Handbook*, Alaska Native Education Board 1976 (62–69).

Like a spruce tree
lying on the ground:
the back-hand
of (the) bear.

We whistle
by the cliffs and gulches:
(the) bear, breathing
or the wind
on a brittle piece of
birch bark,
or wind
blowing on a small, dry
   spruce.

I drag my shovel
on the trail:
a beaver.

At the tip it's
dipping in ashes:
ermine tail.

It really snowed hard
in opposite directions
on my head:
a mountain sheep.

We have our heads
in sheepskin hats:
stumps piled up
with fallen snow.

—P.H.P.

"The Susitna Story" (p. 153)

Shem Pete did not assign a date to the prophecy related in this selection, but it was probably made in the late 1880s. This prophecy can be compared with Anna Nelson Harry's "Lament for Eyak," also in this volume.

The epidemic referred to in the last paragraph was the worldwide influenza epidemic of 1918. It killed thousands of Alaska Natives, including Shem Pete's mother and many other relatives.

Readers might note Pete's frequent use of simile, comparing this literary technique with riddling and use of metaphor in "Ggaadookk," in this volume.

For a more detailed discussion of shamans and seers, refer to "A Talk with Peter Kalifornsky" at the end of this section. See *Shem Pete's Alaska: The Territory of the Upper Cook Inlet Dena'ina* (compiled and edited by James Kari, Alaska Native Language Center, University of Alaska Fairbanks, 1987) for information on Dena'ina territory and a biographical sketch of Shem Pete.

—P.H.P.

"Night Without Dawn" (p. 207), "Tahltan Country" (p. 208), "Traveling in the Land of the Native Art Historians" (p. 209), and "Front Street" (p. 210)

In pre-contact days, most warfare was carried out by surprise attack, usually just before dawn, as the enemy slept in their houses.

Each person had a personal spirit helper which was the spirit of an animal, plant, or object, and which assisted him or her throughout life. The world was populated by physical entities and beings whose spirits affected the outcome of events, and it was through personal spirit helpers that individuals could communicate with this vast population of non-human beings.

"Traveling in the Land of the Native Art Historians" provides a good contrast with "Tahltan Country"; the warriors (or their weapons) have become objects of study. The contrast between dead and living, Native and white, is extended in the former.

—P.H.P.

"O Dark Sister" (p. 217), "Seahorse Music" (p. 219), and "Nuliajuk, A Sequence" (p. 221)

Nuliajuk (also called "Sedna" in many stories) was a young Inuit girl who repeatedly rejected offers of marriage, until she finally fell in love with a suitor. She discovered soon after eloping with him that he was a cruel dog (in some versions, a bird) disguised as a man.

He took her to his home and held her prisoner. She could not escape because he watched her constantly, even tying a rope to her when she needed to go outside to relieve herself. One day her family came to visit her and she saw her chance for escape. She tied the rope to a ball of string, which answered for her whenever her husband asked what was taking so long, a ruse comparable to that used by mallard girl in "Raven and the Mallard Girl" by John Fredson (in this volume). The string's ability to talk is not surprising, given the Inuit talent at string stories (similar to cat's cradle) in which string is transformed into a story and storyteller through performance.

Meanwhile, Nuliajuk left with her family in the *umiaq* (skin boat). When her husband discovered that she was gone, he turned himself into a bird, flew over the *umiaq*, and caused a violent storm to arise. The girl's family realized what was happening and threw her overboard so they could survive. She clung to the side of the boat, but the storm continued. Her father cut off the first joints of her fingers. These fell off into the water and turned into seals. She held on, the storm continued, and her father cut off the second joints of her fingers. These became walrus. She still gripped the boat, and her father cut off the third joints. These became whales.

Nuliajuk tried to hold on with her elbows, but her father struck her in the face with the paddle, knocking out one of her eyes and sending her over the edge. She sank to the bottom of the sea and became the ruler of sea life. She is both feared and revered. Shamans knew that the one way to appease her was to swim down to her abode and comb her tangled hair, untended since she lost her fingers.

—P.H.P.

"K'eła Sukdu, The Mouse Story" (p. 138), "The Gambling Story" (p. 143), "Raven and the Half-Human" (p. 146), "The Old Dena'ina Beliefs" (p. 150), "The Boy Who Talked to the Dog" (p. 148), and "About Shamans and the Men with *Gashaq*" (p. 149)

James Kari, the editor of *A Dena'ina Legacy: K'tl'egh'i Sukdu The Collected Writings of Peter Kalifornsky* (1991, xxviii) points out that Kalifornsky wrote almost all of his texts first in the Dena'ina language, prior to writing the English translations. In general, Kalifornsky favored the writing process over the audio recording of stories. "The Old Dena'ina Beliefs" and "Raven and the Half-Human" are examples of his stories written in Dena'ina. However, "The Mouse Story" and "The Gambling Story" are examples of two tape-recorded stories he told in Dena'ina. James Kari collected and transcribed them in 1974 with those versions appearing in the original *AQR*. The more recent versions shown in this text are slightly different.

Katherine McNamara's interview with Peter Kalifornsky (following this discussion) suggests the inner meanings of Kalifornsky's stories and brings up important points about four types of powerful people: shamans, people whose words come true, dreamers, and skywatchers.

In "Mouse Story," Kalifornsky seems to accept the fact that humans have good and bad sides. In this story the man is rewarded for helping the mouse (his good side), but not punished for being lazy (his bad side). Note that Gujun is portrayed here as a benevolent giant. He is not always benevolent in Dena'ina stories, or *sukdu*.

As in Anna Nelson Harry's "Lake-Dwarves" (in this volume), the question of perspective and size arises. A comparison between the two stories reveals the irony in Harry's tale, while "Mouse Story" is told in a straightforward manner.

The gambling referred to in "Gambling Story" involves gambling sticks in a game commonly played throughout the northwestern and western parts of North America. Specific games vary from location to location, but the general idea of the game is for one player to hold two sticks in his hand, one marked and the other unmarked. The other player must guess in which hand the marked stick is hidden. Each proper guess wins a counting stick (separate from the two held in the player's hands). Often two teams play against each other, and two sets of sticks are hidden at the same time. In this story, the counting sticks were lost, and the man continued playing, betting his belongings and family.

It is possible that one type of gambling game, *kadaq*, was brought north to Alaska by Peter Kalifornsky's great-great-grandfather, who had been sent to work at Fort Ross, the Russian-American Company's fort on the coast of northern California. This game originated among the Pomo Indians and quickly spread throughout the fort and north. Gambling stories involving the Alutiiq version of the game, *kaataq*, are a staple of Alutiiq oral tradition.

The message of "Gambling Story" seems not to be that gambling is bad (it is simply a diverting human activity), but that belief in the old way, exhibited by the loser, is just as strong a power as is the special spiritual power which a shaman has. The story contains a number of motifs similar to those contained in "Mouse Story."

"Raven and the Half-Human," reprinted from Kalifornsky's American Book Award-winning book, *A Dena'ina Legacy: K'tl'egh' i Sukdu*, depicts a monster whose bad side is its human, rather than animal, side. The half-human state of the monster relates to the danger inherent in becoming a shaman, when one first obtains a spirit helper. In this situation, the person is essentially in a half-human state.

—J.B. and P.H.P.

A Talk with Peter Kalifornsky: Sukdu beq' quht'ana ch'ulani, The Stories Are for Us to Learn Something From

We sat in Peter Kalifornsky's house day after day, and he told the stories again as we examined them in the books he had written. He said it was necessary to see the background of these stories, which had been given to him when he was a boy and which he plumbed for their meanings. Dena'ina, he said often, lets you picture what's behind the words, but it takes many more pictures in English to give you the right picture. He meant this notice of *picture* literally. When he was telling, his eyes looked off into the distance as if he were watching something happen, and the precision and flavor of his words exactly described the pictures he could see.

He is a writer in Dena'ina, impelled at first to preserve his language now threatened with death, he fears, by the power of English; but as he came to see the intricate relationship between meaning, sound, and spelling, he reflected more on the nature of the minds from which these stories had come and the nature of the power that had given them to their first tellers.

There are many stories he knows, and they fall into four eras, or cycles, which he identifies in the following way: when the animals were talking to one another; when the first laws and regulations were made; when they were testing belief for truth; when things have been happening to the people lately. The eras come from the first time of the Dena'inas during the stone age, to recent times, perhaps within the last several thousand years. The stories presented earlier lie within that cycle in which Dena'inas test their beliefs in powers greater than their own minds. The stories have been laid before them to show them how the world is composed, and they put to the test the beliefs set forth there. The tests are empirical, performed by experience which often threatens or takes their lives, in order to demonstrate whether there is truth in what is believed.

The discussion given here is an excerpt from the hours of lively, serious, funny, and often stumped talk. Peter's part is the explanatory one; my own is the one of putting questions to him, because there is a good deal in what he was telling that I did not understand, or did almost understand, or thought, wrongly, that I finally understood. For both of us, it seems, this method was an exploration of our own minds and beliefs and ways of knowing. The questions helped Peter approach the explanation of the background of the stories in a way that he no longer has the physical resources to do by himself, that is, in writing.

The stories became cycles, revolving into one another; and each era seems to have its own cycle. Within each cycle, themes recur, and human, animal, spirit persons take form and then reverse form. One thing becomes another, as down reverses to water, as shamans transform to animal spirits, as K'eluyesh seems to become Gujun.

From era to era, the cyclical themes repeat themselves, but in new guises and shapes. And so, through the stories run variously-shaped movements; cycles and recurrences, reversals, repetitions of three. These move, in the mind's picture, both in cycles and in helical continuations, with the dance of reversals allowing nothing to remain static. Everything has its other side; and meaning lies in the whole being of that double face. In Dena'ina, the form of shape and the shape of movement are indicated in the construction of words. In this language, we finally show these only approximately to their originals, relying on our minds, not our experience, to see what the words are showing us of the life of the old Dena'inas.

Here we are talking of the life of their minds.

Imagination and the Testing of Belief

"*Eynik' delnish* – that's how those Dena'inas were," he said. "They had no writing or pencil. They lived life through imagination, the power of the mind."

I asked if this meant they could use their minds to invent, to make what is called fiction. He shook his head.

"The background is, something appears to them that they don't understand. There is something that has a spirit. It goes into a human mind so a person's mind could have a very powerful contact with the other in some way. [In one story,] this man had done a lot of thinking before this. He is wondering. Then, all at once, something like a picture appears in his mind. So he tells the people he has what is like a vision. Whatever this is, the shaman works on it, to see what it might be; but he cannot trace it, because it does not have any spirit or shadow: no way to trace it. It could be some spirit laid before him. For, that picture he imagines is really true. But no, they cannot find a trace."

But how can they know if it's true, then, if they can't find a trace, I wondered.

"They do not know if it's true or not. But when that man said 'All the animals are turned away from us, they had their back to us': they kept this in the minds, until it happened. And it happened. Why did it happen in that way? Maybe for people to realize there's something else besides what they already know or what a human mind can do. So if anything happened they didn't know, they went out to look for it.

"In Dena'ina life," he explained, "they always look forward to see if it will happen [for instance, the animals will disappear] now and again, so they would be prepared and go easy on food, put up a lot of food when they have the chance. The Mouse story was a warning: That first person was lazy and loafing: he didn't think about putting up food for the winter. He runs into that little mouse with the fish egg in its mouth." He laughed gently.

"That would be the answer to him: it would happen, and he would be helped for his kindness in lifting the mouse over the windfall. It did happen that game disappeared and people had something to weaken them.

"This man didn't know what he was doing but was going anyway. Why, and what for?

"It was a reversal: he was lazy but he was kind, too, to help the mouse. And so, 'Now I'll help you save your people.'"

Taking Practice for a Form

"Long ago Dena'inas, they had believings. The way I started that story, they tried for whatever they wanted to become. They tried to take a practice to be a shaman; boys and girls, when they were just becoming men and women."

We learned to fast before communion, I noted; we learned to discipline our wants. Did they do it this way? Did food interfere with the power they sought?

"They didn't eat solid food then," he replied. "If they do, whatever spirit they're praying for will not come into their body. When a person eats, the food takes a place in our body, it makes us live; all this had to be evaporated out of you to make room in your system for what they're praying for."

I asked why he preferred the translation shaman, not medicine person, as I had heard people say elsewhere.

"A medicine man does medicine. But *ch'el'egi* translates, 'he can form a spirit power.' If he is *ch'el'egi* he can form a spirit power. That is, if he become shaman, *el'egen.*

"But this is not the only form of power," he said. "That other person, *nahnaga dnadluni* 'for words to become true': this man takes a form of believing, or religion, in his praying. He would become one who, if he made a wish, his words would come true. This puts us back to where that old Crow[1] could turn himself into human, his wish could become true."

What is the shaman form, I asked him.

"He gets into a form where he can transform his own spirit into an animal to go and do his work for him. On this earth here, whatever there is has his own life. That means every plant, everything has a life of its own."

Does that mean that we should say everything has a spirit?

His answer touched on the Dena'ina doctrine that all beings return eternally, or are reincarnated.

"The spirit combines with a human life. If we didn't have any spirit we wouldn't have any shadow. A life is: we'll look at it this way. A plant has its own generation. It has a life of its own; it couldn't be human. A plant dies out in winter and re-grows again in the spring. Every plant. Whatever is on this soil: that means plant, insect, animals. That means life has to be respected. Us humans, we are here first, but then we have to live and use this what lives for our life.

"So these shamans, when they're praying to whatever plant or animal or insect, they ask this creature for its help so they might have that spirit power. What is spirit? A human, animal spirit? Whatever has life has spirit. Us humans, we have brains that we use for thinking and trying to study. Everything on this soil has its own life, and that is what they are praying to for help. They were asking everything for its help, and giving it their best wishes.

---

1. Peter Kalifornsky usually used the English word "Crow" for "Raven" (*Corvus corax*). In the version of the story reprinted in this volume, the editors of *A Dena'ina Legacy K'tl'egh' i Sukdu* decided to use the word "raven."

"They thought of the form they wanted to be, and it was the good wishes of what they prayed to that let that form come into being. They receive the message in some way, and they turn around and they try to help their people."

I noted that they had to go through a time of danger and nightmares.

"They're getting into the dangers of that form, until they start receiving the power they're praying for. It's in them already then; but the bad part too is still there, to try to make them quit. But if the person is brave he would stay with his work, and this that he is praying to would come to have strength and take hold of his body. When he can transform his spirit into some animal or thing, to go out and see what he wants to see, what he wants to know: he can *see* it. He has received all that power from his praying. Call it power of the spirit."

The evil that is fighting him is a disturbing force, and we talked about it for some time. He reflected.

"What is evil? Something bad will be fighting him. That's what causes him to see all these dangerous things. That puts us back to the Half-animal-half-human, what is called *bad*. The bad thing is fighting him to become one with him; whatever he is trying to be, that bad thing is fighting against him."

Where does this bad come from?

"That bad thing could be same as any spirit. Because that One-side animal told the Crow that the people, the ones-who-sit-around-the-campfire, what they call *bad* he is that one. This spirit is so deep that some way or another it combines. The shaman is trying to receive a power from good things. So the bad one is fighting against him, to get the power from a good thing."

Uneasily, I asked if the bad spirit is part of humans. He laughed wryly.

"What do we do for our life?" he asked. "What we do for our life is not all good. We live along side of bad things. Like now, we look at what we have, to picture the background of this shaman, to see what he tried to do for his people. Same with dreamers, the ones whose words come true, the sky readers: where and how they get the power. The power is working together with good and bad, on both sides. The bad is fighting against him, to become one with him.

"By looking at it this way, I don't think it was bad to be shaman." It was a sore point with him. "Because those people didn't come to use it to do wrong to other people. It was all for good. Because they already suffered on that bad side, before they became shamans.

These men, they suffered and worked hard for the good part of the life, to protect people against anything bad."

Good and Evil

I couldn't see how, in the story of Crow and the One-side Animal, this creature could say Crow treated him nicely.

"That Half-human," Peter explained, "he's what the people-around-the-campfire call bad. 'That's what I am. Now you have treated me nice.' He liked that, for he is a bad person, he belongs to the bad part of life. When the Crow kicked him over and stabbed him: *that's* what he liked. He doesn't mean the baby part. He likes the worst kind of treatment, because he is the bad side of the good part. He expressed that he is the chief of the bad part of being human when he said, 'I like that.'

"He couldn't be just one creature; he had a mixture in him so the picture could show both sides. It doesn't mean animals are on the bad side. The bad side is on our side."

Crow has often been called a "trickster figure," it occurred to me; but Peter's stories of Crow, like other Interior versions, show Crow a little less admirably than he is often viewed from the outside. I asked why Crow acted as he did.

"That old Crow," he said appreciatively but with a trace of disapproval, "he was quite an actor. According to his stories, that old Crow could turn himself into a human, he can talk to the people and do whatever he wants to do; his wish and his word would come true. But one thing: he cannot kill game for himself to eat."

Did Crow make the world?

"In some other Dena'ina stories. It wasn't laid down to me that Crow made the world. So I don't think so. According to the stories we have gone through, seems like in the Crow stories it was laid before him and *became* the stories. If Crow created the world, who would be the Crow today?"

The implications of Crow are great, but here we stopped for awhile. I wondered then about the old lady: is she powerful? He seemed both fascinated and puzzled by her, and his answers became courtly.

"In the Gambling story, when that person came to the shelter, the woman *had* to be first [the first one he met]. She was home, alone. And then, in that Mouse story, same thing. And to follow it, to switch to the man: in that Half-animal and Crow story, there was no woman there. That leads us into how bad and good work together: men and ladies. That's one way of looking at it."

Again, I asked what evil is.

"Evil is something bad. Seems to me some things must have been happening to the people like that, or may have been laid before them as a test, to know what the bad is."

Yet, the Gambling story was about a believer and a shaman, both good, and yet the believer lost everything. He remarked that in the three sets of gambling sticks there is a cycle, and I asked if, then, the cycle is this: living, dying to the shaman, coming back alive to the believer.

"To begin with, that shaman was in the wrong, using his power to do wrong against this person through gambling. And for the shaman doing wrong, it was reversed back to him: the same punishment he gave out. That means that was the end of his shaman work, because K'eluyesh blocked him from transforming into an animal.

"When that second set spun the way the sun goes, that's for the right thing, on the good part. The third set he spun against the sun: that goes into the bad side. The shaman did the bad work, but that same bad form that he did was reversed back to him. So then, what you have here, the life-death-return cycle, it's something like that."

But then, is it wrong if I gamble, I asked him, but right if you do?

"It *has* to be okay. You have to do your part for living, and I do my part. And it gets down to it: we're all gamblers for living. We take chances. Maybe that's why that gambling game story was laid out: to look behind it.

"Human life is a gamble. You have to go out and gamble, take chances, do things."

But why is it a *gambling* story? I persisted, knowing already.

"It's human life," he said.

Truth and Believing

The ceremonial directions were prominent. I asked what it means, to turn the way the sun goes round.

"That is the Mouse and Gambling stories. To go with the sun is to turn to your right, around in a circle. To not go against the sun. They probably had believing just the way the words said: to go with the sun, not against it."

And the water and the down?

"And these people here used water, and then, on that other part there, they used down feathers on this same material in order to let it come back to full size, as they were to come back to being animals.

"The down feather was given by the giant – this was a *gift*. The water was a test form. But that down feather's been used even where there's water. Down belongs to birds that go on water, in the sky, and on land.

"The down feather's something like the reverse of the water.

"And there's another point that puzzles me: anything they do was three: it was always three times. That three seems to go in a cycle all through the stories, Gambling, Mouse, Dog stories. Why is it there?

"In the Gambling story, there is human life cycle: live, die, come back. So there's a combination along the line."

The old giant couple seemed deeply significant to me, and I asked him to explain them.

"The Mouse story doesn't tell us who the old couple is. Gambling story does. That old giant said he *knew* why that fellow came over. The lazy man had helped him; so the kindness was rewarded.

"When this giant was out looking for his child, you could see his tracks, his footprints in the sky. And then that was *naqisten*, his trail over us, the Milky Way. And, I don't know who saw the tracks, but they said that on top of the mountains they would see his footprints. I don't know exactly where, but they say he left his footprints. Whenever his footprints were on top of a mountain, maybe he walked from one place to another. And I don't know how true it is; but it's in the story.

"He would be the head of everything, K'eluyesh, [his name meaning] at the very point: and the rest of the animals would be next to him.

"And Gujun: his name translates to, *over here it will happen.* But it is a funny verb [Dena'ina word].

"In that Gambling story there, when that big old lady was in the house alone, she explained who she was: she said, *shidi k'unk'da jelen.* 'I am the mother again and again.'"

I asked if that meant everything in the world, even humans, came from her.

"Not the humans, though. Mother of the animals, maybe."

I asked about the giants Gujun and his wife: did they make the animals, that is, are they these giants in another guise? He considered this, as we had discussed it before, when he thought it might be possible to think that way. But now he was less certain.

"The story doesn't explain anything about either one of them. And I don't know where the stories started; and *why* are they? It seems to me they were put forward to be studied by humans along the way, in religions. Something is in the stories for humans to learn from. The stories go so far back it doesn't say where they originated from."

Considering the respectful relationship between Dena'inas and animals, Peter himself having always lived as a hunter, I said, But there are people who don't believe in hunting animals. How can they understand these stories?

"Depends on the background you look at," he said mildly. "Whatever experience of the stories those Dena'inas tried, they would go and hand it down to the people. So, there must be some people that were studying parts of the story and tried to make something of it. It said there that if they learned something from the story, they would go out and hand it out to the neighbors. They tried to help one another.

"The animals fear humans. But they have a better smell and better ears. And also, an animal can sense your mind, if you are a danger to him or not. So in the stories they talk to animals. 'Big old man, I'm not for you' is said to the brown bear. That's been experienced: he'll let you alone then. Yet I can't say it's *true*, even though I had my experience with that animal, like I told you, in my hunting."

Why can't you say it's true, I wondered, if you've experienced how the bears leave you alone when you pray?

"I don't know why. It's my feeling and my sense that I am anywheres in the woods not for him, and also that I stayed out of his way and he out of my way. But I don't know what makes that. It's my feeling or my sense that he received my mind contact. Somebody in my place, they might put that for the truth. But I can't, even with my own experience. Because I still don't know the answer to it."

How do you know when something is true then, I asked him.

"This has been happening to a lot of people, but there's no answer to it. You'll be someplace where there's nobody or no animals, and all at once you have that funny feeling that somebody's watching you, something's watching you. That eye penetrating you, sensing you. You may see it or not. But I can't say it's *true*, though you hear it from lots of people along the way. 'I feel like somebody's watching me': that expression's been used among friends for some time."

But you don't know, then, what's out there to cause that feeling.

"No, you don't know what it is."

But, remembering the end of the stories, I asked if stories could tell you what is there.

"No," he said. "This can lead us back to that Crow and Half-human. And that Mouse story. This man told that guy there, 'We *know* you,' even though he didn't see him before. And, 'We know the reason why you came to us.' So in there is some combination that the feeling is that way. The giant knew that person; he expressed himself why he knew him, the reason that one came to him. And that Half-human told the Crow, 'What those you call human, what they call evil, that's what I am.' That combination between good and evil.

"The giant told that man he would help him; that man is on the good side with his kindness, and the giant resupplied him. Otherwise, that man was on the wrong side of the fence, by being lazy and not putting up any food. But at the same time, he showed his kindness, by helping that mouse: to prove there's something alongside bad, on the good part. He came to this giant, and the giant returned that kindness.

"That leads back to the Half-human, when he explained to the Crow that he was on the bad side. So, good and bad is a combination in the human's life. And that is why we don't *know* what's out there when we experience this feeling." He laughed.

"That's digging down to the 'Where's my socks'!"

Word and Spirit

"This goes into that whale hunter, Gashaq, one whose words come true. It's one thing these Dena'inas didn't have any training for, whale hunting. He's the only person there who could call on the wind, according to that story. The one who reads the sky and the shaman cannot call on the wind; they do not have enough power. He's the only person who would call on the wind, and the wind could come.

"The words or the wish is more powerful than the spirit. That shaman cannot take the form of a wish. He has to use his spirit."

He uses the power of water and wind. Peter gestured breath coming from the mouth.

"Wind. The breath is something penetrating, like the wind, the wind penetrates. Our breath penetrates. The sound that we breathe, our voice, that sound follows the wind."

Words are powerful, I said, thinking of the horror of lies here.

"The man whose words come true: he seems to describe religion, or believing.

"He's inhaling and breathing out: that has to do with human life. A human life is lived to study and learn what's on this earth. There's power, religion, human mind, our breath. We have to breathe in to be alive. The whole thing put together, that goes into the human mind." He paused and tapped his head, winking at me. "But me, I don't have that much."

He laughed and laughed.

– Katherine McNamara

Katherine McNamara worked under Mr. Kalifornsky's direction on several versions of his stories and commentaries on their meaning.

ANIMAL HEAD (Punuk Islands / St. Lawrence Island Yupik)
This animal head was carved of mineralized walrus ivory during the
Okvik Period (300 B.C. to 0 A.D.). Photo: Chris Arend.
(Courtesy of the Anchorage Museum of History and Art)

SELECTED SOURCES

Apassingok, Anders, Willis Walunga, and Edward Tennant, eds. *Sivuqam Nangaghnegha Siivanllemta Ungipaqellghat: Lore of St. Lawrence Island.* Vol. 1. Unalakleet, AK: Bering Strait School District, 1985.

Bascom, William. "The Forms of Folklore: Prose Narratives." *Sacred Narrative: Readings in the Theory of Myth.* Ed. Alan Dundes. Berkeley, CA: University of California Press, 1984.

Bauman, Richard. *Story, Performance, and Event: Contextual Studies of Oral Narrative.* Cambridge, MA: Cambridge University Press, 1986.

Birket-Smith, Kaj, and Frederica de Laguna. *The Eyak Indians of the Copper River Delta, Alaska.* Copenhagen: Levine and Munkgaard, 1938.

Ben-Amos, Dan, and Kenneth S. Goldstein, eds. *Folklore: Performance and Communication.* The Hague: Mouton, 1975.

Boelscher, Marianne. *The Curtain Within: Haida Social and Mythical Discourse.* Vancouver, Canada: University of British Columbia Press, 1988.

Breinig, Jeane C. *Re-contextualizing Haida Narrative.* Doctoral dissertation. Seattle, WA: University of Washington, 1995.

Case, David S. *Alaska Natives and American Laws.* Revised Edition. Fairbanks, AK: University of Alaska Press, 1984.

Christianson, Susan Stark. *Historical Profile of Central Council Tlingit and Haida Indian Tribes of Alaska.* Revised Edition of Metcalfe 1985. Juneau, AK: Central Council of the Tlingit and Haida Tribes of Alaska, 1992.

Dauenhauer, Nora Marks, and Richard Dauenhauer. "Alaska Native Oral Tradition." *1984 Festival of American Folklife.* Washington, D.C.: Smithsonian Institute, 1984.

Dauenhauer, Nora Marks, and Richard Dauenhauer. "The Battles of Sitka, 1802 and 1804, From The Tlingit, Russian, And Other Points Of View." *Russia in North America.* (Proceedings of the 2nd International Conference on Russian America, Sitka, August 19–22, 1987, pp. 6–24.) Ed. R. Pierce. Kingston, Ontario, and Fairbanks, AK: The Limestone Press, 1990.

Dauenhauer, Nora Marks, and Richard Dauenhauer, eds. *Haa Kusteeyí Our Culture: Tlingit Life Stories.* Seattle: University of Washington Press, 1994.

Enrico, John, ed. and trans., and John R. Swanton, collector. *Skidegate Haida Myths and Histories.* Skidegate, BC: Queen Charlotte Islands Museum Press, 1995.

Fall, James. *The Upper Inlet Tanaina.* Anthropological Papers of the University of Alaska, 21 (1–2), 1–80. 1987.

Fienup-Riordan, Ann. *Boundaries and Passages, Rule and Ritual in Yup'ik Eskimo Oral Tradition.* Norman, OK: University of Oklahoma Press, 1994.

Fredson, John. *John Fredson Edward Sapir Hàa Googwandak: Stories Told by John Fredson to Edward Sapir.* Fairbanks, AK: Alaska Native Language Center, 1982.

Golder, Frank A. "Tales from Kodiak Island." *Journal of American Folklore.* Vol. 16, pt. 1, 16–31; pt. 2, 85–103. 1903.

Jochelson, Waldemar. *History, Ethnology, and Anthropology of the Aleut.* New York: Humanities Press, 1968.

Kawagley, A. Oscar. *A Yupiaq Worldview: A Pathway to Ecology and Spirit.* Prospect Heights, IL: Waveland Press, 1995.

Krauss, Michael E. *Alaska Native Languages: Past, Present, and Future.* Fairbanks, AK: Alaska Native Language Center, 1980.

Krauss, Michael E., ed. *In Honor of Eyak: The Art of Anna Nelson Harry.* Fairbanks, AK: Alaska Native Language Center, 1982.

Lantis, Margaret. "The Mythology of Kodiak Island, Alaska." *Journal of American Folklore.* Vol. 51, (200), 123–172. 1938.

Lawrence, Erma. *Haida Dictionary.* Fairbanks, AK: Alaska Native Language Center, 1977.

Lord, Alfred B. *The Singer of Tales.* Cambridge, MA: Harvard University Press, 1960.

McBeath, Gerald A., and Thomas A. Morehouse. *Alaska Politics and Government.* Lincoln, NE: University of Nebraska Press, 1994.

McClellan, Catherine. *The Girl Who Married the Bear: A Masterpiece of Indian Oral Tradition.* National Museum of Man Publications in Ethnology, No. 2. Ottawa, Canada: National Museum of Canada, 1970.

McKennan, Robert A. *The Upper Tanana Indians.* Yale University Publications in Anthropology Number 55. New Haven, CT: Human Relations Area Files, 1975.

McKennan, Robert A. *The Chandalar Kutchin.* Arctic Institute of North America Technical Paper No. 17. New York: Arctic Institute of North America, 1975.

Oring, Elliott, ed. *Folk Groups and Folklore Genres: An Introduction.* Logan, UT: Utah State University, 1986.

Osgood, Cornelius. *Ingalik Mental Culture.* Yale University Publications in Anthropology Number 56. New Haven, CT: Human Relations Area Files, 1959.

Osgood, Cornelius. *The Ethnography of the Tanaina.* Yale University Publications in Anthropology Number 16. New Haven, CT: Human Relations Area Files, 1966.

Osgood, Cornelius. *Contributions to the Ethnography of the Kutchin.* Yale University Publications in Anthropology Number 16. New Haven, CT: Human Relations Area Files, 1970.

Oswalt, Wendell. *Alaskan Eskimos.* Scranton, PA: Chandler Publishing Company, 1967.

Partnow, Patricia H. *Alutiiq Ethnicity.* Doctoral dissertation. Fairbanks, AK: University of Alaska Fairbanks, 1993.

Pete, Shem, and James Kari. *Susitna Htsukdu'a.* Fairbanks, AK: Alaska Native Language Center, 1975.

Ray, Dorothy Jean. *Eskimo Masks: Art and Ceremony.* Seattle: University of Washington Press, 1967.

Swanton, John R. *Contributions to the Ethnology of the Haida.* Publications of the Jesup North Pacific Expedition, Vol. 10, pt. 2. New York: G. E. Strechert, 1905.

Tedlock, Dennis. "The Spoken Word and the Work of Interpretation." *Traditional Literatures of the American Indian.* Ed. K. Kroeber. Philadelphia: University of Pennsylvania Press, 1983.

United States Joint Federal-State Commission on Policies and Programs Affecting Alaska Natives. *Alaska Natives Commission Final Report.* Vols. 1–3. Anchorage, AK: Alaska Natives Commission, 1994.

Vanstone, James W. *Athapaskan Adaptations: Hunters and Fishermen of the Subarctic Forests.* Chicago: Aldine Publishing Company, 1974.

Veniaminov, Ivan. *Notes on the Islands of the Unalashka District.* Trans. Lydia T. Black and R. H. Geoghegan. Ed. Richard A. Pierce. Kingston, Ontario: The Limestone Press, 1984 [1840].

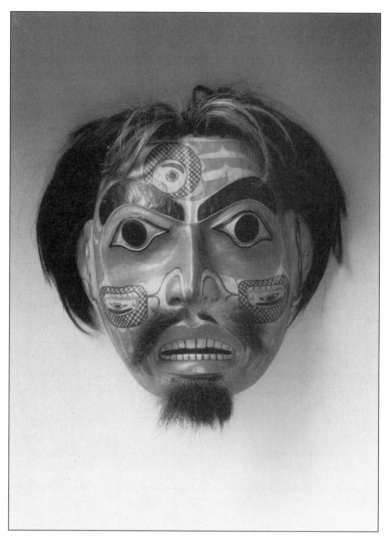

MASK (Tlingit)
Nathan Jackson from Ketchikan, Alaska, made this mask from cedar, bear fur, human hair, copper, and paint. Photo: Sam Kimura.
(Courtesy of the Anchorage Museum of History and Art)

SUGGESTED FURTHER READING

Andrews, Susan B., and John Creed, eds. *Authentic Alaska: Voices of Its Native Writers.* Lincoln, NE: University of Nebraska Press, 1998.

Apassingok, Anders, Willis Walunga, Raymond Oozevaseuk, and Edward Tennant, eds. *Sivuqam Nangaghnegha Siivanllemta: Lore of St. Lawrence Island, Echoes of our Eskimo Elders.* Vol. 2. Unalakleet, AK: Bering Strait School District, 1987a.

Apassingok, Anders, Willis Walunga, Raymond Oozevaseuk, Jessie Uglowook, and Edward Tennant, eds. *Sivuqam Nangaghnegha Siivanllemta Ungipaqellghat: Lore of St. Lawrence Island Echoes of our Eskimo Elders.* Vol. 3. Unalakleet, AK: Bering Strait School District, 1987b.

Attla, Catherine. *K'tetaalkkaanee The One Who Paddled Among the People and the Animals: The Story of the Ancient Traveler.* Fairbanks, AK: Alaska Native Language Center, 1990.

Bergsland, Knut, and Moses L. Dirks, eds. *Unangam Ungiikangin Kayux Tunusangin Unangam Uniikangis Ama Tunuzangis: Aleut Tales and Narratives.* Collected 1909–1910 by Waldemar Jochelson. Fairbanks, AK: Alaska Native Language Center, 1990.

Brown, Emily Ivanoff. *Tales of Ticasuk.* Fairbanks: University of Alaska Press, 1987.

Bruchac, Joseph, ed. *Raven Tells Stories: An Anthology of Alaska Native Writing.* Greenfield, NY: The Greenfield Press Review, 1991.

Burch, Ernest S., Jr. *The Inupiaq Eskimo Nations of Northwest Alaska.* Fairbanks, AK: University of Alaska Press, 1998.

Dauenhauer, Nora Marks, and Richard Dauenhauer, eds. *Haa Shuká, Our Ancestors: Tlingit Oral Narratives.* Seattle: University of Washington Press, 1987.

Dauenhauer, Nora Marks, and Richard Dauenhauer, eds. *Haa Tuwunáagu Yís, For Healing Our Spirit: Tlingit Oratory.* Seattle: University of Washington Press, 1990.

Dauenhauer, Nora Marks, and Richard Dauenhauer, eds. *Haa Kusteeyí, Our Culture: Tlingit Life Stories.* Seattle: University of Washington Press, 1994.

Dauenhauer, Nora Marks. *The Droning Shaman*. Haines, AK: Black Current Press, 1988.

Deloria, Vine Jr., and Clifford Lytle. *The Nations Within: The Past and Future of American Indian Sovereignty*. New York: Pantheon, 1984.

Eastman, Carol M., and Elizabeth A. Edwards. *Gyaehlingaay: Traditions, Tales and Images of the Kaigani Haida*. Seattle: University of Washington Press, 1991.

Edenso, Christine. *The Transcribed Tapes of Christine Edenso*. Anchorage, AK: University of Alaska Materials Development Center. (Now distributed by Sealaska Heritage Foundation.) c. 1983.

Enrico, John, and Wendy Stewart. *Northern Haida Songs: Studies in the Anthropology of North American Indians*. Lincoln, NE: University of Nebraska Press, 1996.

Fienup-Riordan, Ann. *Boundaries and Passages, Rule and Ritual in Yup'ik Eskimo Oral Tradition*. Norman, OK: University of Oklahoma Press, 1994.

Fredson, John. *John Fredson Edward Sapir Hàa Googwandak: Stories Told by John Fredson to Edward Sapir*. Fairbanks, AK: Alaska Native Language Center, 1982.

Haycox, Stephen W., and Mary Childers Mangusso, eds. *An Alaska Anthology: Interpreting the Past*. Seattle: University of Washington Press, 1996.

Kaplan, Lawrence D., ed. *Ugiuvangmiut Quliapyuit: King Island Tales*. Fairbanks, AK: Alaska Native Language Center, 1998.

Kari, James, and Alan Boraas, eds. *A Dena'ina Legacy K'tl'egh'i Sukdu: The Collected Writings of Peter Kalifornsky*. Fairbanks, AK: Alaska Native Language Center, 1991.

Kari, James, transcriber and ed. *Tatl'ahwt'aenn Nenn The Headwaters People's Country: Narratives of the Upper Ahtna Athabaskans*. Fairbanks, AK: Alaska Native Language Center, 1986.

Kawagley, A. Oscar. *A Yupiaq Worldview: A Pathway to Ecology and Spirit*. Prospect Heights, IL: Waveland Press, 1995.

Krauss, Michael E. *Alaska Native Languages: Past, Present, and Future*. Fairbanks, AK: Alaska Native Language Center, 1980.

Krauss, Michael E., ed. *In Honor of Eyak: The Art of Anna Nelson Harry*. Fairbanks, AK: Alaska Native Language Center, 1982.

Krauss, Michael E. *Native Peoples and Languages of Alaska*. (Map). Fairbanks, AK: Alaska Native Language Center, 1982.

Langdon, Steve. *The Native People of Alaska*. Third Edition. Anchorage, AK: Greatland Graphics, 1993.

Laughlin, William S. *Aleuts: Survivors of the Bering Land Bridge*. New York: Holt, Rinehart & Winston, 1980.

Luke, Howard. *My Own Trail.* Ed. Jan Steinbright Jackson. Fairbanks, AK: Alaska Native Knowledge Network, 1998.

Mather, Elsie. *Cauyarnariuq It is Time for Drumming.* Seattle: University of Washington Press, 1985.

McBeath, Gerald, A., and Thomas A. Morehouse. *Alaska Politics and Government.* Lincoln, NE: University of Nebraska Press, 1994.

McClanahan, A. J. *Our Stories, Our Lives: A Collection of Twenty-Three Transcribed Interviews with Elders of the Cook Inlet Region.* Anchorage, AK: The CIRI Foundation, 1986.

Meade, Marie, trans., and Ann Fienup-Riordan, ed. *Agayuliyararput Kegginaqut, Kangiit-llu Our Way of Making Prayer: Yup'ik Masks and the Stories They Tell.* Seattle: University of Washington Press, 1996.

Mendenhall, Hannah, Ruth Sampson, and Edward Tennant. *Uqaaqtuangich Inupiat: Lore of the Inupiat, the Elders Speak.* Vol. 1. Kotzebue, AK: Northwest Arctic Borough School District, 1989.

Morrow, Phyllis, and William Schneider, eds. *When Our Words Return: Writing, Hearing and Remembering Oral Traditions of Alaska and the Yukon.* Logan, UT: Utah State University Press, 1995.

Napoleon, Harold. *Yuuyaraq: The Way of the Human Being.* Ed. Eric Madsen. Fairbanks, AK: Alaska Native Knowledge Network, 1996.

Nelson, Richard K. *Make Prayers to the Raven: A Koyukon View of the Northern Forest.* Chicago: University of Chicago Press, 1983.

Orr, Eliza Cingarkaq, and Ben Orr. *Qanemcikarluni Tekitnarqelartuq One Must Arrive With a Story to Tell.* Fairbanks, AK: Lower Kuskokwim School District, Alaska Native Language Center, 1995.

Pete, Shem. *Shem Pete's Alaska: The Territory of the Upper Cook Inlet Dena'ina.* Compiled and edited by James Kari. Fairbanks, AK: Alaska Native Language Center, 1987.

Ruoff, A. LaVonne Brown. *American Indian Literatures: An Introduction, Bibliographic Review, and Selected Bibliography.* New York: The Modern Language Association of America, 1990.

Snigaroff, Cedor, and Knut Bergsland. *Niiĝuĝis Makax̂tazaqangis Atkan Historical Traditions.* Fairbanks, AK: Alaska Native Language Center, 1986.

Swann, Brian, ed. *Coming to Light: Contemporary Translations of the Native Literatures of North America.* New York: Random House, 1995.

TallMountain, Mary. *The Light on the Tent Wall: A Bridging.* Los Angeles: American Indian Studies Center, UCLA, 1990.

Thornton, Russell. *American Indian Holocaust and Survival: A Popula-*

tion History Since 1492. (Civilization of the American Indian, Vol. 186.) Norman, OK: University of Oklahoma Press, 1990.

Tennant, Edward A., and Joseph N. Bitar, eds. *Yuut Qanemciit Yup'ik Lore: Oral Traditions of an Eskimo People.* Bethel, AK: Lower Kuskokwim School District, 1981.

Wallis, Velma. *Bird Girl and the Man Who Followed the Sun: An Athabaskan Indian Legend from Alaska.* Fairbanks, AK: Epicenter Press, 1996.

Wallis, Velma. *Two Old Women: An Alaskan Legend of Betrayal, Courage, and Survival.* Fairbanks, AK: Epicenter Press, 1993.

Wilkinson, Charles F. *American Indians, Time, and the Law: Native Societies in a Modern Constitutional Democracy.* New Haven and London: Yale University Press, 1987.

Wilson, Shawn. *Gwitch'in Native Elders: Not Just Knowledge But a Way of Looking at the World.* Fairbanks, AK: Alaska Native Knowledge Network, 1996.

Woodbury, Anthony C., ed. *Cev'armiut Qanemciit Qulirait-llu: Eskimo Narratives and Tales from Chevak, Alaska.* Fairbanks, AK: Alaska Native Language Center, 1984.

ACKNOWLEDGMENTS

Alaska Native Writers, Storytellers & Orators: The Expanded Edition would not have been possible without the support of a Heritage and Preservation Grant from the National Endowment for the Arts. The National Endowment for the Arts also made possible the 1986 edition of *Alaska Native Writers, Storytellers and Orators* with a Literary Publishing Grant. That earlier volume would also not have been possible without the hard work and vision of our original contributing editors who joined Ronald Spatz in producing the book: Nora Marks Dauenhauer, Richard Dauenhauer and Gary Holthaus. Additionally, we are indebted to the Dauenhauers for their major contributions to the field of Tlingit oral literature and for their continued involvement in the development of this project through the inclusion of their works and translations, and for their generous help in checking Tlingit and Haida translations and sources for accuracy. Appreciation should also be expressed to James Jakób Liszka who worked with Ronald Spatz in preparing the original grant proposal to the National Endowment for the Arts in 1985.

We wish to express our thanks to all the Alaskan writers who submitted their work for this anthology, to the Institute of Alaska Native Arts, the Sealaska Heritage Foundation, and the Alaska Humanities Forum for their cooperation and assistance in coordinating the collection of manuscripts. Thanks also to the CIRI Foundation, the Alaska Native Heritage Center, especially the Eyak, Tlingit, Haida, Tsimshian Advisory Committee (Helen McNeil, Eleanor Hadden, Beth Garza, Mable Pike, and Jenna May), to Vera Kaneshiro, and to Edna Lamebull and the Indian Education Program of the Anchorage School District.

We owe a special debt of gratitude to Michael E. Krauss for all of his assistance on this project. His book, *In Honor of Eyak: The Art of Anna Nelson Harry,* is an inspiration for all of us interested in Alaska Native languages and cultures. Through his works, Krauss has helped us "sense something of the true meaning of a person's life and of a nation's history" (from the introduction to *In Honor of Eyak*). We are greatly in his debt for the clarity and depth of his scholarship and for his devotion to his subject. So too are we indebted to the staff of the Alaska Native Language Center, University of Alaska Fairbanks, for all of the important work that they have done and continue to do.

We are grateful for the generous assistance of the staff of the Anchorage Museum of History and Art in identifying photographs for use in this book: Patricia Wolf, Walter Van Horn, and Diane Brenner. We are also grateful to photographer Chris Arend and to the late Sam Kimura for his numerous contributions of cover art to *AQR* and for the front cover image for this volume (also used on the cover of the 1986 edition).

It should be noted that, wherever possible, we attempted to identify original sources for reprinted materials at the end of each text. Grateful acknowledgment is also made to the following for permission to reprint material copyrighted or controlled by them: *The Tundra Times*, Alaska Methodist University Press; I. Reed Press; Alaska Native Language Center, University of Alaska; Alaska Historical Commission; Sealaska Heritage Foundation; Haida Society for Preservation of Language and Literature; KYUK's "Yupik Story" (Bethel, Alaska); National Endowment for the Humanities and the Alaska Humanities Forum; Press-22; Institute of Alaska Native Arts; Seabury Press; Yellow Creek Project; Journal of Alaska Native Arts.

Over the years, several administrators at the University of Alaska Anchorage have played key roles in the survival of *Alaska Quarterly Review* as a publishing entity and it is important they be recognized here for their strong and continuing support. University of Alaska Anchorage Chancellor E. Lee Gorsuch's longstanding support for *Alaska Quarterly Review* is a matter of record. So too is his generous commitment to the literary arts and to initiatives that advance an understanding of Alaska Native cultures. Because of his support, *Alaska Quarterly Review* has flourished and *Alaska Native Writers, Storytellers & Orators: The Expanded Edition* has seen publication. Likewise, former University of Alaska Anchorage Chancellor Donald Behrend was responsible for the continuing development of *Alaska Quarterly Review*. Through his decisive administrative intervention a decade ago, *Alaska Quarterly Review* was given office space and the funding to continue publication. Moreover, Chancellor Behrend, along with former Provost Beverly Beeton, also donated their personal funds through the Combined Campaign to supplement *AQR*'s operating budget, support for which we will always be profoundly grateful. The contributions of former President and member of the University of Alaska Board of Regents, Sharon Gagnon (a subscriber to *AQR* since our first issue in 1982), must be mentioned. Her eight years of unflagging support as a University Regent nurtured the development of *Alaska Quarterly Review* in important ways. Her support and her cogent advice have been both inspiring and invaluable.

Undoubtedly, we may have inadvertently omitted the names of people who have helped us. To them we extend our sincere appreciation and an apology.

Finally, we express our gratitude to our subscribers and readers for their loyalty to *Alaska Quarterly Review*. Their support has made all the difference.

THANK YOU SO MUCH ANYWAY (Aleut)
Alvin Amason made this sculpture from acrylic, oil, and mixed media on canvas. Photo: Alvin Amason. (Courtesy of the Decker/ Morris Gallery)

ABOUT THE EDITORS

Ronald Spatz

Ronald Spatz is executive editor and founding editor of the nationally acclaimed *Alaska Quarterly Review*. He is professor of Creative Writing and Literary Arts and Director of the University Honors Program at the University of Alaska Anchorage. A filmmaker and writer, Spatz's short subject films have been broadcast on television, selected for film festivals, and used in schools and colleges. His film, *For the Love of Ben*, was broadcast nationally on public television. Spatz's fiction has appeared in a wide range of national literary journals and anthologies and has been recognized by individual artist fellowships from the National Endowment for the Arts and the Alaska State Council on the Arts. He holds a M.F.A. degree from the University of Iowa Writers Workshop.

Jeane Breinig

Jeane Breinig is Haida (Raven, Brown Bear, Taaslaanas Clan) originally from Kasaan village in Southeast Alaska. One of only three Alaskan Haida to earn a doctorate, she received her Ph.D. in English (American and Native American Studies) from the University of Washington. Breinig is currently working on a book about Haida narrative and has published in *American Indian Quarterly* and *Studies in American Indian Literatures*. She is an associate professor of English at the University of Alaska Anchorage.

Patricia H. Partnow

Patricia H. Partnow is a cultural anthropologist who has worked in Alaska for the past 30 years in the fields of education, oral history and oral tradition, and ethnographic research. She completed her Ph.D. in Anthropology at the University of Alaska Fairbanks in 1993, and her ethnohistoric examination of the Alutiiq people of the

Alaska Peninsula is entitled *Making History.* Partnow is Vice President of Education at the Alaska Native Heritage Center, a nonprofit organization for the celebration, preservation, and sharing of Alaska Native traditions.

HILL CRANE MATING DANCE (Aleut)
John Hoover made this sculpture by carving cedar. Photo: Steve Vento.
(Courtesy of the Decker/Morris Gallery)

MEAN WALRUS SPIRIT (Aleut)
Fred Anderson made this sculpture out of yellow cedar and ivory.
Photo: Chris Arend. (Courtesy of the Decker/Morris Gallery)

PERSONAL ARMOR (Yup'ik)
Jack Abraham's self-portrait was constructed out of handmade paper,
wood, and acrylic paint. Photo: Jimmie Froehlich. (Courtesy of the
Decker/Morris Gallery)

YUPIK ANGEL (St. Lawrence Island Yupik)
Susie Silook, whose prose and poetry also appear in the Contemporary
Works section of this volume, made this carving from walrus ivory and
sinew. Photo: Jimmie Froehlich. (Courtesy of Susie Silook)